SAYING GRACE

By Nov 8th Mon

IN service

Photograph by Robin Clement

About the Author

BETH GUTCHEON is the critically acclaimed author of six novels: *The New Girls, Still Missing, Domestic Pleasures, Saying Grace, Five Fortunes,* and *More Than You Know*. She has written several film scripts, including the Academy Award–nominated *The Children of Theatre Street*. She lives in New York City.

SAYING GRACE

A Novel

BETH GUTCHEON

Perennial

An Imprint of HarperCollinsPublishers

A hardcover edition of this book was published
in 1995 by HarperCollins Publishers.

HarperCollins books may be purchased for educational, business, or sales promo-
tional use. For information please write: Special Markets Department, Harper-
Collins Publishers Inc., 10 East 53rd Street, New York, NY 10022.

First HarperPerennial edition published 1996.

Reprinted in Perennial 2001.

Designed by Nancy Singer

The Library of Congress has catalogued the hardcover edition as follows:

Gutcheon, Beth Richardson.
    Saying grace : a novel / Beth Gutcheon. — 1st ed.
      p. cm.
    ISBN 0-06-017678-4
    I. Title.
PS3557.U844S29   1995
813'.54—dc20   95-8677

ISBN 0-06-092727-5 (pbk.)

03 04 05 ❖/RRD 20 19

For Robin Clements, beloved husband

And for my father, Frank E. Richardson, Jr., honored trustee, who fifty years ago saved a now famous midwestern country day school from impaling itself on a point of history. (In a fraught silence at a meeting of the school community called to decide whether the paralyzed school could continue to exist, he rose and addressed the sitting board, some of them founding members, all elderly rich men unaccustomed to compromise. He suggested that in order to allow for such innovations as parent committees, opening the board to women, and term limits for trustees, they should resign in a body. They all said, "Thank God, a solution," and did so.)

To the woman who sent me the *Elegy* of Yuan Chen so long ago: If you read this, you will know I have never forgotten the story of your son. Here's a patch for his memory quilt.

I owe grateful thanks to many others for various kinds of support and assistance. I thank Wendy Weil and Diane Reverand for their everlasting steadiness, for their professional support, and especially for the pleasure of their friendship. I thank Bitsie Root and Jerri Witt for invaluable suggestions on the manuscript and readers Emily Conroy, Pam Jones, and Cathy Lynn, whose reactions were more helpful than they can imagine. I am grateful for the assistance of John B. Clements, who shares a great deal of Georgia's musical taste. Anyone familiar with the field will recognize that somewhere along the line Rue has met and been deeply impressed by the generous spirit and giant brain of Peggy McIntosh; Rue and her creator both are grateful for the encounter. And last and most I am grateful for the wit, intelligence, and cherished friendship of Douglas Ware.

It was two days before the opening of school when the Spanish teacher dropped dead. *Dropped* is the right word; she was on her knees in the garden, cleaning out the crocosmia bed, when she felt a sudden lightball of pain in her chest, and then was herself extinguished. She toppled face-forward into the fragrant California earth, and lay there, stiffening in the September sunshine, wearing her green-and-yellow gardening gloves. She was otherwise dressed for work. It was the faculty's first day back at The Country School, and the news of her death found her colleagues gathered in Packard gymnasium for a CPR course, performing mouth-to-mouth resuscitation on rubber women.

As her colleagues mourned and comforted each other, Rue Shaw left the gym to hurry across campus to her office. Under the circumstances, she was struck by the illusion the parched campus imparted of a serene and manageable universe. The fields where the bigger boys played football were freshly mowed and green from a summer of sprinklers. As she passed, Manuel was laying down lines in white lime so that all could see the structure of the game, the clear boundary between in and out, good and bad, safe and sorry. Everywhere the scent of cut grass mingled with the smell of eucalyptus.

The offices of the Head, and all the rest of the administration, were in a building known as Home, because it had been the original homestead when the campus was a ranch. The Plum family who pioneered it had grown prosperous and built a grand Victorian farmhouse with wide, covered porches and the latest in gingerbread trim, in which Rue now lived. From there the Plum family had raised livestock and apricots and used the old homestead for a sheep barn. Rue Shaw now bustled into Home through the dutch door, which Merilee kept open at the top to let in the sunlight and the perfume of the outside air and closed at the bottom to keep out the campus dogs and cats. Rue went straight past Merilee's desk to find her assistant head, Mike Dianda. His office, which had once been a birthing pen for lambs, was low and cluttered, with heavy dark beams and small windows. Mike's desk was stacked with papers and books; he had more than once misplaced his telephone and had had to wait for it to ring so he could find it.

In Mike's office, miscreant children sent to be sentenced sat in the ladderback wooden chair facing his desk. But the soft leather chair against the bookcase was only for Rue, for when she came in with mugs of tea at the end of the day and kicked the door closed behind her. Mike was to Rue like the brother she never had. He was tart, smart, handsome, and funny, and as far as she could tell, never afraid to tell her she was wrong. The collaboration was particularly successful because he did not want her job. He would make a fine school head when his life was more his own, but at the moment as a gay man and a single parent he had enough on his plate getting his daughters through school.

"I talked with the mother in Albuquerque," said Mike, as Rue appeared in his doorway.

"How is she?"

"They knew Mariel had a heart condition."

"Did they? Did we know it?"

"I didn't. Maybe Lynn Ketchum did, or Cynda Goldring. They were closest to her."

"Will they have the funeral here?"

"No, they're taking her back to New Mexico. We'll have to have a memorial."

"God. Yes. When?" They both looked at the calendar. Beginning of term was jammed with conferences, trustee meetings, parent council meetings.

Rue said, "I better call Fletcher Sincerbeaux. And Helen Lord, and . . . who else has Spanish in Primary?"

"Would Mrs. Ladabaum come back, do you think?" Mike asked.

"I don't know, isn't she in Florida?"

"Would we want her if she'd come? She was getting awfully deaf."

"Of course . . . I never saw a better teacher. We must have an ear trumpet somewhere."

"Okay, I'll find her," said Mike.

Rue went off to her office to start calling fellow school heads who might have a lead on a Spanish teacher.

On the wall in her office Rue kept a framed motto from Lucy Madeira, a famous East Coast educator. It read: "Function in disaster, finish in style." She often wondered what motto her predecessors, Carla and Lourdes Plum, would have willed her, had they been able to imagine her. The Plum family had proved over time to be as unfruitful as their land was lush, and their line narrowed and stopped with the spinster sisters, Carla and Lourdes, who had made a living conducting a day school according to tenets of their own devising.

Rue had made a study of the "archives" left by the Miss Plums. These artifacts were piled in wooden milk boxes and stored in the abandoned ice house, and included papers, letters, programs from Germans and Christmas plays, books, bottles of Coca-Cola syrup with which they treated children's coughs, woolen bathing suits, theatrical costumes, and some untouched ration books from World War II. The Miss Plums had gaily mixed notions of progressive education which they read about in papers sent out from New York, with their favorite parts of *Science and Health,* the writings of Emanuel Swedenborg, and the teachings of Madame Blavatsky. They believed that babies were born with their souls and their life paths fully formed, so there was no point imposing structure from without that might serve to crowd or cloud the structure within. They believed that every child had an aura which could be read, and that after death, that aura remained on earth, not so much a ghost as an angel, so the clear California air was crowded for them with invisible beings, concerned with the ways of woman and intervening in all her doings.

If the Miss Plums were right in their interesting theories, then no doubt their own auras lingered on the campus of The Country School, interfering in the business of shaping young lives in the ways most likely to confirm their own beliefs. If their theories were in error no one would ever know, because the Depression had put an end to their experiment before a significant sample of scholars could be sent out into the world. Their school was closed, and the

Miss Plums lived by selling off bits and pieces of outer pastures until only fifteen acres remained. By that time World War II had brought prosperity back to the region, and the Miss Plums lived to see others make large profits on land that had recently been theirs. Their joint Will and Testament left what land and money remained for the founding of a Country Day School, on acres that had once been lost in a wide expanse of range and orchard, but by the last decade of the twentieth century formed a hemmed-in green patch of nature, bonsaied between expensive developer houses and an upscale mall called The Countrye Mile. The campus was like a patch of the world as it once had been, but in a jar, with the top off.

   Emily Dahl arrived in Seven Springs by accident, if there are accidents. She had driven north until the children got hungry, and pulled off the highway into the nearest town. Her blond hair was clammy from heat and dirt, and there were half-moon perspiration stains under her breasts on her once crisp lemon-yellow blouse. She kept thinking of things she had forgotten to pack. A favorite pair of gardening shoes she had left outside the back door. A book she was reading, left facedown on the clothes hamper beside the bathtub. The worst was David's gerbil. Fortunately, David had not yet noticed.

She found that Seven Springs was a town of some natural beauty. There were fruit trees, citrus, and apricot, and on the dry hills, avocado. She and Malone and David found a taco restaurant that was air-conditioned. Across the street was a movie house that must have been built in the thirties. It had dusty art deco lettering on the marquee and the front of the theater was faced with black marble. It was cracked now, with pieces missing, but the whole effect was evocative; she remembered the theater in the town on Long Island where she grew up, where the whole eighth grade would show up at the movies on Saturday night. If you liked somebody and he liked you, you would sit apart from the group, in the balcony. There would be frightened bumblings having to do with the boy getting his arm around you while pretending to stretch. You would then die of embarrassment as you waited another hour or so for him to get the nerve to let his arm, lying across the back of your seat, inch down to encircle your shoulders. This, Emily realized, was a memory from a simpler world.

Malone squinted across the street at the movie house while she ate. Eleven years old, she had just gotten her first pair of glasses. She looked like a cross between a beautiful bombshell and a baby owl.

"Mom, *What About Bob* just started."

"Did it? Can you read the times from all the way over here?"

Malone nodded. "You'd only miss a little bit of it and I can tell you what happened."

David said "Are we going to the movies?" David the space cadet noticed everything two beats after everyone else.

"I don't know," said Emily, wondering really, Why not? What else did they have to do that evening? "Sure, if you want to."

"Yea," said Malone and bounced in her seat. This was a New Mom. The Old Mom wasn't so good at actually hearing what other people wanted. The Old Mom didn't tend to consider that someone else's plan might be just as good as hers.

So they went to the movie and ate popcorn even though they had already had tacos, and when they got out it was cool and dark and you could see Venus and the Big Dipper.

"Why don't we find a motel with a pool?" said Emily, and this had met with wild enthusiasm, so they had stayed in Seven Springs for the night. The children splashed and shouted until the manager turned off the pool lights at nine o'clock. Emily could only watch, since one of things she'd forgotten was her bathing suit.

The next morning, over breakfast at a House of Pancakes, they took a poll and decided this town seemed as good a place as any to light and settle. Emily suspected that excess sugar and bread and circuses were behind the choice, since everything they had done since they arrived was an out-of-the-ordinary, somebody's-birthday kind of treat. But the choice was made, and Emily stopped at the office of the first real estate company she saw.

The Coldwell Banker lady, Sylvia French, was a "people person." That, translated, meant she had been out of the job market for fifteen years and had no professional skills, beyond being an extremely nice woman. Fortunately, in Seven Springs there was a market for that. Sylvia had two children in a local private school for which she had run endless cookie sales and book fairs and drives to collect winter coats for the homeless. She was a fountain of enthusiasm for the town, for her school, for her belief in the widely available bounty of goodness life had to offer, and she loved accumulating details about other people's lives. Sylvia was not the sort of woman who needed much privacy. In fact, she abhorred a vacuum, which is how she perceived silence. She sat at the wheel of her big sedan, her glossy cap of dark hair shining, her large brown slightly bulging eyes even bigger behind huge square-framed glasses, chattering as she expertly drove.

"I don't know if this is in your price range but I must just show you these homes because they are *so* affordable, for what they are," she burbled as she pulled into a crescent drive on which stood five or six monstrosities, on parched clay in which not a shrub or field daisy grew, only the odd blade of onion grass and some blackened stalks of what might have been milkweed. The houses were in a half-timbered Tudor style with a soupcon of French chateau thrown in. "Two master suites, two guest rooms, dining room, living room, family room, two-car garage, full basement . . . it's all basically the same floor plan, but they're flopped in this one and that one. So you can choose which way you want the view. Would you like to see inside?" Emily could see through the window of the nearest one that they also had nasty low ceilings, gaudy brass fixtures, and skip-troweling on the walls, like a pretentious motel.

"I think you better tell me the price," said Emily.

"They're asking a million six. It would be closer to two, but so many developers went belly-up in the last three years. . . ."

"Ah," said Emily.

From the plush back seat of Mrs. French's car, Malone caught sight of something promising in the yard. "Mom, are we going to have a hot tub?" Emily didn't answer. She was thinking that at these prices, Malone would be lucky to have her own bedroom.

"Mom," said David from some zone of his own, "Where's Ralph?"

Something in his odd little brain had at this moment come across the memory of his gerbil.

"I'm afraid that's a good deal out of my range at the moment," said Emily, knowing that she was wearing a very expensive watch and shoes, and that cars like her Volvo station wagon, which was currently parked in front of Sylvia's office, didn't come in Crackerjack boxes. How to convey that things were not what they appeared with them, that their circumstances had changed rather suddenly.

"It's . . ." Emily began, and then stopped. Inadvertently she glanced in the rearview mirror at the children.

"I understand," said Sylvia. And amazingly, she did. Sylvia glanced sideways and suddenly understood, from something fugitive in the smile or perhaps from the uncertain way Emily's hand moved to push her hair back, that this very put-together, self-assured, and glossy human had suffered a recent and frightening crack in her foundation, and was trying to keep it from spreading. It wasn't hard to guess the rest.

"Let's try down here in the Lake District," Sylvia said, turning the car away from the parched heights she had been ascending. "It's an older neighborhood, very quiet and safe. I call it the Lake District, of course there's no lake. There's a street called Lake, and a very pretty pond with a playground, and a dog run. Do you have a dog?"

"No."

"Mom," said David a little more insistently, "where's Ralph?"

"We have a gerbil," said Emily. To David: "He's in your bedroom in his cage."

"Here?" asked David.

"Honey, you know he isn't in the motel room. He's in your old bedroom in Daddy's house." Daddy's house. That was the first time it had ever been anything but "our house."

"Who will feed him?" David asked.

"I'm sure Daddy will," said Emily, lying. She doubted that Tom even knew they had a gerbil. It could be weeks before anything caused him to visit one of his children's rooms. She'd have to call a neighbor who knew where the key was, ask someone to take Ralph home till she could arrange to come back for him.

They were driving down a winding street with far more modest houses than the Affordable Homes, fairly close together, under arching trees. These were houses from the twenties, frame and brick, many needing a little paint, or a lot of yard work. "You'll want to be close to The Country School," Sylvia was saying. "The public school, I'll take you by it, it isn't actually a bad school, they've only had one incident, I think, of children in Primary bringing guns to school, but The Country School is so special."

Pressing to hear all her options, Emily learned that the town also boasted a private elementary school run by Scientologists, an Orthodox Jewish school, which was probably the toughest of all academically but you had to take half your courses in Hebrew, and a wildly progressive school called Greenmere, where they did a great deal of "water play" and didn't start to read until fifth grade. Country's most serious competitor was an ex-military school, where the children still drilled in patterned marching, carrying wooden rifles during PE. Sylvia said it was fine academically, but to her mind rather rigid and joyless.

"You better tell me about The Country School," said Emily.

"It's like a family," said Sylvia. "That's the most important thing. You feel that every child matters, that there are no favorites. Every parent too. The Head is a woman named Rue Shaw, and she is really something special. She's smart, she has a sense of humor, and she has principles. Your kids don't just get into the best high schools, although they do that too, they also learn to be really nice people."

I have brains and a sense of humor, thought Emily, with a sudden flash of bitterness. I had straight A's in my major, and all the right connections. Why am *I* not a school head? Why am I not sitting magisterially in a big office with a leather blotter, interviewing prospective parents, reading the latest books on learning deficits? Instead of driving around the middle of nowhere with my children in the back of some strange car because my husband has decided that he wants to boff his nurse-receptionist? A woman named after a fruit? Why was I the last one on my block to learn to fear chaos at midlife?

The outer office of Home had once had a double-height door, so a man, or woman, could ride into the stable on horseback, and dismount in the center of the room, there to curry and brush his horse or wash it down, if it had been a muddy day. There had been a sloping cement floor, with a drain in the middle of the room, where Merilee's desk now stood. The door to this room was now of conventional size, and the visitor walked in to be surrounded by trophy cases, sepia class photographs, and plaques painted with the names of each succeeding class of Country School graduates, including mementos from the days of the Miss Plums. Rue especially relished a photograph of Carla and Lourdes Plum in long white skirts and middy blouses, leading a ragtag little flock of scholars in fencing practice. There was also an autographed picture of Hedy Lamar, whose children had once boarded with the Miss Plums and gone to school here.

What had been the tack room, lined with English and Western saddles, including the Miss Plums' sidesaddles, was now full of office equipment. One large box stall had become the faculty lounge cum sick bay. The other box stall, now enclosed to the ceiling, was the office of the business manager, Mr. Glarrow. Mr. Glarrow was a pale youngish man, quite long and thin, who existed on the edge of this bustle of life like a lost soul. He was brusque and clumsy with his grounds staff—he was *not* a "people person"— and he adored modern technology, although he had no talent for it whatever. Every summer when Rue went on vacation he drove her careful budget out of whack by buying new telephone systems that no one could work or networking software that couldn't be installed because it competed with existing device drivers on the computers, and no one in the office except Rue knew what device drivers were, let alone config.sys files and autoexec.bats, all of which soon came into play when Mr. Glarrow had a new bright idea for making their lives simpler. He was, however, a crackerjack bookkeeper and a terrific steward of buildings and grounds. Rue had never known a manager who could do everything in the job description and was grateful Bill Glarrow could do as much as he could. The fact that he didn't much care for children was not exactly a plus, either, but he worked terribly hard in early morning and evening hours, and rarely left his office during class times.

Emily had been thoroughly taken with The Country School when she visited, although it was still in summer session and she met only the staff, one teacher, and the assistant head, a Mr. Dianda. She had loved the air of the place, which had none of the prim sense of self-importance of the girls' school she herself had gone to in Cedarhurst. But when Emily stopped in two days before school opened, she knew something had happened. The hum of life, the smiles of welcome she had seen all over campus the day she had brought the children to be interviewed, were gone. Faces looked blank, or hurt. People walked together in twos and threes, talking intently. Something was wrong, a family thing. No one looked at the outsider.

In the office, Emily found a plump woman in her mid-forties dictating a newspaper ad to Merilee. She was wearing a long loose jumper of some soft stuff, and she had strong red hair, piled on her head in a haphazard knot. Her eyes were gray, wide, and intelligent. If she wore any makeup, Emily couldn't see it; she had beautiful skin and a fine acquiline nose, and carried herself as if to say that if that wasn't good enough for you, too bad.

Merilee said in her sweet chirping voice, "Oh hello, Mrs. Dahl—this is Mrs. Shaw."

The paragon, the woman with brains and principles. Rue had turned to smile Welcome, and her smile was extraordinarily warm. "Hello, how nice to meet you," said Rue, taking Emily's hand.

"You were still on vacation when we first arrived. . . ."

"Of course, Mr. Dianda told me. I understand you have a son with a brain the size of Montana."

Emily was pleased. "He tests well. He's a little shy, though. He has trouble making friends sometimes."

"Mike told me that too. But there's another little boy in David's class who has some physical problems, so he doesn't play sports and he's mad for dinosaurs. Pterodactyls are his particular field, I think. Mike says David goes in for tyrannosaurs."

"He's interested in pterodactyls too," said Emily.

"Good. No point in specializing too early. Colin's a dear little boy and we've been worried about his being lonely. The class was full, but Mrs. TerWilliams said she couldn't resist David. And in Malone's class, we happened to need a girl, so this has worked out well. Welcome to Country."

"Thank you. . . ."

"Mrs. Dahl," piped Merilee, "did you bring me the health forms?" Merilee had a bright smooth face like an apple, and she spoke with a high-pitched lilt that was so full of good will that no one could say a cross word to her.

"I did, but Mrs. Shaw?"

"Rue."

". . . Rue, thank you. Did I hear you advertising for a Spanish teacher?"

"You did."

"Could I apply for the job?"

"Do you know Spanish? I mean forgive me for asking, since I was about to offer it to Manuel who's out mowing the soccer field. Have you taught?"

"Not recently, but yes . . ." Well actually, not in twenty years, but. She'd been good at it, she felt, and had once meant to go on with it.

"Come into my office," said Rue.

Rue's office was in the low-ceilinged back of the building, beside Mike Dianda's. It too had heavy square beams and small windows. Rue had filled it with soft-blue furniture on a pale green carpet, and on her desk there was always a bowl of flowers from Merilee's garden. Today they were roses. The effect was of a haven, like a favorite book-lined room under the eaves, or a cross between a cave and a garden.

What Emily noticed first, when she followed Rue in, were the boxes of Kleenex everywhere.

"People must cry a lot here," said Emily.

Rue smiled. "They do."

The second thing she noticed was there were no diplomas on the wall. She had a feeling Rue Shaw had some impressive degrees under her belt; she had looked forward to knowing exactly what, from where. She was hoping there might be something a little second-rate, so she wouldn't need to feel one down. She herself had gone to a good but not great women's college, from a very famous Eastern boarding school where she had received a very middling preparation from a faculty superannuated to the point of coma in some cases. It was a school, she liked to say, where girls were supposed to be awash in sentiment and have silver spoons for brains. Still she felt more secure after she'd managed to drop the name. It helped people place her, told them something true about who she was and where she had come from.

Rue apparently had no such need.

Her walls were crowded with framed pictures of children, drawings and paintings from children, handlettered cards and cartoons and certificates of commendation from eight-year-olds. These were interspersed with photographs of her family. There were, side by side, framed antique photographs of two men from other times and places. Each stared fiercely into the camera. One had light eyes and wore a soft hat; the other had puffy cheeks and muttonchop whiskers, and a heavy watch chain across his waistcoat.

"Two of my great-grandfathers," said Rue, noticing Emily's gaze. "The one with the hat was a sheep farmer on an island in Maine. His name was Long. He had eleven children and the boys all had names like Miles Long and How Long."

Emily laughed. "And the other one?"

"My mother's grandfather. A titan of industry."

Emily stopped at a framed snapshot of a girl who could have been Rue herself at eighteen, except that she had a darker quality, too, something deep and intent. Like a cross between Rue and a fawn of some kind.

"I don't have to ask whose child this is. You must have had her by parthenogenesis."

"That's Georgia," said Rue. "Actually she and her father look *exactly* alike." Rue picked up another picture from her desk, this one showing a good-looking man of about forty with blue eyes and unruly blond hair, with a ten-year-old Georgia, grinning, sitting on his shoulders in a striped bathing suit. She handed it to Emily, who said, "Oh my god," and started to laugh.

"What?"

"Cricket Shaw . . . you're married to Cricket Shaw?"

Surprised and pleased, Rue said, "Mostly we call him Henry now."

"Does he still play the saxophone?"

"Only when he's drunk."

"I don't know that I ever saw him sober. My god, I never expected to see Cricket again in this lifetime. What did he grow up to be?"

Rue, smiling, said, "He's a brain surgeon."

When Emily stopped laughing, she said, "I went out with one of his college roommates, Todd Bakeman. . . ."

"Bakelund . . ."

"Bakelund. He was a little odd."

"Still is."

"I had the most tremendous crush on Cricket."

"I don't blame you," said Rue, smiling. "Will he remember you?"

"I don't know," said Emily. Though she did know. He would.

"Tell me about your teaching experience," said Rue.

When Rue got home from school that afternoon her Georgia, Georgia who looked like a cross between Rue and a fawn, Georgia who was somehow the image of Henry when she talked, was packed and ready to leave. Her room was a wreck. It looked as if she had taken out every article of clothing she owned, packed the things she wanted, and left the rest wherever they fell, on the bed, on the chairs, on the floor. Her suitcase, her enormous duffel, her boom box, and her guitar were waiting in a pile to be carried downstairs. The cassettes she couldn't be parted from for twenty-four hours were in a carrying case. A few hundred more were packed in a cardboard box, with her name and her New York address written on it, ready to be mailed. And what looked to Rue like several thousand rejects remained in stacks in her bookcase, along with her Narnia books, her Nancy Drews, her Black Stallion books, and her paperback Great Books from high school English. From now on it was to be no more Dead White Male writers, just composers. She was going to New York to live and breathe music.

Georgia herself was out on the back porch in the glider, with her friend Caroline who had just gotten back from Outward Bound. Rue could hear cries of "Oh my *god* . . ." followed by laughter, as they rushed to fill each other up with every event and detail of the summer they had spent apart. Outward Bound had moved Caroline to take the safety pin out of her nose, Rue overheard, but the change had been temporary. It was back, with a full display of hoops and studs, but at least the safety pin was gold.

Tonight, after family dinners, would be their last evening with their old gang. *Posse* had been the right term for it at one point, but now Georgia rolled her eyes if Rue said it, so she gathered posse was past, along with so much else.

Tomorrow morning Henry would take Georgia to the airport, and Caroline would leave for UC Santa Cruz in a used ambulance her father had bought her. Caroline had already been arrested twice for having red lights and a siren on what was not an emergency vehicle, although she swore she only turned the lights on for, like, a minute. She and Georgia had become friends in high school, right around the time Rue had begun to wonder if she was tempting fate when she said out loud that Georgia alone in her experience with adolescents had never given her parents a moment's unhappiness or worry.

Georgia had been their hearts' delight from birth. She was a large-hearted, bright, wise, and beautiful little girl, and adolescence hadn't made her as hideous as it did most. There was a year when her nose seemed too big for her face, but that had passed, and there had been the famous shouting match the time they caught her chewing tobacco in the bus barn with Manuel, and Henry made her swallow it. This had made Georgia furious at both of them and Rue angry at Henry because it had so upset Manuel. Manuel was a little simple. On this afternoon, Rue could remember being mad at Henry when they differed about Georgia, but she didn't think she could remember ever being mad at Georgia.

Missing her daughter in advance, this morning when Rue left for school she had carried with her a leaden sense of loss that was so piercing that she barely had room for more when the news came that Mariel Smith was dead. If you wanted six children, and you only could have one, Georgia was the one you would want. *Delight* was the word that best expressed Rue's feeling for her daughter. Georgia's brain was very different from Rue's or Henry's; she was quick, inventive, and above all musical, and Rue simply adored her. Rue had begun to worry what would happen when Georgia was gone. The three of them had been so close for so long, she wondered if she and Henry would collapse like a triangle with a missing side.

For Georgia's farewell dinner, Rue cooked eggplant curry, and raita and dahl and fragrant basmati rice, and she herself smelled faintly of cumin. Caroline had gone home to have steak with her family, and Georgia was now upstairs washing her hip-length auburn hair and listening to *Tosca*. Rue thanked God she wasn't playing some ear-splitting heavy metal tonight; but Georgia was good. She nearly always saved her really awful music for when she was out of the house. You tended only to hear it when she had been driving your car and forgotten she'd left the radio tuned to KOL Rock and the volume cranked up to a thousand decibels. Henry had had a few mornings when he'd turned on his ignition and been blasted nearly into the back seat. Rue was spared the early morning assaults because she commuted to campus on foot.

Rue was very glad that school was starting tomorrow, despite the fact that one of the bus drivers had broken her arm, and pressure was already building from parents who didn't want their children in Mrs. Trainer's class, and the Spanish teacher was dead. She loved the first day of school because it was a day full of clean slates and new book bags and happy reunions and hope. And you could say one thing about having the house empty of Georgia tomorrow night. It would make meal planning easier. Since Georgia had become a vegetarian, Henry made sad remarks about "veggie pudding" and "Alpo burgers" on the nights she cooked for Georgia, and when she produced sausage or chops for Henry, Georgia ate cold cereal, looking pained at the savagery before her. Rue was on the fence between them. She liked the meatless meals, but she was constantly allowing herself to be frightened by friends who read women's magazines who warned that if she didn't make a full-time study of meatless nutrition, she would get a protein or calcium deficiency and become demented during menopause, or that all her bones would break, or something.

Dinner was ready, the candles were lit. Henry had come in, opened a beer, and stood around the kitchen humming snatches of the Beatles' song "She's Leaving Home." Every time their eyes met, they laughed, because they were so sad. Georgia breezed in, fresh and clean and wearing a new white t-shirt of her father's, which was huge on her. Her wet hair was twisted into a loose rope down her back. They all took their places at the kitchen table, where they always ate when alone. It was a big room, with wainscot cupboards under the counters and two stoves, the old wood cook stove the Plum family had once used and the thirties-vintage white porcelain number Carla and Lourdes had installed. Tonight there was a bucket of roses from Rue's garden on the cold wood stove.

In the candlelight, and the lingering evening light of late summer, Georgia gave them their pitch. As they had done every night they were all together, for the last fifteen years, they sang "Tallis Canon," in a round. Rue and Georgia began:

> *"All praise to thee my God this night"*

And Henry followed with the same line, as the women sang:

> *"For all the blessings of the light.*
> *"Keep me, Oh keep me, King of kings*
> *"Beneath thine own almighty wings."*

And Henry finished alone:

> *"Beneath thine own almighty wings,"*

in his sweet raspy bass, and Rue felt tears start in her throat. In the silent second that followed the singing she had to wipe her eyes and blow her nose.

Georgia said, "You loved it when I went to camp, Mom. Don't pretend you didn't. You cried till the bus was around the corner and then you hardly remembered to write."

"I wrote *daily*."

"I was the only kid in my cabin who didn't get mail all week. The counselors felt so sorry for me they wrote me notes and forged your name."

"You're a wicked liar."

Henry said to Georgia, "She wasn't crying for you, anyway. She was crying because she knows you're going to sing 'Tallis Canon' at my funeral."

"Oh, good," said Georgia. "Are we? Have you printed the programs?"

"Not yet. No, the new rector at your mother's church gave us all forms to fill out planning our funerals. He's really trying to get us to call our lawyers and put the church in our will, but I thought that was depressing. I've done my funeral, though. I want 'Tallis Canon' and 'For All the Saints,' and 'Oh God Our Help in Ages Past.' And I chose my readings too, but I don't think Father Tom is going to like it."

"What are you having?"

"Robert Frost and E. B. White."

"No gospel?" Rue asked.

"No, I want someone to read White's essay on *The Death of a Pig.*"

"Mom, have you planned yours?"

"No. There are so many hymns I love, I can't decide. Daddy just put 'Tallis Canon' in his because he knows it would make me fall apart. I know you fancy the idea of the widow wailing and sobbing and having to be led from the church, Henry. Would you pass me the chutney?"

"But you forgot, you made me promise not to die first."

"Oh, you'll never keep that promise. Look at all that red meat you eat."

"I don't want any funeral," said Georgia.

"I read about a company in San Francisco that makes coffins out of auto bodies. Wouldn't you like one if you could go in a little red vintage MG?" asked Henry.

"Nope. No funeral. No sacred texts, no ministers especially."

"How about a recital of *Cavalleria Rusticana*?" said Rue.

"Nope."

"So, you want me to record that in your baby book? No funeral, no memorial, just plant the ashes in the garden with a post hole digger?"

"Perfect," said Georgia. "Life is all there is, and life is enough. Too many people miss it, because they're worrying about something else that doesn't exist."

"Okay," said Rue, "but will you let me know if you change your mind?"

"I will if I do, but I won't."

"That's what you said when you were five, about cooked tomatoes."

"Be Here Now. That's my final word. This is great chutney, by the way. Did you make it?"

"Major Grey made it. I made everything else on the table. Everything. I made the napkins, I made the salt cellars. . . ."

"Sorry, Mom. This is great raita, did you make it?"

"Why yes, Georgia, I did. I made it just for you, and I'm so glad you like it."

"Are you all packed, Beezel?" Henry asked.

"Almost. I can't zip my duffel but Sam will do it."

"What's in it?"

"Sheets. Blankets. Shoes. I don't know. Buford."

Buford was her stuffed bear.

"You put Buford in the duffel? I thought he had trouble with claustrophobia."

"He got over that. It was adolescent angst."

"Ah."

"Do you think Buford will like New York?" Rue asked.

"I think he'll love it. He's looking forward to his first subway ride. Don't cry, Mom."

"I'm not. I ate a piece of chili."

"Apart from the Spanish teacher . . . Mrs. Lincoln . . . How does your new school year look, Rue?" Henry asked. "What's going on over there?"

Rue was grateful for the change of subject. She was embarrassed when emotion overcame her, though it happened to her all the time. She said, "I think this may be Catherine Trainer's last year. I'm already getting complaints about her and we aren't even in session."

Georgia said, "Why? I *loved* Mrs. Trainer."

"I know you did, everyone used to. But she went way downhill while Norman was sick, and after he died, she just never bounced back. In the last couple of years, she's just been marking time, as if it doesn't matter what she does because she's a School Character."

"What would happen to her if you fired her?" Henry asked.

"Nothing good. She has one married sister she never sees. She's not trained to do anything but teach. And she needs the money. She's only fifty-nine."

They all three looked at each other.

"Could she get another teaching job?"

"I doubt it. At her age, she's too expensive. And no matter what reference I give her, any other head is going to know I wouldn't have fired her except for really good cause."

"What if she quit?" Henry asked.

"She'll never do that. All her friends are here. The school is her life."

"I assume you've let her know that things are serious," said Henry.

"Of course. I've said everything short of 'You're fired.' But she doesn't hear it. The only part she hears is 'You've worked hard on improving such and such.' The minute I say 'But,' she turns off her receiver. It's as if she thinks we're all family, and you may be annoyed with your sister, but you're stuck with her."

"Well—it *is* the real world. If she can't do the job, you're not running a charity ward."

"She can do the job . . ."

"But someone else could do it better."

"A lot better, I'm afraid. I lost three families last year on her account, and I'm about to lose more. But the Lord provides. We've taken four new kids in the last week. One of the moms is an old girl of yours, Henry."

"How exciting, which one?"

"Her name is Emily Dahl. She's a slim blond, pageboy hair, Georgia's height. About two years younger than I am."

"I'm not placing her."

The doorbell rang. Georgia jumped up.

"Honey . . ." said Rue. "If that's your friends, could you . . ."

"I'll tell them we're eating. They can sit in the living room."

"Tell them to sit outside in the driveway," said Henry. But they all knew that no matter what they did, Georgia's last supper at home as a child of this house was bound to end.

Chandler Kip was annoyed when he left the house. For the fourth time since he bought it, his Jaguar wouldn't start, for no reason that he could see. There was plenty of juice in the battery, it wasn't cold, it wasn't flooded, and it had been running fine last night. He had had to wait for Bobbi to get back from taking Missy to school, so he could borrow her car. She drove a huge Suburban that got about twelve miles to the gallon. It was like driving a tank, but that was what Bobbi liked about it. City traffic scared her, so she needed something heavy that put her high above the road, like a turret gunner, in case she went shopping in LA.

As he hefted the Suburban into the Seven Springs Service on Union Street, he checked himself out in the rearview mirror. He brushed what little was left of his hair back with one hand, and bared his teeth in the mirror to be sure there was nothing caught in them.

He pulled up to the first row of pumps and killed the ignition. The station seemed deserted. A slanted rectangle of sun burned through the windshield across his thigh. He honked the horn and looked around the apparently empty bays of the garage, then around the front seat of the van at Bobbi's detritus, while he waited. There was a gum wrapper wedged between the seat and the back, there were hair pins on the dashboard, there were loose cassettes. Bobbi was listening to an abridged version of *The Joy Luck Club*, he gathered, as she ferried Missy and her little friends to dancing class, to riding lessons, to Campfire Girls.

He got out of the car, walked around to open the gas cap, went to the pump, and started to fill the tank. After three gallons, a voice behind him said, "I'm sorry sir, this is a full-serve island. If you want to do that yourself, you'll have to move your vehicle to the self-serve, see over there. We have big signs."

"Randy," Chandler turned and smiled. "I didn't know where

you were." Randy was twenty and lean, with long arms, big hands, and such big shoulders that he looked as if he'd left the hanger inside his clothes. He took the pump hose from his father.

"I was in the can. Sorry."

"You know, in the last gas rationing crisis, there was a man who closed his station and went home for the night but he left one pump unlocked. When he came back in the morning his whole tank was dry, two thousand gallons. Someone had stood there all night selling his gas and pocketing the money."

Randy bristled slightly. "Thanks, Dad. Next time I go to the can, I'll lock the pumps."

"I didn't mean that. It was just a story. I just was thinking of it, I could have stood here and sold your gas to whoever came in, if you hadn't come back."

"Phil's gas. Don't you think people would wonder a little bit about your suit?" Randy had always been the master of the deadpan. He stood there in his blue overalls, looking at his father's handmade Glen plaid. "They might suspect it wasn't your regular gig. Or, hey, maybe not. It's a recession. Who knows. Maybe they'd think you got laid off and couldn't afford a pair of overalls."

"The people who bought the gas from the guy in the gas crisis must have noticed the station didn't have any lights on."

"You have a larcenous soul. Don't they say you can only con a con?" Randy finished filling the tank of the Suburban, and put the hose back in its cradle.

"So—how's it going?" Chandler asked.

"Okay," said Randy. "Your car in the shop again?"

"It wouldn't start. I don't know why."

"You want me and Phil to take a look at it?"

"No, Bobbi called the Triple A. I guess it's a lemon."

"It's not a lemon, it's a Jaguar. I warned you."

There was a silence. Chandler took his wallet from his back pocket and took out two twenties and handed them to Randy.

"I'll get your change," he said, turning to go to the office.

"Please keep it," said Chandler. He noticed that Randy's hair reached to his shoulder blades and could use a shampoo, and that he had a paperback copy of *The Plague*, by Albert Camus, deep in his back pocket. Randy came back, pocketing the money.

"Thank you."

"You're welcome."

There was another silence.

"Hey Dad, guess what Mom sent me." Randy suddenly smiled.

"You're in touch with your mom?"

"Of course I'm in touch with Mom. What did you think?"

"You just haven't mentioned her in a while, I didn't know. I didn't know if you still knew where she was."

"She's where she's been for two years, Dad. Did you think she was like some field mouse? Drops the litter of micelets in a field someplace and wanders off and forgets to write? I always know where she is."

"Sorry. I'm glad to hear it. What did she send you?"

Randy smiled. "Your college yearbook. She said she didn't have a lot of use for it, and she thought I'd like it. Your senior picture is a gas, man, with your hair curled down over your ears . . . you looked like H. R. Haldeman."

Chandler put his hands on his hips and grinned. "Well thank you very much, how do you even know who H. R. Haldeman is? You have my yearbook? I haven't seen that in *years*. . . . I didn't know it still existed. Your mother had my yearbook?"

"I've got one question, Dad. Tell me about being Tonto Toogood."

Chandler gave a sharp laughing bark of embarrassment.

"Is that in there?"

"Right under your senior picture."

"What, do they have a lot of quotes and stuff under your picture? The same as high school? I'd forgotten that. . . . I guess they did."

Chandler turned away and looked into the distance. He looked back. "Tonto Toogood. I feel like that happened to a different person."

"Apparently." Another car, a Miata with the top down, pulled up to the full-serve pump in front of the Suburban. "Excuse me," said Randy.

When he came back, his father had recovered from his surprise. "So? Tonto?"

"As I remember, it was a fraternity thing. We used to have

Truth or Consequence nights, where you all sit in a circle drinking and people can ask you anything they want and you have to tell the truth."

Randy nodded. And waited.

"One night someone asked me what was my deepest secret, and I told them my real name was Thomas Toogood."

His son stared at him, then smiled briefly, then shook his head, as if to clear his ears. "Your real name is what?"

"My real name is Chandler Kip, but Thomas Toogood is what my birth certificate says."

"Dad—did it ever occur to you to mention this to me?"

"I guess not. To tell you the truth, I think I forgot it."

"It's a hell of a thing to forget. What does it mean?"

"Well, Toogood is Grandma's maiden name. . . ."

"I know. Who's Thomas?"

"I have no idea," said Chandler. His son was staring at him. Now that the subject had come up, it occurred to him that it might be mildly odd that he hadn't thought to tell him before.

"Well didn't you ever ask Grandma?"

"Of course I did."

"Well?"

"I asked her what happened to my real father, and she said, 'Your real father is right in there, go ask him yourself.' Meaning Elmer, lying in front of the TV on his Barcalounger."

Randy remembered Elmer, although he had always called him Grandpa, and he didn't know that that thing he always lay on like a beached whale was called a Barcalounger. Grandpa had wispy patches of steel-gray hair and thick glasses that made his eyes look pink. He was minister emeritus of the Church of Christ. When Randy, aged seven, asked Grandpa what "emeritus" meant, Grandpa said it meant "fired."

"So," said Randy, "your name isn't Chandler and it isn't Kip? And neither is mine?"

"Of course it is. Grandma legally changed it when she married Elmer. She changed hers and mine from Toogood to Kip at the same time."

"Don't you think you might have told me?"

"Why?" said Chandler.

"Because it doesn't just affect you! You were going to let me go through life waiting to look in the mirror and find I'd turned into Grandpa? Elmer? And now it turns out I should be waiting to turn into some guy whose name I don't know, who's head must look like a boiled egg?" He waved his hand at his father's head.

"You get baldness from the mother's side," said Chandler stiffly.

"It seems *you* get everything from the mother's side," said Randy. "Where did Chandler come from?"

There was an embarrassed silence. Chandler glanced at the street, as if willing another car to pull in, but traffic hummed by.

"I think it was a movie star she liked. Maybe a radio actor, from when she was younger. Something Chandler."

Randy looked at his father, laughed, not very nicely, and abruptly walked in a circle around the pumps, as if stillness might lead to an explosion.

"I don't know why you're so aggravated," said Chandler.

"Irritated," said Randy coldly. "Aggravated means 'make worse.' From the Latin *gravis,* serious, heavy, or bad."

"Well excuuuuse me," said Chandler. "What do you want to do, take dueling IQ tests?"

Randy looked at him, angry because hurt, then looked away. His father looked at the sky, as if for answers. He looked at his watch. He looked at the concrete, glittering with mica in the hot September sun.

"You asked me a question. This is the answer. I told my brothers my name wasn't my real name. They decided they should rename me, like Indians name each other after exploits or deeds, so they called me Tonto Toogood. I liked it. But in the end I didn't see what difference it made. My mom gave me a name and then she gave me another name. They both came from the same place. What difference did it make?"

Randy was staring at him as if he couldn't express how dumb his father looked to him. Finally, he said, "Did Mom know?"

"Of course. She was there."

"When you were born?"

"She was there, at Grinnell."

"Why didn't she tell me?"

"I don't know. Ask her."

"Did you make her not tell?"

Chandler flared. "Of course I didn't make her not tell! I'd like to see the man who could make your mother do fucking anything she didn't want! She probably thought all sons should be named for their mothers and men should be left out of the system entirely, I don't know why she didn't tell you. Ask her yourself."

They stared at each other for a long time, Chandler beginning to sweat onto his monogrammed shirt, and his son, burned to brown on his face and neck, the sunburn following the V of his greasy blue overalls that said "Randy" in white stitching over the pocket.

"Have a nice day, Dad," said Randy, turning away from his father. As he walked to the office, he took the book from his back pocket and started to read, as if he were shutting a door behind him. Chandler wheeled and went to the driver's side of the Suburban and climbed in, slamming his door. He peeled out to the curb, only to have to jam on the brakes as a light changed, and he was stopped by a lane of live traffic and left to sit in the sun, confused and angry at his only son.

The campus was looking lush and groomed for the first day of school. The olive and persimmon trees were glossy, and there was a new bed of bright blue campanula mixed with white impatiens outside Rue's office. By 8:15, the parking lot had been filled with Range Rovers, BMWs, Volvos, and Mercedes. Some were driven by moms on the way to work, more were driven by dads on the way to work. The ones with whom Rue most empathized were the moms who drove the carpool in their bathrobes, wearing moccasins on bare feet and drinking a mug of coffee. The only thing Rue liked about the concept of retiring was the thought of sleeping late.

On the central walkway, where the paths led off in long spurs to the Primary building and to the Middle School, Rue stood to greet her children. As they did every school day, every child from first grade through sixth began the day by shaking her hand and saying, "Good morning, Mrs. Shaw." Much as she had dreaded the end of summer and especially Georgia's going, she was surprised by elation at this moment, seeing the children again, seeing how they'd grown and changed in so short a time as summer, seeing the campus fill up again with noise and motion and shining-faced hopeful protoplasm.

"Good morning, Patrick. Good morning, Lillibet. Good morning, Sara. Good morning, Jesse. Jesse . . . What is this in my hand, a dead fish? Oh! It's your hand! That's *much* better. Good morning, Nairi." She had begun this practice sixteen years before, when she took over a school with seventy-seven children left, most of whom were poised to flee. "Seventy-seven," she had reported to Henry when she got back to Boston, "and their IQs match their shoe size."

She had been thirty-two at the time. Most people thought she was out of her mind to take on a school that looked to be on the verge of closing. But her mentor said, "If you follow a beloved longtime head at a thriving school, you'll be fired in three years because no one really wanted a change. It's better to follow a head who was drunk or insane." Rue's predecessor at The Country School, a nephew of the Miss Plums, had apparently been both.

The first thing Rue had decided was that even if they couldn't read or write, Country School children would know how to look you in the eye, call you by name, and give a firm handshake. The tradition caused a great bottleneck now that enrollment was nearing three hundred, but the children liked it, and Rue liked it. There were usually a dozen moments in the course of a day when she feared she was was doing the wrong thing, but in this exercise at least, adding very slightly to the level of civility in the world, she felt sure of doing no harm.

For the first day of school Kathleen Clancy, a dear little girl with Coke-bottle glasses, had brought Mrs. Shaw a tomato she had grown all by herself. It was large and ripe and beginning to split. Rue took it carefully, with warm thanks, shook Kathleen's hand, and wished her a very happy year in second grade.

As she was doing this, a man Rue had never seen before appeared suddenly from the side of her field of vision and started to barge past her and Kathleen, tangled among the little ones. He was dark and very tall with a long angular face, and he moved in a violent rushing way, as one who has been running for a plane and sees that it has left the gate, whose next move is going to be to knock people down and yell at the gate agent. Beyond Home, Rue saw that someone, in spite of the large handpainted sign asking that no one park on the grass, had circumvented the line of cars by pulling a gleaming green Masarati onto the lawn of the preschool.

"Good morning," said Rue, smiling, but subtly blocking his way by holding out her tomato. "Can I help you?"

The man looked balked and angry, as if not used to being questioned.

"Have you seen Malone and David Dahl? I'm Dr. Dahl."

Rue extended her hand and said calmly, "I'm Dr. Shaw."

"Are they here yet? I'd *like* to see my children," he added sarcastically, as if she had personally kept him from them.

"I'll be through here in just a moment, Dr. Dahl. Why don't you wait for me in my office? Right in there, in the administration building."

Rue watched him storm off toward Home.

"Good morning, Lia. Good morning, Ashley. Good morning, Ryan . . . what happened to your foot?"

"A horse at camp stepped on it," said Ryan proudly. He was in a nylon cast that was covered with graffiti. He stumped away.

"Good morning, Jennifer, good morning, Scott. Jennifer . . ."

Jennifer Lowen, a fifth grader wearing all the Colors of Benetton, hopped back to her.

"Could you do me a favor? Would you find Mr. Dianda and ask him to come speak to me? Thank you. He should be in his office."

Mike Dianda, reassuringly tall and broad-shouldered in his tweed jacket and khakis, appeared moments later. "There's a fairly aggressive item stalking up and down in front of Merilee's desk," he said. "Good morning, Shana."

"Good morning, Mr. Dianda."

"I know," said Rue. "Would you please go take over Mrs. Dahl's Spanish class and ask her to come to my office?"

At that moment the warning bell for first class sounded. "Yes, ma'am," said Mike.

"Good morning, Jamie, good morning, Tara, better hop it . . . you've got two minutes. . . . Oh, Royya, thank you!" A beautiful black-eyed girl emerged from a huge silver van and handed her a bouquet of zinnias with their cut stems wrapped in wet newspaper. Rue waved her thanks to Dr. Zayyad, Royya's mother, who was a competitor of Henry's. Rue liked Rita Zayyad a lot.

"I would *like* you to let my children know that I'm here for them," Tom Dahl demanded, loudly, as Rue walked into Home. He was pacing up and down in front of the trophy case.

"I'll be with you in just a minute, Dr. Dahl." She walked past him and handed her flowers and her tomato to Merilee. "Could you find a vase, Merilee? And don't let me go home without the tomato. When Mr. Kip gets here, will you ask him to wait a few minutes? Thank you."

She turned. "Come this way, Dr. Dahl. I don't have much time. I have a meeting scheduled with my Board head. I'm sorry I didn't know you were coming. . . ." She showed him into her office.

Tom Dahl pulled the door shut forcefully behind them. "What is this place? I never heard of it," he demanded, gesturing in a way that indicated he meant the school. Rue stared at him, then sat down at her desk. She was trying to decide whether to play it straight or to get aggressive herself.

She decided to play it straight. "We're an independent country day school, pre-K through 8. We were founded in nineteen forty-eight; our current enrollment is two hundred ninety-eight, and we're quite well known in the mid-coast area. . . ."

"The school my children attend," he said, as if each word were a piece of jerky he had to rip off with his teeth and then spit at her, "The Bonewright School in Los Angeles, where I have paid *full* tuition for both, was surprised to find you expected my children to enroll here. They were kind enough to inform me you had asked for their transcripts. Are you in the habit of taking kidnapped children and hiding them from their parents?"

"I'm not in the habit of requiring legal proof of custody or to see death certificates in the case of widowhood, if that's what you're asking me."

"My wife shows up out of the blue, for no reason, and it doesn't occur to you to ask her if she has the right to be hiding children in some god-forsaken town without telling her husband?"

"Do you think this town is god-forsaken?" Rue asked mildly. "I've always thought it was rather blessed. But you may be on more intimate terms with the Lord than I am."

"You think that Ph.D. makes you smart, don't you?" Rue had hoped that might bother him.

"I don't know if that's a serious question," said Rue, "but I'll give you a serious answer. No, I don't. I don't think degrees have anything to do with making people smart. Doctor."

At that point, Emily walked in.

"Oh, Jesus," said Tom Dahl, wild with disgust. What was his wife doing on campus? He had assumed he could either scoop the kids up and have them back in LA before anyone was the wiser or else bully someone here, who after all wouldn't know Emily from a hole in the ground, into handing them over.

"Emily," said Rue, "Dr. Dahl tells me there's a misunderstanding about where Malone and David are to go to school. I thought the two of you together could probably solve this better than I can. Would you like me to go or stay?"

"Stay," said Emily as Tom roared "GO!"

Just then, Chandler Kip walked in, looking hot and annoyed. Every visible stitch of clothing on his body, including the shoes, had been handmade in London. This was a man who wanted no misunderstanding about exactly how successful he was, but his crisp white shirt was wilted and the top of his head looked uncomfortably pink.

"Chandler, good morning. These are new parents in the school, Dr. Dahl and Emily Dahl. Mrs. Dahl has been kind enough to take over for Mariel Smith. . . ."

"Take over what?" Tom demanded.

"Look, Rue, I can't wait, my car's in the shop, and I have a very important meeting downtown in forty minutes," said Chandler, virtually ignoring the two seething humans who were sharing the office with Rue. "I'll have to call you later to reschedule."

"I'm awfully sorry," said Rue. Chandler waved his hand impatiently, a gesture Rue couldn't quite interpret. He went out and shut the door.

"Took over *what?*" Tom said again, to Emily.

Neither Rue nor Emily answered.

"Emily, Dr. Dahl says I should have asked before, and perhaps I should have. Who has custody of Malone and David?"

There was a silence. Tom glared at Emily. Emily looked as if she were fighting for clarity.

"I do," she said.

"Nobody does," Tom shouted. "There's no agreement, you just left!"

"I do, because if we fight it out in court I'll get them and you know it. You left me, Tom. . . ."

"*You* left the house and stole the car and the children!"

"You want a 'vacation from the marriage' while you're sleeping with your nurse! I've been a faithful, full-time, at-home mother for eleven years! Do you think you're going to get custody?"

"Are you filing for divorce?"

"I will."

"Well then *you're* leaving me. I don't want a divorce."

"Oh for christ's sake!"

"This is a no-fault state. . . ."

"That applies to money, not who's fit to raise children," Emily howled. Rue stood up and handed Emily the nearest box of tissue as she burst into tears.

"Dr. Dahl, I'm going to ask you to leave. If you are going to have a custody fight, it should not be in my office."

"I'm taking the children."

"Not unless you show me a court order."

"*She* can't show you one!"

"What should we do, put them in a foster home?" Emily yelled at him.

"I'll sue you," said Tom to Rue viciously.

"I'm sorry to hear that," said Rue.

"I want to see them," he said.

Rue looked at Emily. Emily said, "They're in class. It's their first day of school."

"I can't wait here all day!"

"If it were me, I would," said Emily.

"I work for a living," said Tom nastily.

"So do I," said Emily.

"At *what?*"

"I really think," Rue said, "that you should have your lawyers work out regular times for your visits, Dr. Dahl. But you *are* welcome to stay and have lunch with us. The children will be free then for forty-five minutes."

Tom Dahl stared at her. He stared at his wife. Moments passed. Suddenly, he turned and stalked out, slamming the door explosively behind him.

"Well," said Rue, looking at Emily. "The year has begun."

Emily sat down and began to shake. "I'm sorry," she said. "I'm sorry. . . ."

Rue opened her office door and called, "Merilee—is there any coffee? Would you bring us some? Do you mind?"

"I've got to get back to my class," Emily said.

"Take a deep breath," said Rue. Emily did, and it was ragged, like sobs. "Again," said Rue. Merilee came in with mugs of coffee.

"I'm terribly sorry," said Emily more calmly. "I thought he didn't know where I was." She blew her nose. "I'm sorry, it really isn't like him . . . it's just that I broke all the rules. He's supposed to be able to hurt me and reject me, and I'm supposed to stay and take it, because I'm a mother. He can't believe I walked out of his cage. He can't believe I won't come back and climb back in and pull the door closed behind me. Maybe I can't either. I wonder if he's put down fresh paper for me. Shoveled up all the old doots and bird seed."

"I take it you don't have a lawyer yet."

Emily shook her head.

"I've got a good one for you. Ann Rosen. She's on our Board, she was my president for four years. She's smart and she's not afraid of bullies and she gets it over quickly. At least that's what I'm told. Would you like her number?"

Emily nodded. It looked to Rue as if she still didn't believe things had come to this.

Merilee came to the door. "Excuse me . . . the auction committee would like just a minute, if your nine o'clock is canceled. . . ."

"God, I'm sorry—" said Emily for the third time, jumping up.

Rue said, "Why don't you come have supper with us tonight? I know Henry would like to see you. Bring the children."

The auction chairpersons trotted in, carrying clipboards and mugs of coffee.

"You don't have to . . ." said Emily.

"You don't know. We have an empty nest for the first time tonight . . . you'll be doing us a favor. Come at six." Emily, teary, nodded and ran out. The auction chairs, both fit and bright-eyed in spandex and sweatshirts, began to chatter. The annual auction fundraiser this year was to have a Gay Nineties theme.

That evening, Rue missed the moment when Emily and Henry met. She was in the garden, cutting flowers for the table. Emily came to the front door with the children, found it open, and came through the house, following the smell of cooking, to where Henry stood in the kitchen, making pesto. She stood in the doorway watching him. The same tall, long-torsoed body, the same thick blond hair, stiff and wiry and curling over the silver side pieces of his glasses. His hair had more gray than hers, but of course he probably didn't dye his.

He looked up, about to speak, and saw her. She was wearing pressed blue jeans and a fresh shirt, and her hair was pulled back and sleek. His mouth hung open a moment. Then he grinned and said, "Well, waddya know. It's *you*." He put down the spoon he was holding and put his hands on his hips and stared. After a while, Emily said, "Yes, it's me. And this is Malone, and this is David. Malone, this is my old friend Dr. Shaw. Who used to be called Cricket." Malone went to shake hands. David went to shake hands. Emily went to shake hands, but Henry kissed her on the cheek, his hands on her shoulders. They smiled at each other.

"I'm so glad to see you," said Emily, broadly smiling.

"Me too you," Henry said. "You're certainly aging well." Then Rue came in.

"So you *do* remember each other." She was pleased.

"Yes," said Henry. "Very well. It's just this habit women have of changing their names."

"Men too. Henry," said Emily, and they both laughed.

Rue turned to Malone. "Do you like *Mad* magazine? Or Pogo?" Malone nodded. "If you go to the top of the stairs and turn right, you'll find a room with big stacks of them." The children thanked her and thundered out.

Rue looked at Henry looking at Emily. "So, what *is* her name?"

"Goldsborough," said Henry.

"How nice. How eighteenth century. You should take it back," she said to Emily. "I don't usually give personal advice, but having met Dr. Dahl, I think I would take back Goldsborough immediately."

Emily took the advice.

School had been in session for a week and a half. Emily Goldsborough was, to put it mildly, having a problem with the eighth grade. Oddly, she found that handling fourteen-year-olds had virtually nothing to do with what she had learned in primary grades during her ed courses. The wizard of the class, running the show behind masks and curtains, was a sharp-faced boy, Korean by birth, with the distinctly un-Korean name of Kenny Lowen. The worst thing was Emily could never catch Kenny at anything. Out of the corner of her eye she would see a note being passed, or a conversation in sign language, but when she whirled to look, it was always someone else holding the note, or stifling laughter.

Hughie Bache had once gone ostentatiously sound asleep in her class, causing the other boys to come unglued with amusement. Students would get up and walk around without permission and even leave the room. When Emily asked what they thought they were doing, they would say with mock surprise that Miss Smith always let them, or they thought class was over, or that they needed the bathroom. She'd sent Glenn Malko to Mr. Dianda three times. What she didn't know was that Margee Malko had come in to complain to Rue that Mrs. Goldsborough was picking on her son.

Mike Dianda came repeatedly to observe Emily's classes, but when he was there the children were angels. The small sarcastic woman who taught history in the class next door kept coming in to ask if Emily could keep the noise down. Emily thought it was a rude question. If she could, she would, wouldn't she? At home at night she was tense with despair. She'd always been better with small children than teenagers, but she'd never had this kind of trouble. She didn't need this fear of failing. She'd failed enough, at more or less everything up to now, or at least it felt that way. Certainly at being a wife, if you asked Tom. And if she hadn't yet failed as a mother, she hadn't really been tested, had she? Anyone could be a decent mother with a big car, a full bank account, and nothing to do all day except work on her tennis and remember someone's dentist appointment. Try it working full-time at something you stink at, with so little money you have to say "No" every time your children ask for something, in a dingy little house that looks to your daughter like the kind of house people's maids live in. Try doing that and still keeping your sweet and loving temper.

Cynda Goldring, who taught English, made a point of sitting with Emily at lunch. Cynda had a glossy flip of dark hair, big white teeth, and incredibly long fingernails, such that Emily wondered how she could hold the chalk. She told Emily comforting stories.

"You'll get better, and the kids will let up on you. You think these kids are tough? I used to teach public school until one of my eighth graders tried to rape me in the girl's room. He was seventeen and weighed about two-twenty. I took a forty percent pay cut to come here, and believe me, it was worth every penny."

Cynda made her laugh, and so did Janet TerWilliams, who taught second grade and drove a new BMW. The bad part of the job was the job. The good part was that for the first time in fourteen years, Emily belonged to a group other than her family, and she found that you form a different kind of bond with people with whom you share work. She found herself measuring time a different way and valuing money a different way. She felt a longing to succeed that was entirely different from wishing to win at games; it was a matter of identity. When she taught in the younger grades, she had moments of hoping she was going to be really good. Certainly she was learning a new respect for the mixture of tact, kindness, imagination, and skill that went into this job. She thought of teachers in her children's old school whom she had hardly seen as people like herself; she'd seen their ordinary clothes and heard their occasional grammatical mistakes, and known only that they hadn't had fancy educations like hers. She wondered now if she'd ever had any idea of how hard it was to be good at what they did. She began to take home information on teacher enrichment workshops and seminars she hoped Rue would send her to. She hired Ann Rosen, and instructed her to file for a divorce.

*　　　*　　　*

"Her class control is terrible," said Mike Dianda. "She didn't command their respect from the beginning, and I don't think she can recover."

Rue pushed a paperweight around her desk. The parking lot gossip vine had it that Mrs. Goldsborough was nice but clueless. Several eighth-grade girls aiming at competitive high schools were worried they wouldn't score well on their admissions tests. There had even been complaints from other teachers—well, from Lynn Ketchum—about the noise from Mrs. Goldsborough's classroom.

"I guess I better start interviewing," said Rue. "Will you go on working with her, though?"

"I will."

"Did you get to observe Roberta Shaftoe?"

"I spent an hour in pre-K this morning."

"And?"

"I don't see how we can keep her," said Mike. "She won't come to school without a hat. If her hat of the day comes off her head, she gets hysterical and yells 'Where's my bankey?' over and over, even if it's right at her feet. She treats the other children like objects in her fantasy life. This morning I saw her yell 'Danielle, the phone is ringing!' and then answer the phone herself, as if Danielle were inanimate."

"What kind of hats?"

"Baseball yesterday. Mickey Mouse today. Her small motor skills are terrible. She can't cut out a paper doll without cutting off its head. She can't write her name. She's terribly fearful of loud noise and new situations."

Rue sighed. The Shaftoes, delighted with The Country School, had just donated $2,100 to the Capital Campaign fund for a bronze plaque to be set in the new gym lobby floor, with their names on it.

And then there was the Bird Feeder Affair.

At her own expense, and with her own little hammer, Catherine Trainer had hung a bird feeder outside her classroom window and was loopy with excitement when there appeared among the robins and mourning doves first a dark-eyed junco and then a western tanager.

"A western tanager!" she had babbled to all who would listen.

"Oh, it was lovely with its little red skullcap and that golden breast. You know you almost never see one. You hear them sometimes, but they're terribly shy. You hear them call *piit err ick!* The children were *so* excited!" She went on so much about it at lunch that Bill Glarrow, the business manager, actually left his office during class hours and went over to the middle school to view the bird feeder. The next thing you know, he had torn it down and was going off with it.

Malone gave a fairly merciless accounting to her mother of the spectacle Mrs. Trainer then made of herself. She stopped her history class in midsentence and shouted at the window, "What do you think you're doing?" Then she sprinted from the classroom, and the delighted children ran to the windows in time to see her catch up with Mr. Glarrow and give him a great angry push with both hands. Malone demonstrated how Mrs. Trainer had *pushed* and the astonished look on Mr. Glarrow's face before he gathered his wits and saw who was attacking him.

"What on earth do you think you're doing?" she had howled at him, red in the face. Surprised into indiscretion, Mr. Glarrow had pointed and shouted back, "Look what's happening! The birds are sitting on that branch up there, waiting to get at the feeder, and they're shitting all over the camellias!" The children were overcome with delight. They looked down and saw that the hedge of dark green leaves below them was glazed with white, a virtual birdy toilet. "Those are specimen shrubs!" Mr. Glarrow had yelled. "Do you know what it would cost to replace them? It's not a cold climate, for god's sake, the birds have enough to eat!"

Apparently Mrs. Trainer and Mr. Glarrow then had a race, speedwalking, to see who would get to Rue first. Mrs. Trainer won, because Mr. Glarrow had to stop outside the office to put down the bird feeder. By chance Rue appeared in her office doorway just in time to see Mrs. Trainer burst into the reception area, and Catherine beetled into Rue's office and threw herself into a chair. They were in Rue's office for about ten minutes when Catherine came out calmer, but sniffling and still talking about the dark-eyed junco, and went back to her class.

Then Rue went in for a talk with Bill Glarrow, and after a while he stumped off to the middle school. Emily later learned he had

been sent to apologize to Mrs. Trainer for not discussing his decision with her before he acted upon it, although Rue agreed that he
was perfectly right to prevent the death of the camellia bushes,
dark-eyed junco or no.

The parking lot was ablaze with gossip by next morning, with
the moms of fifth graders retailing this story to anyone who would
listen.

$\mathcal{C}$handler Kip had not been anyone's first or even second choice for president of the Board of The Country School. He was fairly new to this Board and had no other experience with nonprofits. He had no talent for building consensus; his management style was to give orders and expect them to be taken. As with many self-made people, appearances were very important to him, and he didn't have much tolerance for deviation from what he considered normal.

Rue had had an unfortunate confrontation with Chandler the first month he was on the Board. Her assistant head had been hired away by a school in New York, and Rue wanted to hire Mike Dianda. Since hiring the staff was in her job description, she foresaw no problem. But she mentioned her choice to the Board as a courtesy, and Chandler made a great fuss. It was bad policy to promote a member of the faculty to management, he claimed. Rue gave several good reasons why it was not. Mr. Dianda was weak, Chandler then claimed. Discipline would be his province, and Mike Dianda couldn't "play in the traffic." Rue, baffled, insisted that the opposite was true. His judgment was sound, he kept a cool head when all around him were losing theirs, and he had excellent rapport with both faculty and parents. The objections went on without making definitive sense until Ann Rosen said, "Chandler . . . are you trying to tell us Rue shouldn't promote Mike because he sleeps with kangaroos? Because we know that, and we don't care."

Chandler had turned crimson, and there had been laughter. Because Ann Rosen read him absolutely right, he dropped the discussion. Because Ann Rosen was his social equal, he couldn't hold such a grudge against her as he felt entitled to. But Rue was his employee, an overweight, self-important schoolteacher, and because of her, he had been humiliated. Rue, who did not feel herself to be less than Chandler's equal, did not notice that she had made an enemy.

Nobody thought that Chandler would be a perfect Board president. But it was a time-consuming job, and usually thankless, and for the last year and a half, Chandler had made it clear that he actively wanted it. The other more likely candidates actively didn't. When at a faculty retreat (which Chandler had been too busy to attend) the Board vice president began to weep during a role-playing exercise and announced that he had at that moment decided to retire from public life and devote himself full-time to undergoing Jungian therapy, the nominating committee was left with no other candidates. They decided the school had weathered worse things; it would weather Chandler.

"It's only for two years," Rue had said to Henry. "How bad can it be?"

Rue had a full agenda when she arrived at the California Chuckwagon for her first weekly lunch with Chandler Kip. The Chuckwagon was a cafeteria with wagon wheels next door to Chandler's office, where you stood in line to order Stew 'n Biscuits or Doc's Rattlesnake Chili and then ate at formica tables and were done in twenty minutes. That was all right with Rue; whenever she was off campus for more than an hour, something seemed to blow up or catch fire.

Rue explained about the problem with the Shaftoes, and Chandler nodded. She reported that Emily Goldsborough wasn't working out and they were seeking a replacement. Chandler concurred. Chandler reported that he had had an angry call from a mother of a second grader who claimed her daughter was being abused by her teacher.

"By Janet TerWilliams? I can't believe it. Who was this?"

"Helen Blainey."

"Ah," said Rue.

"She said her daughter was made to sit in a corner for half an hour. The child had been humiliated."

"Did she tell you what her daughter did to deserve it?"

"Her point was that the child is seven . . . what *could* she have done?"

"She announced in a loud voice that there are too many fucking Jews in this school," said Rue.

"Oh." Chandler noticed that two people at the next table

turned to stare at them. He tried to look as if he and Rue had sat down together by accident.

"If she does it again, I'm going to expel her," Rue added. "I hope I'll have your support."

Chandler broke off a piece of sourdough bread, rolled it into a pill, and ate it. "That seems hard on a seven-year-old."

"It's the mother I'm expelling. I discussed this with Mrs. Blainey the day it happened. You can see what kind of support I got."

"Okay," said Chandler, "I'll tell her I'm backing you up."

"Thank you," said Rue, feeling an unexpected wave of gratitude. Maybe this wasn't going to be so bad.

Chandler wiped some bread in the grease on the plate left by his Blanket Roll Hash. He wasn't finding this job at all as he had expected. He was used to conducting business in a decisive world of move fast, cut to the chase, on to the next. The men he worked with respected and enjoyed this style. With Rue he found himself continually in a mushy world of six sides to every question. He felt like a basketball superstar who finds he's been traded to a football team. He wondered how to regain his footing.

"I had a talk with Oliver Sale the other day," said Chandler. "You know he works for me?"

"Yes," said Rue. The Sales were relatively new to the school. They had moved out from Sheboygan a year and a half before and put their children in public school, but it hadn't worked out. Rue had taken both children in the middle of last year, under some pressure from Chandler Kip. There was a girl, Lyndie, now in fifth grade, and a boy named Jonathan in junior kindergarten who was passing strange. Jonathan had a walleye and he licked the palm of his hand all the time, as if he were a cat trying to calm himself. He also had a trick of sticking his tongue way out as if he were trying to get it into his nose. He was not an attractive child and seemed racked with anxieties. Late last spring Rue had asked the Sales to come in to talk about Jonathan, but they hadn't responded to the message. That was fairly unusual. When parents were paying X thousands of dollars a year, they usually wanted all the attention they could get, and they virtually always snapped to attention at any hint that a child was not working out at Country.

"I don't know how well you know them," said Chandler.

"Not well."

"He's a very bright guy, genius level."

Rue only nodded. To her Oliver Sale was a tall and angular but flabby man who seemed to glower even when he tried to smile. His head was strangely proportioned, as if it had been necessary to cram all his features together at the bottom of his face, and leave the other two-thirds for forehead. The wife, Sondra, was more approachable, although nervous, like Jonathan. Rue's memory was that when they came in for their interview, Oliver did all the talking.

"Oliver says that Lyndie doesn't seem to have any homework. They ask what her assignment is and she doesn't know."

Uh oh, thought Rue, here we go. She said, "I'll speak to Mrs. Trainer."

"Thank you. You know I've heard *nothing* but complaints about Catherine Trainer since I joined the Board? I'd like to raise a point of curiosity. We're in a recession here. Teachers are a dime a dozen; they're stacked up over the airfield waiting for a job like this. Young kids with good degrees who would cost half as much as Mrs. Trainer. Isn't that true?"

"In a way."

She looked at him, feeling weary. Oh, he was going to be one of these kinds of presidents. She wished they could all be like Ann Rosen, intelligent and supportive, good at leading the baying hounds away from the wounded deer, so that Rue could do her job while Ann channeled the Board in directions that strengthened the school.

"In what way?" Chandler asked.

Rue said, "It isn't true that good teachers are a dime a dozen. There are plenty of teachers, but not plenty of good ones. Mrs. Trainer has been one of the best teachers I ever saw. She has a history with the school that is worth a great deal to the faculty, to the alumni, and to me."

Chandler smiled, and took another roll. "Well, those points are well taken."

"Thank you."

"But in my business when we have a a difficult personnel issue, we make a clean cut and go forward. We aren't sentimental and no one expects us to be."

"Can business really be as simple as that?"

"Yes," he said, though they both felt instantly that this was a lie. They sat silent another moment.

"Let me ask you a question," he said with an air of beginning over. "Just for my information. When a teacher is past it, what does it take to decide you're cutting her too much slack?"

"It's a matter of judgment. The important thing is that I have to be sure to think with my own brain and not let parking-lot politics think for me. I've had years when a particular teacher will come under fire for no reason known to God or man, and then the storm blows out to sea and the next year's class is delighted with her again. And when I do decide that a longtime employee of the school is ineffective, there are right ways and wrong ways to handle it. So I have to do what I have to do in the right way, at the right time."

Chandler seemed annoyed by this answer, and shot his cuffs to display heavy mother-of-pearl cufflinks. He put one hand in his pocket and fumbled around, a gesture that looked habitual, like looking for a lighter and then remembering you don't smoke any-more. He put his hands back on the table, folded together. Finally, he said, "Do I understand you to say that you are going to fire her? In the right way, at the right time?"

"You do not."

"What then?"

"I'm saying that it is improper for school parents, and most especially for Board members, to interfere with the head in person-nel matters. Maybe we should schedule another board retreat, at your convenience, to review this sort of thing."

There was an uncomfortable silence, during which they both looked around the room, as if suddenly enchanted with the decor. Each had come to the meeting determined to establish a rapport, hoping to make a new start with each other. Rue felt chagrin that once again she had let her impatience show because a new trustee knew so much less about schools than she did. Of course he knew less; it wasn't his job. He hadn't been at it for eighteen years. Chandler, for his part, had agreed to be president in the hope of serving the community, and also, of course, for the pleasure of wielding a big stick. He had told the Sales that he would take care of this. Now what was he going to tell them? It was embarrassing, and Rue knew it.

"Let's talk about the auction," he said.

"Let's."

"I'm concerned about the theme," said Chandler.

"You are? Gay Nineties? I thought it was very clever. We've found a collector to lend us some antique bicycles, with the huge front wheels. The eighth-grade girls will wear leg-o'-mutton sleeves and bustles. Imagine how much they'll learn about how uncomfortable women's lives used to be, these little ones who spend their lives in sweat clothes."

"I don't like the overtone of homosexuality."

"Chandler!"

"Well, I don't. I asked my wife what she thinks of first when she hears the word *gay* and she agrees with me."

"That's the silliest thing I ever heard!"

"Thank you very much. It's not a lifestyle choice that should be associated with The Country School."

"It's not a lifestyle choice at all! It's a lovely word, with many meanings. This decade a hundred years ago was called the Gay Nineties, and that's what it's always been called."

"What about Merry Nineties?"

"You're not serious."

"Do you realize that from the beginning of this lunch, you have brushed off or belittled every single thing that I came here to say to you?"

She paused. She could see that in fact she had but . . . but . . . did she really have to deal with this? Maybe she could get Ann and Terry to sit down with him and explain to him what the job was. Maybe she could talk Terry into taking it over next year. She said carefully, "I can see that it seems that way to you, and I'm sorry. But the auction is run by the Parents' Council. Firing is done by me. If you are going to overstep your bounds in areas like this, I'm going to fight you tooth and nail. It isn't good for the school."

"And you are *the* authority on what's good for the school?"

"In this case, yes."

"I think I better go," said Chandler quietly, and he went. It was the first time in her seventeen years of leadership at the school that a Board president, man or woman, had stuck her with the check.

Life had not been entirely fair to Catherine Trainer. It was not fair that Norman should have died the way he did. He never smoked. He didn't drink, except a thimble of wine at Passover. And yet he got a ghastly cancer when he was only fifty-seven, and lingered, getting paler and thinner and less and less himself as his immortal spark was replaced erg by erg with man-made drugs. He lingered on in the hospital bed in the downstairs den long after he knew, where he was, or even who he was, and long after he lost all control of his bladder or sphincter muscles, which at least he never knew, thank god. Catherine used to race home from school at lunch and immediately after class to be with him. She started recycling lesson plans and putting off grading homework as Norman's suffering grew, and she was the only one who could soothe him. It turned out not to make much difference, either the putting off or the soothing of Norman. School went on in a blur, and so did Norman. Finally she had to have a nurse in the daytime, while she was at work, but she nursed him alone every night and all weekend. In the last months, he was so drugged that he could hardly be said to have slept night or day; he just slipped in and out of trances of pain. And she slept sitting up in a chair beside him. Once she let the doctors bully her into letting him be carried off to the hospital. But the minute he saw her in the morning, in his first lucid moment in weeks, Norman made her promise to take him home and never let them take him again, and she kept the promise. She was holding his hand when he died, although there was so little of him left by then that he slipped away without a ripple, and she missed it.

Norman Trainer had been the only person left alive who didn't call her Catherine. He had called her Caddy, as she had been called when she was little. Now no one called her that. Grandchildren might have, if she had any. She always thought that she would teach her grandchildren to call her Caddy, as she couldn't imagine she would ever feel old enough to be Granny. But to have grandchildren you had to have children, and she was lacking those.

She and Norman had had a full life though. Norman was an electrical inspector for the city, which was a terribly interesting job. He was always meeting new people and visiting new sites, and people always liked Norman. He had honest eyes. And she had her children at school. No one but Norman knew to what extent they became, in her mind, her own children. She yearned over the little ones in the preschool, watching them grow up on their way to her. She followed the big ones as they moved to the upper school, and then off into the big world. She followed them around the campus with her eyes; she followed them in her mind's eye when they physically departed. She had never missed a Homecoming at The Country School in all her nineteen years. She loved to see the grown-up strangers approach her, great twenty-five-year-olds whom she had taught when they were ten, and see them smile and exclaim "Mrs. Trainer!" You could see in their eyes how they had loved her. And they knew that she loved them.

Catherine made fifth grade fun. If she did an Egypt project they all made a model of King Tut's tomb. When they studied the Age of Discovery, they made model Ninas and Pintas and sailed them on the carp pond, and then they studied the People of the Americas and did things like making a whole meal of foods eaten by Incas.

She taught her children to sprout beans in little dishes as the Natives of New England had taught the Pilgrims to do, to avoid scurvy in the long winters. They made popcorn, of course, and they read about pemmican, a convenience food made of sun-dried strips of deer or buffalo meat, packed in leather pouches with melted fat for energy, and often mixed with dried blueberries or cranberries for flavor and vitamins. The children felt this would be fun to make but too disgusting to actually eat. Likewise the cooking methods of the nomads of the plains, the tipi-dwelling Sioux, Cheyenne, and the like. Catherine taught how they trailed their tipi poles, skins, and fur robes along behind their horses or women (the two beasts of burden) on the trail, but they didn't carry any pottery or cookware. For a cooking pot they used a buffalo stomach, which they would fill with meat and fat and whatever vegetables might be gathered, then bury it in a hole filled with steaming hot rocks, and let it simmer. Then they dug it up and ate the stew, and then the pot. The children thought that would be gross, if you didn't wrap it in aluminum foil before you buried it.

A favorite project was the Sweat Lodge, which the fifth grade built each year on its Indian Overnight. For safety this was held on campus at the school. Parents helped each year to erect three genuine Cheyenne tipis, whose poles were stored in the Bus Barn and the skins in Catherine's garage. The skins were actually marine duck, now smoke-stained and painted all around with pictograph accounts of battles and buffalo hunts. Every fall the children helped to cut and peel new tent pegs and lacing pegs from shrubs on campus, as the Indians would have. On the night of the Overnight, Catherine and Norman cooked and served maize (corn on the cob) and stuffed buffalo gut (hot dogs) in the Mess Tipi. The tipi was furnished in the ceremonial way, with the doorway to the east and the altar at the back, and the children sat cross-legged on blankets around the fire, passing food hand to hand. After dinner they did ritual prayer dances, chanting chants they had written, and then they told ghost stories until the last streaks of light were gone from the sky. Then the children were sent to bed, the girls in one tipi and the boys in the other.

Norman and Catherine used to sit watching the firelight until the worst outbursts of whispers and laughing had subsided and every child had been escorted by torchlight to the bathroom at least twice. At first light, they all got up and began building the Sweat Lodge. While the children sweated, Catherine made bread dough, which the children wrapped around green sticks and cooked over the fire until it was black on the outside, though raw on the inside. They ate this dripping with butter and authentic Indian wild grape preserves, which came from a somewhat unauthentic Welch's jelly jar. Norman cooked jerky strips (bacon) over the fire, and then the parents arrived in their Volvos and took their sticky Indians home to sleep it off.

Since Norman died, Catherine had to arrange each year for a supportive dad to do Norman's part of the Sweat Lodge ceremony. She could cook the bacon, but she couldn't carry the bucket of hot rocks. She was wondering whom she would choose as she drove to school, a half hour earlier than usual because she had to meet with

Jennifer Lowen's parents before class. She had already had an interminable meeting with Mrs. Lowen last week, but Rue said they wanted to come back for more. Maybe Nicolette Wren's father would help with the Sweat Lodge. She was a nice little girl, Nicolette.

Corinne Lowen sat beside her husband, Bradley, on the couch in Rue's office. She was a pretty woman, with short perky hair and big, intelligent eyes with long lashes. Bradley was neat and small with a cherubic smile, who always wore shiny black loafers. He was a CPA whose clients included most of The Country School community. Catherine had often heard it said that he was so kind and funny that Seven Springs was the only place where people actually enjoyed tax time. He was holding his wife's hand, with absentminded affection, when Catherine came to the door. Rue sat at her desk.

"Come in, Mrs. Trainer," said Rue as Catherine tapped at the doorjamb, a bright little birdlike sound. Catherine, a once pretty woman whose colors had faded, like an Ektachrome print exposed to years of sun, tripped in and perched on a chair with her back to the windows. She was wearing a denim dress with mother-of-pearl snaps and deep pockets filled with erasers and paper clips and treats for the campus dogs. The Lowens, facing her, looked out over green campus, glowing in sunlight, a little haven for lucky children, Catherine thought. She had always liked the Lowens. She had taught their little Korean son, Kenny, four years ago, and they got on famously. He was a bright one, Kenny.

"The Lowens have some concerns," said Rue to Catherine, "about the way the school year has started for Jennifer. I thought we all ought to discuss them together." Catherine knew the drill, of course. It was a game they all had to play. Overinvolved parents fretted to Rue, Rue was elaborately attentive about it, then Rue and whatever teacher was being second-guessed had to meet with the parents and explain to them the long view. Half an hour from now Catherine would be free to go back to her children, where she would teach a special unit on bird-watching as her science class, and they would have the kind of fun that made the children love her, that instilled love of learning in a way you couldn't measure.

"We are concerned that Jennifer doesn't seem to have any home-work at night," said Bradley. "At ten, it seems to us, she should be developing the habit of homework. Besides, if she doesn't have any, then she wants to watch television."

"Children work at such different speeds," said Catherine blithely. She was trying to remember what homework she *had* assigned. Math worksheets, well of course most of the children did those in class, and had there been spelling to study? Yes . . . and a chapter to read in geography, by the end of the month, and jour-nals. Of course. She could not see a problem. "I think it's very posi-tive that Jennifer is such a committed student that she does all her homework at school."

"We don't, Mrs. Trainer," said Corinne. "We think she's bored. We would like to see her challenged. And she wrote a composition last week that you haven't handed back yet. She was very proud of that composition. It's discouraging for her not to know her grade."

"We think writing is important," said Bradley.

"The curriculum says that in fifth grade the children write com-positions every week," said Corinne. "We want to know if that's happening."

"And math," said Bradley.

"The children are keeping journals," said Catherine. "They make notes about the books they are reading. They make science notes on the flowers and birds on campus."

"Is Jennifer supposed to be doing that?"

"Of course."

"And is she?"

"I assume so," said Mrs. Trainer.

"Don't you know?"

"She was writing a book report on *Pippi Longstocking,* I know."

"And what grade did she get?"

"I don't grade the journals on a weekly basis."

"How often do you?"

"Well, that's hard to say. Every week is different." Really, thought Catherine, she was ceasing to enjoy this. Did these people think she was a robot? Did they think teaching children was like making shoes?

"So do you know for a fact whether she's written in her journal at all?"

"I'm sure she has," said Catherine, sounding impatient.

"You're sure? Does that mean you know for a fact? Have you graded her journal at all?"

"I think we understand your concern," said Rue, deciding it was time to impose her body between the ravening tigers and the tethered goat, although the goat seemed oblivious to the danger. It was clear to her that Catherine hadn't the faintest idea what home-work her class was doing, and didn't seem to care. "I'm sure we all agree that Jennifer should be asked to perform up to her ability. Suppose Mrs. Trainer and I work together in the next few weeks to arrive at a program we can define to you."

"So we know what she's supposed to be *doing*," exclaimed Corinne. So we can ride herd on her, so we can cross-examine her on every comma, is what that meant, thought Catherine. She'd had a child in last year's class whose homework always reeked of ciga-rette smoke, because his chain-smoking mother went over it line by line, or did it for him. Jennifer isn't as bright as Kenny, she thought, in case you hadn't noticed. She felt sorry for poor little Jennifer, being hounded to meet an impossible standard, being taught to grub after grades instead of loving to learn for its own sake. She was beginning to feel really cross with these people.

Now came the jockeying for Rue's ear. The Lowens wanted to stay after Catherine left, so they could demand to have Jennifer switched to the other section. Catherine wanted to stay after the Lowens left, to justify herself and complain about the Lowens. Fortunately, Merilee came to the door and said, "Mrs. Shaw, when you're done, could I have a minute?" and Rue gratefully said, "Of course."

The Lowens left reluctantly, not at all reassured. Catherine left reluctantly, to go and find some sympathy in the faculty lounge. When they had gone, Merilee shut the door behind them. "Lee wants to move to Colorado," she said, and burst into tears.

Rue's heart sank. "Oh, Merilee." Merilee's husband had recently taken early retirement with a huge golden parachute. Ever since, he'd been pressuring Merilee to retire as well.

When the storm of tears was over, the nose blown, Merilee said,

"He's found a house he wants to buy, where he can fish. That's all he likes to do, besides work. He likes to fish."

"What about you?"

Rue knew without asking that what Merilee liked was her garden and her job and her church. None of them portable. "We'll be closer to the children . . ." said Merilee in her kind, piping voice, and started to cry again. The children were both in Massachusetts.

"I can't imagine the school without you," Rue said, and meant it. "What will I do?" She was wondering equally what would Merilee do. Retirement struck her as an awful prospect, if you loved what you were doing. As she knew Merilee did.

Merilee said, "I've been thinking about that. Why don't you give the job to Mrs. Goldsborough?"

"Brilliant," said Rue. "That's brilliant. Oh, Merilee."

Emily sat in a deep chair in Rue's office, looking defeated.

"I knew I wasn't doing very well, but I didn't think I was going to get fired."

"I'm not firing you. I'm offering you a job that pays better."

"But I wasn't doing well, was I?"

Rue let a moment pass. "No."

"I don't know how to be a secretary—"

"You're smart, and you're sensible. You'll be my backstop. . . . I make mistakes, and I need a friend to catch what I drop and point me in the right direction. I can teach you what you don't know."

Emily was not used to being found wanting, especially in her own eyes, and lately she was getting a steady diet of it.

"I feel like I got called to the principal's office and expelled."

"That happened to me," said Rue.

Emily had expected Rue to comfort her, which would have annoyed her. This, however, was interesting.

"You got expelled?"

"Yes, from boarding school."

Emily looked at Rue with new eyes. "*You* did? What did you do?"

"I thought the school was a wicked place. It was encouraging all our snobbery and self-importance and not teaching us all that much. And the rules were irrational, designed to make us easy to handle, not to teach us anything about being decent members of a community. So I decided to try to break them all."

Emily didn't know what to think—of her own boarding school self, who indeed had been a "good" girl, quite satisfied with the status quo, or of Malone, who was showing signs of becoming quite a burr under the saddle as her hormones kicked in.

"And did you? Break them all?"

"Most of them. But I didn't mean to get caught."

"Were your parents furious?"

"Let's say they were in character. My mother was embarrassed . . . as if something had happened to her, not to me. I remember her saying 'Rue, ever since you were a little girl, you've seen everything from your own point of view. You can never see till it's too late how much you are annoying people.'"

"Oh dear," said Emily.

"Of course, it hurt so much because it was true. I hope it's less true now."

"What did your father say?"

Rue smiled. "He, who always *did* see other points of view, saw that apart from being stunned and angry and ashamed of myself, I had never failed before, and I was frightened. I thought my life was ruined. No other school would take me, I wouldn't get to go to college, and my whole life would be blighted by one mistake. So he came to me that night after dinner, when I was holed up brooding, and he stood in the door and said, 'Rue, it's silly for a girl like you to worry what to do with her life. You should just become queen of a small country.'"

Emily laughed. Rue laughed too, her wonderful rich, deep laugh.

"What school was it?" Emily asked.

"A New England one where my mother had gone. I was the first person from our town to go away to school. Maybe the last."

There was another silence. Rue sat quietly.

"I think I could have handled the eighth grade, if it hadn't been for Kenny Lowen," Emily said at last.

Rue did not seem surprised. Instead she offered, "I once heard a psychologist say that when he studied groups of children, he couldn't necessarily pick out the ones from what we used to call broken homes, but he could always spot the ones who were adopted."

"Not that you'd have much trouble with Kenny; he looks about as Jewish as Reverend Sun Yung Moon."

"Which makes it worse for him. He does seem to have an empathy problem."

"I'd say he's an evil little shit."

"I was using the technical language. It's too bad he's so bright; it makes it so easy for him to manipulate the other kids. Do you want to think about this job for a day or two?"

"Either way, I can't have the teaching job?"

"No. I'm sorry."

"Then I want it."

"Good."

Emily found that her position on campus changed dramatically with her new job. She was no longer a gear in a machine, she was the closest thing to the main axle. If she had foreseen what the advantages were, she'd have begged for the job in the first place. In many ways, she soon knew more of what was going on than anyone else on campus, including Rue. Not necessarily all of it was useful, but nearly all of it was interesting, in the way that family gossip is interesting to members of the family. There were many things that people wanted Rue to know but did not want to be seen to have told her. The faculty made publicly a unified front but among themselves were full of feuds and annoyances. Teachers who wanted Rue to know that Charla Percy had spent three times her budget on new classroom furniture, told Emily. Teachers who wanted Rue to know that Marilyn Schramm was not doing her share of cleaning up the mess in the art room, told Emily. Teachers who wanted Rue to know that they all felt threatened when she let the Lowens terrorize Catherine Trainer, told Emily.

And parents who wanted Rue to know that they might withdraw their children if their children got Catherine Trainer next year, told Emily. Parents who thought Sylvia French was siphoning money from the hot lunch fund, told Emily. Sometimes parents told Emily other parents' secrets for the hell of it, so she'd owe them one if they wanted her to tell a secret to them.

The first week in October got off to a great start. Lynn Ketchum had planned an eighth-grade class outing for Wednesday, to see an exhibition of memorabilia honoring Anne Frank, the famous teenage martyr and diarist. Unfortunately, the Jewish parents of the class were incensed.

"Why on earth?" Mike Dianda asked.

"It's Yom Kippur," said Rue. It was so terrible they both began to laugh.

"We'll have to reschedule."

"Can't," said Rue. "It closes Friday. It was the only day she could get the reservation."

"I can see why," said Mike, and howled. There seemed nothing for it but for Rue to turn her bow into the wind and accept the storm, and they knew it would blow. It was true that the nonobservant Jewish families would rather have their children see the exhibit on Yom Kippur than not see it at all. It was also true that the observant ones were deeply offended, and right to be. Rue felt that maturity, or civility, or perhaps she meant sanity, consisted of the ability to hold in the mind as many points of view as a situation required and retain the ability to function. It appalled her how often she herself failed to meet her own standard, considering that she knew that she at least was trying.

And at this moment she only laughed because it wasn't funny. There was no doubt at all that anti-Semitism was alive and well, or alive and ill, on their little stretch of America's Gold Coast. Last Rosh Hashanah, she'd had an angry visit from a Fundamentalist faculty member, who complained bitterly because the second and third graders had been taught to sing a round in Hebrew for flagraising. She said it was offensive, if this was a school with no religious affiliation, to teach the children songs of spiritual significance.

The music teacher pointed out that it was a secular song, it just happened to be in Hebrew. No one was satisfied.

There were sadder things to consider. The parents of Roberta Shaftoe, the prekindergartner who wouldn't come to school without her hats, demanded a meeting with Mrs. Shaw.

"I think Mrs. Yeats is making a mountain out of a molehill," said the furious Dudley Shaftoe. "Roberta is very musical, she loves color, she's very quick at rhymes . . ."

"Mr. Shaftoe, Roberta's teacher is spending sixty percent of her time dealing with one child in the class. It simply is not fair to the other children."

"I don't understand. At home she plays by herself for hours."

"That may be true. But in a more stimulating setting, she is very easily upset. A child is not ready to participate in a normal kindergarten program if she becomes hysterical several times a day because she's lost her hat."

"But she's made so much progress!" exclaimed Mrs. Shaftoe.

"In what way?"

"Last year, she wouldn't go to school at all, except in full costume!"

Mr. Shaftoe added aggressively that they had had Roberta tested and had been told that she was absolutely "not abnormal." Rue asked permission to speak to the therapist, which the Shaftoes readily gave.

"Did you find that Roberta Shaftoe was *not* abnormal?" she asked, after being told which diagnostics had been used. The psychologist was shocked.

"Of course not," he said. "I found that she was not *psychotic*."

"Do you believe that she can thrive in a normal academic setting?"

"Not a chance," said the therapist. He added, once assured that the remarks would never be repeated, that he thought he had never seen a stranger child in his life. He said he thought she might be possessed.

Rue was just hanging up and wondering if maybe now she could begin the work that she had been trying to get to for two days, the high school recommendation letters, when she heard the words she had come to dread, the words that were measuring out her life in coffee spoons: "Rue, do you have a minute?"

It was Catherine Trainer at the door, wearing the puffy-sleeved blouse and dirndl that made her look like a superannuated extra from a movie of *Heidi*. She was holding a Kleenex box in her hand and looking grave.

"Come in," Rue said, unnecessarily. Catherine had taken the chair across from Rue.

"I was moving some desks to make room for a spelling gauntlet when this fell out," said Catherine, handing over the box. Rue wondered what a spelling gauntlet might be, but decided not to ask. She picked up the box. It was well stuffed with lined papers, each sheet tightly folded to a tight square, such as could be concealed in the palm and passed to someone else under the teacher's nose. Rue took one out and unfolded it. On it she found three distinct ten-year-olds' handwriting. One wrote mostly script; the other two printed. Rue found the theme easy to follow. There were rude drawings, scatological doggerel, and conspiracies, all aimed at insulting, excluding, and driving to despair a plump, gormless child named Nicolette Wren.

"Well, this is charming," said Rue. "Can you identify the authors?"

"Jennifer Lowen, Malone Dahl, and Lyndie Sale."

Rue's heart sank. Poor Emily. And poor Catherine, who didn't know that both the Lowens and the Sales were leading the pack howling for her blood.

"Please send them all to see me."

"They're at Art."

"Please pull them out and send them here immediately."

Catherine nodded and bustled out. When she passed Emily's desk, she deliberately looked at the ceiling.

Fifteen minutes later, three little girls in skirts and sweaters, with their little stick legs looking long and bare above white socks, marched in single file through the front office. Malone looked sheepish as she passed her mother's desk on her way to Mrs. Shaw's office. Emily looked after them, puzzled.

The girls found Mrs. Shaw sitting at her desk, grave and un-amused. She looked larger and older than when she was smiling.

She asked them to close the door behind them and sit down. They felt her gaze on their faces, like heat, as each caught sight of the Kleenex box full of notes. Mrs. Shaw was looking at them like some flesh-and-blood Buddha as the terrible silence lengthened.

Rue took a piece of lined paper from the box, opened it, and studied it. She looked at the girls, and they looked at the ceiling and floor. Rue pointed to a paragraph and asked, "Who wrote this?" Both Jennifer and Malone were darting looks at Lyndie, who was looking at her lap. "Lyndie, will you read this aloud, please?" Rue handed her the paper, and after a moment of resistance, Lyndie read:

> "My Dad has a machine for recording phone calls. Why don't we call Nicolette and tell her we want to be best friends, and she'll be excited and then afterward we can play back the tape and laugh."

Rue gave her a long look. She chose another paper with a different handwriting and looked at the girls with raised eyebrows.

Reluctantly, Malone raised a finger. Malone managed to take the paper and read without ever looking up enough to look at Rue's face.

> "Did you see who came and sat beside me at lunch? GROSS. She ate all the white stuff out of her cookies and then licked them. I got up and left her alone at the table."

Rue looked from face to face again. The girls were not enjoying this.

She chose another piece of paper, a paragraph from the third hand, the one who favored green ink.

"This must be yours, Jennifer." She handed her the paper and pointed to a paragraph. Jennifer began to read.

> "If you're captain again at recess, be sure Miss Asswipe gets chosen last."

Rue said, "I want each of you to take home the paper that I just handed you and have your parents sign it. I want them back on my desk before class tomorrow morning.

"Both parents?" Lyndie asked.

"One will do. Now, why don't you tell me what is so serious about these notes." Nobody spoke. "Jennifer."

"We wrote them in class."

"That's not a good thing, but that's not what bothers me."

"Bad words," said Jennifer.

"No, it's not the bad words."

There was a silence. Rue looked from one to the other.

"They're mean," said Malone.

"They are very mean," said Rue. "They are extraordinarily unkind. I've been thinking a good deal about what I want to say to you, since Mrs. Trainer left to go get you, and I've decided that I shouldn't say very much. But I've made a short quiz for you." She handed them each copies of a paper. The girls had no idea what a struggle she'd had not only to write so fast, but also to make the computer print in three columns. Gravely, they read to themselves:

A	B	C
"I have the right to choose my own friends, and no one can make me be friendly to a girl I don't like."	"I have my friends, but I try to get along with everyone."	"I must be nice to everyone."
"When someone offends me, I ought to tell her off."	"When someone offends me, I can choose to tell her, or I can decide to let it go."	"When someone offends me, it's better to ignore it."
"When I don't get my way, I get mad."	"When I don't get my way, it's not the end of the world."	"I don't expect to get my way most of the time. Other people are usually right."
"People in authority make mistakes, and when they do, I ought to complain."	"When a teacher makes a mistake, it may be because she's human. I make mistakes too."	"People in authority should always be obeyed. It's better that way."

Rue let it sink in for a moment. Then she said, "When you were in third grade, you were all like A. But when you're as old as I am, you can be like A, or you can choose to be different. You have choices to make right now about what kind of person you want to be. Now, who do you want to grow up to be?"

She looked from one to the other.

Malone said "B" in a low voice.

Rue looked at Jennifer and she said "B."

Rue looked at Lyndie and Lyndie said "C."

$\mathcal{M}$alone came into the kitchen (with the spatter linoleum floor she so admired) where Emily was cleaning vegetables for soup. She got herself a diet drink from the refrigerator and sat down to drink it.

"What's up, honeybunch?" Emily knew this wasn't an idle visit.

"We got sent to Mrs. Shaw today," said Malone.

"I noticed. What was that about?"

"I don't really know," said Malone in a grieved voice. "See, Jennifer is having a birthday party, and the school says if she has more than half the girls, she has to have all of them!"

Malone waited for her mother to sympathize with her outrage, but her mother was apparently too stupid to grasp the situation.

"Yes?" said Emily.

"Well—it isn't fair, that means she has to have Nicolette *Wren* and Bharatee and that will *ruin* it!"

"In what way?"

"Mom, you don't understand, Nicolette ruins everything!"

"Honey, why don't you tell me what Mrs. Shaw wanted to see you about."

There was a pause, as Malone heaved some deeply put-upon sighs. Finally she produced from her pocket a piece of lined notepaper, much folded, with three different handwritings on it.

"Mrs. Shaw says you have to sign this."

Emily put down her knife, wiped her hands, and took the note. When she had read it all, she put it down, and looked long and hard at her daughter.

"What do you have to say for yourself, Malone?"

"I don't know."

Malone was staring at the table. Her face was sullen.

"What do you think Nicolette is feeling tonight?"

"Nothing. . . ."

"Malone. What do you think Nicolette feels when you treat her that way?"

Silence.

"Do you think she doesn't notice?"

"She doesn't act like she does."

"So that means she isn't hurt? Haven't you ever pretended not to mind when someone hurt your feelings?"

Silence.

"I won't tolerate unkindness, Malone. You don't have to like Nicolette. But you do have to treat her with common courtesy."

Emily peeled another carrot into the sink, then spoke again.

"I think you're so wrapped up in your new friends that you're not thinking for yourself. I want you to spend some time away from them so you can remember that it's important to think with your own brain. You are grounded for a week."

"MOM!" Malone roared, and burst into tears. "That means I can't go to Jennifer's party!"

"I'm sorry. You can go to school and come home, but other than that, you stay in the house. No play dates, no riding your bike to the mall, and no telephone."

Malone leaped up, threw her empty soda can into the sink, making a clatter, and stamped out of the room. Emily stood still at the sink.

Malone slammed back into the room, her eyes streaming and her mouth contorted with angry sobs. She had unplugged the phone in her room and brought it downstairs. She slammed it violently onto the table and shouted, "You say you're sorry, but you're not. You're not sorry about anything! You won't even let me have my own feelings!"

"You can have your feelings, absolutely. What you can't do is behave horribly."

"Who says? Are you so perfect?"

"No."

"Is that why we live in a house with a floor that looks like someone threw up on it?"

"Malone, go to your room until you can control yourself."

"This isn't *fair* . . ."

"MALONE!" Emily shouted. Malone marched out of the room

and up the stairs and when she slammed her bedroom door it made the house shake.

Oh great, Emily thought, now I'm a child abuser. For a long time she felt a pulsing rage at Tom for putting her in this position, having to work all day for less than he paid his bimbo nurse, and then at night deal all alone with an angry baby woman who seemed perpetually premenstrual. She felt an irrational cloud of anger at everyone who was happily married and didn't particularly deserve it. She made herself stop and think whether she would like to have Tom there with her right then, in a mood to help, and had to admit she didn't. What she really wanted was to turn back the clock to a time before all that had gone wrong began. She wanted to choose a different path and be successful and admired and loved. By somebody.

She wanted to go upstairs and apologize to Malone. Go ahead, grow up to be a selfish bitch, Malone, just be pleasant to live with. It was tempting.

After a while she went to call the Lowens hoping for some comfort from them, since they were going through the same thing with Jennifer.

Only they weren't.

Corinne Lowen was very cool. "We aren't very pleased with having Rue Shaw tell us how to raise our children. A private party is private, and my daughter should be allowed to invite whoever she wants. They can't *force* someone to like someone else. There have always been girls who were more popular than others."

"Oh," said Emily. There was no mention of the notes, she noticed.

After a glass of wine for courage, Emily dialed the Sales, and got Oliver.

"I'm Malone's mother, one of Lyndie's friends," she said. "I wanted to talk to you about their meeting with Mrs. Shaw today."

There was a pause. "Did you want to talk to my wife?" Oliver said.

"Has Lyndie told you about their meeting with Rue?"

There was another pause, and then a clunk, as if the phone had fallen on the floor. When he came back on the line, Oliver Sale said, "What did you say your name was again?"

Emily told him. "I'm a single mother," she said, wondering if she'd ever get used to saying that. "It's hard to discipline when you're on your own. I thought it would make an impression if we made some kind of united front."

"I'll tell Sondra you called," said Oliver. "Maybe she knows something about this."

Emily got off the phone and decided to finish the bottle of wine. Tomorrow she was going to have to listen to the most painful wailing about how unfair she was, and how Lyndie's mom and Jennifer's mom were on their side and why was she such a bitch? Malone would have learned a valuable lesson from this whole episode. That unkindness is unacceptable? No. That actions have consequences? No. That her mother is a bitch. Thank you, Mrs. Lowen and Mr. Sale, and the horses you came in on.

It was Sunday morning, the second weekend in October. There had been a strange warm wind all night, so that Henry had gotten up in the middle of the night to turn on the air conditioner. Now in the cool, gray hum of morning, Rue and Henry had slept past nine.

Rue woke slowly, feeling as if she could go on sleeping forever, watching the movie inside her eyelids.

Henry was awake, she could tell, because he was lying on his back, but he wasn't snoring. She rolled over and wrapped an arm across his chest, and he made a shoulder for her head.

"I had strange dreams," Henry said with his eyes closed, as if he were still having them.

"Mine weren't strange at all. I dreamed we were taking Henry Kissinger kayaking."

"Really? How did that work out?"

"He liked it because he thought the kayak and his life vest were bulletproof."

Henry laughed.

"What were your dreams?"

"Oh—they're mostly gone—no wait. You and I were living in Maryland, on the shore, and my father was alive, and we had a puppy."

"Did we? What kind?" Rue had always wanted a dog, but Henry and Georgia were both allergic to animals.

"It was one of those ones that are all fur, with little legs sticking out. Maybe a collie. You know what I mean. Well it looked like an ostrich."

Rue laughed, a gravelly belly laugh.

"Did you like it?"

"Oh," he said, "I *loved* it. Now I'm sad."

"Maybe we could get a poodle. People aren't supposed to be allergic to those."

"Don't they yap?"

"Not big ones. Or a manx."

"What's that?"

"It's a cat that behaves like a dog. It has no tail, and its back legs are longer than the front ones so it looks like a bobcat."

"Or a stock car."

"Yes, or a stock car. You could paint your numbers on its sides." She rolled over onto her side, and he fitted himself against her back, with an arm around her. They lay together, at peace and drifting. After a while Henry said, "I want to go back to sleep, but I can't, I'm too hungry."

Rue took his hand, which was curled around under her chin, and kissed it.

"Would you like breakfast in bed?"

"I would. You're a saint."

"It's a well-known fact," said Rue, and slid out of bed. Behind her, as she put on her bathrobe, Henry took her pillows and mounded them up with his own, and rolled onto his back and prepared to snore.

The house was warm and still outside the artificially cool bedroom. Rue padded barefoot down to the kitchen to put the kettle on. Then she went outside to get the Sunday papers. The *New York Times,* which she rarely had time to read, arrived on Saturday night wrapped in bright blue plastic. It lay on the doormat on the Plums' front porch, overhung with Victorian gingerbread. The Santa Barbara paper was down on the brick path. Beyond, in the front garden that faced across the lawn toward school, were the beds of roses Rue had begun to plant when she learned she would have no more children after Georgia. Soon it would be time to dress them for winter.

Rue picked up the papers and went back into the front hall. They took both papers because Rue liked the *New York Times Book Review,* but Georgia liked the local funnies and Ann Landers. Rue wondered if Georgia read the paper in New York. It was lunchtime, her time, if she was up. Rue opened the Santa Barbara paper to look at the headlines, and in the kitchen the phone rang.

The kettle began to whistle as well, as she answered the phone.

"Hello!" said the familiar voice, overly loud as if not trusting he could be heard so far away.

"Dad—Good morning! Can you wait a minute?"

When she came back, he said, "I've been trying to call you."

"I'm sorry—have you? We had to turn the air conditioner on. It's hot here. I forgot that when it's on I can't hear the phone ring."

She didn't like to have a phone in the bedroom, because people from school called at all hours. When Georgia was out at night they kept the door open until she came in, so they could hear either the phone or her return. When Georgia was in, the phone was usually for her anyway.

"It's quite cool here," said Jack.

"Is it?"

"Yuh." The way he said it, it had two syllables. "I hauled my boat this weekend."

"Did you. So early?"

"Yes, I did. It's been cool, and it's been wet. And my sailing pals are getting to where they say they can't get in and out of rowboats. I threatened to put a derrick on the float to lift them in and out. . . ."

Rue laughed. But she knew her father hated the telephone. If he'd been calling since earlier this morning, it wasn't to chat.

"So—how is everything?" she asked.

"Fine, everything's fine." There was a pause. "Your mother's had a little shock." He said this lightly. Rue took a deep breath, knowing he hated fuss, and that shock meant stroke.

"I see. When?"

"Oh—I guess it was about Friday night. She had an awful headache, and when she woke up in the morning, she said she couldn't see so good. So I took her over to Ellsworth."

Rue knew they would both hate this. That meant a forty-minute drive for her father each way and doctors who didn't know them. There had been a hospital in the next town all their lives, but it had closed. It was said to be inefficient to duplicate expensive equipment, keeping two hospitals in the one county.

"Is she still there?"

"Yuh. They did some tests of some kind, said they'd know something Monday."

So he was alone in the house. She doubted he'd slept a night alone in that house in forty years. He was clearheaded and resourceful, but she didn't like to think of it.

"Daddy, do you want me to come?"

"No, no. No need for that. I just wanted you to know."

"Thank you—how did she seem after the tests?"

"Well—a little confused . . . she didn't sleep very well. She can't find some words she wants when she tries to talk."

"Is there any paralysis?"

"Doesn't seem so. Did I tell you about when Howard Schwarz had his shock?"

Howard was a banker who had retired to farm on the little neck of land on the coast of Maine where her father grew up. He called his farm Schwarzcroft. Howard was smart and kind and very good with sheep, and he and her father were good friends.

"I don't think so—tell me."

"His daughter came to the hospital and Howard couldn't talk for two days. Then he could say a few things, but they couldn't tell if he didn't know the answer to things or if he just couldn't get the words out. So Kate set to asking him questions. She asked him what his name was, and he knew that. She asked him where he lived, and he knew that. So she said 'Dad, do you know what religion you are?'

"And Howard, he chewed at it and then he said 'I'm a . . . Jerk.'" Rue's father laughed, and Rue laughed, because no one would have thought this was funnier than Howard.

"I said to Kate, 'You know, he is kind of a jerk.' She laughed."

"Is Howard all right?"

"Howard? Oh, yes he's fine. Got all his lambs slaughtered. He's flushing the ewes, getting ready for breeding. I heard he killed a coyote in one of his pens, but I haven't seen him to ask about it."

"Give him my best, please, Daddy, when you see him. And Velma."

"I will."

There was a little silence. "Dad—would you like Georgia to come? She's right there in New York. She could be there tonight."

"No, no, that's not necessary."

Another pause.

"What are you going to do the rest of today?"

"I'm going over to Ellsworth in an hour or two."

"And when you get back?"

"I'll probably have my supper over there, and when I get back I'll go to bed."

Rue smiled to herself. She always thought that if everyone were as literal and direct as her father, the world would be a simpler place and a good deal more amusing.

"And tomorrow, you'll get some results?"

"They say so. Then we'll know where we are."

"Will you call me as soon as you do know?"

"I won't call you from the hospital. I'll call you when I get home." She understood that he meant he might want to say to her more than he wanted her mother to hear, and it wouldn't occur to him to use a pay phone in the hospital hallway.

"Does Mother have a phone in her room?"

"She does." He gave her the number, and the doctor's name and number.

"Give her our love, Dad. And I'm going to let Georgia know, just in case. You might just feel like having some company, or some help with the driving."

"No need," he said. But she knew he actually would love it, should Georgia just appear. At least she knew *she* would love it. After she said good-bye, she made a breakfast tray and carried it up the stairs. In the bedroom, she opened the blinds and got carefully back into bed with Henry, who returned half the pillows to her side of bed, sat up, and said what he always said: "This looks great." Before she told him about the phone call, she sat in the sun, looking at the exposed surface of the half grapefruit, halved. It was glistening full of clear pink juice.

"If you could take a picture of health, wouldn't it look like that?" she asked Henry.

"If I say yes, do we have to go on a grapefruit diet?"

She laughed. "No, I was just wondering how many years we have, to feel really well, and have all our marbles. . . ."

"Are you hoping for a lot? Or for quick oblivion?"

"A lot. My parents have never been really happy, and now they're starting to die."

"I think your father is happy."

"He's content, because he has a talent for it. But it hasn't been a happy marriage. It hasn't been the kind of marriage where you bring out the best in each other. . . ."

She told him about her father's phone call. Henry said he would call the hospital in Ellsworth in the morning, and make sure everything needful was being done. Rue thanked him.

"So how many Sunday mornings do we have together, before we need diapers and everything?"

Henry looked thoughtful and then said, "Eighteen hundred and twenty."

"Really?"

"Yes."

Rue squeezed grapefruit juice onto her spoon and drank it. "It's nice to have a doctor in the house who knows these things. Did you subtract the Sundays when you go duck hunting?"

"Oh . . . seventeen hundred and eighty-five, then."

"I hope that will be enough."

"I'm worried we'll run out of this good jam before then."

"There will be Sundays when we'll be downstairs cooking pancakes for our grandchildren."

"The little nippers. And they'll get butter on the funny papers. . . ."

"And knock over the maple syrup."

"And we'll get to poke them and play with them as long as it's fun, and then we'll make Georgia take them away."

"You'll have to fix that log swing in the back before they get here."

"I will."

Henry reached across Rue to co-opt the magazine section. Rue poured out hot tea and put on her glasses.

It was two weeks later, mid-October, when a sharp-shinned hawk appeared on campus and began eating the little birds that Catherine Trainer cherished to the point of fetishism. She noticed the hawk at once, circling high in the sky and then turning sharply to dive. She almost screamed as she saw it intercept and stick its sharp talons into some helpless little oriole. She fancied it was an oriole; it was really too far away to see. Perhaps it was a robin. At first she thought the hawk would go away. Sharp-shinned hawks were growing rarer, and they usually hunted in forests, not in open areas.

It did not go away, however. Soon the population of local songbirds and doves was frightened into silence. Even the escaped pair of African gray parrots that usually lived in the school's live oaks disappeared, although they were themselves too large and well armed for the hawk to eat. Catherine Trainer was beginning to feel overwrought at the situation. What if the hawk ate her lazuli bunting? That is, if it was a lazuli bunting, and if it ever came back? What if she had waited three weeks for another glimpse of the tiny technicolor handful of feathers, with its loud sweet jumble of *chips* and *pits*, and it chose this moment to return to her, and the *hawk ate it?*

That was what was going on in Catherine's life the day Lyndie Sale showed up at school with a broken arm.

Lyndie came into class as the bell was ringing. She had a yellowish bruise on her cheekbone, and she looked unkempt. Her hair needed a good brushing, and her clothes were the same she had worn the day before, looking as if she might have slept in them.

Lyndie took her seat in the back of the room.

"We are having a pop quiz this morning," Catherine announced, and everyone groaned. Catherine had found a copy of a test she had given on California missions several years before, and decided it would be interesting to spring it on them. Not to mention that it got her out of having to work up a lesson plan.

Jennifer Lowen and Malone Dahl began to whisper to each other. "Is this going to count towards our grade?" Jennifer asked as Catherine passed out the quiz sheets.

"Of course," said Mrs. Trainer serenely.

"That's not fair!" said a number of voices together.

"No? Why not?" Catherine had heard this before, a few thousand times. She handed quizzes to Jennifer and to Malone, and then to Lyndie. She noticed that Lyndie took hers with her left hand. The right wrist, lying across the paper to hold it still while Lyndie fished in her backpack for a pencil, looked swollen taut and twice normal size.

"Have you hurt yourself, Lyndie?" Mrs. Trainer asked gently. Lyndie looked up at her a little like one who has been startled from sleep. She looked as if she was so clouded with pain that she had forgotten others could see her.

"A little," she said.

"That looks awfully sore. Did you put ice on it?"

"No." The rest of the class had now turned to look at Lyndie. Mrs. Trainer briskly moved away, passing out the rest of the tests. "Read the questions over carefully first, and in a minute we'll begin," she said, and went back to Lyndie.

"Do you think you can write?" Catherine asked her.

"I think so." Catherine looked doubtful. But she looked at her watch and said, "Class—ready? Please begin."

Then she went back to her desk and sat over her attendance book, watching the room sharply, as she always did during tests. Bobbie Regan was sticking his pencil into the back of the girl in front of him. Catherine told him to stop it. Malone Dahl was moving swiftly through the test. Jennifer Lowen, who daydreamed in class and only heard half of what Catherine said, was looking worried and not marking the paper. Lyndie, she saw, could not hold a pencil in her right hand.

Finally, she said, "Nicolette, will you be my proctor, please? Come to the front of the room." Nicolette waddled up, bringing her pencil and test paper with her. Nicolette was bottom-heavy and beginning to get little breasts, but did not wear a bra. Her hair was in black ponytails. Mrs. Trainer installed her at the teacher's desk. "Please work until twenty past, and then bring your papers up to Nicolette. If I'm not back by then, begin to read chapter four in your geography reader. Lyndie, come with me."

Once outside in the sunshine, Catherine asked permission to look at the arm. She probed it gently, and Lyndie nearly jumped out of her skin.

"I think this is broken, honey," she said. "What happened? Did you fall?"

Lyndie nodded. She kept her head tucked down, as if the bright sun hurt her eyes.

"We better go see Mr. Dianda." As they walked, Catherine asked, "Did this happen while you were playing? Did you fall outside?" Lyndie seemed to be thinking this over. "I fell off my bike," she said. "In the driveway."

"In the driveway! That must have hurt! Did you skin your knees too?" Lyndie looked at the ground. Her legs were bare and bony, but not skinned.

"Was this yesterday afternoon? Where were your parents?"

Lyndie was silent. Catherine looked at her intently and decided to leave her mouth closed for a bit.

After a while Lyndie said, "I fell in the driveway but that's not really when I hurt it."

"I see."

"Last night, well you haven't seen my house, but there are these stairs? And I had a tray in my hands, I was bringing my TV dinner down to the kitchen. So I couldn't see my feet when I got to the stairs, and I tripped and fell all the way down."

"No wonder you're all banged up! And it must have made quite a mess!"

Lyndie looked questioning.

"The tray. You must have had glasses and food and forks and things all over the place."

"Oh, yeah. Oh it was a mess. The gravy got on the rug."

"But didn't your parents put ice on the wrist? Or think about taking you to the hospital?"

"They weren't home."

"Then the babysitter?"

Lyndie looked at the ground some more.

"They must have noticed this morning, how swollen it is. . . ."

"My dad was kind of upset this morning. I thought if it didn't get better I'd show Mrs. Shaw."

Catherine was finding this troubling. Lyndie looked up at her sharply, a pleading look, and then away again. She put her good hand in Mrs. Trainer's and held it as they walked.

"Didn't anyone hear you fall?" she asked. Lyndie said nothing. Catherine patted her good hand, which felt little and hot and gritty. Lyndie started to cry.

"Mrs. Trainer? There's a ghost in our house." The little girl looked up and her face was full of fear.

"A ghost, Lyndie? That sounds terrible. Do your parents know?"

Lyndie shook her head forcefully. "No one can hear it but me! I told my brother, one night when it was crying, and he couldn't hear it. . . ."

"You heard it crying. Is it a child ghost?"

"No it's an awful woman, and it weeps and weeps and I hear it after the lights are off, limping up and down the halls. And it comes to my room and stands there outside the door and I'm afraid it will come in."

"How terrible!"

"It wants something!" said Lyndie. "No one would believe me. If Jonathan can't hear it, they won't hear it, and they won't believe me!"

"Would that be so bad? You could tell your parents, and even if they didn't believe you, they could comfort you, or help you to feel safer."

Lyndie looked at her as if she must be mad.

"The ghost pushed me down the stairs," she said. "It came up behind me and went like this . . ." she demonstrated a straight arm, such as Catherine had used on Mr. Glarrow when he took her bird feeder, "and I fell down and broke a glass. The glass broke. It *hates* me, I think it wants to kill me!"

Catherine had stopped, and the child stopped too, and looked at her very directly, as in agitation she finished this story. Catherine met her gaze, as if making her a promise.

*   *   *

They went into Home.

Catherine and Mr. Dianda together examined Lyndie's arm. "She fell down the stairs," said Catherine to Mike.

"Is that what happened?" Mike asked Lyndie gently. Lyndie nodded, holding back tears. "We better get you to a doctor," said Mike. "Thank you, Mrs. Trainer." And he and Lyndie went out to drive to the hospital.

In the afternoon, while her class was at PE, Catherine sought out Bonnie Fleming, the school psychologist. Bonnie was a waiflike young woman, a trapezist and a dancer with broken knees, who had learned massage when her own injuries had become chronic. From physical therapy she had progressed to psychotherapy. Rue had hired her on a hunch to be on campus several days a week, "making herself available." Bonnie had a manner about her, quiet but magnetic, that Rue thought might be useful. The day she presented herself for her interview, Rue was showing her the campus when one of the runaway African gray parrots, which never let people get near it, had come down low in the live oaks, followed them from tree to tree, and finally flown out and settled on Bonnie's shoulder.

"Hello, bird," Bonnie had murmured to it, completely unsurprised. "Hello bird. You got away, didn't you? You got away and now your pin feathers have grown out and you can fly, can't you bird? Good for you." Rue had been amazed.

Catherine Trainer found Bonnie sitting under a tree, crocheting what looked like a snowflake in fine linen thread. Bonnie was wearing a black leotard, a long Indian wrap skirt, and ballet slippers. Catherine tried to guess her age but couldn't. Her long neck and torso bent and moved as she sat cross-legged, as if she needed to be constantly subtly stretching, warming her muscles in case her dance should begin.

Bonnie looked up at Catherine's troubled face and gave her a welcoming smile. Catherine settled down on the grass beside her. It was very nice to find her out here under a tree, this psychologist girl. Catherine had never talked to a psychologist and would not have liked to be seen going into one's office.

"Look at that bad blue jay," said Catherine. "Look how close he comes to you."

Bonnie nodded and made a noise in her throat at the bird.

"Do you know a lot about birds?"

"Hardly anything," said Bonnie. "I like them though." She made the sound again and the jay cocked his head at her. Catherine watched the bird, and then told Bonnie all about Lyndie, and Bonnie listened carefully.

"Tell me again where she was bruised," she said.

"Here. And here. That *I* saw. Do you know the Sales?"

"Not Mrs. Sale. I met Mr. Sale when he came to the science building to donate a computer."

Catherine stared at the grass. "Don't you think something terrible is going on? When a child is hurt and tells different stories about what happened? To make up a thing like that ghost?"

"Children make up stories for so many different reasons."

"But she went to bed with a broken bone in her arm! And didn't tell her parents?"

"I agree it sounds like something's wrong. But I wouldn't want to say what, based on so little information. Would Lyndie like to talk to me?"

"What will you do if she tells you a ghost pushed her down the stairs?"

Bonnie laughed. "I kind of liked the ghost. I'd like to hear more about it."

Catherine said, "When a child is injured and can't tell how it happened the same way twice in a row, it means someone beat her up."

"It *can* mean that."

"The police came and talked to us! It's a classic case!"

"Catherine, children get hurt a lot of different ways. And they tell big stories for a lot of reasons. She's got your attention by doing it, hasn't she?"

"We signed that piece of paper. From the State of California. If it even *might* be child abuse, you have to report it. If you *suspect*."

Bonnie looked troubled. "Have you talked to Rue?"

"No, she isn't here. I heard her mother is sick."

"That's too bad. But the child has had medical attention, for the moment. I think we should talk to Rue. There could be all kinds of ramifications we don't know about."

"You're probably right," said Catherine.

*   *   *

But Catherine didn't really think Bonnie was right, and thus didn't hear what she said.

Catherine thought about the ghost, the angry weeping woman, and felt a strange stroke of pity for her. She thought about that poor hurt little girl, trying to be brave, and the look in her eyes as she told Catherine her story. She thought about it all evening, and talked it over with Norman, as she did everything. And by morning she had come to believe that Bonnie had quite agreed with her, certainly Norman did; that when a person is being misunderstood or hurt it is terribly important that she learn that somebody cares, and believes her. So before she left for class Friday morning, Catherine telephoned Child Protective Services.

Rue's mother had grown querulous and miserable in the hospital, and her father had determined to take her home. He couldn't tell Rue on the phone what exactly had been so desperate, but he said she hadn't taken to it, and they better get her out. "Do you want me to come?" Rue had asked.

There was a brief pause before her father said, "No, no, we'll be fine." So Rue said, "I'll be in Bangor tomorrow night, and I'll rent a car, so don't worry, and don't wait up; I won't be in before midnight." When he didn't tell her not to come, she realized he'd been wanting her for days.

Even at the top of the airplane stairs, as you stand above the tarmac in Bangor, the crisp smell of fir washes over you, cleansing ether from a northern world. The airport was virtually deserted at ten o'clock at night. The car rental desk had closed but the agent left Rue's contract and car keys with the airline baggage handlers. She was soon driving alone on nearly deserted roads, with black pine woods on either side of her, opening here and again to farmers' fields. She drove carefully, watching for deer, and grateful it still lacked two weeks of hunting season, a time that had grown increasingly frightening throughout the state. During November even the dogs wore blaze orange and her father reported that Howard Schwarz braided blaze orange into his cow's mane, and painted C-O-W on her sides with dayglow paint. A woman in Brewer had been killed hanging out wash in her own backyard, and another in Surry found some drunk had shot her donkey.

She had an hour and a half to home, to sort out her feelings about seeing her mother stricken. Jeannette was a proud and cool woman with a great need for others to see her dignity. Rue hoped they would not embarrass each other. She hoped she could be some help to her father without making him feel that he needed help. The car was underpowered and the upholstery reeked of cigar smoke.

As she drove she kept the windows open to the pine-perfumed night air, although the temperature was certainly in the forties. She wondered what Henry was doing. Then she wondered what Georgia was doing, and liked knowing they were in the same time zone. She tried the radio but it was AM only, and at this time of night she got a jumble of overlapping stations, either hard rock or call-in shows, the strongest signal being KDKA in Pittsburgh. She turned it off and drove in cold scented silence.

There was a light on in the kitchen when she pulled into the yard of the house where she grew up. The house was a nineteenth-century farmhouse, with boxy little rooms to hold heat and wood-burning stoves in the kitchen, parlor, and best upstairs bedroom. She was struck at how much it was like the house in which she now lived, except that the California rooms were breezier with much bigger windows, since the farmers there were not facing three months a year of subzero weather. When she was a little girl in this house, they used to live in the kitchen and keep the stove cranked up to a zillion in winter. You got used to piercing cold outdoors, so that a windless day and five above zero seemed positively balmy, but when you were inside, you wanted to be warm through your bones.

Rue went in the back door quietly. The familiar smell of the kitchen swamped her so that she stood for a moment in the door-way, breathing it in as if every minute of the years she had lived here was still here and you could smell them.

She hoped her parents were asleep, but when she closed the kitchen door softly she heard her father stir in his chair in the par-lor. She went in to him.

He looked just the same. Lean, with a long-jawed lined face, thick hair, and pale blue eyes. If he had been asleep he didn't look it. He got up, kissed her, and told her in the same words he always used that it was awfully nice to have her home. She felt as if she had just come back from boarding school.

"Is Mother here?" she asked. She had still been in Ellsworth when they last spoke. He nodded.

"I told her you said not to wait up, but she wants to see you. She slept a lot of this afternoon, so don't worry about waking her."

"How is she?"

He considered this question carefully.

"She's not too bad. I don't think she can see too awful good. She says the headache is better."

This gave Rue very little idea what to expect. But she left her father, saying she wouldn't be long, and climbed the stairs.

In the bedroom her parents had shared for fifty-odd years, her mother lay looking so waxy that Rue's heart nearly stopped when she saw her. She thought she must have died since her father went downstairs. But as she walked softly across the floor, her mother's eyes opened, and her spirit, which must have been floating nearby, went into her body and animated it, so that at once, as if by conjuring, the object became a woman. Jeannette smiled, and Rue bent over to kiss her cheek. Her mother pulled herself up on the pillows.

"I made him take me out of there," she said. Her speech seemed entirely normal, as near as Rue could tell.

"I know you did. Good for you."

"They put a needle in your arm and leave it there, so you're attached to this . . ." she couldn't finish the description, but gestured such that Rue knew she meant the IV bottle, hanging from its aluminum cart beside her bed, which might have been dripping in drugs or just sugar water to keep her strength up.

"I guess they have to do that," said Rue, though she knew from being a doctor's wife that it was often done out of routine and not reason. "I bet you hated it."

Her mother nodded and rolled her eyes as if her daughter was a mind-reader. Rue was unused to having her mother's approval, let alone to having her mother think she had any special gifts, so it was a new experience to be thought a mind-reader, and where her mother was concerned she dreaded new experiences.

"I had to tinkle," said her mother in a stage whisper. "I didn't tell him this. I had to tinkle in the middle of the night and I rang the bell, I rang and rang and rang, and nobody came."

"Oh, Mother . . ." said Rue. "Where were the nurses?"

Her mother made a face. It was a deep mystery.

"Finally a nurse came down the hall and I shouted, "Yoo hoo—yoo hoo—and she came, and I said 'I have to tinkle,' and she said 'I'm not on duty on this floor.'"

"Oh *Mother.*"

"And off she went, trip trap, trip trap." This was the noise the goats made crossing the bridge in *The Three Billy Goats Gruff*. The copy of the story that her mother had read aloud was in the next room, as was apparently her whole childhood. And her mother still spoke in a code to her daughter, special words and signs that only she and Rue shared, that only Rue would know. Trip trap, trip trap, the nurse went away, and—what did that make Jeannette? The troll?

Rue waited to hear the end of the story. Her mother was looking at her, a look full of drama. Finally it dawned on Rue that the end of the story was that . . . she needed to get up, and nobody came, and she had a needle in her arm, trapping her in the bed and . . . the inevitable had happened.

"Oh *Mother!*"

"I couldn't tell Him," she said, meaning of course her husband of fifty-four years. "I just told him I wouldn't spend another night in that place."

"I'm shocked. I'm glad you put your foot down."

"I did," said Jeannette.

They both looked at each other and Rue began to picture exactly what kind of commotion her mother had made, before and after this disaster. She said gravely, "I like the yoo-hoo part." And began to smile. Her mother demonstrated this high point, so that Rue pictured her, upright in her hospital gown, yodeling at the goat-footed nurse.

"How long can you stay?" asked her mother.

"Till Sunday. I have a three o'clock plane." She hoped her mother would be pleased with almost the whole weekend.

"Three o'clock? Can't you stay for Sunday supper?" her mother asked, as if only willfulness or thoughtlessness could explain this odd planning.

"I'm sorry—I can't."

Her mother seemed to sag a little. Then she said, "Do you have exams?"

Rue was momentarily frozen.

"No, I have a job, Mother. I run a school. You know that."

"Of course I know that," her mother said smoothly. There was a brief pause. "I meant, is it exam time at school? At Country?"

After a moment Rue said, "No, it's only October. We don't have exams until right before Christmas."

"I don't believe in this new business, you know," said her mother. Rue waited. Finally her mother said, "This not giving grades. This business where they don't have tests. Life is a test. They have a new principal here at the Consolidated, she's got the whole town in an uproar. . . ."

"Yes, I know you feel that way." At Country, there were no letter grades until fifth grade, and no exams until seventh. She had no way of knowing if her mother remembered this and couldn't resist provoking, or if she had eliminated it, along with so much other unwanted information. Her mother kept all Rue's swimming ribbons and award certificates framed in Rue's old room. She had her National Merit Scholar certificate over the wood stove, and her college and graduate degrees beside them. It still pained her that Rue wouldn't give her her Phi Beta Kappa key, so Jeannette could have it put on a charm bracelet for her.

"How is Georgia . . ." her mother asked. She was clearly reluctant to let Rue leave, though her fatigue was now palpable.

"She sounds very well, Mother. She's at The Juilliard School, in New York, you know."

"The Juilliard School!" Her mother made a sort of actressy face of delight. "Juilliard! Mother wanted me to go to the Conservatory, too, you know. But I said Juilliard or nothing." Rue did know. This was a seminal story in her mother's history, and every time Rue told her about Georgia, the news got routed to a side track, while the great engine of her mother's disappointment came charging up the main line with fresh news from 1938.

"Georgia—at The Juilliard School. And she's playing the . . ."

"Singing, Mother. She's a soprano. Lyric."

"Soprano!" exclaimed her mother, losing interest. She herself had played the piano.

"Mother—you should try to sleep. We'll have plenty of time in the morning."

"I don't need much sleep," said her mother. Rue thought she had just been asleep, with her eyes open, and snapped herself back.

"I know. That's good—I'll see you early, then." She got up. "Would you like this light on?"

"No—no—not this one. I want the one in the bathroom." Rue went into the bathroom and turned on the ceiling light. The old white tiles had been replaced by something plastic and textured, with baskets of blue flowers on each square. The old claw-footed tub was freshly scrubbed, and her father had put out her mother's monogrammed towels. The towels had been a wedding present and now had loose threads along the warp at each side where the hem had worn away.

"Not that . . . not that one the . . ."

Rue turned on the light built into the mirror, and turned off the overhead light.

". . . one beside the . . . oh the . . ."

"Mirror, Mother." Rue came out and left the door standing open.

"No that's too . . ."

Rue closed it until there was just a sliver of light and looked toward the bed. Her mother waved her hand toward the ceiling. Rue opened the door a few more inches. The hand dropped, satisfied. Rue went back to the bed and stood looking down.

"I'm sorry to be such a . . . nuisance," said her mother.

"Don't be silly. I'm so glad to be here." Her mother nodded.

"Are you ready to have this light off?"

She shook her head NO. "Leave it for Daddy."

Rue tiptoed out to find her father sitting on the bed in her childhood room, with the light on and door open, waiting for her. She went in.

"I thought you might sleep in the guest room while she's sick," said Rue.

"No, we'll do all right," he said. She looked at him in the light and thought he looked drained.

"I'm sorry to keep you up so late."

"It's good for us. Change in routine." He stood up, and she realized with a shock that he was now hardly more than an inch taller than she. "There were some phone calls for you, earlier."

"Important?"

"Fellah sounded pretty druv' up. It was a Mr. Herring."

Rue thought for just a moment to get from herring to kipper. "Kip," she said.

"Yes. And Mike, he called twice."

"Thank you, Daddy. Sleep well—do you mind if I use the phone in the kitchen?"

"That'll be fine."

"Can I bring you anything?"

"Not a thing." She watched him make his way quietly into the darkened bedroom and close the door behind him.

She watched him walk off, and when his bedroom door closed behind him, she made her way back down the narrow darkened staircase to the pitch-black kitchen. For a moment she couldn't find the light switch; she was feeling for the switch in her kitchen at home.

hat's *it*," yelled Chandler Kip into the phone, when Rue returned his call at 10 p.m., Pacific Time. "That's it, she's a nutcase, she's making a laughingstock of the school. I want her fired, Rue, and if you won't do it, I'll do it myself."

"No, Chandler, you will not. Look, could you hold on just a minute? Hold on, I'll be right back to you. I'd like you to tell me again what happened." Rue was cursing herself for not getting through to Mike Dianda before she called Chandler. Mike's line had been busy for ten minutes and it was getting late to call. She did not want to have this conversation without knowing both sides to the story. The kitchen was cold and the coals in the wood stove were almost ash, and she'd had a long day and frankly didn't want to have the conversation at all. But. She put new kindling and a couple of birch logs into the stove, and went back to the phone.

"She called Child Welfare and told them Oliver Sale, my firm's general counsel, broke his daughter's arm," Chandler announced, and Rue's heart sank. "This is an upstanding member of the community and a valued colleague of mine," Chandler's voice was rising, "and he is very upset. *Very* upset. And so would *you* be, if you suddenly found the police at your door because some harebrained . . ."

"Chandler, please stop shouting at me. I can't make a sensible decision if I can't find out what happened."

"I just told you what happened!"

"In the first place, it's not police who come, it's a social worker, and they don't go to the house. In the second, Mrs. Trainer didn't call them without a reason."

"How do you know, you're three thousand miles away! Wouldn't you be upset? If the police or whoever came prancing on campus to decide whether you're fit to raise your own child . . ."

"Chandler, stop shouting at me."

"This is a man with an impeccable reputation, and now of course this rumor is all over town, Oliver Sale beats his kid!"

"Stop shouting at me."

There was a moment of silence. Finally Rue said, "I take it Lyndie has been injured in some way."

"She fell down the stairs in the dark and broke a bone in her wrist."

"I see."

"And she told Mrs. Trainer that. She told her exactly what happened!"

"And whom else did she tell?"

"Oh *whom* else? Could you stop for once talking like you've got a goddamn hot potato in your mouth?"

"Yes, I can. Sorry. Did she tell Mr. Dianda?"

"I suppose so, he took her to the hospital."

"And she told the doctors, I suppose."

"Look, I have to get back to Oliver. I told him I'd have an answer for him tonight. What am I going to tell him?"

"Please tell him that I am extremely sorry that this happened, and I'd like to meet with him and Sondra on Monday."

"I'm not going to say that, Rue, I'm going to tell him that Mrs. Trainer is fired."

"You can't do that. You can set policy, but you cannot do my job for me."

"This *is* policy."

"It absolutely is not."

"Rue, let me be clear. I am taking this personally. I want you to consider this as if it had happened to me. *Your* teacher, a useless neurotic, who I've warned you about before, has accused someone very close to me—a lawyer, Rue! She's accused him of a felony, he could be disbarred, did you think of that? I told the Sales I would give it my first priority, as if it had happened to me. To *me,* do we understand each other? I told them it would be taken care of."

"And so it will. But if it's taken care of by anyone but me, you'll be looking for another school head."

Chandler hung up.

Rue dialed Mike Dianda and got a busy signal. She waited five minutes and tried again. Still busy. Mary or Trinnie must be on, probably doing homework with a friend across town. She called the operator and told her it was an emergency.

$\mathcal{M}$ ike, it's Rue."

"We've been trying to reach you all day!"

"I know, Chandler got to me. Tell me what you know."

"First let me tell you about the Oliver Sale School of Charm. He called me this afternoon and said if I didn't put you on the fucking phone he was going to come over and rip it out of the wall."

"Lovely."

"Only he didn't say Mrs. Shaw, he said Mrs. Shay."

"How soon did he get around to his close friend, the President of the Board?"

"Right quick."

"Oh, god. Well I'm ready. What happened?"

"Remember the speech you make before school opens, that no one should call CPS without talking to you first, unless they think you are the abuser?"

"Yes."

"Someone didn't hear it. Someone has a trap door in her brain that she opens and drops out all the information she doesn't want."

"Why do I always think of Catherine when you say these things? Did she talk to you, at least?"

"No, she talked to Bonnie."

"Nothing like following procedure. And Bonnie told her to call CPS?"

"Bonnie expressly told her *not* to, until she discussed it with you. Catherine of course was in my office in tears for at least an hour this afternoon. She had done the *only* thing she could do, it's up to her to protect that little girl, and there's a hawk on campus eating birdies that has something to do with it. . . ."

"Oh god."

"She said Norman told her she was right . . ."

"She didn't."

"Rue, I couldn't make this up."

"Just do one thing for me, don't ever tell anyone else that. If that gets around, she's completely cooked."

"I know. But I have to tell you, when she finally told me what Lyndie said, I felt she was right. I could kill her for not telling us first, but I think she was probably right to make the call." He told Rue about the conflicting stories and about the ghost. Rue drew in her breath.

"Oh, no, the poor little thing," she said.

"Really."

"Clearly *something* is wrong . . . but god, I'd have wanted to talk to her, I'd have asked her to talk to Bonnie . . ."

"I did say to Oliver Sale, this afternoon, that while I was sorry about what had happened, I thought Lyndie was asking for help, and it would be wise to consider family therapy. He began to rave about how he was so much smarter than any goddamn therapist, he took a psych course once at the U of Chicago, and believe me, he knows it *all*."

Rue sighed. The wood stove was finally beginning to throw some heat, but she wished she could cross the room to put the kettle on. It occurred to her that she'd given her parents a cordless phone for Christmas, and wondered what they had done with it. Found it too complex to work, she imagined. You have to remember to turn it on.

"So I take it a Child Protection worker paid us a visit."

"Yes. Now as you know, it was Grandpersons' Day, so the campus was crawling with visitors. Right before lunch a behemoth appears at Emily's desk. We got Lyndie out of class and gave him an office to use."

"Mine."

"Yours. When he finished, middle school was just going down to lunch, so they all got a good look at him. He weighed at least three hundred pounds, and his stomach hung halfway to his knees, in two bags inside his pants. I think he was Rumanian. In any case, he did not speak English as a first language, or as a second, that I could tell."

Rue groaned.

"Lyndie was very upset when she left. Every kid in the middle school saw Man Mountain, and of course in ten minutes they all knew what he had come for. He stopped to talk to me before he left."

"And? Did he speak enough English to understand about the ghost?"

"She never told him about the ghost. Lyndie told him she tripped in the dark, that the arm didn't hurt till she got to school, that everything is fine at home and she's a happy little girl, and he figured that settled that. Then he got up to leave and stepped in Bucket's dog dish. Broke it right in half and never noticed."

Rue laughed, but it wasn't funny. "Oh lord, this is a real mess."

"Yes. It took until two o'clock for the news to reach Chandler Kip. I had a nice talk on the phone with him, and then a nice talk with Oliver Sale, and then Mrs. Sale came home from her aerobics class and they both appeared on our doorstep."

"Both Sales."

"Yes."

"I don't know her at all—tell me."

"He came in in his gray suit and his white shirt and his big black shoes, and she came in after him, this little bit of a thing all in neon spandex. It was like Beauty and the Beast. It was like one of them is in black and white and the other one's in color."

Rue laughed.

"I explained about the form we all sign, and I said these things happen and we would like to help in any way we could, and that was not the right thing to say. He began to roar at me, what kind of goddamn help did we think they needed, who did we think we were, he's an upstanding citizen, a member of the bar, his mother belonged to the Eastern Star and his wife's father works for the FBI."

"Does he really?"

"Yes, apparently. So he went on flailing at me and she stared around the room. She has a figure that must be half plastic, at least."

"Did she talk?"

"Not much. She clearly *hates* Catherine Trainer. She doesn't want her fired, she wants her killed."

"Are they going to withdraw?"

"I don't know. I don't think they know yet."

"If you had to choose one word to describe the wife . . ."

Mike thought carefully. "Flighty? No, that's not it. She did keep staring around and making little motions with her head, like a bird. But wait, I'll get it."

"Frightened?"

"That seemed like part of it. But it was more that she seemed disconnected. I'd say she has an inappropriate affect, but that's not one word. I wouldn't say she was a relaxed or happy woman."

"I'll see for myself soon enough. I don't know that I'd be too relaxed, married to that man."

"No."

"I don't suppose you brought up the subject of Jonathan?"

"You know," said Mike, "it just didn't seem like the time."

"So where do we stand?"

"They wailed away at me until they wore themselves out, and now they're back in their corners having their brows mopped and their mouthpieces fitted, waiting for you."

"Great. Okay, now, talk to me about Lyndie. Have you seen her?"

"She didn't want to talk. She seemed mortified by Man Mountain."

"Is *she* frightened?"

"I can't tell. She's too angry. And not much inclined to trust me, at the moment."

"I see. Now, where do we stand? The family refuses therapy. If they leave the school the children may be in danger and no one will care, but if they stay, then it's our problem, but there's nothing we can do. And of course it's entirely possible that Lyndie makes up stories to get attention. She may even *hurt* herself to get attention. What's your gut feeling?"

Mike said, "My gut says Oliver Sale could certainly throw a child down the stairs. But Lyndie . . . I don't know. I don't know. You better talk to her yourself."

They sat in silence for a while, on opposite edges of the continent.

"Do we know what house they live in?"

"Why do you ask?"

"What is the chance it really is haunted?"

Mike didn't laugh. She could tell he had thought of this himself. "At that address, I'd say not much. That section was all developed about the same time; it's the California Palazzo style, vintage nineteen seventy-six."

"Of course, we don't know how ghosts behave, exactly," Rue said. "There may be haunted places that no one died in. There may be ghosts who haunt people, not places."

"It might be one of the Plums!" Mike exclaimed. "It's an angel gone wrong and it followed her home from school!"

"I hope it isn't that. I don't want to have to explain it to Protective Services."

"Or the accreditation committee."

"Listen, before I get back, will you talk with Catherine, tell her you want to see her at least once a week, to talk about class preparation and lesson plans and anything she needs help with?"

"I already did."

Rue breathed relief. "Thank you."

There was another silence. "How's your mom?" Mike asked.

"She's better than I expected. It's good that I came."

"Good. I'll let you know if there's any more excitement."

"Let's hope not. I'll see you Monday."

Rue sat for a while in the bright kitchen surrounded by blackness. Then she damped down the wood stove, turned out the lights, and went upstairs. She had to clear her Raggedy Ann and Andy dolls off the pillow before she could get into bed.

The first thing Rue did Monday morning, after Flag Raising and taking attendance, was send for Lyndie.

Lyndie came to the door of her office and stood like a wraith, waiting for Rue to notice her. Rue was shocked when she did. Lyndie's skin looked gray, and her hair, which she had worn in fat pigtails last week, was hacked short. She did not look directly at Rue but stood staring at the floor.

"Come in, Lyndie," Rue said, and Lyndie did. She took a chair far from Rue's desk and perched on the edge of it. Rue got up and shut the door, then went to take a chair closer to her. She waited a moment or two hoping Lyndie would speak, but the girl looked steadily at the carpet.

"You've got a new haircut," Rue said. Lyndie nodded. "I like it."

Lyndie didn't reply. She did not, apparently, care whether Mrs. Shaw liked it or not.

"How is your arm, Lyndie?"

Lyndie was wearing a lightweight cast, strapped on with Velcro. Under it a dirty ace bandage held her wrist stationary. "You've got a V-wrap bandage there, I see. I used to know how to wrap that, from Girl Scouts. Does your mother wrap it for you?"

Lyndie shrugged, and Rue couldn't tell if it meant I don't know or I'll say anything you want if you'll leave me alone.

"Does your arm hurt much?"

Again, Lyndie didn't bother to answer.

"Lyndie—you seem very angry about something." There was a pause. Lyndie stared at her shoe, and then nodded.

"Is it anything I can help with?"

No answer.

"If you tell me what you're angry about, or who you're angry at, maybe I can do something about it."

Lyndie suddenly looked out the window. She stared at the sky, her face hard to read.

"Are you angry at me, Lyndie?" The girl shook her head no. Then she looked at the floor again and said bitterly, "Mrs. Trainer."

Rue sat up. "You're mad at Mrs. Trainer?" she said softly. "Did she do something bad?"

Lyndie looked at her fiercely. She looked like an animal that's been beaten in an unfair fight.

"I told her a secret, and she told."

Rue took a deep breath. "That *is* bad," she said. "I always think of Mrs. Trainer as someone you can trust."

Lyndie looked as if that made Rue a bigger fool than even Lyndie.

"Are you sure she knew it was a secret?"

Lyndie nodded angrily.

"I don't suppose you can tell me what it was about?"

Lyndie apparently did not think this deserved an answer.

"Lyndie, it seems to me that a bad thing has happened here, and I don't know quite what to do about it. I'm sure Mrs. Trainer thought she was doing something for your good."

She could see she was getting nowhere.

Emily came to the door. "Mr. and Mrs. Sale are here, Rue." Lyndie looked alarmed. Rue said, "Ask them to wait just a minute, please." To Lyndie she said, "Your parents are very upset about what happened Friday, and I want to talk with them about it. Would you like to stay?" Lyndie shook her head.

"You go on back to class, then, and I'll find you later and we'll decide what to do."

Lyndie didn't move. She stared at Rue, a deep, stubborn, demanding stare. Rue found it both frightening and touching. Again, she had the image of Lyndie as a hurt animal that can't tell you where it hurts so you have to guess. On an impulse, she said, "I'll tell you what. Go to the library and tell Mrs. Nafie I sent you. Ask her to help you choose a topic and show you how to look it up in three different reference books. If you have time before I come to find you, you write me a one-page paper on what you've learned. Is that all right?"

Lyndie nodded. For the first time since she came in, there was some light in her eyes. She stood up, and Rue stood too, and put a hand on her shoulder. Lyndie jumped as if she'd been burned.

Rue spent an hour with Oliver and Sondra Sale, during which she heard in detail how humiliating, intrusive, uncalled-for, and stupid they found having their private business exposed for the whole town to discuss. They were upstanding private people, Rue learned, and to be the subject of rumors, especially ugly and false ones, was a great and serious harm. Rue bowed to it.

"In Mrs. Trainer's defense," she said once, "she felt she was obliged by law to act as she did. It's up to the State to evaluate the . . ."

"Section one-one-one-six-six of the Penal Code, I'm a lawyer, Mrs. Shaw," said Oliver. "'Knows or *reasonably* suspects' is the language. Are you saying this was reasonable?"

"I'm only saying it must have been reasonable to her."

"I find this incredibly offensive," he said, and stood up. Sondra went on staring at her skirt. "There was nothing wrong with Lyndie when I drove her to school. I think she had an accident here, on the playground or in class."

"Why do you think she would not tell us that's what happened?"

"How the hell do I know? She's protecting someone—another student. Even a teacher. Where's the piece of paper for parents to sign, that if they know or reasonably suspect that a child has been injured at school, they should sue the hell out of the place to make sure it doesn't happen to anyone else?"

Rue listened as quietly as she could. Toward the end of the hour, when she began to be aware of the press of other matters that were stacking up outside her office, she said, "There is no way any of us can change what happened. But I don't have a clear sense of where we should go from here."

She was waiting to hear that they were withdrawing their children and filing suit. But instead, Sondra Sale said, "We demand that you fire Catherine Trainer. Lyndie has been upset since the moment she met that woman. She's a danger to the children."

Rue looked at her, slightly thrown. She said "I'm afraid I can't agree. She may not be perfect, but I am quite sure she is not a danger to anyone."

"She's a danger to us!" Oliver roared. "Look at us! Do you want to go through what we just went through?"

"I can't apologize any more than I already have. I understand your point of view, but I am not prepared to fire Mrs. Trainer at this time."

That was the moment. They would stand, they would announce that they withdrew their children, then they would march out, call their lawyers, and call Chandler Kip.

To her surprise, they stayed seated.

"We want Lyndie moved to Mrs. Douglas's class immediately. Today," said Oliver.

"I'll have to talk to Mrs. Douglas, her class is full. But I'm inclined to think that is the best thing to do."

"It isn't the best thing," said Sondra. "Lyndie has friends in her class. She'll have to start all over again. The best thing is to fire Mrs. Trainer."

There was a silence. After a minute, Rue stood up. "I understand your feelings, and I'm taking them very seriously. Thank you for giving me so much of your time. I hope we'll be able to go on from here and make this a really good school year for Lyndie." She was fairly amazed when the Sales stood up and filed out. She'd begun to fear they might fall upon her and beat her. Or worse: simply stay all day.

Emily was at the door with a list in her hand and a stack of pink telephone messages. Before she could start, Mike slipped in and dropped into the chair Oliver had left.

"One minute, Emily," said Rue. "I'll be done as soon as I can." Emily handed her the messages, went out, and closed the door.

"They're staying. They want Lyndie moved to Evelyn's class. I'm inclined to do it."

"God, Rue. You're going to have eight other families in here by carpool time, demanding you move their children too."

"I know. I'll just have to weather it. Mike, what am I going to do? This has to be Catherine's last year. I don't think she's slipped as much as they say, but the rumors are getting corrosive."

"If only she had let *me* make the call. If only she'd let you do it."

"Yes, I know, thank you very much. I haven't taken enough flak."

"I'd have done it," said Mike.

"You have nerves of steel." Mike smiled and flexed a bicep like Charles Atlas. Rue told him about Lyndie's anger at Catherine.

"I can't send her back to that class now. She couldn't learn with that kind of mistrust between them."

"Does she want to switch?" Mike asked.

"I think so. Though the mother said she's made close friends that she doesn't want to leave. Malone Dahl and Jennifer Lowen?"

"Yes—but Emily says that Malone and Lyndie made friends at first because Malone was new. Now that she's finding her way with Jennifer's friends, Malone's cooling off on Lyndie."

"Because Malone's a climber?"

"Not only that. They were never a perfect match. Lyndie is . . ."

"Weird," said Rue.

"Well, yes."

"So the question is, Is that the cause? Or the effect? Is she weird because something bad goes on at home? Or is the family uptight because one of the kids is weird?"

"*One* of them?"

Rue thought for a moment about Jonathan Sale, and then she thought about Georgia, and she wondered what it would do to you to have a baby, hoping it would grow to be bright and funny and loving, have a happy life, and instead you got . . . Jonathan Sale?

"Sometimes I wonder how anyone has the heart to have children at all."

"I spent a little time with Lloyd Merton this morning. He had Lyndie in his class last year. He told me something that will make your hair fall off."

"Tell."

"He's quite good friends with his opposite number at Seven Springs Middle, I forget her name, Joan . . ."

"Thor. I know her. Good teacher."

"Lloyd ran into her somewhere and asked her how Lyndie had been in her class. Lyndie was having a hard time adjusting, he thought. Joan told him that early in the year, Lyndie came to her in tears and showed her some mean notes someone had left in her locker. 'Lyndie is a poop,' that kind of thing. Lloyd says that Joan is absolutely certain that Lyndie wrote the notes herself."

Rue felt sick. She and Mike stared at each other.

"I think I better talk to Bonnie," she said.

Bonnie listened to all that Rue told her.

"Complicated," she said.

"You mean you're not going to tell me that Colonel Mustard did it with a knife in the library?"

"Nope, sorry. I'd have to talk to the whole family."

"I don't think that's going to happen. But if you have any chance to observe Lyndie, or even make friends with her, I'd appreciate any insight."

"Of course."

"Have you got any advice for me about Chandler Kip, by the way?"

"He's a typical One," said Bonnie.

"One what?"

"On the Enneagram. He's a One, a typical Achiever."

"What, pray tell, is an Enneagram?"

"It's an ancient system, probably Zoroastrian, for recognizing personality types. There are nine."

"And what is the use of it?"

"It's useful to remember people are different. Otherwise you can make the mistake of thinking all failures are failures of character. If Chandler is a typical One, then by definition, he's convinced he can do your job better than you can."

"I already knew that. Let me ask you this. Leaving aside her type for a moment, do you think Catherine understands how hard she is making it for me to protect her?"

"No."

"Does she have any sense of how much dissatisfaction there is with her performance?"

"No. She's a . . ."

"Don't tell me . . ."

"Two. But not such a typical one."

"I'm beginning to feel she's a typical birdbrain, and I don't have much hope of getting her to hear me."

"No," said Bonnie. "I don't blame you."

They sat silent for a moment.

"What's a Two?" asked Rue.

"A Helper. It's a personality that gets its satisfaction from a feeling of being of service. It's not a very intellectual type, and it can be a person who's so focused on Doing Good that she doesn't see the big picture."

"I see," said Rue. "I thought maybe it was a person who was prematurely deaf."

Henry was very glad to have Rue home again. He'd lost a patient over the weekend, a young woman who had had four operations for brain tumors and was scheduled for a fifth. The tumors were technically nonmalignant, but that hardly mattered if they kept blossoming like cauliflowers inside her nonexpandable skull. The patient had been gallant and funny in the face of excruciating headaches, and though Henry knew he was going to lose her, he was taking it hard.

"Tell me about your parents," he said.

"Are you sure we're finished with Myrna?"

"I'm supposed to be so objective. What kind of a sick idea is that? Your patient is an object. Do you think there are doctors who believe that?"

"Only the men. The women doctors are all models of empathy mixed with inner strength."

"That's what I thought. I wish I'd stuck with obstetrics."

"Ob-Gyns lose patients too."

"I'm sure they don't," he said. "I have an idea. Why don't we run away?"

Rue laughed. Henry and Rue were out for a walk at dusk. They walked holding hands and chose a route up into the hills, away from traffic, alongside groves of orange and avocado trees. The land was dry, but the air was fresh with spicy smells from the bark and the fruit and the drying eucalyptus leaves beneath their feet. This was a new luxury, this evening walk. When Georgia had been at home, Rue insisted on having supper early, so Georgia could get on with her homework. Now they often stayed outside together, walking and talking over the events of the day, until the blue streaks of last light, and ate supper late, by candlelight.

"That's a great idea," said Rue. "When I was ten I decided to live in a tree when I grew up, like the Swiss Family Robinson. No one would know I was there, and no one could find me when they were mad at me."

"My idea is very similar. We are perfectly matched. My idea is we go to Canyon de Chelly and live in the ruins up on a cliff. The roofs are all gone but it won't matter, it never rains there."

Rue looked at him with wide eyes. "I've *always* wanted to do that."

"Fine, let's leave tomorrow. Let the parents all beat their children senseless, let Mr. Herring run the school since he knows how." Henry was a great fan of Rue's father's habit of naming people by association. He treasured new examples of the genre. "I missed you a lot," he added.

Rue stopped walking to put her arms around him.

"I missed you too. I'm sorry I wasn't here."

"I feel pulled in too many directions," he said. "My patient is dead and all my partners want to talk about is joining an HMO. My wife's three thousand miles away, her school is on fire, and I miss Georgia."

She held him and nodded. She missed Georgia too.

"Will she be shocked, do you think, to find we've fled the scene and gone to live on a cliff?" Rue asked.

"Of course not, she'd be *proud*."

"I think you're right," said Rue.

After supper Rue ordinarily got into bed with a book while Henry, who needed little sleep, sat up in his study. Sometimes he watched old movies on cable, or wrote to Georgia, and sometimes he played war games on his computer. But this fall, unbeknownst to Rue, he spent at least an hour every night reading aloud into a tape recorder. For years Rue had been saying that she wanted to reread

Ovid's *Metamorphoses*, but she was never going to have time. He was reading them to her as a Christmas present, so she could listen to them while she worked in the garden. They were quite harrowing, he found, but haunting. He always had trouble giving Rue anything; she seemed to have everything she wanted. This year, all fall, he was looking forward to Christmas.

The scene of the October trustee meeting resembled Gettysburg after three days of fighting. The field was trampled and covered with gore, and hardly a blade of grass was standing. Bodies lay everywhere, and only Rue, Ann Rosen, the killer divorce lawyer, and Chandler Kip remained in the fray.

Rue and Ann Rosen had planned a reasoned discussion of personnel issues, especially the hiring and firing of teachers. Chandler had derailed that by announcing his own topic: he wanted to abolish Annual Giving. He sat in his $1,600 suit and his $200 necktie, and reported that it was offensive and unnecessary to ask hardworking families for donations over and above the tuition they already paid. Schools should run like businesses. If the school couldn't run on the money it earned, then tuitions should be raised.

"Chandler, this isn't a hardware store!" Ann Rosen had snapped. That was the first salvo, but it had been met with a roar of returning fire from Chandler's side. Now Ann and her allies sipped coffee from paper cups in hollow-eyed silence as Rue tried to hold the fort.

"When the *Wall Street Journal* publishes a list of the twenty best colleges in the country, the first measure, the first, Chandler, is how much *more* the college spends per student than the cost of the tuition. Harvard costs $20,000 a year and it spends $50,000. On every undergraduate."

"They have a huge endowment. We don't."

"How do you think they *got* a huge endowment?"

"They established themselves in a noncompetitive environment. Men got rich before the days of income tax, they went to Harvard, they could afford to be generous. The world has changed."

"Women went to Harvard too," said Ann Rosen wearily. "*I* went to Harvard." Chandler ignored her. "But I admit, it was after the income tax," she added, and Sylvia French laughed. Chandler glared at them.

"It's uncharitable not to have Annual Giving," Rue said. "If you raise tuition to cover operating costs, you're going to lose students every time you do it, and they'll be just the students you don't want to lose."

"I don't agree. This is an entrepreneurial world. The schools that should survive are the ones that do the best job for the least money, and the people who should go to them are the people who can afford them."

There was a groan from Ann Rosen. She whispered something to Sylvia. Terry Malko, sitting next to Ann, was taking notes in a tiny handwriting with a beautiful gold and red lacquer fountain pen.

"Suppose," said Terry, "instead of Annual Giving, we have giving for special projects. You could give a computer to the second grade, let's say, if you know your child's classroom needs one."

"So you can give money in a way that benefits your own child?"

"Exactly."

"That's just what we *don't* need," Rue said. "We are trying to build a community in which everyone understands that what is needed on this earth is the decent survival of all. Not a world in which the rich get richer and the poor get poorer. And not a ghetto where your children meet only other children whose backgrounds are just like theirs! That is unfair to your children, and it's not an education. We are trying to teach our students that in this world you repay the gifts you've been given, with interest. You don't grab up as much as you can and scramble up a ladder with it, kicking at the hands on the rungs below you. And the first and best way we teach them that is by setting the example ourselves."

"Amen," whispered Ann Rosen.

"Yes, Amen," said Chandler in a nasty tone. "Except I wasn't aware you had been ordained, Rue."

"I'm sorry to be pompous, it's a failing of mine," said Rue. "But this school has a mission, and what I said is an important part of it."

"Then we have an important disagreement," said Chandler quietly. "I believe that this country was built by individualists. The revolution was fought by men who weren't afraid to say 'Bullshit' to bullshit, who wouldn't pay taxes that exploited them without giving them any return. The economy, and the character of this country, were built by men who go their own way, take care of their own, and who aren't afraid of competition. That's what *I* think this school stands for. And I'm prepared to put it to a vote." Rue stared back at him appalled.

"And women," said Ann Rosen, as she made an X on a tic-tac-toe grid and pushed the paper over to Sylvia.

"What?" said Chandler.

"Men and women. The revolution was fought by men and women. 'The national character was built by men and women who.'"

Chandler didn't get it. He turned questioning to Terry, who smiled slightly but didn't speak. Chandler let it pass. Terry turned to look at Ann.

"I move we vote to abolish Annual Giving. Second?"

Rue said, "Chandler, it's late. Don't you think it would be a good idea to poll the community before we do something that will be very hard to undo?"

"We can't respond to that motion, Rue, since you're not a voting member of the Board. Is there a second to my motion?"

"I move to table the motion," said Ann Rosen.

"Second," said Sylvia French. Rue thanked them with her eyes. Just then, the door to the music room, where they were meeting, surrounded by pictures of musical notes and shelves full of Orff instruments, opened. Looking very apologetic, buffed and coiffed like a model, Chandler's almost beautiful wife poked her head in and waggled her fingers at the group. "Hello . . . sorry . . . sorry to interrupt . . . shall I wait in the car?"

"No, come in, come in, of course not, come in, Bobbi," said everyone except Chandler. Bobbi scooted in and sat in a tiny chair against the wall, as if by achieving stillness quickly she could erase the interruption, and perhaps her presence.

Chandler looked back at the table. His motion was unseconded and he felt suddenly that his control of the group was at an ebb, now that he was being picked up at school as if by his mother.

"My car's in the shop. Again," he said, and got a murmur of sympathy.

"Damn Jags," said Terry. "They're pretty though." Everyone agreed.

"Well," said Chandler. "There's a motion on the table. All in favor?"

Everyone said 'Aye,' except Chandler. He took a breath.

"Motion to adjourn?"

"So moved," said Sylvia.

"Second," said Terry.

"Meeting adjourned. Thank you all," said Chandler, standing.

Everyone else began to talk wearily and gather papers and pens and handouts. Bobbi popped up and went to rub against her husband, like a cat marking territory.

Henry had built a fire and was waiting for Rue with a glass of wine beside her chair.

"How did it go?"

"Unbelievable," she said, sinking into a huddle and accepting the wine. "I thought the big issue would be personnel and the budget. I thought maybe I'd get chewed on some more because the Lowens are so mad that I moved Lyndie Sale out of Catherine Trainer's class but I won't move Jennifer. But no." She described what had happened.

"I think I should ask Chandler to join my men's group," said Henry.

"What men's group?"

"I think we should get together in the woods some weekend and do some drumming and chanting and then talk about what shits our fathers were until we all burst into tears. I think it would do us a world of good."

"You know, it might. I'm out of ideas."

"We'll be Men together. We'll stride around the woods carrying big sticks to show what Men we are, and we'll talk about natural selection and kill small animals with our teeth. You can spend the afternoon with Bambi, learning to do your nails."

"Bobbi."

"I'm sure it's Bambi. She works so hard on those doe eyes."

"I could have a major revolt on my hands," said Rue. "Without Annual Giving, I couldn't afford Mike's salary. It happened to a friend of mine in San Diego. The Board made him balance the budget by firing staff. He spent all day doing two people's jobs and nearly had a nervous breakdown. The teachers lost faith in him because he could never give them time when they needed him. The parents began to run roughshod over the teachers, all the while complaining that Todd was unresponsive."

"What happened?"

"Half the faculty quit. Then the Board fired Todd. Then half the parents withdrew their kids. The school lost its niche in the ecology, to adopt Chandler's point of view; all the normal kids went off to a rival school and liked it fine, and now Todd's school is running with about a fifth of the enrollment they had had, as a school for children with learning disabilities."

"I bet Chandler's father brought him up to be a real Man, don't you? I wonder if he was breast-fed. I bet he wasn't; I think I'll ask him."

"Please do," said Rue. "I think it's important for Men to be close to each other."

"Me too," said Henry.

At the November Parents' Council meeting, Emily Goldsborough brought up the subject of the Annual Giving campaign. There was hot debate. Some parents felt embarrassed by it because they couldn't afford to give. Some of the long-term parents were still smarting because once Rue had addressed a financial appeal to the grandparents who had attended Grandpersons' Day. This had unexpectedly turned up the fact that some of the medical or real estate or software millionaires who sent their children to Country had parents of their own who lived in trailers. The grandparents would have liked to give to the school, but they couldn't, and they didn't for a minute enjoy having this brought home to them.

Rue was pointedly given to understand that it was confusing enough, in this land of opportunity, to encourage and enable your children to succeed, only to see them succeed so far as to be virtually living on a different planet from you, not to mention making you and your own experience incomprehensible to your Gold Coast grandchildren. The whole mess was thoroughly aired again at the November Parents' Council meeting, and Rue apologized again.

The parents, mostly moms, then got into a long discussion of the value of scholarships, and found that they were good. Rue ventured to mention the importance of trying to raise faculty salaries. Most, though not all, came to agree that it was wrong for your child's teacher to be paid an annual wage that was less than the cost of your car. So, in the end, a fairly strong consensus was reached that Annual Giving should continue and discussion moved on to the subject of the auction. Its theme: the Merry Nineties.

Chandler was thoroughly put out when he heard about the meeting. He did not for a moment believe that it was not Rue who had opened the Annual Giving discussion to the parents. He felt undercut, he said, completely unsupported by her, taking a complex issue of Board business and airing it in public. Furthermore, he was turning the pressure up again about Catherine Trainer. At this year's Indian Overnight, two children were almost hurt when Nicolette Wren's father, helping Catherine with the Sweat Lodge, chose the wrong kind of rocks to heat and one of them exploded.

"It was Catherine who nearly lost an eye," Rue pointed out.

"That's her problem. What I'm concerned about is her judgment."

"It was Buster Wren's poor judgment. Catherine told him what kind of rocks to get, and he didn't admit he couldn't tell the difference."

"She was in charge. It was her fault."

"I am in charge, so it's my fault," said Rue. "As it happens, no one was hurt, though I agree, somebody could have been. We go through our Doomsday Preparedness drill before every outing, and now we will add this to the list. What do we do if war breaks out? What do we do if someone gets appendicitis? And what do we do if the rocks blow up?"

"Do you think you're being funny?"

"Not at all. I assure you. Last year, the upper school science trip was unable to get back from Santa Catalina because there were riots in Los Angeles and no one could get to the airport. We were prepared. Blair Kunzelman rerouted the whole trip through the Ontario Airport in Orange County because in our Doomsday List, we asked, "What if we can't use the LA Airport?""

"Do you know," said Chandler, "that three different times this year, when I've approached people about joining the Board, I was asked if I know why we don't fire Mrs. Trainer?" Rue felt cold. She had not known this, and unfortunately, she could believe it. Silence seemed like the only safe response.

After a moment Chandler added, "If you're going to insist on the Annual Giving thing, you're going to have to give in somewhere else."

"I will when I can, Chandler. There are times I can't."

"You work for me, you know."

"All too well."

"Well . . . think about it." He brushed the crumbs of his tuna fish sandwich from his knees, rose from the couch in Rue's office, where they had been closeted for lunch, and walked out. Rue could have told him before he left that he had a piece of lettuce between his teeth, but she was too annoyed.

As Rue's birthday approached, her first in nineteen years without Georgia in the house, she began to suspect that Henry was up to something.

"If you give me a surprise party, I'll file for divorce," she said one morning at breakfast.

Henry looked distressed. "But you loved the party Janet Ter-Williams gave Carl."

"Carl likes surprises. I don't. I have enough of them all day long."

Henry looked sad, and when he trudged off to work, she had a feeling he had a few phone calls to make.

For her part, she arrived at school that day to discover that a school parent, Jerry Lozatto, the local BMW dealer, whose daughter had complained that Bobbie Regan teased her too much, had concealed himself in some bushes on campus, waited for eleven-year-old Bobbie to come along, leaped out, and attempted to beat him to death. You could hear the yelling halfway to town.

Fortunately, the PE teacher jumped in and wrestled Mr. Lozatto to the ground. Rue arrived just in time to see this edifying sight, a member of her faculty rolling around in the dirt outside the science lab, trying to get a hammerlock on the father of the Pink Fairy of last week's middle-school pageant. The fifth- and sixth-grade boys were entranced, especially at discovering that Mr. Kunzelman was so inept at wrestling. The girls were stealing fascinated looks at the expression of horror on poor Patsy Lozatto's face.

"Say Uncle!" Blair Kunzelman was yelling, though it was by no means clear that he was winning.

"Get off me, you asshole!" was Mr. Lozatto's considered response.

"Would you both get up, please?" said Rue.

After some more shoving and grunting, they did. They were

both red in the face and covered with twigs and dirt and stains from dried chokecherries.

"I was just trying to teach this kid some manners when this *asshole* . . ." Mr. Lozatto suddenly uncoiled and gave Blair a shove as Blair began to yell, "You were *killing* him! He's *eleven!*"

Rue put her hand on Mr. Lozatto's arm and drew him away from Blair, who continued to glare and stand poised, fists clenched.

"When this *asshole* jumped me," Jerry Lozatto went on.

"Mr. Lozatto . . . I think we should talk about this in my office. . . ."

Mr. Lozatto made one more halfhearted lunge at Blair, who jumped backward. "I don't want to *talk*, there's nothing to talk about!" Rue was walking him away from the children. Mike Dianda, who was standing behind her to be sure she didn't get hurt, began to herd the children off to class.

Rue walked Jerry Lozatto to the parking lot, talking reasonably about making an appointment to talk everything out, but he was still blustering and quacking and erupting in cries of how he was just teaching some manners to that little Mick from Hell.

Rue then spent the morning on the phone with the boy's parents, trying to reassure them.

"He has guns, you know," cried Angela Regan. "He's insane. He wears a handgun strapped to his leg. Ann Rosen went in to buy a car from him, and he showed it to her."

Rue thought she wouldn't be surprised if the Regans took Bobbie out of school, but instead, just after lunch, she received word that it was Patsy Lozatto who was being withdrawn and, furthermore, that the Lozattos were suing the school for "failing to provide a safe environment for their daughter."

Since the conversation about surprises, Henry had made no more mention of her birthday, and Rue began to think he might really have forgotten it, which would be another kind of surprise and not a good one. On the morning of the day, he failed to wish her happy birthday when he kissed her good morning. He had gone off to work whistling.

When Rue arrived at school feeling rather sad, and missing Georgia keenly, there were flowers on her desk from Mike. Cards and cookies and grubby little pieces of candy were handed to her all morning by various preschoolers, which raised her spirits. Then she went out to collect attendance, and Janet TerWilliams's second grade presented her with a book they had been working on for a week. It was dedicated to Mrs. Shaw on her Birthday, and was a book of proverbs. Janet had given each child the first half of a maxim, asked each one to complete it, and to draw an illustration to go with it. Rue sat down in the class and examined each page while the author of it squirmed and beamed. The children all crowded up to her when she had finished, wanting to know which one she had liked the absolute best.

"I can't choose at all, I have so many favorites," said Rue. This was a lie, however. She had two clear favorites. Ashby McCann advised, "Don't cut off your nose . . . to see what's inside," and Chelsea Malko wrote, "You can lead a horse to water . . . but you can't make him walk backwards, unless you pull the heels just right." "Thoughts to live by," she told the children.

Back in her office, she studied the day's agenda that Emily clipped to her door each morning. Then she went out to the front office.

"Didn't I have a meeting with Kenny Lowen's parents at two o'clock?"

"Mr. Lowen couldn't make it. They're coming in Monday."

"Oh. Well, what about the TGIF?" Every so often the faculty had a potluck Thank God It's Friday party, to which Helen Yeats brought sweet-and-sour meatballs, Catherine Trainer brought Jell-O mold with marshmallows, Blair brought beer and wine, and others brought brownies and cakes and spicy chicken wings and fruit plates and cheese. Sometimes there was a special occasion, sometimes it was just to gather together and howl. Today, Rue had rather thought it might be at least a little bit in honor of her birthday.

"Oh, we're going to do it in two weeks," said Emily, who was rooting around in her drawer with a look of annoyance. "Somebody took my staple remover!"

"Ah," said Rue.

Emily began searching another drawer while explaining, "Pat Moredock has a root canal at four, Cynda is gone for the weekend, and Rosemary Fitch has to take her dogs to the vet."

"I see," said Rue. She went back to her office and sat down. She almost never had an afternoon with a clear calendar, and today of all days, she didn't really want one.

The back door of her office opened, and Henry stepped in.

"Hello, dearie," she said, feeling silly, because she was suddenly struck by how handsome he was. "Who let you out of your cage?"

"I've cured everybody. There are no more sick people in California. I came to see if you were free for lunch."

"I was just going to go down to the kitchen. Do you want to come? I think there are tacos."

"Sure. Or, no . . . why don't you come with me? We could try something new."

"Something that will only take forty minutes?"

"Sure. Maybe we'll eat hot persimmons off the sidewalk."

Rue located her purse and left a note on her door saying she'd be back at quarter of one.

Henry took her to a new restaurant at the top of the tallest building in Seven Springs, which meant six stories up. It was called the Cafe on the Square. They had a great view of the vistas of malls and parking lots and houses and lawns that stretched out across what had so recently been cattle country. There they ate risotto and drank red wine. Rue kept worrying about the time, but Henry (who was a stickler about punctuality) seemed unconcerned, and Rue had to admit there was nothing specific she had to be back for. One of the art teachers, Pat Moredock, had lately shown signs of hysteria, claiming that Marilyn Schramm had stolen all her rulers and that no one respected her subject, the proof being that even Rue had yanked Lyndie Sale, Jennifer Lowen, and Malone Dahl out of class without asking and never apologized. Rue had planned to meet with her, but it could wait.

After lunch she settled happily into the front seat of Henry's car and felt so content that it took her a minute or two to realize that he was not driving toward school; they were headed north out of town, toward the freeway.

"Henry . . . I'm already late!"

"No, you're fine."

"Henry!"

Looking pleased with himself, he drove faster, heading north. Rue watched his profile as he studiously avoided looking back.

"Am I in the grip of a wicked conspiracy?" she said at last.

Henry smiled more broadly, though he was trying not to.

"You and Emily have been plotting!"

"You've been driving her crazy . . . every time she got your calendar cleared for the afternoon, you'd schedule something else."

"And I was feeling so sorry for myself that they postponed the TGIF! Where are we going?"

"Oh, we're just going to drive until we fall off the edge of the world."

It took about four hours for them to get to Big Sur.

"Oh, Henry!" Rue said.

The road was densely lined with huge, crooked Monterey Pines. It curved in S-hooks along cliffs above bays cut deeply into the shoreline. The water far below was pale and roaring. Often the beaches were filled with surfers in wet suits, although the air was already quite cool, and the water must have been frigid.

"We're going to Esalen," said Henry. "We're going to sit in a big hot tub with strangers and talk about our sex life. And eat brown rice and gruel and get rolfed, and learn the Primal Scream."

"We are not."

"I've packed my bell-bottoms. And sandals. I'd have grown back my Fu Manchu mustache, but I thought you might suspect something."

"You're lying. We passed Esalen five minutes ago."

"Did we? Damn."

Henry had made reservations at a resort his doctor friends had told him about, high in the redwoods overlooking the sea on one side and deep fog-filled ravines on the other. It had a four-star restaurant and miles of paths curving through rock gardens and Japanese tea gardens and drought gardens of cactus and euphorbia, and exotic shrubs and flowering trees. Their bedroom had a fireplace and the biggest bed they had ever slept in together. Henry had packed a suitcase for Rue and had done quite a creditable job. He'd remembered socks and underwear, and she was especially touched that, given a choice of what he most liked to see her wear, he had chosen an old, soft, gray cashmere dress that she'd had as long as she'd known him.

"Is this your favorite?" she asked as she unpacked her suitcase, madly curious to see what he had thought of and what not.

"It is, actually. At first I couldn't find it."

She had been worrying lately about the Yummy Mummies in the parking lot in their tiny tennis dresses, their big shirts over leggings, that Oh-I-forgot-to-put-on-my-pants-look, and wondered if Henry wished she were more in vogue.

Over dinner, they didn't say a lot. Henry had never looked more handsome, Rue thought, carrying twenty more pounds than when they had met, and his blond hair at last beginning to go gray. She was thinking of the year they met, when she was a senior and he was starting med school. He was famous for wild behavior, but with her, he'd been serious and trusting. He talked about joining the Peace Corps. Rue had been with him when he learned that his father had died and had gone with him to the funeral. She had been unprepared for the depth of his grief. They had stood side by side at the graveside on the shores of the Chesapeake. . . . Rue had been wearing this same gray dress.

Henry's mother, whom Rue met for the first time that weekend, was very proper, very ineffectual. She had no reserves of strength to share with her children and had retired, with apologies, halfway through the reception that followed the burial, although the house was full of neighbors and relatives.

Henry's only sister, Sybil, a freshman at Bennington that year, had come home for the funeral but managed to stay hors de combat in the matter of social responsibility. Henry's father had been sick for some time, with complications from heavy smoking, and had serious pains from angina, arthritis, and possibly gout. Sybil had borne a lot of the burden of catering to him during her last years of high school. She delighted Henry by coming to the funeral in a black miniskirt and boots with her hair down to her butt and her eyes lined with kohl. During the reception she cleaned out her father's medicine chest and, over the course of the weekend, took all the pills.

Rue realized she was smiling.

"What are you thinking about?" Henry asked.

"Sybil. Floating around the house the weekend your father died, and your mother sighing over how well Sybil was taking it, and how she'd always had inner resources."

"I was pissed she even took all the codeine."

"And now you can write your own prescriptions. Sybil always thought that's why you went to med school."

"You were wearing that dress."

Rue noticed. "We were so young."

"I always felt my life started when I met you," said Henry. Rue, surprised by a rush of feeling, reached for his hand.

"And now we're starting over again," she said.

"I'm expecting it to be easier this time. I don't have to get over being such an asshole."

"It won't require a whole new wardrobe."

"Unless we decide to retire and move to the Seychelles."

They sat quietly, content to be together, and to let their thoughts wander.

"I don't suppose Georgia remembered my birthday," Rue said at last.

"It seems not. I should have reminded her."

"No, you shouldn't."

After dinner, they planned to walk up the ridge, but a light drizzle had begun to fall.

"Let's go to the Japanese Baths then," said Rue.

Henry was shocked. "We don't have bathing suits!"

"The little card they put in our room said Bathing Suits Optional. Which means Bathing Suits de Trop."

"I thought you said this wouldn't require a new wardrobe."

"Come on," said Rue. "Let's just look."

The bath house was deserted. Steam rose from the water and you could see the stars through intermittent clouds through the open lattice of the roof.

"Come on," said Rue.

"What if other people come and want to have group sex? Or laugh at my penis?"

"That will be bad," said Rue. She had put her clothes in a locker and was slipping naked into the water. Henry eventually joined her, and no one else arrived, and they floated under the stars, whispering and kissing and giggling, until Henry said he was too wrinkled and had to go home.

They spent the next day hiking on the headlands. The weather was cool and bright and wild. The hotel packed them a lunch and lent Henry a backpack.

In the morning, they talked about the Peace Corps. They had never gone because they couldn't afford it. Henry had to pay off student loans.

"If we had gone, how would our lives be different?"

"You wouldn't have finished your Ph.D."

"That's probably true."

"Would it matter?"

"I don't think so. Not very much. That last year in Cambridge was fun though."

"It was. Remember the house in Somerville?"

"Whatever happened to that strange guy who always wore bicycle clips and kept all those canaries in his room? And made margaritas in the blender when his girlfriend came, and they never seemed to eat any food?"

"Was he in physics?"

"Economics."

"And that couple from the law school with the little MG that wouldn't start when it rained?"

"She's a judge now. In Arizona."

"Are they still married?"

"Oh, no. He had a pants problem."

"Did he? When did he find the time?"

"You might well ask."

"And remember the girl from your boarding school who went back and told everyone you were living in a commune?"

"Oh, I loved that! Quelle scandale."

They stopped to admire the view. Henry said, "Why don't we go to the Peace Corps now?"

"You're kidding."

"I'm not. We could go to Africa."

"Or Indonesia. Where they ate Michael Rockefeller."

"Why don't we?"

"Are you tired of cutting open heads?"

They began to walk again.

"I'd love to try something else," he said. "You know. Save lives. Save the world. Something modest."

"You could work with children. Come over to school, we're about to have a chicken pox epidemic."

They let the subject drop for a while and soon stopped for lunch. They ate leaning against a rock, looking west across the ocean. There were gulls and occasional pelicans. Rue thought of Catherine Trainer, and how she would love the birds here.

When they started to walk again after lunch, Henry brought up the subject of starting over again, but in a different way. "We've never talked about how long you want to stay at Country," he said.

"No, but of course I think about it."

"What do you think?"

"The world is changing. The school is changing. Remember when Georgia was born, how people talked about the whole child, and started schools where they believed in granola and banning television and not letting children play with guns? Now, no one gives a shit about any of that. Now they just want to get their kids into the best high school, so they can all go to Stanford or Yale, and if they don't know anything about peace or the downtrodden or being a good person, who cares?"

"Well, some of them care, or they wouldn't send their kids to you. They'd all be over at Poly."

"I hope that's true."

"Are you ever going to write a book?" Henry asked her.

"Me?"

"You used to talk about it, when you were in graduate school."

"I used to talk about retiring at fifty and doing a bachelor of science."

"I thought that was a great idea. Aren't you tempted?"

"Are you having a midlife crisis?"

"Maybe."

They stopped on a bluff and looked out over the Pacific.

"I want to go somewhere," Henry said, unconscious that he was flexing his arms and shoulders as if preparing to brachiate. "I want to see something different. Remember how it felt, when we all thought we could stop the war and change the world and raise little boys who wouldn't grow up to be sexist assholes? And little girls who *would* be sexist assholes and want to run Morgan Stanley?"

Rue looked at him. He looked as if he felt caged. She *did* remember what it felt like to be so young and to believe your generation was different. She smiled and touched him. She said, "Remember, we thought that if we *lived* to fifty, we would stop war and landfills and no one would eat meat?"

"No one would use Saran Wrap or plastic cartons; we'd all keep glass bottles and those reusable bowl and bottle covers that looked like shower caps?"

"And wash everything over and over," she said. "That was before we knew about the drought."

"What we thought," said Henry, "was that you could change the world by behaving as if what one person does makes a difference."

"That's it," said Rue, taking his hand. "That was it." She was remembering what it was like when she first fell in love with him. She felt she had made a difference in *his* life, just by being herself. And she felt as if he had made her life make sense.

"I'm not dead yet," said Henry, "and I want to feel like that again."

She turned to meet his eyes. What was this? It was serious.

"But you *do* make a difference . . . think of your patients."

"I think of them. I think that there are two people in my own practice who could do exactly what I'm doing as well as I'm doing it. But I could use my training in places where it's really needed. I'm sick of conversations about health plans. How about going where there isn't any health plan because there aren't any doctors?"

Rue didn't know what to say. She felt as if she *was* making a difference. She didn't think that teachers were interchangeable, or that schools were. She thought that what she did could change people's lives. You could argue all day about whether it was less noble to affect these lives than the lives of children starving in Somalia. She was doing what she was trained to do. Children were children. The ones at Country were hers. They had lives to live, and gifts to give.

"What about Georgia?" Rue asked. "If we left the hemisphere?"

"She'd be fine," said Henry. "A kid who doesn't remember her mother's birthday is not pining for home."

"That doesn't mean she doesn't need us to be here when she needs us."

"You've got to give her up, Rue. She's gone."

"I know she's gone, Henry," said Rue, slightly annoyed. She didn't think Henry was any more blithe than she about admitting Georgia was gone. In fact, she thought he was looking for drama and romance as a way of distracting himself from the loss. Not just of Georgia but of that whole part of their life together. At that moment, she realized that she profoundly did not want to go to Somalia. She wanted to finish the work she had started, in her own time and her own way, until the pattern of the life work she had chosen emerged from the background whole, so she could see its meaning and carry that forward into the next part of her life. Whatever that was, whenever it was time. It wasn't time yet. Rue did not like to have change thrust upon her.

"I think about those days before we had Georgia," she said, "and I don't feel like a different person. I feel older, but I don't feel as if I had dreams and then forgot them. I feel as if I'm doing what I was meant to do."

"You are very lucky," said Henry.

The sun was high in the afternoon sky, and they chose another path and walked on.

Work Day was a sort of family outing at The Country School. Parents would bring their own tools and paint, rake, build fences, level brick paths, or weed the flower beds. Emily was delighted to sign up, since what she should have been doing was ripping up the linoleum in her own kitchen so she could put down a subfloor and lay some decent tiles. She had promised to do this to show Malone she loved her, even though Malone said, when she had to miss Jennifer Lowen's birthday party, that she thought her mother was a complete turd and would think so till the day she died. Even on your wedding day? Emily had asked. Yes, said Malone. Emily would be allowed to attend the wedding and could stand in the receiving line, but inside Malone would still think she was a complete turd.

When the Work Day dawned sunny, Emily decided her floor would wait. She gathered up the kids and took them up to school. The children went off to help Manuel in the garden. Emily found herself assigned to help Henry and Chandler Kip build a picket fence at the preschool.

They had a great time, after Henry and Chandler straightened out what kind of music they were going to listen to. "You're kidding," Henry bellowed. "You don't know 'There Ain't No Instant Replay in the Football Game of Life?'" Chandler seemed unsure how to take Henry's sense of humor.

Henry insisted that to be politically correct they would have to let Emily use the Skilsaw while the men hammered. (This was probably the safest course as well as the most correct, since Chandler did not appear to have much experience dealing with the physical universe.) Then they tried to get Emily to mix the concrete to hold the uprights, but she said it was entirely too domestic, all that measuring and stirring. She *liked* the power saw. "Measure twice, cut once," Henry kept saying. He said that was the way they did it in the operating room, when they started on the skulls.

Late in the morning, Malone appeared with David, who was weeping.

"What happened, Lovie—are you hurt?" she asked David, who burrowed into her arms, sniffling.

"Lyndie decided to torture him," said Malone. Malone was upset.

"What do you mean?"

"She found this file thing that was pointed, and she asked me what it was for and I didn't know, so she went over to David and started poking him with it."

"Had he been bothering you?"

"No! He was just digging a hole! He went 'Stop it, that hurts,' and she just kept on, and I went 'Stop it Lyndie, you're hurting him!' But she didn't stop!"

Emily studied Malone's indignant face. She stroked David's hair.

"Poor you," she said to him. David nodded. Malone looked to her mother as if there must be an explanation for this, but Emily didn't know of one.

"Thank you, honeybunch. David can stay and help us. Will you help us?" she asked him. He nodded. Malone shrugged and went off. Emily went back to work, troubled. She had noticed Lyndie wasn't very patient with David, but this was like pulling the wings off flies.

Rue had spent the morning gardening with some new kindergarten parents in the shrubbery beds around the gym, and together they walked to the outdoor barbecue hosted by the Lowen and Malko families. Bradley Lowen was cooking hamburgers, Corinne Lowen and Margee Malko were dishing up pasta and potato salads. As Rue was joined by various campus pets and the young mothers were joined by their happy dirty spouses and children, converging from other parts of the campus, Rue was surprised to see Sondra Sale standing by herself in the lunch line.

During registration this morning, Rue had seen Sondra drop off her children and drive away, as if she thought the point of the day was free Saturday babysitting. Surely she couldn't have thought

Jonathan was going to be of substantial assistance laying brick or planting pear trees, or Lyndie either, with her arm in a cast. Corinne Lowen had had to delegate two eighth graders to babysit Jonathan. He had walked off between them, licking away at the palm of his hand. Lyndie had gone off to find Malone and Jennifer.

Now, as Rue looked around for a table full of parents she didn't know well, so she could join them for lunch, she noticed Sondra Sale standing silent with a plate in her hand. She was dressed in spotless white denim; Rue wondered if she had come to work and those were indeed her work clothes. Then her attention was taken by Terry Malko, who put an arm around her shoulder and said, "Chandler just told me a joke. Want to hear it?"

"I didn't know he knew any," said Rue.

"What's the definition of a preppie?"

"What?"

"Someone who was born on third base and thinks he hit a triple." They both laughed.

"I knew you'd like that," said Terry. He hurried off to make sure there was enough ice in the washtubs full of soft drinks. Terry and Chandler both had achieved enough success in business to become more Republican than the Social Register, and certainly their children were being raised to expect the best of everything. And yet she knew that if anyone was supposed to feel the butt of that joke, it was Henry, and by extension she herself.

She chose a table with two young couples and their preschool children, and asked if she could join them. Happily they cleared a sleeping infant in a car seat off the table to make room for her. "I'm Rue Shaw," she said. "We know!" they caroled. And there began happy talk about what each adult had been working at for the morning, and what a nice day it was, and how at their old school there was nothing like this, no sense of belonging, no way to help or to feel that the school was your own. As Rue ate, she noticed Henry and Emily in line, with paint on their hands and clothes. And to her surprise, she also noticed Sondra sitting apart on a stone wall, picking at a plate of lettuce leaves and talking to Bonnie Fleming.

*   *   *

"How can you eat that cake and keep that figure?" were the first words Sondra addressed to Bonnie. It had none of the flavor of an opening gambit signaling a wish to make an acquaintance. Bonnie felt it was a literal request for information. She looked at her plate piled with salads and bread and a slice of coconut cake.

"I don't eat meat or cheese," Bonnie said. "Maybe that's it."

Sondra looked at Bonnie's long-boned willowy figure, a flat appraisal. It was like the look of a child who has not been told that it's impolite to stare. Or ask personal questions.

"You're so thin," she said to Bonnie, almost as if it were disagreeable of Bonnie to be so.

"I think a lot of it is genes," said Bonnie. "My mother is very thin as well."

"I was real fat when I was a teenager," said Sondra, putting a leaf into her mouth.

"You have a beautiful figure now," said Bonnie.

Sondra nodded, chewing. "I work at it. I have to take about four aerobics classes a day or I blow up like a cow. Lyndie could get fat when she gets the curse. That's what happened to me. I watch her diet, but I see the signs. She could really blow up."

"Are you Sondra?" Bonnie asked.

Sondra nodded. It was as if she thought everyone here must know who she was, since they all seemed to know each other. That's what the world had kind of seemed to her for her whole life, like a big group of people who already know each other and you don't.

"I'm Bonnie." Sondra said, "Nice to meet you," and for a while they both chewed, like horses side by side in their stalls.

"I used to dance," said Bonnie, "so I got a lot of exercise. Now I don't get as much as you. But I have today; Mike Dianda and I have been double-digging a plot for a kitchen garden, so the science classes can grow vegetables. Whew! that's hard."

Sondra looked at her with that flat gaze. "Mr. Dianda? The one in the office?"

"Yes."

"What is he, is he her secretary?"

"Mrs. Shaw's? No, he's the assistant head."

"I thought assistant was secretary."

"It's more that she's the president and he's the vice president."

"Oh," she said. "So he's important?"

Bonnie nodded. She wanted to say that in the great scheme of things they were all important, secretaries and presidents, but she hadn't sensed in Mrs. Sale any sense of humor, let alone any sense of her own affect. Lacking that, she was unlikely to take any pleasure in even the gentlest teasing. Alas, they would share no bonding laughter.

"Isn't he a fairy?"

Bonnie was so surprised that she didn't react. Sondra was looking at her in the usual flat way, again seeming unaware of any possibility of giving offense. Bonnie wondered if this disconnected manner had to do with living with such a frightening man as her husband. Had she retreated into childishness? Or had she married him because she was poor at reading nonverbal clues and thus had not noticed what seemed so obvious to others, his angry arrogance, the way his knotted body seemed to announce his discomfort in the universe.

Bonnie said, "Yes, he is." That seemed to satisfy Sondra, who then reverted to her primary topic, which seemed to be food.

"My mother was a cook," said Sondra. "Once she won a Pillsbury bake-off, you know you send in your recipe to the magazine and it's a contest?"

"Did she really?"

"Yes, but she couldn't go get the prize because you have to tell your name and what you do, and they check, because there are rules, you can't be professional, you can't work for the magazine, things like that."

Bonnie was lost. "It was a chicken recipe," Sondra went on, "that you rolled in cornflakes, and then you cooked it with pineapple. Hawaiian. We had lived in Hawaii once. But we were in St. Louis by the time she won."

Bonnie suddenly remembered something Mike had said about his first conversation with the Sales. "Your father was in the FBI, wasn't he?"

Sondra nodded. "He was an agent. He's retired now. We moved a lot, and we kept changing our names."

"Because he did undercover work?"

Sondra nodded.

"It sounds very interesting."

Sondra said nothing.

"Was it?"

"No. It was lonely."

Bonnie nodded. "Of course. I should have thought of that. I hope you have brothers and sisters, at least, to keep you company?"

"I had a brother, Craig."

"Oh, I'm sorry," said Bonnie, sympathetic.

"Why?"

"You said 'had.' Did he die?"

"I don't think so. He was kind of an asshole, and he and my dad fought a lot. So he joined the navy when he was sixteen and we never saw him again."

Bonnie stared at her, searching for signs of anger or distress. But Sondra was very matter-of-fact. So she had a violent father? So a violent husband seems normal?

"You couldn't find him if you wanted to?"

"I tried once. After he left we moved a few more times. And changed our names. So he couldn't ever come home. But when I got to Chicago a man told me how to get the navy to help me find him. And we tried, but he'd been discharged six years. They had an address and I wrote, but it came back."

"This is a sad story, Sondra. It makes me feel like crying."

Sondra looked at her, surprised. And then it seemed, grateful.

"Yeah, I was sad."

After lunch Chandler said to Henry and Emily that he had to be going. Driven mad, no doubt, said Henry, by having to listen to "All My Exes Live in Texas." Henry and Emily and David painted their fence by themselves. At one point Henry went to get cold beer. When he came back he said, "Do you know that fart Chandler didn't go home at all—he's over at Primary helping make a rock garden?"

"That hurts my feelings," said Emily, opening her beer.

"I thought it would."

They worked side by side in comfortable silence. Emily liked that. Tom Dahl, her ex-husband-elect, couldn't stand a conversational vacuum. And Henry was good with tools. Tom couldn't plug

in a lamp without banging his head or hurting himself. Thank god
he'd become a dermatologist, not a surgeon, Emily thought.

Henry brought up the subject of career changes, which Emily
thought was a nice thing to call having your life blown up in mid-
stream because your husband wants to marry a woman called
Bannany. He made her feel it was exciting to be choosing a career
when she was old enough to know what she would really enjoy
doing.

Emily said she might like to write or take a degree in psychology.

"Why not both?" Henry said.

"Indeed, why not?" Emily said and smiled.

"My own plan," said Henry, "is to open a bed-and-breakfast in
the Seychelles."

"You want to give up surgery?"

"I want to go where there are no brains at all."

"Will Rue like it?"

"She is greatly looking forward to it. I will do all the cooking
and she will make the beds. Georgia will fly in to visit us in her private jet when she is a star of La Scala. She will bring us our grandchildren to play with us, and as soon as they get sunburned and
cranky, we'll wave our hands and she will take them away."

They went on painting in the sun. After a while, Emily said,
"You know, it really helps me to see a truly happy marriage. It gives
me faith."

"I'm glad," said Henry.

On the Monday after Work Day, Lyndie Sale was late going down to lunch because the librarian, Mrs. Nafie, had asked her to stay after class and help put some books back on the shelves in alphabetical order.

Lyndie's friends had trotted off to lunch without her, and the whole time she worked, Mrs. Nafie burbled about how kind and quick and bright Lyndie was. When they were done, Mrs. Nafie thanked her effusively. What a deep, interesting child, Mrs. Nafie thought. She felt that Lyndie would profit from extra attention, from knowing that certain adults thought she was special. She'd taken an extra interest in Lyndie ever since the day Rue had sent her to the library to learn to do research. Mrs. Nafie had helped her look up UFOs and remembered that Lyndie seemed to feel an interest bordering on jealousy in the reports they found of people who claimed to have been kidnapped by aliens.

Lyndie arrived at the kitchen to see that her whole class had already gotten their food and chosen their places at the tables outside under the live oaks. Jennifer and Malone were sitting together, and Nicolette Wren was sitting with two of the boys. When Nicolette laughed, she opened her mouth so you could see the chewed food, Lyndie noticed, staring at her with narrow eyes. There was no one for Lyndie to sit with. She had to get her tray and stand in line with the third graders. There was Malone's horrible little brother. That fat cow Mrs. Nafie was coming along to get her lunch too. Lyndie wished all her clothes would fall off right now, with everyone watching.

Lyndie didn't know the name of the mom who was ladling soup. It was one who was all teeth, like a horse.

"What kind is it?" Lyndie asked.

"Chicken noodle," said the horse.

Lyndie said, "Okay." She hated the noodles in chicken noodle because they were slimy and dead-feeling, but she could leave them. She put the paper bowl of soup on her tray without another word and moved down the line to choose a muffin out of the bread bowl. She'd get an apple too; she wasn't going to eat any of that gummy Mexican bean shit that the next hot lunch mom was offering her.

Behind her, some third graders were having a giggling fit. One of those complete, lose-it, giggling fits that you get sometimes when you're a little twit. They were limp with laughing and tumbling against each other, and one bumped Lyndie from behind so that her soup slopped over the bowl and soaked her tray, ruining her paper napkin. Lyndie turned around, and with one savage sweep of her hand, upended the little girl's tray so that hot soup splattered over her clothes, and everything else on the tray—milk, silverware, bread and butter—crashed and splattered to the floor. The little girl roared with surprise and burst into tears. The nearest hot lunch mom began yelling at Lyndie.

"She bumped me!" Lyndie roared back, tense with outrage. "She bumped into me first, she spilled my soup!"

Rue did not anticipate with pleasure calling the Sales to tell them Lyndie was being suspended for a day.

It was Homecoming Saturday. Rue was standing outside the gym listening to the roars from the bleachers as Country duked it out against Poly Sci, their perennial football rival. Poly Sci had some huge ringers on their team, and Blair Kunzelman, Country's coach, insisted on playing every boy who suited up, at least for a few minutes, while the coach at Poly played only his varsity best. But Country had a great quarterback, tiny Larry Gerard, and at half-time today, the score was 13–7. It was an exciting game.

Rue was walking with Serge Korfus, father of a second grader. He had just announced they were thinking of withdrawing. Lily Korfus's best friend in her class had moved away, leaving her lonely. The tuition was a stretch for a family who had another little one in diapers, and May Korfus had come home from serving hot lunch upset by what she had heard about the new math approach used in third grade.

"My wife and I both went to public school," Serge Korfus said apologetically. "We're in a pretty good district. To be frank, it's hard to justify the tuition here."

"We'd be very sorry to lose Lily," said Rue. They were interrupted by a girl of about eighteen calling Rue's name.

"Nina Bennett! How nice to see you, dear!"

"Almost my whole class came back. We wanted to see the drinking fountain in the gym that we made the tiles for with Mrs. Moredock."

"You hadn't seen it installed? Isn't it great? You're all memorialized now, forever. Nina, this is Mr. Korfus." Nina was a glowing girl with a happy, open map-of-Ireland face. Mr. Korfus said he was pleased to meet her.

"Is Georgia coming home for Thanksgiving?" Nina asked.

"No, she's staying in New York. The dorms stay open."

Nina, who looked as if she herself rarely missed a meal, asked, "Where will she have Thanksgiving dinner?"

"Probably Horn and Hardart. She doesn't eat meat anymore, so turkey is out anyway. Frankly, at the moment she seems to be eating music. I'm delighted more of your class is here. Who came?"

"Arlene and Christin and Colin and . . . really almost everyone. Sheila couldn't come, she's in Massachusetts."

"Is she?"

"Yes, she started at High, but she didn't like it so she transferred to Exeter."

"Nina, Mr. Korfus just asked me a question, sort of, and maybe you should answer it." She turned to Mr. Korfus. "Nina graduated three years ago and now she's at the top high school in Santa Barbara." And to Nina: "How are you getting along?"

"I love it."

"You're not lost in such a big place?"

"I like it that it's big."

"Was Country too small for you?"

"Not at all, but my class from here, we're like brothers and sisters? I feel like I always have them. And I do have Colin, he's in my calculus class."

"And how are you finding the work?"

"Easy. Oops—God that sounds *so* conceited."

Rue smiled. "After all the complaining you guys did. So you're well prepared?"

"Definitely. We've done much more writing than kids from other schools. We've done harder work, and we've read more. And people can't believe when I tell them about the memory maps."

"Thank you, Nina, I'll pay you later. Are you all going to play volleyball?"

"Absolutely."

"Good girl. I'll come find you."

Nina waggled her fingers to say "Later," and started off.

"Nina," Rue called, "you're looking terrific."

"Thank you, Mrs. S. You are too!" Rue laughed.

She and Mr. Korfus walked toward the lunch tables. "Unsolicited, I promise," she said to him.

"A nice girl."

"Awfully nice. She had a lot of trouble when she first came to us. She had a chip on her shoulder, and she was round as a butterball."

"Super bright?"

"I'll tell you a truth I rarely tell parents. A school like this is most important for the unspecial child. There are very bright children who will get an education anywhere. And there are children with special needs who are much better served in public schools. But for the child who could get lost in the crowd, the one who needs to be strengthened and shaped and hardened off before you plant her outside in the cold ground, we change lives. I truly believe that we do."

"Do you think Lily is an unspecial child?" he asked, raising an eyebrow.

"If I did, I wouldn't know my job very well. But I still think we have something special to offer her. One of our graduates was a Presidential Scholar last year, and there are only a hundred and forty-one in the whole country. But don't tell anyone I told you that."

"All right. But why not?"

"I'm supposed to be opposed to awarding prizes. We don't do it here. But believe me, the world does it soon enough when they leave us, and somehow, we can't help but notice."

They had stopped to watch a sack race pitting six seventh-graders against six graduates who ranged in age from nineteen to seventy-two. (They often had students from the Miss Plums' days back at Homecoming.) The seventy-two-year-old was a former nun, and she appeared to have some special training in sack racing; she was burning up the track. Rue wondered if it was something they practiced at the Order.

Mr. Korfus asked, "What's a memory map?"

"Come back in June and I'll show you. By the end of the year, every one of our sixth graders can draw an entire Mercator projection of the world from memory."

"You're kidding!"

"I'm not. Lyndie, what is it?"

Lyndie Sale, her face streaked with dirt and tears, was running toward her wailing. Rue excused herself from Mr. Korfus and gathered Lyndie in, leading her to a stone wall where they could settle and talk.

"Jennifer Lowen pushed me! Look, she knocked me down and I scraped my knee and my *hand hurts!*" She wept, waving her right hand, sticking out of her Velcro cast. Rue clucked and took the hand, gently feeling the little wrist bones. There was some grit in the heel of the hand, but unless Lyndie was in shock, there was no pain in her wrist or hand.

"Mrs. Shaw!" Jennifer Lowen had arrived at a run, with Malone Dahl and Carly Cort behind her. Jennifer was furious.

"Mrs. Shaw! I did *not* push her! She said she was going to tell you I did and I never *touched* her!"

"You did!"

"She did not, Lyndie, that's a lie!" exclaimed Carly and Malone indignantly. Their faces were like thunderclouds.

"Shshshs," said Rue. "Quiet down. One at a time, please." She looked quietly at each of them in turn, and her look had the effect of a calming touch. Their faces, suffused with hot emotion, regained a more normal appearance. Rue watched carefully how they held themselves and who looked at whom. There was no guilty exchange among the three leaders. All of them looked hard at Lyndie, with serious, shocked expressions. God, fifth graders are horrors, Rue thought to herself.

"Jennifer, suppose you tell me what happened."

"She lies!" cried Jennifer. Rue tipped her head slightly, a warning move. "We were talking about riding lessons. We started jumping this week. Carly jumped a two-rail fence! And I jumped once and refused once."

"This is at Meadow Wood?"

The little girls nodded.

"Do you take too, Malone?" asked Rue.

Malone shook her head. Rue happened to know that since meeting Jennifer, Malone had gone horse-mad. She had borrowed every Black Stallion book in the library, and was now plowing through *King of the Wind*.

"I'm asking my dad, though, I think he might let me take. I'll ask him at Christmas."

Jennifer burst out: "Lyndie said she didn't have to go to Meadow Wood, because she had a stallion in her backyard. And I was like, 'No way.' I was like, 'Okay, Lyndie, what do you do when the horse trots—what's it called what you do?' And she didn't even know that. You should see her yard, it's the size of a . . . it's the size of a . . . bathroom!" She started to giggle and so did Malone, and Carly, because Jennifer was so bold and so droll. They got control of themselves, though, since it was clear Rue was not as easily amused.

"So she was like, 'Yes I do, I have a gray stallion in the back yard, and I ride him bareback,' and we were like, 'Come off it, Lyndie, liar liar pants on fire,' and she started to *cry.*" Her voice dripped with scorn at such baby behavior. Malone and Carly stood behind her nodding, their faces set in stubborn intensity.

"And then she got up to run away, and she just like stumbled . . ."

"She didn't even go all the way down!" Carly added.

". . . and she turned around and made this *face* at me, and she was like, 'I'm going to tell! I'm going to tell that you pushed me and hurt my broken arm!'"

There was silence for a moment, as Rue considered Jennifer's face. Slowly she turned to Lyndie.

Lyndie looked at her fiercely and said, "She did! She did push me, and I hurt myself." Rue gazed at *her* for a while, waiting for her eyes to waver. They didn't.

Rue said, "I don't think anyone in this story has much to be proud of. But, fortunately, you are all going to win because you're going to learn to do something very important, and knowing how to do this will help you all your lives."

"What are we going to do?" said Jennifer, hoping it would involve horses.

"Apologize. You first please, Jennifer."

"For what?"

"You tell me."

"She's the liar!"

"Did you hurt Lyndie's feelings?"

There was silence.

"Did you hurt her feelings, and did you know that's what you were doing?"

"At least I didn't tell stupid lies, like I'm too stupid to tell . . ."

"SSSt," Rue cut her off. "Apologizing does not include justifying yourself. Do you know what to do or do I have to show you?"

After a long pause, Jennifer raised her eyes to Lyndie's face, and said in a low voice, "Lyndie, I'm very sorry that I hurt your feelings."

"Thank you," said Rue. "Carly?"

Carly apologized to Lyndie, and then Malone.

Rue turned to Lyndie.

"What?" said Lyndie.

"Your turn."

"I didn't do anything!" Rue looked at her for a long time. She saw a thoroughly miserable child, but beyond that, she wasn't sure what she was looking at. At last she said, "You tried to get your friend in trouble."

"She pushed me. . . ."

"SSSt," Rue cut her off. "You tried to get your friend in trouble. Now you can insist on being right, and be lonely, or you can apologize, and maybe get your friend back. Your choice." She and Lyndie looked at each other for a long moment.

"Jennifer," said Lyndie, almost inaudibly, "I'm sorry I tried to get you in trouble."

"Thank you," said Rue. She looked at the four little girls standing before her. Their faces had changed. It was as if saying the words had changed the furious feelings they had brought into the fray.

"I'm proud of you all, that's a hard thing to do. Much harder than fighting and holding grudges. Is there something you all like to do that you could do together right now?" Rue knew perfectly well that there was nothing fifth-grade girls liked more than hanging out complaining about bossy, unfair grown-ups, and she was pretty sure they could find some sheltered place to do it.

It was a Monday afternoon in mid-November. Carpool was over and the campus was quiet. Rue was in her office doing the payroll for Bill Glarrow, who was on vacation, when she heard a scream from the parking lot.

Cynda Goldring was not an hysterical woman, but when Rue reached her, she was crying. Emily was there seconds later, and the two of them stood with her beside her car as she blew her nose and apologized.

"I know, I've completely wrecked my mascara," she said. She had, indeed. There were dark, wet puddles under her eyes. "Sorry. I'm okay now. I shouldn't have screamed."

"What happened?" Emily asked. She touched Cynda's shoulder, comforting, but Cynda shrugged it off. She was back in control.

"You won't understand why I made such a fuss. It just surprised me. "

"What?"

"Get in the driver's seat and look in the rearview mirror."

Emily climbed in and did as she was told. At first she inhaled sharply, then swung around to look at what she was seeing in the mirror.

"That is absolutely *sick*," she said, scrambling out of the car.

Rue got in. She looked in the rearview mirror and saw written in black ink on the leather above the rear window were the words, *Die, You Bitch.*

As Emily had done, she whirled around to look straight on. The writing was careful, skillful mirror writing.

Rue got out. "Was the car locked?"

Cynda shook her head no.

"Nevertheless . . . some little beast came out here in daylight, bold as brass, and climbed into your car and took his time doing that."

Cynda nodded.

Emily asked, "Do you have any idea who?"

Cynda shook her head. "The eighth graders are terrors. But I *like* the bad ones! They all know that!"

"You're not having special trouble with anyone?" Cynda shook her head.

Rue and Emily looked at each other. Now what should they do? Should they urge her to ignore it? Should she be frightened? Who would do a thing like that?

She stood looking miserable for a moment. Then she said, "I didn't need to make such a fuss. I'm not usually such a baby. It's just that Elliot and I decided to get divorced this morning."

"What?" cried Emily.

Rue whispered, "Oh, no!"

"It's all right," said Cynda. "We were hardly speaking to each other. We didn't even like to pass each other in the hall. It's just that now that it's over and he's going I feel a little . . . jumpy."

"Maybe Elliot did it," said Emily.

"Not a chance, he's not clever enough," said Cynda.

"This is somebody bright and really malicious," said Rue.

"I guess I better start locking my car," Cynda said. She climbed in.

"Are you sure you're all right? Do you want me to follow you home?" asked Emily.

"No, really. I'm fine." Cynda turned on the engine and pulled out of her parking space rather suddenly. She drove off leaving Rue and Emily staring at each other.

"This job is a laugh a minute," said Emily to Rue.

"Tell me about it." They stood in the sunshine.

"Did you know Cynda and Elliot were unhappy?" Emily asked.

"I noticed they were never together. He never came to faculty lunches, or anything." They started walking back to Home.

"What's he like?" Emily asked. "Maybe he'd like me."

Rue laughed.

"I wasn't kidding," said Emily.

"I know you weren't," Rue said, and briefly patted Emily's arm. "Don't worry, we'll find somebody for you."

The weeks leading up to the Christmas break had become a complicated time in the life of The Country School. Under the Miss Plums, all had been serene. There was a Christmas pageant telling the story of the Annunciation and Nativity from the point of view of the Angels. The first and second graders performed in the entr'actes, dressed in nightgowns and spangly wings, but the action was controlled from Gabriel's headquarters, which looked a lot like the newsroom of a big city paper.

An angel would run in dressed in a big suit. "Boss, they only got as far as Bethlehem and it looks like the Lord is going to have to sleep on the ground."

"Oh, we can do better than that," Gabriel would say, taking his feet off the desk. "Get down there and disguise yourself as a pig or something, and tell the animals to take care of them." Then the lights would move to the stable scene. A pig would appear on stage and whisper to the oxen and the sheep, and pretty soon a nice clean manger full of straw would be ready to receive the infant. At the end of the performance Miss Carla Plum would remind the audience that In Those Days angels appeared on earth dressed as shepherds of the first century just as today angels were all around you, looking exactly like ordinary people. And who knows what they wear in heaven, she would say, and the audience would laugh as their children appeared dressed as sheep, shepherds, and newspapermen for curtain calls.

Miss Lourdes Plum then would play the piano and lead the school in Christmas carols. There was a wassail bowl after the program, and Miss Carla Plum appeared in a Santa Claus costume with a pillow under her tunic and a cottonball beard taped to her face. She handed out sweets and oranges and told everyone they should look for miracles every day, not just at Christmas.

Now there was no Christmas celebration at Country. Instead

there was a Festival of Holiday customs, featuring costumes, music, song, and story from three foreign countries each year, if possible represented by families in the school. This year the countries were Nicaragua, Tibet, and Armenia, and preparations were by no means going smoothly. The Nicaraguan family was staunchly pro-Contra and had run afoul of another mom on the committee whose brother had helped prosecute Oliver North. The mom from Lhasa knew very little of the holiday folkways of her country; she had grown up in Nepal in a house the size of Vaux Le Vicomte, in which the king of Tibet was being held prisoner on the second floor. She was a charming woman, beloved by all and now married to a venetian blind salesman, but the exotic holiday treats she remembered best from her childhood, which she reconstructed from a yellowing recipe written in Hindi by the family cook, turned out to be brownies. The Missirlians were preparing a huge map labeled Armenia, chunks of which the rest of the world tended to call Iran, Turkey, or Russia. They were also preparing tableaux vivantes depicting the Armenian holocaust and diaspora. This was actually quite popular, but it had caused unfestive feelings in the Hikmet family, Turkish-Americans whose five children had been attending Country for a span of sixteen years.

Rue and Mike Dianda were drinking mugs of herb tea in Mike's office. It was the end of a long day.

"What else?" Rue asked.

"Well Pat Moredock seems to be going crackers. She is keeping a diary of her grievances, and she's started stuffing pages from it into my mailbox every day," said Mike. "Also, she went to the store to buy a couple of hacksaw blades and some construction paper, and came back with receipts for two hundred and seventeen dollars."

"Worth of hacksaw blades?"

"No, she bought twenty soldering irons, and a few bales of cop-perfoil, and she had her whole trunk full of sheets of stained glass."

Rue covered her face with her hands.

"Bill Glarrow made her take it all back, but she's bitter. She says the teachers teaching academics can spend money without asking first. I pointed out that they can't, but never mind."

"She thought she'd teach stained glass in an elementary school? Can you imagine the insurance?"

"Insurance, nothing. We'd have to build an entirely separate studio. You get tiny little shards of glass in everything when you cut glass."

"Speaking of insurance, the Lozattos are now suing us for fifty thousand one hundred and seventy-five dollars."

"What?"

"Yes. They asked that Patsy's tuition be returned, so I sent it back. . . ."

"Minus one hundred seventy-five dollars for processing. The contract *says* it's unrefundable."

"And Jerry Lozatto signed the contract. The insurance company wants to settle the suit, but Ann Rosen is so mad now that she won't."

"Good for her."

"And someone in the eighth grade took forty dollars from Cynda Goldring's wallet."

They sat in silence, finishing their tea. "I better go talk to Pat Moredock," said Rue, sounding as if it was the last thing she wanted.

"Take Bonnie with you," said Mike.

"Great idea, thank you. I will."

Rue and Bonnie found Pat Moredock cleaning up her studio. It was a large bright room lined with gray and orange tiles, with art projects stacked on every surface. On the long workbenches in the center of the room lay gray life masks, eerie eyeless visages that the sixth graders made by applying surgical cast material to each other's Vaselined faces. The masks were drying now, after which the students would paint them so that the masks became a statement of identity. Sometimes the most apparently sunny children would paint their masks in dark, disturbing colors, or color one-half one way and the other side quite different, or paint on strange scars.

"So interesting," said Bonnie to Pat as she walked from dead face to dead face. "Since sixth graders all wear masks anyway."

"Do they?" said Pat. She had been expecting a more conventional compliment. She was used to people making a great fuss about the sunny color that flooded the room, the artwork and materials everywhere, the feast of possibilities she provided the children.

"I think so. They're so frightened of standing out of the crowd, and yet angry that we don't see how they're special."

"I think they're all special," said Pat stiffly. She went back to wiping down tables and putting the caps back on the jars of tempera paints.

"Oh, yes, but do we see in what individual ways? Behind these little blank faces?" She gestured to the masks.

"Oh yeah, oh yeah," said Pat, with her back to the room. Pat was a big woman, with iron-gray hair, inexpertly curled. She wore large loose shirts and skirts, and in the studio, a denim apron. She moved soundlessly in thick-soled brown Hushpuppies. She was very busy putting things in order. Rue couldn't interpret her tone, or for that matter, her meaning. Was she agreeing with Bonnie? Or brushing her off? . . .

There was a pause. Rue, listening, found herself looking at a shelf of cubbies stacked with drawings. She took down a pile and began to leaf through them. They were designs, or in some cases pictures, that incorporated letters of the alphabet. Here was a clever one in which a large K had become a tree with a rake leaning against it.

"You already washed those once," Bonnie said next. "The brushes."

"I did not," said Pat, quite aggressive.

"You did," said Bonnie gently. "I watched you."

"Would you mind telling me what you're doing here? I know my time isn't as valuable as the Latin teacher's or the math teacher's, but it's mine, and I'm fond of it." Rue went on paging through the drawings. That sentence didn't make much sense, she thought. She's so angry about something that it's making her speechless.

"I'm sorry," said Bonnie. "We did come for a reason. We want your advice."

"Oh," said Pat. "All right. Do you need me to sit down?"

"Do what you have to do."

Suddenly Rue felt herself go white. She was looking at a drawing that was very different from the others in the stack, which she judged to be by eleven- or twelve-year-olds. It was a picture of an Arnold Schwarzenegger–like character looking into a mirror. It was more a cartoon than a portrait but it was extraordinarily well done.

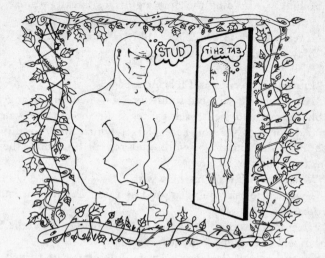

Over the muscleman's head was a thought balloon. "STUD," the figure was thinking, as he looked in the mirror. In the mirror, a very different male figure looked back. He was a puny-limbed, sagging creature. In his thought balloon, in perfect mirror writing, were the words *Eat Shit.* Around the drawing was a frame of thick, wonderfully drawn branches, with twigs and leaves and words woven along. Half the words were normal, and the other half were mirror writing. The straight writing gave words like *Jock . . . Macho Man . . . Punk Cruiser.* The mirror ones, cleverly disguised among leaves and tendrils, said *Asshole* or *Suck My Dick.*

"Pat, what are these?" Rue held up several of the drawings.

"Oh, aren't those clever? Those were done by the sixth grade two years ago."

"This year's eighth grade."

"Yes."

"Who did this one?"

She carried the drawing with the mirror writing to Bonnie and Pat. She could see that Bonnie saw at once why it interested her.

"Guess." Pat made a face.

"Tell me."

"Kenny Lowen."

Bonnie was holding the drawing. "This is extraordinary," she said.

"It really is, isn't it? He's incredibly talented. But awful."

"May I take this?" Bonnie asked.

"Well . . ."

"I just want to copy it. I'll bring it back."

"All right," Pat said, but suddenly again she sounded angry. She turned and went back to her sink. She ran the water and searched for a while for her sponge, which was on the floor. Eventually she found it, swore, and resumed washing the paint stains from the porcelain.

"What did you want my help with?"

"I wanted to ask you what kind of a year Lyndie Sale is having in your class."

Pat stopped scrubbing again. "Lyndie Sale . . . Lyndie Sale. I think fine. Let me get my grade book."

She walked off, leaving the water running. Rue turned it off. "Can't stand running water," she said to Bonnie. "Georgia's got me trained."

Pat came back from her office with a ring-bound notebook. "Lyndie Sale . . . got a B+ for her fantasy map and a B on her tie rack. She had trouble handling the stain. Other than that she's doing fine. Why?"

"No special reason. She gets along with the other children?"

"Always has."

"But you haven't seen a change this year?"

"I don't think so."

"Well. Thank you. That makes my life simpler."

"You're welcome."

"I'll bring this drawing back Tuesday," said Bonnie.

"No problem." Suddenly there was a feeling that Pat was in a hurry for them to leave. So they left.

They walked across the wide lawn toward Home, looking at Kenny Lowen's drawing.

"Are you going to show it to Cynda?" Bonnie asked.

"What do you think?"

"I think yes. What about the parents?"

"There's no point now. I certainly would have if Pat had seen fit to show it to me at the time he did it. But hold on to it. I think we're going to have a rough year with him."

"I think you're right. What are his parents like?"

"Bradley's a sweetheart. Very bright and funny and kind. Corinne is one of those intense moms who lives through her kids, and she's very competitive. They have a daughter in Catherine Trainer's class."

"Jennifer Lowen? That's his sister?"

Rue nodded. "Kenny was the most adorable toddler. But always a dickens. Jennifer is entirely different. A princess, with all that that implies."

"Interesting family."

"Tell me about Pat Moredock. Did she really wash the brushes twice?"

"Not only that, I watched her take the tops off the paint jars and then screw them all on again."

"We seemed to scare the hell out of her. What *is* that?"

"Don't you know?" Bonnie asked.

Rue felt a sudden shift of terrain, a momentary blankness. Was there something right in front of her she couldn't see?

"I have no idea. Do you mean you do?"

"Of course."

The two women stopped and looked at each other. Bonnie was puzzled. Rue was feeling rather frightened.

"Well?" said Rue. "What is it?"

"She was drunk," said Bonnie.

Rue gave no reaction at all for a moment, except to blink.

"Are you sure?"

"Absolutely. Haven't you ever seen anyone drunk?"

Rue looked completely bewildered.

"Poor Pat," she said at last. "Now what am I going to do?"

"We better talk about it," said Bonnie. "Does she have any family?"

"A daughter at college. She's divorced."

"Mother? Father?"

"I think so. In the south someplace. Maybe Arkansas. Should we do an intervention?"

"Well, wait. How drunk is she? How often does it happen? Is this temporary or chronic?"

"I see what you mean."

"I know of a case where a business did an intervention on a longtime bookkeeper. They sent the woman off to a dry-out farm. She'd been functioning at a pretty high level, so they didn't figure her for a hard case. She did the whole course, and then on the way back to San Diego, she got off the plane in Denver and got so drunk in the airport she wound up in jail. After that the company fired her, and her family wouldn't take her. Her sister says she was arrested a year later stark naked, up in a tree. Throwing things at people."

"So you don't just bust in on someone who's operating without a safety net."

"I'd give it careful thought."

They walked in silence. "I'm exhausted," said Rue. "I think I'll go home to my husband."

"And have a stiff drink," said Bonnie.

"And a big cookie," said Rue.

They both laughed.

Bonnie said, "That should work. I'll see you on Tuesday."

And they parted.

Chandler Kip and his wife, Bobbi, were giving a Christmas party for the faculty and trustees. Their vast half-timbered Tudor house was filled with decorations of the Olde English variety. There were strings of twinkling white lights winking in the many-paned leaded windows. There were pine boughs on every mantel-piece and tucked behind every picture frame. There were pine ropes twined along the long curving bannisters, tied with red velvet rib-bon, and clutches of mistletoe hanging at every doorway. The immense Douglas fir in the front hall was so tall Bobbi had had to have the top four feet cut off, so it seemed to grow into the ceiling. It was strung with popcorn, cranberries, and paper snowflake chains made from silver paper. Instead of electric lights, it was lit with candles, clipped to the boughs in genuine antique Victorian holders. Unfortunately, every time someone opened the front door the candles flared, threatening to ignite the paper chains. That, or half of them blew out. Bobbi, who had only spent a full month of her life planning the decor for the holidays, had been called a moron by her husband, and had wept much of the day. Chandler had now solved the problem, sort of, by employing their nine-year-old daughter, Missy, to sit beside the tree throughout the party holding a fire extinguisher. Missy, who appeared to be borderline anorexic, was a ballet fanatic, and agreed to this duty if she could be dressed as the Sugar Plum Fairy.

Oliver and Sondra Sale were the first to arrive. Oliver was wearing his usual gray suit, white shirt, and black tie. Sondra was in a forest green form-fitting cocktail dress, and her blond hair was violently coiffed. They found Chandler in his Savile Row tweeds, wearing a red Christmas vest printed with tiny green holly wreaths, applying sandpaper to the ornate iron handrail that had recently been installed to aid the infirm in ascending the front steps.

Chandler's mother, though not old, was infirm and had arrived to spend Christmas and most of January.

"Merry Christmas," announced Oliver as he preceded his wife up the stone walkway from the four-car garage. The walkway was lined with paper bags half-filled with sand and lit from within by votive candles. Each bag had been stenciled with Christmas motifs by Missy. At least Chandler believed that Missy had done it, as he had paid her a quarter a bag for the job. Actually Bobbi had found that Missy was getting spray paint all over the green marble kitchen counters, and she refused to move out to the garage because there was no TV out there, so Bobbi had done the bags for her. In doing so, Bobbi had gotten red spray paint on her fingers, and when she removed it, the mineral spirits also removed most of her nail polish, so she had to have her manicure redone this morning at a cost of $32, including tip. Chandler, who vetted his Visa bill minutely with a calendar at his side, would need to know why she had had two manicures in one week. But by then it would be January, and Bobbi would have thought of some excuse. Missy, meanwhile, had made $2.75 on the deal.

"Bobbi let the damn contractor put the wrong kind of paint on this thing, and it's started to blister," Chandler told the Sales. He gave the railing a last fierce swipe, put the sandpaper in his pocket, and gave Sondra a kiss on the cheek.

"You have a lovely home," said Sondra.

"Are we early?" Oliver asked.

"Right on time. Bobbi's in the kitchen trying to make eggnog," said Chandler.

"I'll go help her out," said Sondra, with relief. She handed Chandler the white beribboned poinsettia she was carrying and started off in the wrong direction.

"No the kitchen is that way," Chandler called after her. Flustered, she turned and looked at Chandler, who was pointing. She nodded once and went off again, walking stiffly on high heels.

"Come in, have a drink, how are you?" said Chandler, shepherding Oliver in through the front door. Oliver seemed to tower over him, as if he would have to duck to fit through the door. The candles fluttered wildly on the tree as the door opened.

"Come say hello to Mr. Sale," said Chandler to Missy. Missy

put down her Christmas red fire extinguisher and arabesqued her way across the stone floor to Mr. Sale, for whom she performed a deep curtsey. Oliver bowed in return, and the skeletal little girl in a silver tutu and pink tights pirouetted back to her place beside the tree. Chandler hoped she wasn't going to keep *that* up all evening; if she did, she would soon be knocking into waiters with drink trays and waitresses with platters of canapes. He led Oliver into the den, where the bartender was setting up.

They both ordered spritzers. "How's Lucky Lyndie?" Chandler asked.

"They kept her overnight to be sure she didn't slip into a coma," Oliver said. "Sondra spent the night with her and brought her home this morning. She's got a hell of a goose egg on the back of her head."

"That must smart."

"I'm getting rid of those rollerblades—I think they're dangerous as hell. She just got out of a cast, you know."

"Have you ever tried them?"

"No, have you?"

"They're a lot of fun," said Chandler. "I was going to get a pair, but my orthopod had a fit." Chandler's son, Randy, had introduced him to rollerblading. It hadn't been easy, the last few years, for them to find things they could do together or interests to share. Randy fought savagely with Bobbi if he was allowed in the house. Bobbi thought he'd taken his father rollerblading in the hope he'd break both his arms. But Chandler didn't see it that way.

The doorbell rang, and Chandler went to answer it. It was Pat Moredock, the art teacher. She was wearing a candy-cane bracelet and a Rudolph Reindeer pin with a tiny electric bulb for a nose, blinking on and off. When Missy saw her, she flew across the room and leaped into Pat's arms, crying, "Mrs. Moooooredock!" Art was Missy's favorite subject. "Daddy, can I show Mrs. Moredock my room?"

Chandler closed the door so carefully that the candles on the tree barely flickered at all. Missy took Mrs. Moredock by the hand and dragged her toward the stairs.

"Why don't you let Mrs. Moredock get a drink first?" said Chandler. To Missy's disgust, Mrs. Moredock seemed to think this was a good idea. But once she had given her coat to a butler and let the bartender pour her a hefty scotch on the rocks, she consented to be led.

Next came Janet TerWilliams and her husband, Carl. They had brought Helen Yeats and Charla Percy with them, and all exclaimed over the originality of real candles on the tree. Helen went to very few parties where butlers waited on her, and to her especially, the warm, twinkling house smelling of pine and fragrant wood smoke seemed like a wonderland.

Rue came to the party determined to be on her best behavior. She and Henry arrived rather late, on purpose, not much liking cocktail parties, which Henry called bun fights. They brought Emily Goldsborough with them. The driveway was already full of cars, and they had to park far out on the road and walk in. The pathway, lit with lumières, reminded Rue of Christmas in Maine, and she thought again how odd it was to feel a warm evening wind in the early darkness that meant December, and to pass along a rock garden of cactus on her way into a house full of evergreens and Christmas music.

The party had spread throughout the downstairs of the house by this time. It had not been announced as a dinner, but the buffet in the dining room was so lavish, with roast beef, turkey, and ham, huge bowls of boiled shrimp, crudités, cheese puffs, platters of cheese and fruit, and salvers of hot chicken livers wrapped in bacon, that most of the guests were making a meal of it.

Rue soon found herself trapped by a trustee who believed that her son was being picked on by one of the most beloved teachers in the school. Rue urged her to call for an appointment, so that she and Mrs. Percy and the McCanns could sit down together. Carson McCann agreed that that was the way to handle it, then went right on regaling her with tales of Mrs. Percy's bizarre and unjust behavior to little Ashby.

Blessedly, Henry cut in.

"Do you want some dinner?" he asked Rue. "I'm going to eat as much meat as I can, before Georgia gets home." They made their escape.

"I'm going to find a place to sit down."

"Try the library," said Henry. "I'll bring you a plate."

"Chandler—what a beautiful party," said Rue. They had all come together in the hall.

"Have you met my mother?" Chandler indicated the tiny woman at his elbow who was peering up at her through very thick pink-tinted glasses. She was looking anxious, and she was wearing a velvet dress covered with cabbage roses in which she must have been half-cooked.

"How nice to meet you, Mrs. Kip. I'm Rue Shaw. Have you come to visit for the holidays?"

Rue had bent over nearly at the waist so as to be heard in the din echoing from the stone floor.

"I'm not supposed to stand up so long. I have varicose veins," Mrs. Kip replied, as if it was callous of Rue not to know this.

"Come with me, I'm determined to sit. Come into the library." And Rue led Mrs. Kip away, hoping that Chandler would be grateful to her. In the library, they found Pat Moredock sucking on a glass of scotch and talking about her childhood to Lloyd Merton, who taught fourth grade. There was room for Rue and Mrs. Kip on a couch near the fire, but Mrs. Kip found this to be too warm. Finally, Rue got her settled in a ladder-backed rocking chair in the corner, beside which someone had artfully arranged a basket full of soft balls of yarn and a selection of knitting needles, and another basket of colorful seed catalogues. All along the tables and window-sills there were pots of forced paperwhites, the bulbs in white gravel. The perfume was enough to put you to sleep.

Rue sat down by Mrs. Kip in a soft chair closer to the fire, and almost at once they were joined by Cynda Goldring and a date, a good-looking man named Doug with a large mustache. These two were both feeling merry. Rue introduced them to Chandler's mother.

"We were just trying to decide whether Jesus knew in the cradle that he was the Messiah," said Cynda. "I'm sure he did, because of all those Renaissance pictures where he sits on his mother's lap but looks about thirty."

"I don't think he could have," said Doug. "If he knew from birth, why don't we have a record of his miraculous childhood? We know nothing of his childhood, except that he and Joseph walked to England, being carpenters."

"He did not go to England," said Cynda. "I've been to England."

"He did."

"Do you have proof?"

Doug began to sing:

> *"And did those feet*
> *In Ancient Times*
> *Walk upon England's Moun—tains Green ..."*

Henry came in, carrying plates of food.

> *"And was the hoo—ooly Lamb of God*
> *On England's pleasant pas—tures seen?"*

"That doesn't prove anything," said Cynda. "Those are questions, not answers." Doug, who sang well and knew it, boomed on:

> *"And did the Coun—tenance Divine*
> *Shine forth upon our clou—ded hills?*
> *And was Jeru—uu—salem builded here*
> *Among these dark Sa—tan—ic Mills?"*

"Oh, darling, you're just in time," said Rue to Henry. "We're having a very Christmassy conversation." He handed her a plate full of shrimp and cocktail sauce, some cheese, and some grapes. He sat down himself on the edge of her chair.

"This is perfect. Thank you," said Rue, admiring her plate of food.

"Blake wrote that," said Doug proudly.

"I *know* Blake wrote it, I'm an English teacher," said Cynda.

"Are you?" Doug asked.

Henry asked, "How long have you two known each other?"

Rue turned to Chandler's mother. "Mrs. Kip, please have some of these shrimp."

"I don't eat shellfish, I'm allergic," she said darkly. "Bobbi knows it."

"She's very kind, isn't she," Rue said. "Your daughter-in-law," hoping that Mrs. Kip was not going to begin abusing her hostess. "She's done such a pretty job with this room. With the whole house."

Mrs. Kip looked as if Rue were a half-wit.

"My son was a straight-A student," she said pointedly. "He went to Grinnell, he had a full scholarship." This seemed not to follow, but Rue was afraid that it did. She was fairly sure that Mrs. Kip was complaining of her daughter-in-law's mental capacity.

This suddenly reminded Doug of another of his points about Jesus. "And what about those rather rude things he says to his mother?" he resumed. 'Woman, what have I to do with you?' He said that in public. At a wedding. If I did that, my mother would tear my ears off."

"Suggesting that he *did* know he was divine. He knew he could get away with being smart, because he was the Messiah," said Cynda.

"It only proves His mother thought so. But it wasn't very Christ-like of him," said Doug.

"Why shouldn't it be that your spiritual nature accrues throughout your life?" Rue asked. "An embryo, in utero, starts out so undifferentiated that it could conceivably become a fish. Or a dog. It has gills for a while. But its humanity accrues throughout gestation. Why shouldn't it be the same with your spiritual life? That once born, you make choices, or follow your path, and gradually as you pass your tests or fail them, as you choose your fights and learn from them or don't, your spiritual nature evolves?"

"Building up layer by layer, like lacquer?" Cynda asked, interested, and looking at her amazing fingernails.

Suddenly Mrs. Kip wriggled out of her chair and stumped out of the room.

"So that he had the potential to become the Christ in the cradle, but he didn't achieve it until decades later," said Doug.

"And would that mean that there are others born with the same potential?" Cynda wondered.

"I don't see why not," said Rue. "I don't know how else you explain the Buddha, or the Hindu holy men, or the Prophet Mohammed."

"Or Emanuel Swedenborg, or Joseph Smith, or Mary Baker Eddy," said Henry enthusiastically.

"Henry, go do something useful. Go see if Emily needs to be rescued from Bud Ransom."

Henry rose and went, smiling.

"So at what point did Our Lord know he was the Messiah?" asked Doug. "You know, the gospels don't ever say there were wise men and a star, let alone a stable. Matthew says there was a table in a room, and later a couple of astrologers from Iran. Luke says there was a manger and shepherds, but he also says there was a poll tax in the reign of Herod, and there wasn't, so why would Mary and Joseph be on the road at all and have to stay at an inn? Why wouldn't they stay in Nazareth?"

"Rue," said Cynda, "if humanity accrues throughout gestation, and birth is the culmination, and life is a spiritual gestation, then is death the next birth?"

"If you were in the womb, and you somehow had intimations of what birth was going to be like, wouldn't it sound horrible?" Rue asked.

"It would. It would indeed."

"All those lights and noise. The air on your skin. Learning to breathe."

Just then Chandler hurried into the room. He came over to where Rue, Doug, and Cynda were sitting and stood over them.

"Excuse me," he said crossly. "But can any of you tell me what happened to my mother?"

They all looked at each other.

"She left us. I thought she was going to get food."

"I tried to make her share my food, but she didn't like shrimp."

"Is something wrong?"

"She's gone upstairs to bed," said Chandler, furious. "All she would say was, she didn't think she liked my fancy friends."

The three looked at each other. Rue stood up.

"Chandler . . . I'm sorry. I don't know how we offended her but I'm awfully sorry we did. Would you take me to her?"

"For what purpose?"

"I would like to say good night to her and tell her how sorry I am. I'd like to tell her I look forward to seeing her another time."

"I don't think so, Rue. I don't think that would strike her as a good idea."

Fortunately, that was the moment that the Christmas tree finally caught on fire.

W̶e were being clever," said Rue in the car, miserable. "We assumed that we all agreed that was a clever conversation to have." Emily, from the back seat, watched the exchange.

"Excuse me," said Henry, "but I happen to know you were talking about your most deeply held beliefs."

"But I was talking about them lightly. She misunderstood. She thought we were being facetious."

"Rue . . . you're not perfect. You can't get it right all the time. Chandler will get over it."

"I'm not worried about consequences. I'm sorry I offended my host's mother. My employer's mother. I'm sorry I gave pain when I didn't mean to."

"Chandler's a jerk and so is his mother," said Henry. "Don't worry about it." He happened to look in the rearview mirror and found that his eyes met Emily's.

The next day was Monday, the last half-week before Christmas break, and on Wednesday, Georgia would be home.

The day began with Corinne Lowen, Kenny Lowen's mother, on the phone yelling bloody murder at Lynn Ketchum because Kenny had gotten a B in history. The Lowens had already had an hysterical hour-long meeting with Rue the week before because Kenny's B– in PE was keeping him off the honor roll.

"PE should not count toward the honor roll," Bradley Lowen kept intoning. "It is not an academic subject."

"I understand that," Rue kept responding. "But these children are very grade-oriented, and the teachers say that if the grade doesn't count, they won't make an effort. I can't keep good art or music or PE teachers if the students don't take their classes seriously."

"You call Blair Kunzelman a good teacher?" Bradley demanded.

"Yes, I do," said Rue, hoping her nose wouldn't start to grow.

Blair was much loved by the boys who cared about team sports, but he fancied himself quite the jock, and his judgment in handling the less athletic boys was not always the best. In her experience it was hard to find a good PE teacher with perfect social skills.

"Kenny's a fine athlete. He just isn't interested in PE," said Corinne Lowen. "He's too smart for it. He gets bored."

"I understand that. But we believe that the whole program counts. We feel it's a good thing to learn to do your best at the task at hand."

"But it's keeping him off the honor roll!"

"You know that the high schools don't see the honor roll. It will have no effect on his future."

"But he's the brightest kid in the class!"

"He may well be."

"Then how can he not be on the honor roll?"

"Because it's just that. It's an honor. It's not something he's entitled to because he's bright."

They had gone on like that for a dozen inconclusive rounds, until they wore themselves out and went away. *What are they going to be like when I tell them that Kenny's the psychopath who's been harassing Mrs. Goldring?* Rue wondered.

In any case, they were now onto Ms. Ketchum, the gray-haired, fleshless, bitter-looking teacher of history whom Rue knew to have a razor tongue and an even sharper mind. She was not the sort who was thought to have a way with children, but there was something in her unflinching dry irony that her students loved. Especially the bright ones, whom she favored. Rue knew Lynn was one of the few teachers in school who was not completely fed up with Kenny. But apparently Corinne Lowen didn't know that, or care.

Lynn repeated the conversation to Rue while Rue took notes. Lynn's reporting was close to verbatim; she had a wicked ear for speech patterns.

"I said, 'Good morning,' and she screamed, 'What the hell is this B for?' I said, 'History.'" Rue made a successful effort not to smile.

"She yelled, 'How could Kenny Lowen get a B in history? Do you know what they said to him at CTY in Los Angeles last summer? They said, *This boy should be in college-level calculus. This is one of the brightest students we ever taught. He has the potential to be a mathematician of world-class importance.'*

"I said, 'No, I didn't know they said that.' She said, 'Well that's what they said. Now you tell me how that same boy could get a B in an eighth-grade history course?'"

"I said, 'Did they also recommend that he take their advanced course for another thousand dollars next summer?'"

Rue couldn't help smiling at that. She put her hand over her eyes, as if she didn't want to know what was coming.

"She screamed, 'Well of course they did! He's too bright for classes he's in, he needs advanced-level courses!'"

"I said, 'If he's too bright, why didn't he get an A in my class?' She said, 'That's what I'm asking you!'"

"I said, 'Then I'll tell you. He has failed to turn in four homework assignments, he made careless mistakes on his midterm exam, and he did a mediocre job on his *You Are There* assignment. Which he turned in late.'"

"She said, 'You call it mediocre because it's Kenny. If it were Sharon Poobah or Johnny Slipperyrock you'd give it an A. You penalize him for being bright.'"

Rue made a gesture of annoyance but Lynn waved it off. Parents didn't scare her. "I said, 'You are quite wrong. I have standards and I apply them equally. He did B work in my class. There were four students who got A's, because their work was clearly better.'"

"Then she said, 'Don't you have some kind of warning system when a child is going to get a poor grade?' I said, 'Yes, we do. If your child is going to get a D or an F, we let you know at least three weeks in advance.' She chewed on that for a while, and then I said, 'If you would like me to warn you if Kenny is going to get a B, I can certainly do that.' She yelled, 'This isn't about A's or B's!'"

Rue rolled her eyes.

"I said, 'Then I'm afraid I don't understand.' And she said she was sure I didn't, and hung up."

Rue took a deep breath. "Thank you, Lynn."

"No problem."

But they both knew it was a big problem. The Lowens were

close friends with half the parent body. But they had a troubled boy on their hands, and they didn't want to hear it, and sooner or later, they were going to shoot a messenger.

Next, it was time to go monitor Charla Percy's class, to ascertain whether or not Charla was making a scapegoat of Ashby McCann. "He's never had any trouble with a teacher before!" Ashby's mother had kept asserting over the eggnog and the Santa Claus cookies she was compulsively eating. This was quite untrue; Ashby had been in trouble with every teacher he'd had since he was a three-year-old in preschool. Furthermore, his two older sisters had adored Mrs. Percy. But the McCanns did not then reason that maybe Ashby was a problem, but rather that Mrs. Percy had changed. They were full of wild theories about what had changed her: she was an unhappy newlywed, her husband traveled too much, she was under stress because she was African American and her husband was white, she was having trouble with her stepson and displacing her anger on Ashby. Rue was glad Charla was in her early thirties, or she knew the next thing she'd hear was that Charla was in menopause.

Rue had listened respectfully. This was the sort of situation that ended with everyone angry at Rue. The faculty, because Rue listened to such tales at all, saying she was far too submissive to wilding parents. The parents, because she listened and then failed to agree with them.

Rue sat through an uneventful forty-five-minute period in which Charla taught the children to recite aloud "A Visit from St. Nicholas." Charla first explained that St. Nicholas was a character from European folk tales, descended from a German figure known as Bellsnickle, who was thought to appear at Christmastime jingling bells and carrying a sack of willow switches with which he would punish naughty children. No Christ child, no presents. Another desanctified holiday tradition, quite correct. The children loved the class and behaved well, including Ashby, and soon all could recite the poem en masse.

The class then went to recess. Cora Alba-Fish was on playground duty. Rue stood at the side of the playground and found that the children shyly approached her one by one. As one came near, he or she would suddenly blossom into technicolor, transformed from a distant, uniformed widget into a quirky, pulsating spirit-filled person. Sasha Petrie wanted to tell Rue all about her new puppy. After she danced off, Courtney Leavitt offered to make Rue a potholder because she had a kit at home. She would make her one tonight. Brendan Bramlett sidled over to tell her that he was going to Hawaii for Christmas. He took Rue's hand and held it while he fidgeted and talked.

Suddenly there arose a clamor from the other side of the yard, where Ashby McCann, Tod Bitter, Chelsea Malko, and Drew Miles were playing Four Square. "Ashby—you're out! Get out of the square!" yelled Tod and Chelsea.

"No, but we made a new rule . . . !" Ashby yelled back, meanwhile staying in the square and bouncing the ball, bat-bat-bat, and not looking at them. The three others ran wailing to Mrs. Alba-Fish.

Rue watched as Cora led them back to the square where Ashby stood alone, bouncing.

"Ashby," said Cora, "Do you understand why your friends are upset?"

Ashby bounced the ball. "Well we made this new rule where . . ."

The others yelled, "No, we didn't Ashby; you just said there was a new rule after you were out. . . ." Cora quieted them and asked again, "Do you understand why they're upset, Ashby?"

Finally, he said, "Well, I guess I'm out, but . . ." and dropped the ball and walked away.

The other three children reclaimed their places and went back to their game. Brooke Humphrey came shyly to tell Rue that her big sister was coming home from boarding school. As Rue listened, she watched Ashby edge back toward the Four Square game and begin to harass the players. He kept sticking his foot into the square and then pulling it out again or reaching in to bat the ball, stopping the play. "Ashby, get out!" "Ashby, get away, you're out!" "Mrs. Alba-Fish!" wailed the three playmates.

Rue went back to her office to take careful notes.

Wednesday evening, an hour before the Holiday Traditions program was to begin, Chandler Kip walked into Rue's office. Rue's desk was stacked with boxes and bags wrapped in bright paper and tied with ribbons, and with plates and tins and jars of cookies and nuts and homemade jam she had been given for Christmas by parents and children and faculty colleagues.

"Merry Christmas," said Rue. "Want a cookie?"

"I've just come from the Curriculum Committee," said Chandler.

"You called a special meeting of the Curriculum Committee?"

"Starting immediately after the New Year," said Chandler, "we want every faculty member to write out the curriculum they plan to follow for the rest of the year. We want to know what topics will be covered, what texts used, what field trips, special assignments, and term projects are planned. Every Friday, we want a report on every subject taught by every teacher, on what they covered that week, and if they have not kept to their schedule, an explanation of why not. And a prospectus for how and when they will make up the missing material."

Rue just stared at him. Chandler stared back. Rue was running over in her mind who was on the Curriculum Committee. Mike Dianda, who was gone today, attending his daughter Mary's class lunch, Chandler, Carson McCann, Bud Ransom, Terry Malko, and from the faculty Rosemary Fitch, who'd been out all week with the flu.

"Well?" said Chandler.

"Chandler, have a cookie."

"I don't want a cookie. I want to tell my committee that you got the message."

"I got it."

"And you will explain it to the faculty at the opening of next semester?"

"Absolutely not."

A beat. Chandler got rather red in the face and began drumming his fingers on the edge of Rue's desk. He liked to stand over people who were sitting, she noticed. He liked to loom over people. She returned his gaze unflinching. She didn't know how long he was going to keep it up, but she was prepared to sit there till breakfast, if necessary.

Finally, Chandler said, "You will not give this message to the faculty?"

"I will not."

"This is a direct order from your employers."

"Chandler . . . please sit down."

"I prefer to stand."

"Fine. You are my employers, but not in the sense that you're the boss and I'm the hired hand. This is a nonprofit institution of learning, not a bolt factory, and I am the trained professional who runs it."

"I know, I know, I've heard your speech. Now you hear mine. The Board establishes policy, and that is what we are doing. We have no say in who you hire or fire, fine. I understand that, and I understand why. But we feel that our families pay a great deal of tuition, and they have a right to know what it's going for. They have a right to be assured that their children will be at or above grade level in every subject when it comes time for them to be measured."

"Wait a minute. Are you asking me to ask my faculty to demonstrate to you that they are using all their class time to cram your kids so they'll do well on standardized tests?"

"This is a school. Education is our product. . . ."

"So you want the curriculum to be shaped by what can be tested, even though those tests are biased, and at best can only measure a fraction of what goes into becoming a sound, moral, well-adjusted, curious human being?"

"Education is our product," Chandler repeated, as if she had not interrupted. "The quality of what we are selling must be measured. Like it or not, life works like that. When Country students go out in the world we want to be sure they're prepared to compete."

"To compete with whom?"

"With the competition! With students from Poly Sci and Arthur Academy, and from Harvard-Westlake and from Burke's and Hamlin's!"

"I couldn't disagree with you more."

Surprised, he was silent for a minute. Finally, he said, "I find it difficult to see how we could disagree. We've made a simple request for some quality control."

"Then listen. First, it's an offensive request. You are not trained or qualified to 'control' the quality of teaching here. Nor is it in your job description. The quality of teaching is the business of the talented professionals I hire. If something changes in a teacher's work, and there is a legitimate question of quality, you or any other concerned party can bring that question to me, and I will evaluate and deal with it. . . ."

"So you're upset about control."

"Please let me finish. No, I'm not upset about control, because I believe the school's Statement of Philosophy is so clear on this subject that you don't have a leg to stand on."

"May I remind you that two of the members of the Curriculum Committee are lawyers?"

"Please let me finish, Chandler. I am upset because you are suggesting that the policy of this school *should be* to prepare our children to compete against others and win."

Chandler looked at her, truly puzzled. Yes, he thought, for once off balance. That was exactly what he thought. What on earth could be wrong with that?

"Why don't you tell me what you think our policy is," he said finally.

"Our policy, our stated mission, is to prepare each child to do his or her own best, according to the particular gifts he or she has been given. We prepare them for success by helping them to help themselves, to believe in themselves, to discover and respect their own talents, to strive for excellence for its own sake, and to respect and applaud the different tastes and talents of others."

"Yes," said Chandler. "So?"

"SO. You're talking about preparing them to compete with others, to beat others, to think that winning, scoring highest, getting prizes, leaving others in the dust, is the goal of life. So that every year, two or three of them will succeed, in your terms, and the rest will feel like second best. Or failures. I am teaching them the opposite. I'm teaching them that what matters is to feel successful when you have done the best *you* can. And if your gift is in art or music or playing soccer or memorizing the phone book, you accept that gift and do the best you can with it. You don't feel like a failure because your gift wasn't measured on the ERB. And you rejoice in belonging to a community that values difference, where we don't applaud only winners, we work together for the decent survival of all."

There was a long silence. Finally, Chandler said, "Are you finished?"

"Almost. You think human community is a pyramid, with the winners on top and the failures at the bottom. I think it's a net, in which everyone matters and has something essential to offer. I think my model will produce more, and happier, truly useful and satisfied humans than yours will. I may be wrong, but it's not negotiable. Accept my view, or fire me."

There was another long silence.

Finally, Chandler said, "I better go. We'll be late for the program."

"I think you'll be very proud of Missy."

"I'm sure I will. I'll see you over there."

"Yes." He turned to go.

"Merry Christmas, Chandler."

"Merry Christmas."

She waited until he had left the room and then opened a tin with a picture of Santa Claus on it, and fiercely bit the head off a frosting-covered gingerbread man.

The Holiday Program was, in the end, a love fest. Everyone was relieved that the term was over and filled with anticipation about the program and about whatever holiday they were going home to celebrate. The family from Armenia had substituted folk dances for Holocaust tableaux. The red and green iced brownies from Tibet were a great success. The third graders sang holiday songs from Nicaragua, and second graders recited "A Visit from St. Nicholas," and Missy Kip, along with five other fourth graders, dressed in red long johns, appeared on stage as balletic elves in a play about *The Grinch Who Stole the Holidays*. At the finale, the whole student body, from junior kindergarten to eighth grade, stood in a ring hand-in-hand around the auditorium, surrounding and enclosing the audience, their parents, teachers, older siblings, and baby ones, and sang a lovely round with overlapping verses about two neighbors' houses, one with a glowing Christmas tree and the other bright with Hanukkah candles. It left out the Buddhists, Jains, and followers of Islam in the school family, but everyone felt embraced by the spirit of it, and as always, it gave Rue a lump in her throat. So when the lights came up, and she found that the person standing beside her in tattered blue jeans and an unfamiliar coat of some ancient mangy fur was Georgia, she burst into tears.

There was always at the end of the program a speech of thanks and farewell to send people on their way. Mike Dianda, seeing that Rue and Georgia were hugging each other and that more and more of the upper schoolers had joined the hug to welcome Georgia home, decided he better take the microphone.

"I see that our leader has lost control of herself again," Mike said, "but don't worry. I Am In Charge. I know that tonight we all want to thank the Holiday Program Committee, especially Corinne Lowen . . . (applause), Mrs. Stevens, who worked so hard on the music for the show, and of course all the children. (Applause all around.) Have a wonderful vacation. Merry Christmas, Happy Hanukkah, Happy Holidays to all . . . and (looking toward the knot of huggers who were becoming a spectacle) Welcome Home Georgia!" There was laughter and applause.

There had been a tradition on nights when Georgia and her high school friends appeared at school plays, or to square dance with the little ones at Western Night, for the upper schoolers to stamp their feet and start a chant of "Geor—gia, Geor—gia, Geor—gia," a request for her to sing. It had begun when Georgia, as a surprise, had come from high school with her girl group and crashed a middle-school dance. They took over the mike and sang "Don't Say Nothing Bad About My Baby," and "It's in His Kiss," and "To Know Him Is to Love Him," and sixth graders thought they might flop over and die, they felt so sophisticated. The girl group continued to strike at unpredictable moments: dances, flag raisings, and once even at a father's kindergarten breakfast, where they sang "It Isn't Easy Being Green." Tonight, as soon as they saw her, the eighth graders began stamping and chanting, "Geor—gia, Geor—gia," and soon the younger children had taken it up, whether they knew what it meant or not.

Perhaps they hadn't really expected her to sing; they didn't know if she *could* sing without her group. But Georgia, blushing but wearing a quizzical grin, handed her mother her disgraceful coat and went forward.

The eighth graders shushed the crowd. Georgia stood, a small figure in torn jeans, with hip-length red hair. She was wearing a slouchy gray sweater that came halfway to her knees.

She did nothing visible to prepare herself, and showed no nervousness. She just stood very still for a moment, then took a deep breath and began to sing.

She sang the *Panis Angelicus* of César Franck in a soaring soprano that was darker, stronger, and richer than any of them had heard from her before. The high notes seemed to be made of silver. Mrs. Stevens, who knew the aria well, tried an experimental note on the Kurzweil, and found that with perfect pitch, Georgia had begun in exactly the key in which the piece was written. She pushed the organ button and played the accompaniment.

When the aria ended, there was a long moment of silence and then a roar of applause. The eighth-grade Georgia claque shouted for more, but she gave a deep bow, then ducked her head and scurried back to her parents as people applauded, and here and there a voice shouted, "Georgia—'He's a Rebel,' or Georgia—'Poor Little Fool.'"

Her father looked her in the eyes, and said, "Wow."

Georgia shrugged and smiled, and said, "Plus ça change," looking at him straight. Anyone watching them would have had the impression she had done it for him.

Henry, Georgia, and Rue walked slowly, very happily, across campus in the moonlight. Their house was full of light, waiting for them.

"So what is this rainbow ribbon, Georgia," said her father, inspecting her.

"That's for gay *rights,* Daddy."

"I see. And what's this red one?"

"AIDS support. Don't you read?"

"No, we're very sheltered here. You aren't trying to tell us something, are you?"

"What would that be?"

"This earring."

"The skull and crossbones?"

"Is that what it is? I'm too old to see in the dark. Now what is the significance of the one ear?"

"It's not the one ear, it's *which* ear."

"I see. And what does it mean?"

"Left is straight. Right is gay."

"Left is right and right is wrong?"

"If you see it that way."

"Rue, is she trying to tell us something?"

"She's trying to tell you that Truman isn't president anymore."

"He *isn't?*"

Rue put her arm around Georgia's shoulders and Georgia wrapped hers around her mother's waist.

"Hey," said Henry. "I feel left out."

"You're the wrong height," said Rue.

"Me and my friends went to see . . ."

"My friends and I," said Henry.

"Oh, did you go too?" Georgia asked.

"So," Rue prompted. "You and your friends . . ."

"Went to see Jan Morris speak at Town Hall."

"Was she wonderful?"

"Wonderful!"

"Isn't he the one who climbed Mt. Everest and then became a woman?" asked Henry.

"Yes, Daddy, she is."

"What did she say?" Rue asked.

"Well, after the talk, there were questions, and someone said, 'You've been a man, and you've been a woman. Can you talk about what you've learned from that?' And she said, 'Let me put it this way. Women are like computers. And men are more like . . . Waring Blenders.'"

Rue and Georgia both roared with laughter.

"I don't think that's a bit funny," said Henry.

"Yes, you do," said Georgia, and began to tickle him.

"I do not. And I don't remember giving you permission to . . . GROW UP!" And as he spoke he wheeled and began to tickle her with both hands. Georgia screamed and ran for the house, laughing, with her father on her heels.

Rue walked slowly after them, feeling she might have been so happy sometime before in her life, but if so, she couldn't remember when.

rdinarily the face-off with Chandler before the Holiday Program would have shaken Rue badly, and she and Henry would have talked it out from every angle. But Rue was so glad to have Georgia home, and her presence put things in such a happy perspective, that she decided to forget it. Instead, in the next days, Rue and Georgia spent hours shopping together, decorating the house, and planning the Christmas dinner. Rue was to be allowed to braise a goose, for the nonvegetarians. Georgia was going to make vegetable tempura, some curries, raita, and Japanese buckwheat noodles with miso. Rue would make sautéed Brussels sprouts, cranberry chutney, and pecan and apple pies. They had a wonderful time making lists, and going from the Safeway to the health-food store.

Georgia had brought home a knapsack full of cassettes of the music she was listening to. There was some jazz, some rap, a lot of blues, and a lot of what she called "alternative strangeness." She also had a pirate tape of *The Ghost of Versailles* made by a friend of hers who sang in the Met chorus. She wanted CDs of *Einstein on the Beach* and of the *Death of Klinghofer* for Christmas.

There were also a lot of long-distance telephone calls that involved stretching the downstairs telephone cord until Georgia was sitting in the coat closet.

Finally, Rue said, "Forgive my curiosity, but . . ." and Georgia laughed and looked shy.

"I won't ask if you don't want me to."

"No, that's all right. I've been admiring your restraint."

"Well?"

"It's just Jonah."

"Do I know Jonah?"

"No. He's a senior. He's training to be a conductor. He's incredible, he can play five instruments, and he can sight-read a score and hear all the voices at once . . . most people think he's a genius."

"What five instruments?" Rue was rolling out pie dough. She knew it was better to keep her back to Georgia, if she wanted her to feel safe when she was telling something new.

"Clarinet, saxophone, trombone, piano, and electric bass."

"Some combination."

"You should hear him play the bass. . . ."

"Do you have any of his music in that pile of tapes?"

"A couple of cuts upstairs. It's fairly outrageous."

"Honey, anything more avant garde than Karla Bonoff sounds outrageous to me. I'm still interested."

"Do you like ska?"

"I haven't the faintest idea."

"Sometimes, if he writes vocals, he asks me to sing."

"Are they songs, then? That he's writing?"

"Sort of."

Rue turned around. She could see by the light in Georgia's eyes that this was no ordinary professional admiration.

"Mine are songs," said Georgia, encouraging. "The things I write are recognizably songs. And he still likes them."

"Oh, good," said Rue. She lifted her pie crust into the baking tin, trimmed it, and crimped the edges. She covered the bottom with pinto beans to weight the crust and put it in the oven. Then she started assembling the brown sugar, pecans, vanilla, and butter for the pie filling.

"Is that Jonah's sweater?"

"Yes."

"He must be tall."

"Six-four."

"Where is he from?"

"Brooklyn."

"I'd like to meet him."

"Yes, you would. You'd like him. What are you putting in now?"

"A little bourbon, and some grated orange peel."

"Is *that* the secret?"

Rue smiled. "One of them."

"Would you teach me to bake?"

Rue turned and looked at her. "You've never been interested in baking. You don't eat desserts."

"I know, but I think I'd like to learn."

Rue smiled and turned back to her saucepan. Georgia was in love, and with someone who liked sweets.

On Christmas Eve, Georgia was going caroling with her friends from high school. Rue had planned a high tea by the fire before she went out. She had made scones, and they had a choice of home-made jams and cookies and tins full of nuts and dried fruits that the school family had given them for Christmas. She made shirred eggs and warmed some Black Forest ham for Henry as well, and this being California, there was also a bowl of fresh strawberries. It had been a Christmas Eve ritual to have high tea together in the early evening and then a quick cold supper after midnight, when they got back from church and hung their stockings from the mantelpiece.

After tea on Christmas Eve when Georgia was little, Henry used to read aloud *A Christmas Carol.* Some years he read selections from *The Pickwick Papers,* which one happy year gave Georgia such a contagious fit of the giggles that the reading had to be stopped so they wouldn't wet themselves.

Rue noticed that Henry had put his *Pickwick* on the table beside his favorite chair, in case this evening there should be time to read a little after tea and before Georgia's friends came to take her away.

"I *love* this tea," said Georgia, pouring cream into her cup and heaping in sugar. "What is it?"

"Lapsang Souchong."

"Just the smell of it reminds me of Christmas Eve."

Rue was toasting the scones over the fire.

"Could you pass me the dead pig, Georgia?" said Henry. Georgia passed the ham and eggs, and accepted a hot scone from her mother. She heaped hers with jam and whipped cream.

Rue looked wistfully at her rail-thin daughter and ate a hot muffin with a little sugarless jam.

"Is that all you're having?" asked Henry. "Have some dead pig," and he passed the plate over. Rue took some eggs.

"It's just that we're going to eat all day tomorrow. Of course Georgia could eat all day every day and not gain an ounce."

"Good genes," said Henry, knowing she took after him.

The phone rang. Both Rue and Henry were surprised when Georgia said, "Excuse me," and dove into the back hall to answer it. They had long had a family rule against talking on the phone during meals. But soon Rue heard the now-familiar sound of Georgia stretching the phone cord to where she could settle herself in a nest of rain boots and tennis racquets on the floor of the coat closet. Even with the door mostly closed, they could hear happy murmurs, long silences, and the occasional exclamation or peal of excited laughter.

"What's all this then?" Henry asked Rue.

"We have a boyfriend."

"We do? Is that whose sweater that is?"

"Yes," said Rue. She was surprised he had noticed the sweater, not that Georgia had had it off since she got home.

"I knew it wasn't mine," said Henry. "Too big. Does this mean she'll stop going off with all my shirts?"

"I wouldn't think so. A first serious boyfriend is different from getting married and moving to New Zealand."

"So this is serious?"

"Oh well. That may be the wrong word—it seems more euphoric than serious."

"What's its name?"

"Jonah."

"I hate him already."

"Have a scone." Rue held one to him on the end of her toasting fork. He took it and piled on some jam.

"Does it have a last name?"

"Not as far as I know. He comes from Brooklyn, he's a senior, he's training to be a conductor, and is widely considered a genius."

"Does that mean he can't be told not to call when we're eating?"

"I think it might."

There was a whoop of joy from the coat closet, followed by the scuffling sounds of Georgia hauling herself to her feet and hurrying back to them.

"I'm sorry," she said, as she picked up her napkin from the floor and sat back down to her half-eaten scone. She scooped some strawberries onto her plate for good measure. "Guess what—Jonah has a recording contract! He's been sending our tapes around to A&R people, going around knocking on doors, and this morning Combat Earache offered him a contract! He's going to make a record!" She looked from one parent to another, eyes glowing and cheeks flaming, fully expecting to be told that this was the single most astonishing and elating piece of news to be heard since man first walked on the moon.

Henry and Rue both looked at her. Rue said, "Well *how* exciting, dear," thinking this could be good news or terrible and she had no idea which.

"What kind of record?" Henry asked.

"I don't know what you'd call it. Sort of grindcore with a lot of blues influence."

"So this is not destined to premier at the Met."

"No, Daddy."

"Well just give me a clue. Where would one expect to hear this music?"

"Clubs. Concert halls, when he gets famous."

"Will there be stage diving involved?"

"*No,* Daddy. Where did you hear about stage diving?"

"But there will be amplifiers?"

"Of course!"

"I'm just looking for information. Is this contract for him or for a group?"

"A group, I guess. He uses pick-up musicians for gigs, but now he'll be able to put together a band, to tour."

"And how will that work out with his studies?"

"Daddy—do you know how exciting this is? Do you *know* how many wannabes there are in New York, going from label to label with their demo tapes, who would kill to get a chance to make a record?"

"I have some idea."

"Well then stop the third degree! This is exciting!"

"It *is* exciting, Georgia. It's absolutely thrilling," said Rue. Then the doorbell rang, and Georgia leaped up again. She stuffed another chunk of muffin into her mouth and scrambled out. Soon she was back, with Caroline and Mary and Shana and Rochelle, her old pod from high school. They came to the door to say, "Hello Dr. Shaw, hello Mrs. Shaw . . . Merry Christmas!" while Georgia put on her coat. Then they were gone, the door closed behind them, and outside they could hear the excited piping voice of Georgia telling her news, and then the shouts of amazed excitement and the slap of high fives as her friends gave her the appropriate reaction that had so escaped her parents.

Georgia was still pink with excitement when she slipped into the pew beside her parents at five minutes before eleven. Rue had a basket of gift-wrapped presents at her feet, and to her surprise and pleasure, she saw that Georgia had brought four presents with her too, wrapped in Rue's most expensive paper. "You remembered!" she whispered to Georgia.

"Of course. I brought them all this def stuff from New York." Rue suddenly felt her eyes fill with tears, to think of Georgia, nineteen, on her own in that terrifying city, with an allowance that barely covered what she needed for subway tokens, shopping for Christmas presents for homeless children on the coast of California.

The doors at the back of the church opened, and the organ began "O Little Town of Bethlehem." The choir came down the aisle singing and carrying candles, and behind them, a twelve-year-old Joseph with a burnt-cork beard carried a staff and led a Shetland pony, on which was seated the blue-robed figure of Nicolette Wren. She was sitting sideways, bareback, and was clutching the pony's mane with both hands, leaving the Baby Jesus she was supposed to be cradling dangling from her bosom with no visible means of support. Apparently, he was strapped to her body under her robes in some sort of infant carrier. Rue was pleased to note that Joseph was African American, feeling that this gave good representation to those who thought of Our Lord as the Lion of Judah, and Ethiopian. She wondered why in the world poor Nicolette had been cast as Mary, however, since she was clearly terrified of the pony. Then Rue remembered that Buster Wren was on the vestry.

Following Joseph and Mary came two sheep who kept trying to escape into the pews. These were being admirably managed by an efficient border collie whose master, dressed as a Magus, was about twice as tall and three times as old as the rest of the cast. Then came two smaller Magi carrying ornate boxes. One was Asian, and one was a girl. Far overhead, in the vaulted arches of the sanctuary, there was a large glittering star with a tail like a comet's, being drawn along a wire by some form of pulley. The two little Magi kept their eyes piously fixed on the star, while the tall one kept his eyes fixed on his sheep.

As it happened most years, some sort of miracle occurred once the members of the tableau reached the manger scene. Mary was helped from her ass by Joseph and she neither fell nor dropped the baby. The infant Jesus was (with some effort) disentangled from his mother's bosom and laid in the manger, where he seemed to disappear in a cloud of straw. The pony then stood quietly, and the sheep lay down and went to sleep. The congregation listened, once again to the familiar verses from Luke, and they sang all the favorite Christmas carols. Rue found herself in tears over and over again to have Henry on one side and Georgia on the other, with Georgia sight-reading the alto and Henry singing the bass.

Standing between her husband and her daughter, surrounded by people she knew and did not know, all of whom share a membership in this community, whose many bodies made one body and whose many voices sang one song, she wondered if she could find the words to explain to Mrs. Kip how she felt elated and transformed by belonging here. Inspired in the literal sense, she felt that as they sang they breathed in air that belonged to one spirit. She wished for a chance to say to her, "You thought I spoke lightly because I don't believe, but that's not it. I speak lightly because it doesn't matter which parts of a narrative I believe or don't believe. What matters is that I belong to a community that believes in a pattern life. I believe in the *experience* of belonging to this community. I can feel what it does in my life, it's not a mystery or a matter of doctrine, it's as experiential as eating dinner."

She thought of it again as she was falling asleep, with her arms around Henry and her cheek against the back of his shoulder. Of course, saying things like that to people whose beliefs were otherwise made no sense. No matter what she said, neither Chandler nor his mother was going to get the point of her. Never mind. Her job was to do what you have to do and let the storm blow until it blew over. They were entitled to hate her if they wanted to.

Christmas morning, Rue was down early. She had to get the goose ready, put all the leaves in the table, and get out the tablecloth and napkins and start ironing the creases that always settled in, since she didn't have a linen press or a drawer long enough to store the tablecloth rolled. She called her parents in Florida where they had somewhat unwillingly gone to visit her mother's brother. Her father said the trip had been fine and it was raining. Her mother seemed almost entirely recovered, he reported, and they were on their way out to eat something called fried conch for lunch. Fish for Christmas. Rue said, "You should see what *we're* having."

Rue found that her stocking and Henry's were half-stuffed with presents from Georgia, and that hers and Georgia's had presents in them from Henry. That fox—when had he done that? He must have gotten up in the middle of the night. She brought out the bag of stocking presents she had been collecting and wrapping since summer and added them to Georgia's and Henry's stockings.

At nine she made a breakfast tray with fresh orange juice and hot tea and the rest of the muffins from last night, and carried it up to Henry. She got back into bed with him.

"Merry Christmas, sweetheart," she said, kissing his shoulder. He pulled himself awake and sat up. He stared at the tray for a minute or two, and then said, "Oh, bliss," and retrieved the extra pillows from his side of the bed that he always threw on the floor. He propped them behind his back so he could sit up straight. She transferred the tray to his knees, and made him take his vitamin pill, and while he ate, they talked about Georgia and Jonah, and about Christmases in Maine when Georgia was a baby, and Christmases after they moved out here, and Christmases when they themselves were children. When he'd eaten everything on the tray, she kissed him and took it back downstairs, and he got up to take a shower. In her room, Georgia was up and dressing. Rue was surprised she wasn't going to sleep until noon, and she hurried to make coffee for her.

Nothing went quite as planned for the rest of the day. Somehow they blew a major fuse when Georgia put a bagel in the toaster and a cup of coffee in the microwave at the same time as the dishwasher was running. Then Rue discovered that the chestnuts she needed to stuff the goose were gone; Henry had given them away a week ago to a young lady who was going house to house gathering food for the needy.

"You gave them my chestnuts? What do you think they'll do with them?"

"What are *you* going to do with them?"

"I told you, stuff the goose!"

"Well, I didn't know that. We never had goose before. What if I don't like it?"

"You'll like it. Will you see if Tagliarini's is still open, and if it is, go buy me three cans of chestnuts?"

Henry trudged off.

They were still opening their stockings when Emily and Malone and David arrived with an armful of flowers. Soon after that Charla Percy and her husband arrived, then Catherine Trainer, and Consuelo Cole, the new Spanish teacher, and Dr. Coburn and his wife, Dr. Klein, and their three hulking teenagers. In the middle of this the phone rang and Georgia disappeared into the closet for half an hour. When she emerged, she was so excited that Rue looked at her and thought to herself, My God, he's asked her to marry him.

She only hoped Henry hadn't noticed. Henry was serving sherry and Bloody Marys by now. Georgia, keeping her own counsel, became a whirlwind in the kitchen since her tempura was not yet cooked, and she still had to make the condiments for the curries. Rue was in and out of the kitchen, passing crudités, refilling the platter with hot cheese puffs, refilling the ice bucket. Each time she came in, she studied her daughter, who was flying with inspired efficiency from saute pan to mixing bowl, chopping board to oven. Georgia was brimming with excitement and happiness, and she didn't want to talk to her mother.

Well. She'll choose her time, thought Rue. I'll have to wait.

At last Charles and Craig MacEwan arrived from church. Rue met them at the door. "Are you full of Christmas spirit?" she asked. Craig was the parish administrator, and it was his job to distribute the turkeys and presents that had been collected for needy families.

"Half full," said Charles.

"Half empty," said Craig.

"Did you have enough presents?" Rue asked.

"We have a hundred left. We'll save them for next year." They were shaking off their wet raincoats and stuffing scarves into their sleeves and wiping their feet. Henry appeared as if by magic with a tray with two drinks.

"The one with the celery is the Bloody Mary," he said. Craig took it and said, "Bless you, my child."

Charles took the Bloody Shame. Craig said, "There was a woman who came in and said, 'Do you have my stuff?' We said what's your name and she showed us a welfare card. We said no, so she showed us another, and another. She had five welfare cards. She was listed as having twelve children when she has two. There were eighteen boxes of presents there for her."

Craig had finished his drink. "It took her so long to assemble it all that by the time she was ready, her car had been towed."

Rue laughed, appalled.

"Guess what kind of car. A '91 Jaguar convertible."

"Have another drink," said Rue to Craig.

"Thank you, I intend to."

"Will the cook say grace?" said Henry.

They all stood around the table, which was covered with hot dishes, while the sideboard was lined with salads and relishes brought by the guests.

"Which cook?" said Rue.

"The one who cooks meat," said Henry.

They bowed their heads. "We thank you," said Rue, "for all your goodness to us. We thank you for our health, for our friendships, for your love and for each other's. We think today of all those who have less than we do, and we thank you for perhaps the greatest blessing of all, the gift of being able to give. For these and all thy many gifts, Lord, make us truly thankful. Amen."

"Amen," chorused the table, the chairs scraped back, and everyone sat except for Henry, who was carving. There were many thoughts around the table as people digested the grace and prepared to digest the food. The three hulking teenagers were wondering what all that vegetable-looking stuff was at Georgia's end of the table and hoping the goose would go around. Malone Dahl was thinking that one of the hulking teenagers was quite cute. David Dahl was hoping his mother wouldn't make him eat any raw tomato. Catherine Trainer was thinking it was indeed blessed to be able to give, and she hoped her nephews in New York City would like the bird house she had sent them. Dr. Coburn was thinking how much he liked Brussels sprouts, and Dr. Klein was thinking how much she liked latkes and wishing there would be some. She hadn't done much about Hanukkah this year, and she wished she had a wife who could cook.

Henry said, "Georgia, what would you have said if we let you say grace?"

"Well, of course, I would have asked that all the wicked people at the table wearing leather and eating animals would learn to stop it, and . . ."

"Thank you, that's what I thought. We'll give you another chance next year."

"Would you like some eggplant curry?" Georgia said to the youngest hulk, who was nearest her. It shook its head briefly no.

"Eggplant makes him throw up," offered its brother.

The oldest hulk, which had a tattoo on its wrist, said "What is grace for?"

Its father looked shocked.

"You know what grace is for . . . we say grace at Thanksgiving and Christmas. . . ."

"I know we do it, but I don't know what it's for. If its important, why do we only do it then? If it isn't, why do we do it at all?"

"I think that's a good question," said Henry. "Is this thing all dark meat, dear?"

"Yes, Henry."

The hulk with the tattoo said, "I'm not like, being rude. I want to know. Is it an incantation? Like, magic? How is it supposed to work?"

"What's your tattoo for?" asked his father crossly.

"Decoration," said the hulk, as if he had now heard a truly stupid question.

"Grace is not decoration," said Rue. "But I don't know if it's magic. Although I'm all for magic where I find it."

"Perhaps," said Charla, "we can arrive at a definition by elimination."

Atta girl, thought Rue. That's a teacher.

"I don't think it's incantation," said Georgia, "but it's ritual. The question is ritual what?"

Dishes were passing hand to hand now. Those who wanted wicked goose flesh were passing their plates to Henry. Charla and Georgia were hoping to have the tempura all to themselves.

"What does ritual mean?" Malone asked. She had decided that the hulk with the tattoo was the cutest, really.

"Should we get a dictionary?" said Dr. Coburn.

"Oh, heavens no, that would spoil the fun," said Henry.

"Ritual is something that is repeated in particular ways at particular times."

"That's all? Just things you repeat?"

"Like 'Who stole the cookie from the cook—ie jar?'"

"No, not like that," said Georgia. "It's something that symbolizes a meaning."

"Spiritual or ceremonial," said Dr. Coburn, feeling with relief that they were getting somewhere.

"But if you have no idea what the meaning is, then the ritual won't work."

"Now wait, that's arguable," said Henry. "When me and my friends go out in the woods and beat on drums and talk about what shits our fathers were . . ."

"My friends and I, Daddy."

"Oh, you go in for drumming too?"

"This conversation is deteriorating," said Rue.

"Speaking of drumming," said Georgia, "I thought our grace today was full of meaning."

All eyes turned toward her. This sounded as if it was going to be interesting. Uh-oh, thought Rue, here it comes.

"Did you, dearie?"

"Yes. I've noticed something since I've been away. I've noticed that people who feel blessed and lucky are the ones who aren't always watching their backs or saying 'I've got mine, Jack.' The ones who have always been lucky and safe and had enough of everything are the ones who dare to keep giving things away. And who dare take risks. It's the ones who feel pinched and unsafe and mean who hunch over their bowls and snarl when people come near."

Oh my god, thought Rue, she's not getting married, she's going to join a cult. She's going to join Mother Teresa. We're never going to see her again.

The others listened expectantly. They could tell she was going somewhere, they just couldn't guess where.

"It's the people who haven't felt lucky, and blessed, who have to say Me First, and I Win, who are always looking for systems to keep them safe, who think they aren't all right unless they're beating somebody else." Her eyes were bright. She was full of passionate conviction.

Rue was tearing apart inside. On one hand, she was fiercely proud of Georgia. On the other hand, she was terrified that her beloved only child was about to take a vow of silence and become a nun.

"That's very well put, Georgia," said Henry.

"Yes, it is," murmured Emily. She was unable to take her eyes from Georgia's face. It was as if she were seeing Cricket again for the first time.

Georgia took a deep breath. She was smiling as if she would bubble over. "So . . ." she said, "I have something to say."

That much had long since been evident to all.

"You always taught me . . ." she looked to her mother, and then to her father ". . . you always taught me that we have an obligation to use our gifts. To find the thing that we can do that nobody else can do."

From opposite ends of the table, Henry and Rue nodded at Georgia. Then they looked at each other. Henry had finally gotten out from behind the eight ball. What the hell is going on? his eyes asked Rue.

"So," said Georgia, "I have to say truly that the world is full of sopranos with well-trained voices who want to sing Santuzza. And in the long run it won't matter if it's me or somebody else. But no one can write the songs I'm writing. No one can sing the new music we're going to make."

"We?" said Henry.

"So Jonah and I are leaving school. We're starting a band called Brain in a Jar," said Georgia.

You are carrying this too far," said Henry, coldly furious. They were sitting in their bedroom, talking in low tones to keep from waking Georgia. It was hours past their usual time for sleep, and the room was cold. Rue was wearing a nightgown and bathrobe and a pair of Georgia's aerobics socks. Henry was naked under his bathrobe. It was the first, and worst, fight they had had in many years.

"I think she has a right to make her own mistakes. It's her life," said Rue softly. Her voice was almost pleading. She was horrified to feel so far from him, and part of her wished he *would* behave like a Victorian patriarch, and simply forbid Georgia to leave school.

"If she was four, and she wanted to light her hair on fire or bring a toaster into the bathtub with her, would that be her right?"

"She's not four."

"But she's not right! She's infatuated with this Whale fellow, she's thinking with her . . ."

Rue interrupted him. "I don't think you're qualified to say that."

"Qualified! Who do you think you're talking to? I'm her father, what kind of qualifications do I need?

"You would have to be her. She. You would have to be nineteen."

"Rue, I know this is a long-standing principle of yours, everyone gets to decide for himself who to be and what path to follow, but sometimes children need to be protected from themselves. When she was little, there were times when we shut her in her room and told her to stay there until she could control herself. This is one of those moments! She's talking about changing the course of her life in a way she can never undo, and she hasn't even *thought* about the consequences!"

"She has now, since we spent the whole evening yelling at her."

"We didn't yell at her, and she didn't think at all. All she did was tell us the decision was made. Do you think, if she drops out now, and two years from now she gets sick of greasy spoons and sleeping bags and she wants to go back to Juilliard and have a grown-up professional life, do you think they are going to take her back? Of course not, they're going to give her place to someone who's shown some commitment, some vocation!"

"We don't know that. They might grant her a leave of absence."

"She isn't asking for one. She's dropping out." He picked up a small book that sat on the table between them, held it in midair between finger and thumb, then opened the fingers. The book dropped. What had been where it belonged, ready for use, now lay on the floor, face-down, with pages crumpled, and Rue had to fight to resist picking it up.

"You talk about gifts, Rue. You talk about people's obligation to use their god-given gifts. That girl has an incredible set of pipes, and she has a brain and she has an ear. She could be Jessye Norman, with proper training . . ."

"She doesn't want to be Jessye Norman."

"She did last week, and she may next month."

"I wish you wouldn't yell at me, Henry, this isn't my idea."

"I can't help it. It *is* your idea, as much as any one else's. You've been telling her since she was in Pampers that it's her life to do what she wants with."

"That's not fair. I never told her that without also making it clear how responsible she is to all the people who are affected by what she does."

"Is she showing that she heard that part?"

"Some things have to be learned, not just received."

"Oh, bull. You just can't back down because this is a page from your sermon. And because you pander to her, because you can't bear to be at odds with her."

This was true, and Rue knew it, though she didn't care for the choice of words. She felt so profoundly cold at the moment that she couldn't tell if it was from the chill in the room or some ague of misery that had come to live in her bones forever. She couldn't bear being at odds with Georgia, but it was no worse to her than being at odds with her husband.

"If we acted together," said Henry, "if we showed a united

front, and we both told her we didn't want her to do this, we might be able to get her to finish the year. And by then everything might have changed. She might change her mind, she might convince us . . . but if you won't stand by me, then she's gone."

"It's not a matter of standing by you! I'm listening and I'm trying to agree with you, but I can't! I don't! I think she has a right to do this, whether I think it's a mistake or not!"

"Does she have a right to be supported while she does it?"

"Not a right, no. I wouldn't want to think of her in want. . . ."

Henry stood up and began to pace. The bare floor was cold on his feet; Rue noticed he confined himself to the area of the rug.

"That's it, I see it. You are going to let her commit professional suicide, and then you're going to send her money behind my back."

"Are you willing to starve her into submission?"

"I would hardly choose those words for it. I would give her the opportunity to feel the consequence of her actions."

Rue stared at him. She suspected, with an awful misgiving, that he was absolutely right. That that's what they should do . . . and that she wasn't strong enough to do it. That if Georgia asked her for money, Rue would be unable to deny her.

As if he could read her mind, Henry said, "You think this is principle, Rue, but it isn't. It's just sick. And I'm going to sleep in the guest room. I'm too angry to get into bed with you, and I have to sleep, I'm on call tomorrow."

And he walked out. In a moment, Rue ran after him. She gathered an armful of blankets from the linen closet and went into the guest room, where Henry had just discovered that the bedside lamp was unplugged. In rising from plugging it in, he banged his head painfully on the corner of the bedside table. Then he pushed the switch and found it still didn't go on. Rue put the blankets on the foot of the bed and went back to the closet for a bulb. She returned and handed it to him. He took it and screwed it in, handing her the dead one. Then he got into bed, still wearing his bathrobe, either too cold or too angry to appear naked before her, and turned off the light again. Rue stood by the door, hoping he would at least say good night. But he didn't want to talk to her anymore, and standing there, shivering with shock and exhaustion, she wasn't sure it was such a good idea anyway.

She flipped the wall switch that turned out the overhead light, went out, and shut the door behind her.

Sometime after dawn, which was late at that season, Henry, with feet like ice trays, slipped into bed with Rue and put his arms around her. She had been too miserable to sleep soundly, and instead was floating in a slightly lurid half-sleep, missing him, and apologizing to him, and feeling that he was unreasonable and completely wrong, or else that she was, but wishing he would just come back.

"I had a terrible dream," Henry whispered.

"Did you, sweetheart?" She turned and put her arms around him so that she could feel him all the way down to his cold feet. He hugged her as if he was amazed to discover he still had that option.

"I dreamed I was marrying somebody else. I didn't love her, and she didn't love me, and you were right there, and I knew you were the love of my life, but you didn't do anything to stop me, and I had to go on even though I knew it was a terrible mistake."

Rue stroked his hair and pulled the covers up to his chin.

"Did you know her? The one you married?"

"I don't think so. She was young and built like a fireplug. It was terrible. And I knew that for the rest of my life, instead of her understanding me, I would have to explain my life to her. And even if she listened, even if she understood, then she'd start explaining *her* life to *me*. I'd have to go spend Christmas with her, in places like Texas, and meet her family, and they wouldn't care anything about *The Pickwick Papers*. It was really terrible."

"It sounds terrible," she said. They held each other.

"I woke up and couldn't figure out where you were."

"I know," she said.

That was enough to say for the moment. They held each other, and presently felt finally warm again for the first time in many hours, and then slept again.

A little later, Henry was up, showered, and dressed for work, before Rue realized he was gone. He sat on the edge of the bed with a present wrapped in Santa Claus paper in his hand. Rue sat up.

"I was so mad at you last night I forgot to give you your present."

"I thought the fancy Screwpull was my present."

"No." He handed her the package and watched her open it.

In it were the cassettes he had secretly been recording for her all fall. They were carefully labeled Ovid's *Metamorphoses* read by Henry Shaw. They both looked at the title and started to laugh. Rue kissed him, and they clung to each other.

"Henry—I love you," she said.

"I know."

eorgia left them on December twenty-ninth, a week before they expected her to go. She wanted to spend New Year's Eve with Jonah.

Henry and Rue had scarcely known a happy moment since Christmas Day. Rue had come to understand that a strong source of pain to Henry was that his little one, two years shy of her legal majority, was going to leave the dorm, pack her duffel bags, and move into some sort of slum flat with a hairy man. She was going to put her socks and underwear into his drawers. She was going to cook for him, or maybe he was going to cook for her. They were going to treat each other as if they were a couple, as he and Rue were a couple. It caused Henry a piercing sorrow, and he and Rue had somehow managed to keep that aspect of his distress completely out of the conversation. He knew it wasn't rational or especially noble, but that didn't mean the pain wasn't real.

They had learned a good deal more about Jonah in the awkward days since Georgia's announcement. He was twenty-three, which sounded old to be a college senior. He had a lot of hair, they gathered, and was more than ordinarily pierced, though when Henry wanted to know exactly what was meant by that, Georgia laughed.

"Why won't you tell me?"

"Why do you want to know? You'll just start in about ritual self-mutilation, and scarification."

"Well, isn't that what it is?"

"No."

"Then what is it?"

"Daddy, why do you even ask? You're not going to understand."

She was right. He wasn't. And yet, he felt terribly hurt and balked, like a person standing at a door that has always opened at a touch, and hearing someone on the other side turn the latch to lock it. He couldn't understand if she didn't even *try* to explain, could he? Could he? So why wouldn't she try?

The answer was painfully obvious.

"Doesn't it hurt her too?" Henry asked Rue. "Why does she seem to take pleasure in telling us she's going where we can't follow her?"

"Think of all the times when she was little we closed doors to her, understood things she couldn't, and went places without her, leaving her behind."

"But we didn't do it *in order* to hurt her."

"We did it."

Henry and Rue spent some time talking about their own rages at their parents when they were Georgia's age. "That was different. Our parents were horrors," said Henry.

"I grant you. But maybe we are too."

They learned that Jonah's parents had been divorced when he was twelve, and that he had been an emancipated minor since he was fifteen. He had left Brooklyn and lived over a classmate's garage in New Jersey. He went to high school in New Jersey and turned the friend's garage into a recording studio. In an odd detail, Georgia informed them that he had made quite a good living performing as a magician. There were two expensive restaurants in New York that let him go from table to table performing sleight of hand for the customers. He collected tips.

"And that was it? His parents didn't support him?"

"I think his dad helped a little, sometimes."

So. Jonah, widely thought to be a genius, was as well a magician. It figured.

When they asked if he was handsome, she'd say, "Sort of," and laugh. Clearly, wildly attractive to her. They gathered he didn't read much. He was extremely streetwise, she said, which seemed like a good thing to be if you were a kid running wild in New York.

He had never lived in the dorms at Juilliard. Too expensive. He had an apartment in the East Village, above a head shop. Henry was appalled to learn that such things still existed. Jonah did not drink at all, Georgia said, but she conceded some marijuana.

"Would your friends like him?" Henry asked.

"Which friends?"

He named the girls and boys she had gone to Country with. Georgia conveyed that this was typical of parents in their dotage, to assume that your friends from your babyhood were your real friends because they belonged to the part of your life they had shared. But she deigned to answer. "Everyone likes Jonah, Daddy. Everyone."

He asked if Jonah had ever been in trouble with the law. Rue expected Georgia to resent this question hotly, but she didn't. She just said no.

They asked these questions and mulled over the answers, looking for clues that would make it all right. They wanted some sort of message from Georgia's magician. Word that he loved Georgia, that he would protect her. No word came. It seemed as likely that Georgia was supposed to take care of him. Her ideas of what their housekeeping would be like were sketchy at best. Similarly, her grasp of what the bills would be, and who would pay them. They had an advance from the record company. Georgia herself hoped to get some session work.

"What's that mean?"

"Recording sessions, Daddy. Commercials. Back-up vocals." Spoken as if it were a chore to have to explain every last jot and tittle. Couldn't they infer anything? Were they even trying to?

So, she wasn't even asking them for money. She thought she could drop out of school, out of the ring of safety they had provided her all her life, and get along on magic. "Or on her own talent," Rue pointed out halfheartedly. But she knew Georgia was leaving her in a way she had never expected. She stood up against Henry for Georgia's right to choose, but she was doing herself no favors with Georgia. Georgia was going, no matter what they did. The more they tried to hold her, protect her, prepare her, remind her that she carried their hearts with her wherever she went, the more eager she was to be gone.

And then, much sooner than they expected, but not before they began to wonder how much more they could take, she *was* gone. She left them Jonah's address; he didn't have a phone. Henry asked if he could pay to have one put in, and Georgia just rolled her eyes.

Henry actually called Juilliard to ask about Jonah Wachtel,

beginning to fear that he didn't exist. How could a person with no telephone number be shown to exist? He did indeed, said the woman in the office. One semester shy of completing his degree, he was majoring in conducting and minoring in composition. Was he on scholarship, Henry had asked, knowing that there was no way on earth the woman should give him this information. But the woman was feeling chatty. The office was closed for vacation; she was just the bookkeeper, doing some overtime filing. As such, she was in a position to know that Jonah Wachtel paid all his fees himself, often in cash.

"Oh Christ," said Henry to Rue, "he's a drug dealer."

Rue was so heartsick that she couldn't think of anything to say. She and Henry had never been farther apart, not since the day they met. They couldn't comfort each other, and they hadn't made love in a week. She wanted to believe what Georgia believed. She wanted to believe she would be happy, that she was off on a great adventure, that she would be back soon full of tales and triumphs, and their house would be full of happiness again.

Henry saw Rue as delusional. And he believed that if she had seen this situation straight, that Georgia could not have held out against them. That she would have been angry perhaps, but she would have stayed in school until June, and by then, everything would have been different. His daughter would not be shacking up with a hairy much-pierced magician in some slum where they didn't have telephones. What if he had to reach her? What if there were an emergency?

Chandler Kip and Terry Malko were having lunch at the Cafe on the Square, the fanciest restaurant in Seven Springs, at the table where Henry had once given Rue lunch on her birthday. They had each, in different ways, had a fairly upsetting Christmas.

Chandler's mother, touchy and overtalkative, was not getting along well with Bobbi. She kept developing new food allergies and phobias, and no sooner did Bobbi catch up with them than she changed the rules and was unable to eat something else. So far there had been shellfish, chocolate, dairy products containing lactose, then all dairy products ("mucus-producing," Mrs. Kip announced at the table, making Missy gag), anything with wheat or corn flour in it, and the flesh of animals raised on hormones. For the last week Bobbi had been driving into Santa Barbara where a health-food store sold venison, rabbit, and beefalo, frozen in gray brick-like lumps, that were range-raised and grass-fed. Missy said the venison tasted like fish and wouldn't eat it. Mrs. Kip, triumphant, wouldn't eat it either, saying Bobbi had cooked it wrong. Chandler had to gnaw away at it, smiling, and last night he had given up and swallowed a piece that was too tough to chew and nearly choked to death. Bobbi had to perform the Heimlich maneuver. It was humiliating, but thank god he had married a stewardess, who knew how to do these things.

Chandler had also had an unhappy encounter with his son, Randy. He'd gone to visit him at the gas station two days before Christmas, and taken him his presents. Randy was sullen. Chandler had asked if he was spending Christmas with his mother, and he said of course not, she was four hundred miles away.

"There are buses," Chandler had said.

"I only have two days off. You know I work, Dad."

"There are airplanes."

"Are there airlines that give scholarships?" Randy asked rudely.

"I'd have paid for you to go," Chandler protested. "All you had to do was ask."

"Really? And how was I supposed to know that?"

Chandler was silent. He had certainly refused to help Randy with money at other times, when he thought he could force him into line that way or simply because he was angry at him and wanted his power acknowledged. He should have thought to ask Randy what his plans were. He felt rotten that he hadn't.

"Is it too late?"

"Is Christmas Eve too late? I'd say so, Dad. I told Phil I'd mind the store since I didn't have anywhere to go. He took his family to Hawaii."

Chandler asked what Randy *was* going to do, and he said, "Oh, maybe I'll put on my turquoise polyester suit and clean my fingernails and go to LA for a big Christmas dinner at the Beverly Hilton. Isn't that what you'd expect a gas pump guy to do?"

Chandler didn't answer. As he turned to leave, Randy said, "Hey Dad, look, I gave myself a present!" Chandler looked to see that on his knobby wrist his son was wearing an ID bracelet. It was engraved Randy Toogood.

"Very nice," Chandler said, and left, feeling a soul-killing sense of failure he could discuss with no one.

Randy knew why he wasn't invited to their house. He knew perfectly well. It didn't make it any better. The boy was twenty years old. He had been alone on Christmas. Meanwhile, Terry was happily sharing his Christmas ordeal.

The Malkos' Christmas had been noisy and expensive. Margee's whole family came to stay with them, and Margee and her mother had a painful relationship. Nevertheless, Margee insisted that her parents have the master bedroom and that she and Terry sleep on the convertible in the TV room. Terry had spent the entire two weeks needing a different tie or a fresh pair of socks that he couldn't get at, because Grammy or Grampy was taking a nap, or a bath, or "having a lie down." Throughout the visit their son Glenn was impossible, acting smart with his grandparents. He spent half his time, it seemed, over at Kenny Lowen's house. "I think the kid's a juvenile delinquent," Terry said. "It must be genetic. He's like the leader of their Tong."

"Can't you keep them apart?"

"Are you kidding? They have bikes. They have money for the bus. The only way I could keep them apart would be to move to New York. Bradley and Corinne are completely clueless. I told them that two different times when Kenny had been at our house, the level in the gin bottle went down about three inches. One of those gallon bottles? You could see them look at me, like, poor guy, he doesn't know his own son is stealing booze from him. But kindly explain to me why it only happens when Kenny's been there?"

Chandler had had times like that with Randy—more than he cared to remember. Would Randy have turned out different if he'd gone to private school? Small point in asking now. Chandler's first wife didn't speak private school, nor had Chandler then.

"Wonderful food," said Terry.

Chandler nodded. Terry was expertly boning his fish so that the spine and ribs came out all in one piece, like a xylophone. Chandler's own plate looked as if his fish had been blown apart by a bomb. Every bite he took had slivers of bone in it. He felt that trying to eat it now expressed some sort of death wish, and he couldn't face another choking episode within twenty-four hours.

"Speaking of trouble," said Terry, "did you hear that Georgia Shaw is dropping out of Juilliard?"

"No," said Chandler, putting down his knife and fork. "Where'd you hear that?"

"Margee heard it at Tagliarini's. She's dropping out to live with her hippie boyfriend and join his band."

Chandler began to laugh. "Oh my god. You mean Our Leader, the perfect mother, is having trouble with the Perfect Child?"

Terry agreed this was unexpected; he knew Georgia fairly well and thought she *was* very nearly a perfect child. In fact, the way Georgia had turned out was one of the strongest reasons people had trusted Rue's judgment so thoroughly when it came to their own children.

"Margee says that Rue is putting a good face on it. 'Isn't it perfect, the darling is moving to the East Village with some druggy bass player, what an adventure.' But Henry has gone ballistic."

"Well, no kidding," said Chandler thoughtfully, abandoning his attempt to eat altogether. He thought about the terrible moment in a marriage when you disagree about a kid. The pain. The way the fight turns into ego, the way I was brought up against the way you were brought up. He pictured screaming fights at the Shaw's house, plates smashing. It didn't make him any more sympathetic. It affected him as weakness always did: it made him want to kill her.

When Terry finished his fish and they'd ordered coffee, Chandler said, "I want to talk to you about this curriculum thing." He gave him a version of Rue's reaction to the decision of the Curriculum Committee. Terry listened and nodded.

"I'll tell you frankly how I feel about it," said Chandler. "Let me run this up the flagpole."

The waiter brought their coffee and cream, and Terry sent him back for skim milk.

Chandler said, "The Lowens are fed up with Catherine Trainer, and so are a lot of people. I am. She's an irrational ditz, and I wouldn't want her teaching *my* kid, and that trick she pulled, accusing the Sales of child abuse, was the deal breaker as far as I'm concerned. In the meantime, the McCanns are upset with Charla Percy, and I don't know what kind of excuse you can make for an ass like Blair Kunzelman. Now, that's a lot of unhappy Board members. The fact is, and you know and I know it, that in business there comes a time when a person goes stale in the job. Anyone can see that a new head at Country would get rid of the dead wood on the faculty. Any new head would. So why won't Rue Shaw?"

"There *are* reasons," Terry pointed out. "As a lawyer, I have to say that firing has to be done right. And even when it's done right, it's hell on the morale of the other employees."

"But the real reason," said Chandler, "is they're friends of hers. She hired them. They socialize together. She's a woman and she doesn't want to hurt anybody's feelings. Now, let me run this by you. Every goddamn time I ask Rue to do something she doesn't want to do, she stops the conversation cold and says, 'You'd have to fire me.'"

Terry sat up straighter.

"Boom, end of conversation. 'Drop it, or fire me,' and then 'have a cookie,' she says. Like it's unthinkable. Like it's her school. But I say it's *our* school. *We* pay the tuitions, we sit on the Board.

Where did everyone get the idea that the school won't run without Rue Shaw?"

"Interesting," said Terry. "But what grounds could you find for firing her? She's been there a long time and the school is in very good health."

"I think the length of her tenure is a problem. Is she the right person for the challenge of the nineties? I'm not sure she is. She's too attached to her own way of doing things, and these are changing times. You have be ready to change with them."

Terry thought about it. At last he said, "Firing a head can be very upsetting in a school. And Chandler, it's a hell of a lot of work. Have you thought of that? Searches? Interim heads? And guess who most of it would fall on."

"I'm perfectly aware of that. I'm just not afraid of it. I think it might be good fun to shake things up, roll the dice. Personnel is a long suit of mine. I think I could find someone I can work with."

Terry was silent again, thoughtful. He was a trial lawyer, and he liked action. He liked conflict and tumult; he often said he liked to be "where the plates rub together." But he also liked Rue, although they had had their run-ins. And he couldn't help thinking of Chandler's in-house counsel, Oliver Sale, who struck him as one of the strangest birds he'd ever met. Terry thought the guy was just too thin-skinned, too odd and angry to be a good lawyer no matter how bright he was. So he wondered exactly *how* strong Chandler was on personnel. Finally, he said, "But you have to have grounds. You can't just take someone's life work away."

"That's not so hard. This curriculum review thing, for instance. 'The Board finds her intractable. Won't respond to reasonable requests for information, for accountability. Won't report to the Board, even when asked.'"

Terry began to see what he had in mind.

"Interesting," he said, thinking it was daft, and wondering what was driving Chandler.

In the first week of January, Emily Goldsborough was putting shelf paper in the kitchen cabinets when Malone and Lyndie came downstairs. Jennifer Lowen had gone to Baja for New Year's with her family, so Malone had nobody else to play with. She and Lyndie had been riding their bikes outside. Malone was very jealous of the bike Lyndie got for Christmas, which she said was like totally cool.

"Mom, can we make pull taffy?"

Emily said sure. Malone started telling Lyndie how totally cool pull taffy was.

"Haven't you ever made taffy?" asked Emily, climbing down from the counter.

"I had a box of saltwater taffy once," she said.

"That's different," said Emily. She began to get out the sugar and lemon extract and to look for the candy thermometer. Then she read the recipe aloud step by step for the girls, as they took turns measuring and pouring.

The girls knelt on chairs beside the stove so they could stir constantly and watch the sugar water turn to syrup. Emily, back on the counter with her shelf paper, kept warning them to watch the thermometer.

"If you get it too hard, you'll have brittle, not taffy. We did that once, by mistake. When it cooled, it got so hard you had to break it with a hammer." Lyndie seemed engrossed, as if being introduced to alchemy.

"Okay Mom! It's at Soft Crack!" Malone shouted, turning off the heat in a panicky way.

"I'll be right there."

"No Mom! It's ready now!" Malone hopped on one leg.

Emily climbed down. Lyndie watched, mystified, as Emily took off her watch and her rings. Malone too took off the silver ring with tiny turquoises that her father had given her for her tenth birthday. "Take off your ring, Lyndie, and give it to her. And you better take off your bracelet too." Lyndie looked at Emily, questioning. Emily nodded.

Emily turned the taffy out onto a buttered cookie sheet to cool. Then she turned to the girls and with soft butter, greased their hands and wrists so the taffy wouldn't stick to them as they worked it. She did Malone first, so Lyndie could see. Malone accepted these ministrations with professional calm. Then Lyndie offered her hands. Emily started buttering, but Lyndie flinched. Emily turned over her left hand to examine the underside of the arm. There was a long red angry welt there.

Emily reached as if to touch it and Lyndie pulled her arm away.

"Is it very sore?" she asked. "What happened?"

"It's not that sore, I just don't like to touch it."

Lyndie held her hands out again. Carefully, Emily finished buttering her.

"Here, let me roll up your sleeves for you." Lyndie obediently stood while Emily did this, taking care not to touch the welt. Lyndie and Malone, with their buttered hands in the air before them, looked like surgeons ready for the operating theater.

Emily tested the taffy and found it still too hot.

"What happened there, Lyndie? Did you burn yourself?"

Lyndie said, "I was rude to my father at Christmas dinner."

Emily turned to look at her. Lyndie seemed blandly unaware of any non sequitur.

"So then what?"

"So, they sent me to my room, but I wouldn't stay there."

Emily tested the taffy again. It was still hot to handle, but she cut the lump in half with a buttered knife. She handed one lump to Malone, who sucked in her breath and passed it from hand to hand.

"Too hot?"

"Just a teeny bit."

Emily picked up the second half, juggling it for a moment. "I think it's all right now." She handed it to Lyndie.

"Now you just keep pulling, like this, until it gets so you can't see through it. And it gets stiffer." Malone demonstrated, and Lyndie, fascinated, copied her movements, pulling her taffy out in a thick rope, then smushing it back together and pulling again.

"When it gets really stiff, we'll put it all together and both pull, like a tug of war."

"Cool!" said Lyndie. The girls worked away.

"So you didn't want to stay in your room?" prompted Emily, trying to sound casual.

"No. I didn't like being locked in. I was afraid the house would burn down."

Shocked, Emily kept her mouth shut, hoping Lyndie would keep talking, as kids do in the back seat of a car, as if driving made you deaf.

Malone asked, "So what did you do?"

"I kept screaming and pounding on the door until they let me out."

"While they were eating dinner?" Malone was impressed.

"Well, they were almost finished."

"So they let you out?"

"But then they were really mad because I was like yelling, "If you don't let me out I'll break the fucking door down," and I was pounding on it and kicking it, and my father was like right outside the door." Both girls started to laugh. "He'd come to let me out. And I'm like, 'I'll break the fucking door down' at the top of my lungs. He was pretty mad when he opened it." She suddenly sobered at the thought of that.

"So . . . then what happened?" Emily finally asked. And Lyndie seemed suddenly to remember Emily was there.

"So . . . he let me out."

"I mean, the welt."

Lyndie shrugged.

"This is getting pretty stiff, Mom. Do you think it's ready?"

Emily looked at it. "I think you can combine." Excited, ready for the next stage, they pressed their two lumps together. Then Malone held on tight while Lyndie pulled away from her. They both began to laugh.

"Don't forget to twist it as you pull," said Emily. Malone, remembering, showed Lyndie how to twist and braid the strands as they pulled.

Emily went to get powdered sugar in which to roll the finished rope of taffy before they cut it into bite-sized pieces. She somehow knew she wasn't going to get the rest of the story. She didn't want to push, for fear of saying the wrong thing.

She was glad the girls were getting along so well. She'd had a painful time listening to Malone describe the presents Jennifer Lowen got for Christmas and was just as glad the Lowens were out of town for a while. As she finished the shelf paper she could hear peals of laughter coming from Malone's room, and when the girls piled down the stairs again to get Cokes, Malone asked, "Can Lyndie spend the night?"

Emily said, "Of course. We'd love to have you, Lyndie. Why don't you call your mom and ask?"

So Lyndie went to the phone, and they watched as her face fell as she listened to her mother on the other end of the line, and then she hung up and said her dad was on his way to pick her up.

"Why?" Malone asked. Lyndie had closed in and shut down. "I don't know," said Lyndie. And suddenly there was nothing on the list of things that had been fun all afternoon that she felt like doing anymore. So the girls went out and sat in the driveway, and then Oliver drove up and swung Lyndie's bike into his trunk, and the two drove away.

"She forgot to take her taffy," said Emily. She had put Lyndie's share in a plastic freezer box, each layer dusted with powdered sugar so the candies wouldn't stick together.

Malone followed her mother around the kitchen for a while as Emily got ready to make chili for supper. She seemed deflated, as if having the fun of the afternoon let out so suddenly had left her weakened and smaller.

"Do you want to help? There are all these onions to chop," said Emily.

"No, that's all right," Malone sighed, rather missing the point. She sat for a while, looking at the floor.

"Mom?"

"Yes, honey."

"I'm worried about Lyndie."

Emily stopped what she was doing and turned. "You mean the burn?"

"You know what she just told me? While we were outside?"

"What."

"She told me she's afraid to go home because there's a ghost in the house. It's an awful angry ghost that cries all the time, and it wants to hurt people. And she's the only one who can hear it or see it."

"She can *see* it?"

"Well I think so, I know she can hear it. The house will be quiet and suddenly it will be there, right behind her, crying. And it hits her and knocks into her, and tries to hurt her, and whenever she tries to tell her mom and dad how scared she is, they get mad. They think she's lying! She was in the kitchen trying to help, and there was something cooking in one of those black frying pans, the heavy ones, and it was blazing hot and the ghost grabbed her arm and held it against this red hot pan, and when she screamed, her parents were like, 'Goddammit Lyndie, why are you always doing these stupid things, like don't you have eyes,' like she likes hurting herself?"

Emily felt chilled as she listened.

"That's a terrible story, Malone."

"I know! I felt *terrible* watching her drive off! She wanted to stay here! I think her parents are mean. Do you believe in ghosts?"

Emily thought carefully, before saying: "I think there are a lot of things in the world that are harder to understand than some people think."

"I believe in them. I knew a girl at daycamp who saw one. Maybe I should spend the night there. Maybe I would see it too."

"That's very brave of you. I'm not sure I'd be that brave."

"Should I call her? You could take me over."

"It's not polite to invite yourself, honey. You can ask Lyndie when you see her if it would make her feel better to have you sometime, and then if she invites you, we'll see."

Emily was at Rue's door on the morning of the first day of the new term. Rue came in from flag raising, and Emily followed her into her office, saying, "Do you have a minute?"

liver and Sondra Sale sat across the room from each other in Rue's office.

"I know this is painful for you," said Rue, gently.

"Do you?" asked Oliver. His voice was quiet, but his anger was so great, it was frightening. "Do you have any idea what you are doing to this family?"

Rue took a deep breath.

"I don't want to claim to know anything that I don't know. Would you agree with me that Lyndie is showing many symptoms of being a very troubled girl?"

"Do you have any idea what it's like to live with her?" Oliver burst out.

"I'm sure it's difficult."

"You're damned right, it's difficult!"

"Oliver . . . please. I am sorry for anything that I do that adds to the pain this situation is already causing."

"I should fucking hope so. . . . Why the hell are we here, may I ask? What business is this of yours?"

"Can you tell me how Lyndie got a nine-inch burn on her arm?"

"She burned herself on the stove," he said, hissing with contempt for her inability to grasp this simple and utterly mundane fact.

Rue bowed her head and studied her fingers, laced in her lap.

"You are here, to answer your earlier question, because we feel we have seen a change in Lyndie in the last few months. I don't know what is causing it. I was hoping we could talk about some of the possibilities."

Sondra Sale unexpectedly dried her eyes and burst out now, with some passion.

"I'll tell you one thing—that dyke you've got teaching PE! She comes on like Rebecca of Sunnybrook Farm, but she has a temper, believe me! They never know what she's going to do next! It's very upsetting to Lyndie. She has terrible pains in her stomach—that's just since the start of the school year. I think she's getting an ulcer!"

Rue decided that this outburst was so unreasonable it was best ignored. She said, "When a child is as unhappy as Lyndie seems, and when there's a personality change unexplained by obvious stress or trauma . . ."

"We just gave you an explanation, but you're not listening."

"I am listening. But Miss Flower teaches PE to one hundred and twenty-four other children who have not developed ulcers. Received wisdom demands that we examine the system the child lives in."

"System. The system she lives in. Do you mean the family she lives in?" asked Oliver.

"Yes."

"Is that just ours, Mrs. Shaw? Or is it yours too? Does your daughter belong to a system?"

"Yes. Of course, she does."

"And how's it working?"

Oh, thank you, Chandler Kip, thought Rue. "Not very well at the moment. Thank you for your interest. Is there any chance that the three of you would consider family therapy?"

Oliver couldn't stay in his chair. He got up so fast he nearly propelled himself against the wall of the narrow room. He looked like a higher primate in a suit, so full of adrenaline that he wanted to charge across the savannah or rocket up a tree and tear a lemur's head off.

"Family therapy," he boomed. "Are you kidding? This is the only country in the world where you have an angry, vengeful, self-destructive child tearing a family apart and blame the parents!" He turned to stare out the window to the primary playground, where Charla Percy's second grade stood in a circle in the sun, learning Morris dancing.

"Let's not debate that, let's move on. Sondra, are you with me?"

Sondra, weirdly, had been staring at, and had now picked up, a teacher's magazine that was lying on Rue's table. She put it down and said, "Yes. Of course."

"I don't know what is going on in Lyndie's life. She may be in a phase that will pass. She may be in some kind of trouble that one or both of you don't understand. But this much is clear. She is quite symptomatic, to use the professional jargon, for which I apologize. She is sometimes depressed, she can't control her temper, and occasionally hurts others. She is, I agree with you, Sondra, very upset by inconsistency in adult behavior. And she is extraordinarily accident-prone. Every one of the symptoms I've mentioned has been confirmed by several, even many of the adults and children who work with her. And every one of those symptoms is typical of a child who is being abused. I'm afraid I don't have any choice. I am legally compelled to call Child Welfare at this point. I am sorry."

"If you're sorry, why the hell are you going to do it?"

"I meant, I am sorry for the pain you are all in. And I'm sorry not to have the wisdom of Solomon. But I have to do what the law requires. I don't know what is the symptom and what is the cause, but Lyndie needs some kind of help you seem unwilling to get for her. That alone forces my hand."

There was a long, cold silence. Finally, Oliver said, "Would you be doing this if we had gone along with your therapy idea?"

"No, I wouldn't. At least, not immediately. Are you willing to change your mind?"

"Absolutely not."

"May I ask why not?"

"Absolutely not . . . you've done enough for one day." He stood up, and Sondra followed suit, like a whip that's been cracked.

On the second Monday of the term, Chandler Kip walked into Rue's office, unannounced, and dropped a paper on her desk.

It was a report from Child Protective Services. It was written by Myra Dobkin, MSW. She had visited the Sale family and interviewed father, mother, and child. She saw a normal preadolescent with a nice room of her own, two parents who were tense, perhaps, but understandably so, and no reason to pursue the matter further. Chandler stood over Rue, glaring, as she read it. The Sales had withdrawn both their children from The Country School.

"Rue—Mrs. Bathhurst is here," said Emily timidly from the open door. Chandler walked out of the office, leaving the report. The set of his shoulders said I Will Not Forget This.

Martine Bathhurst must have passed him in the hall. She was a frail woman, underweight and defeated-looking. She had curly graying hair and huge eyes. She had one child in the school, an almost pathologically shy seventh grader called Leila. Leila's father had died when she was ten. Martine worked as the hostess at Cafe on the Square and spent everything she had to send Leila to The Country School.

Martine took a small cassette player from her handbag and set it on the desk between her and Rue. She pushed the play button. Rue heard a woman's voice say, ". . . Okay? I'll call you then. All right, bye-bye." Then a dial tone. Martine was staring at the machine, so Rue did too. Next she heard an echoey noise of an open connection and what sounded like muffled words far from the phone. Then a heavily distorted voice said, "Hello, Martine. I'm going to kill your daughter, I watch her everywhere. I know when she's home alone. I'm going catch her and kill her and fuck her when she's dead."

Martine clicked the tape off. "This is the fourth one," she said. "Leila's so frightened she won't sleep in her own bed. She comes to work with me at night and does her homework in the kitchen."

"Play it again," said Rue. When she'd heard it she said, "Do you mind if Mr. Dianda listens?"

Martine shook her head.

When Mike had heard it he said to Rue, "It's not a man, it's a kid." She nodded. Martine did too.

"That's what I thought," she said.

"What is it we hear as he's hanging up? What are those words?" Mike asked. He rewound the tape and listened to the end again and again with the volume up.

"In the background. It's "'Hey you, something . . .'"

Mike shook his head. "I think it's 'Hugh.' 'No, Hugh.'"

They listened again. This time Rue thought she heard the same thing. A voice far in the background, muffled, as if the people in the background had hands over their mouths.

"I have other tapes," said Martine. "I erased the first one, but I got extra cassettes and I've kept the others."

Together they listened to three other tapes. The same message, with minor variations.

"It's the same voice each time," said Rue.

"Definitely."

"Do you know who it is?" Martine asked.

Rue and Mike looked at each other.

"We have an idea," said Rue. "Could I keep these tapes?"

Martine said she could.

"If we can't solve it you should go to the police. But give us a day or two."

Martine agreed. She left, unsmiling.

"Why would they choose Leila?" Rue asked Mike.

"She's weak. She has a Don't Hit Me way about her that makes you want to hit her."

Rue looked at her watch. "Where are they . . . Mrs. Ketchum's class? Good."

Mike went to Lynn Ketchum's class and explained briefly that he needed to talk to a few of the boys, one at a time. It was important that they not be able to compare notes. Lynn understood perfectly and gave a class reading assignment so that there would be no writing or talking that she didn't see.

Mike said "Glenn Malko, could I see you outside, please?" He watched the eyes. Hughie Bache, Jose French, and Robey Hearne couldn't help but glance at each other.

"Glenn," said Mike when he had him outside, "someone has been leaving threatening messages at the Bathhurst house, and I think you know who it is."

Glenn stonewalled emphatically. Gosh, Mr. Dianda, that sounds like a terrible thing, I don't know a thing about it.

Next he asked for Hugh, who said, "Really? I don't know anything about that, but I'll tell you if I hear anything."

"It's funny, it sounds like someone is talking to you on the tape." He saw Hughie lose momentum for a second.

"Me? Talking to me?"

"It sounds like one of your crew saying, 'Hey, Hugh.'"

A pause. "I can't explain that Mr. Dianda. I don't know anything about it." Mike let him go.

Next was Robey Hearne, a nice kid, a Beta male, who was sometimes allowed to tag along with the Alphas. When Mike said, "I think you know who's doing it," he looked stricken.

"Me?"

"Yes. I think you know. Don't you?"

Robey looked panicky.

"I don't know if you know Leila, Robey, but she and her mother live alone, and they are both very very frightened. And I think you also ought to know that if we can't solve this here, within the school community, we will turn the tapes over to the police." Mike held his gaze steadily as he said this.

After a long pause, Robey said, "I wasn't there, but I heard about it."

"Did you? Who told you?"

Robey was terribly uncomfortable, but he said, "Glenn and Hughie."

"And did one of them make the calls?"

"No, it was Kenny Lowen."

In Rue's office, Glenn denied it, Hughie denied it, and Kenny Lowen denied it. Robey said he didn't want to get them in trouble, but they had even told him at recess last week what the message was. Rue asked him to repeat it but he couldn't bring himself to say the F-word to her. He had to go outside and tell it to Mr. Dianda. Asked who else knew, he said Jose French, although Jose hadn't been with them either. Eventually Jose confirmed that he too had been told by Glenn and Hughie that they'd watched Kenny make the phone calls. He made them from Hughie's house in the afternoons, before Hughie's parents came home from work. When Rue asked why Leila, none of them knew. Jose said Leila danced with Kenny once at a middle-school dance.

Rue was amazed at the volume of calls that poured in on her that afternoon and evening. There were people whose children had told them disturbing things about Kenny. There were friends of the Lowens who said pointedly that an offense committed away from school and not in school hours was not her jurisdiction. And there were parents and teachers of the eighth grade who were sick of dealing with Kenny and wanted him gone.

The next morning, first thing, she had a visitation from Kenny Lowen, flanked by his mother and father. The two parents looked fiercely at Rue. Corinne Lowen was so upset she was shaking.

"We've had a long talk with Kenny," said Corinne, "and he has something to tell you."

"I'm ready to hear it," said Rue, expecting a confession. The Lowens were ethical people, and she knew they would take this seriously.

With that, Corinne pulled from the paper bag she was carrying a finely bound copy of the Torah. "This Torah was given to Kenny on his bar mitzvah by his grandfather."

Kenny looked at Rue with a face as calm as an untroubled brook. His shining hair was combed neatly across his forehead, black as crow's wings. He wore a clean oxford-cloth shirt, with a Star of David on a chain around his neck. He put the Torah on his knee and his left hand on the Torah. He raised his right hand, as if he were in court. "I swear on this holy book," he said, looking straight at Rue, "that I never made threatening phone calls to the Bathhursts or anybody else." He handed the book to his mother, and she put it back in her paper bag.

The Lowens stared at Rue. She stared back at them.

"Well," she said at last, "I understand." The Lowens rose and walked from the room. When she was sure they were out of the building, she put her head down on her desk and yelled toward the office next to hers, "Miiike!"

Rue was glad she was scheduled for her weekly lunch with Chandler that day. She wanted him to hear this one from her.

"I have to act before the end of the day, but I wanted you to be warned before I do it. They're not going to go quietly," said Rue.

"Now wait a minute. The boy came into your office and swore on a bible, in front of his mother. Isn't the Torah a Jewish bible?"

"It is, but . . ."

"You have no proof except the unsupported accusations of his classmate."

"Classmates. Three. And they all correspond exactly to the tape."

"Maybe they're out to get him."

"Chandler—they're good boys with no reason to lie. Kenny Lowen is a terrorist. If I let this go, there'll be no stopping him. This boy is not in normal bounds."

Chandler remembered that Terry Malko had said to him much the same thing, but he was too angry at Rue for what she had done to Oliver Sale to see anything her way.

"I'll tell you what—if my child came into your office and swore on a Bible in front of her mother and God and everybody, and you didn't believe her, I'd go to court and have you pounded into the ground halfway to China."

"I'm sure they will. But Chandler—he's guilty. He's frightened Leila Bathhurst and her mother out of their wits. He's made anonymous threats against Cynda Goldring and probably stolen money from her. I've got to protect the school, and frankly I've got to protect him. He needs help, and his parents are in complete denial."

"God, I hate this feel-good babble. Could we stick to English?"

"Sorry. I thought that was the clinical term."

"Why don't you give Kenny a warning, and then if he gets caught at anything else, we can talk about something stronger?" Chandler demanded.

"He won't get caught again. We've got one chance, and it's right now."

"And if you take it, the Lowens will sue the shit out of us. The school, Rue. The Board. They'll sue *me*, Rue."

"But . . ."

"Leave it a minute. Let's talk about the curriculum reports," he said.

Rue stared at him.

"I thought we agreed to drop that," she said.

"You agreed, I didn't. The academic policy group has decided that every teacher will write up a full year's curriculum, starting now for the remainder of the year, and report weekly, in writing, on her progress through agreed-upon material."

"Weekly? In writing? Chandler, we've been through this! You can't just add hours a week to their work week. They're already so underpaid that it's embarrassing."

"I don't know what you mean. Our salaries are well within the norm for independent schools in California."

"They're not within the norm for other professionals. Dentists, for instance, or doctors or engineers."

"Oh, don't give me that crap! These are elementary teachers, for christ sake. They spend their days with ten-year-olds! That's why we want to monitor what they're doing!"

"I see. Because we pay them badly, they don't deserve our respect?"

"Respect is paid in coin of the realm. Give me an honest answer, if you can. Is Catherine Trainer bright?"

"I think she's as bright as Marvin Schenker."

Marvin Schenker was a retired local dentist whose great square blue stucco house abutted the campus. He had taken the school to court on the average of once every two years on claims ranging from his tulip beds having been ruined by the cook's cat (the culprit turned out to be a skunk who lived under his porch) to a complaint that a temporary classroom ruined his view, even though the classroom faced only a toolroom and garage, neither of which had any windows.

"Rue—why do people become teachers?"

"Because they love children. Because they remember the difference a good teacher made in their lives, and they want to make that difference to someone else."

"You know what I think?"

"Tell me."

"I think they become teachers because they're like children themselves. They don't really want to compete in the real world. They may be bright, they may not, but they want to live in this cocoon where we're all a family, and you're the mommy and I'm the daddy."

Rue stared at Chandler.

"So you think what we do here is not the real world," she said.

"Not compared to running IBM. Designing rockets. Sitting on the Supreme Court. Frankly, no."

Rue drank some water and ate the last of her asparagus.

"Thank you for sharing. I think at this point we had better agree to disagree."

"If Lloyd Merton had what it takes to get a six-figure job in industry, or to go to med school or law school, would he be pissing his life away in fourth grade making thirty-two thousand dollars a year?"

"Yes! Lloyd Merton graduated Phi Beta Kappa from Yale!"

"He did?"

"Yes, he did!"

"Well, Rosemary Fitch, then."

"Look, if you don't think what we do here matters, then why are you on this Board?

"I do think it matters! Of course it matters! It matters too much to leave it all to people who get paid the same as my cleaning lady!"

"If it matters, why don't you pay them as much as you pay your dentist? I think forty dollars an hour would be about right. More for teaching kids like Kenny Lowen, charge those like root canals."

They were talking so loudly that others in the restaurant were beginning to stare.

"You're talking nonsense," said Chandler rudely.

Rue was wondering why she shouldn't plunge a fork into his heart.

"Will you please call a faculty meeting and explain the new policy?"

"No, I will not. I can't ask my faculty to take an hour a week extra from the time they need for grading and course preparation, and I certainly can't ask for more of their own time. Is there some way we can compromise?"

"Let me put it this way. If you cost the school thousands of dollars in legal fees by firing a student who swore on a bible he was innocent, I'll tell you what part of the budget it's going to come out of."

"You *can't* hold the faculty hostage, we have lawsuit insurance. . . ."

"With a ten-thousand-dollar deductible. You cannot have your way on every issue, all the time. You're the one who brought up compromise."

They stared at each other for a long time. When the waiter appeared, Chandler ordered dessert, so Rue ordered black coffee. The negotiation began.

ue had two shocks before bedtime that night. The first was administered in the parking lot of Tagliarini's mall, where she had walked after school to get a couple of inches of smoked salmon as a treat for Henry. When she came out into the parking lot it was the last light of the short winter afternoon. In the far corner, in front of a yogurt shop that was always empty at this time of year, she saw the dark green Maserati convertible that belonged to Margee Malko. It was the only Maserati in town, as far as Rue knew, certainly the only one with license plates that said GR8HIPS.

In the driver's seat was a man who looked, from the back, like Terry, but Rue couldn't be sure because he was locked in a kiss with a woman who was definitely not little blond Margee. Rue was almost jealous . . . imagine being so in love you would neck in your wife's car in a parking lot the size of the Tagliarini mall, in a town the size of Seven Springs. She had less than no desire to kiss Terry Malko, handsome though he was in a sort of meaty way, but it had been many years since she had been out of-her-mind in love like that. She hoped she didn't know the woman.

She wanted to step backward into the store and into the moment before she saw them. It was such bad news for Margee, for Terry too, for little Chelsea, and for Glenn, who was making a rocky beginning to adolescence.

But having not stepped back fast enough, she found out in the next instant what bad news this was for her too. The woman kissing Terry was Ann Rosen.

Ann Rosen, former president of the Board, was perhaps the smartest person on it, and had for years been Rue's staunchest ally. Mr. Rosen never came to school events, but Rue believed he was an artist of some kind. Ann was a lawyer, as was Terry. And she was running for mayor.

*　　*　　*

"What can they be thinking of? Do they *want* to get caught?" she asked Henry. She wished she'd gotten twice as much smoked salmon. Life was too short to do without, if it was going to be full of this sort of shock.

"I doubt it. In my vast experience, when people do that kind of thing it's because their apertures have closed down to about here," he made a tube with his hands and looked through it at Rue's face, "and the only thing that is real to them is each other."

"You certainly can't choose a place like that to park and imagine no one will see you, unless you're fairly impaired. What am I going to do?"

"Nothing. You're going to pretend you didn't see it and hope it goes away."

"Does that kind of thing *go* away?"

"I think it can. If you can give it up, and if you have nerves of iron."

Rue thought about Margee, about Terry, about Ann, and felt terribly sorry for what was coming.

The second shock of the evening arrived by telephone. Though shock is the wrong word. It was at first just a curiosity, mildly disturbing, but soon forgotten.

The phone rang during dinner. She reached behind her to the phone on the kitchen wall, as she never would have done when Georgia was at home, and answered it. Although Henry was in the middle of a description of the young father whose brain he had trepanned that morning.

Rue held up her hand apologetically. It might be Georgia, the gesture meant. If it's anyone else, I'll get rid of them.

But when she said "Hello?" no one answered.

She said "Hello?" again, and listened. After a time she said, "If you can hear me, I can't hear you. If we have a bad connection, please call back." Then she hung up.

"Nobody there?" Henry asked.

"I thought there was. I could hear breathing," she said. He looked up from his plate.

"Who would do that? Any candidates?"

"Not really," she said, not truthfully. It could certainly be

Kenny Lowen. But it could be any copycat in the school community, since the Leila story was all over town. What she thought of was the look of frustrated rage she'd seen on Jerry Lozatto's face when their suit was heard, earlier in the week, and the judge ruled against the Lozattos.

"You haven't heard the end of this," Jerry had snarled, looking directly at her, as they stood at the bank of elevators after the hearing. When an elevator arrived, Jerry Lozatto had refused to ride down with her and Ann Rosen, who had defended the school.

"What more can he do?" Rue asked Ann.

"Nothing. Forget it," said Ann. "He's a macho asshole."

The phone rang again. Henry rose to answer it for her, but Rue had already picked it up, and this time it was Georgia.

don't understand you," said Henry. They were staring at each other over the coffee cups. They did not yet know—although they would by two in the morning—that Rue was so upset she had accidentally made caffeinated coffee. "She's joined a band called Stool Sample and you think it's great?"

You're right, you didn't understand me."

"I *heard* you say, 'That's great, dearie.'" He imitated her phrasing, deadly accurate.

"She has not joined the band, she's singing back-up vocals for them in the studio. She's being paid a hundred and twenty dollars an hour, that's what I said was great."

"Why didn't you say this whole thing is infantile, which is the truth?"

"Because it's not what I think."

"Stool Sample? You think that's funny?"

"I think it's a *little* funny . . ."

Henry picked up a magazine that was lying beside his place, rolled it into a cylinder, and hit the table with it. Wham! The coffee cups jumped, and Rue flinched.

"She could have sung at the Met! She could have sung *Tosca*, if she just had the . . . the . . . character, the maturity . . . you think you put enough sugar in that?" he asked suddenly.

Rue stopped what she was doing and was surprised to find a spoon in her hand, halfway between the cup and the sugar bowl. How much had she put in? Her hand didn't seem connected to her brain.

She put the spoon down. "You have a mean streak, you know it? It's not as wide as your father's, but it's plenty bitter to the person who bites into it."

Henry got up and began clearing the table. After a while he said, "You didn't know my father. When you met him, he was dead."

"I know what you've described."

"Maybe I lied. Maybe he was an old sweetheart, and I was just a whiny little wuss, complaining."

"I doubt it."

"Why am I the only one who has to apologize for his parents? What about *your* mother, with her cooking sherry bottles full of vodka, too hung over to be polite half the time and everyone pretending she has the flu?"

"Be careful, Henry. There are things that shouldn't be said."

"Like what? Like I'm lucky it's sugar with you and not vodka?"

She looked at him steadily for a long beat. He held her gaze. "Yes," she said. "Like that."

"She tells you she's singing for a group called Stool Sample, and you . . . what is that? What *is* that, Rue, except saying 'Up yours' to you, and to me, and to everything we've tried to do for her?"

"It's life! It's an adventure! She's full of hope, and full of a sense of the ridiculous, and I'm glad she's finding work doing what she wants to do. I'm grateful she's being paid so well. If I got a hundred and twenty dollars an hour I'd be a billionaire."

"You're grateful that you don't have to decide whether or not to send her money, because that's the deal breaker."

"I didn't realize it was a deal breaker, Henry. But now that I know it, I'm very grateful. Yes."

"You know what's wrong with illegal drugs? You know what the real hidden cost is? Twelve-year-olds . . . *ten*-year-olds can make a living on the street, dealing drugs, working for drug dealers. If you have a kid in trouble who can say, 'Fuck you, I'm gone, I'll make my own living,' you can't help them! You have no control, you can't keep them home until they can grow up enough to make decent decisions. . . ."

"Henry, I love you," said Rue wearily. Though there was not much love in her voice.

"I know you do. So what?"

"I think you're having some kind of midlife crisis, and I don't know why. Georgia is not ten, she is not dealing drugs, she is just making decisions for herself that you wouldn't make for her. But it's her life."

"Don't tell me one more time whose life it is. It's *our* life. All three of us. I'm tired of being talked to as if I'm out of it. I feel as if I have two teenaged assholes in this family instead of one."

"Thanks, Dad," said Rue.

It was the second night in a month that they slept in separate bedrooms.

$\mathcal{M}$argee Malko, usually so little and trim and perky, was weeping in Rue's office. She had come in to school in an old turquoise jogging suit, as if she hadn't the energy to get dressed. Her face bare of makeup, Margee looked older than usual, with crow's feet and laugh lines and a little sag along the jawline all on view. Rue, feeling a hundred years old herself and as if her insides were made of lead, waited for Margee to stop crying. Rue had slept a total of five minutes the whole night, after the fight with Henry. She didn't know if Henry had slept; he had dressed and left the house before she came downstairs.

Glenn Malko, age thirteen, was being suspended from eighth grade for the afternoon. He was sitting in the outer office now with Emily, reading a back copy of the yearbook and fooling with his shoelaces. He had drawn an obscene cartoon in the lab book of a new girl, Louise Chang. Louise had complained to Rosemary Fitch, the science teacher, that she was being sexually harassed, and rather than give him a lecture or detention, which would have made him more glamorous to his peers, Miss Fitch had made Glenn clean out the guinea pig's cage. This greatly amused Kenny Lowen and Glenn's other pals. At recess, passing Louise and Leila Bathhurst near the volleyball court, he reportedly had said, "It's just like you bitches to get me in trouble."

Margee, far from defending or justifying Glenn, as Rue half expected her to do, had more or less imploded.

"I don't know why I can't seem to keep a grip on myself these days," she said, shaking her head, blowing her nose, and making an unsuccessful attempt at a girlish laugh. "I'm the proverbial Water Works."

Rue, feeling like an assassin, finally managed to ask what she always did in such situations: "Is there something going on at home I should know about?"

Margee shook her head no. "I just can't cope with Glenn." And she wept again.

"Is he difficult with you?"

"*Awful*. It must be my fault . . . he says terrible things about women. He teases Chelsea all the time. He goes into her room and hides her stuff, just to upset her. He took twenty dollars from my purse last week."

"How do you know?"

"The maid saw him do it. When I confronted him, he said he hadn't and that Gladys probably did it herself. I tried to tell him this is a woman who's supporting four children, I tried to tell him that it was cruel to blame her for something that could cost her her job."

"Did he understand?"

"No. At least, if he did he didn't let me in on it. I wish you'd expelled that damn Kenny Lowen, Rue . . . we all do. There's a petition going around."

Rue sat silent. "How is Glenn getting along with Terry?"

"He's better with Terry. He doesn't dare be rude to his face, anyway."

Rue wished she could think faster. She knew she should be making an articulate speech at this point about actions and consequences. She couldn't comfort Margee, she couldn't even offer the sop of suggesting family therapy. Terry would refuse . . . what could he do? Go into therapy and lie to the therapist about having an affair, with his wife and children looking on? That would help a lot.

Finally, she said, "When Glenn gets home, he is going to spend the afternoon writing me a letter, describing what he must do—and not do—to make it through the rest of the year. With the understanding that if he can't live up to the standards he describes, he will be expelled."

"I think that's a great idea," said Margee.

Oh no you don't, Rue thought. Or at least, you won't once you've thought about it. And even if you do, Terry won't. You'll be back here within the week feeling that I've betrayed you. One way or another, this will end up being my fault, because I didn't expel Kenny Lowen, because Ann Rosen is a friend of mine and I suggested her for the Board. . . .

"I'm glad you do," said Rue. "Margee—if I could suggest, no television this afternoon or tonight?"

"Oh right," said Margee. "Of course." She got up and went out to collect her criminal.

Reluctantly, Rue put in a call to Chandler to explain why Glenn was on probation, and ask for his support, especially important since the child was the son of a Board member.

Rue had been working on the budget for the upcoming year all through the long weekend of Martin Luther King's birthday. She had to present it on Thursday at the January Board meeting, and she was trying desperately to arrange enough of a surplus to give the teachers a six-percent raise.

She had a $90,000 budget allotment for capital improvements that she couldn't seem to whittle down. Late last year a leak was discovered from the underground gasoline storage tank that had been used for thirty years for fuel for the school's ancient buses, the truck, and the maintenance equipment. What at first had seemed an annoying unexpected $10,000 expenditure for testing and patching had ballooned to $50,000, mandated by the county water district to have the tank removed, followed by inspections of the water table to be made by an expensive engineering firm but paid for by the school, for the next three years, at $10,000 a pop. Worse, during the digging to remove the tank, which had completely destroyed the brand-new parking lot, it was discovered that the pipe system that carried water to Home and out to the bus barn was not only not copper, it wasn't even plumbing pipe. It was electrical conduit, apparently installed in the years of shortage immediately after World War II. Rue was extremely afraid that the whole plumbing system, absent the pipe that served the new gym, would prove to be conduit and have to be replaced.

It was frustrating to be spending such huge sums on buried pipe when the sixth-grade teacher couldn't afford the subscription to *National Geographic* that her son wanted for his birthday. On the other hand, Rue was glad of an excuse to stay closeted with the computer through the long weekend. She and Henry were treating each other with elaborate consideration, hoping that through good manners and ordinary kindness they would gradually return to the sense of affection and safety they had always provided for each other. She was afraid to ask Henry how it was feeling to him; for her, it wasn't working. She felt far from him, and wary.

She was in the business manager's office going over the capital expenses when Emily appeared at the door.

"Rue . . . there are three fifth-grade moms here to see you . . . they say it will just take a minute."

She looked at her watch. "Who are they?"

"Barbara Wren, Inez Cort, and Corinne Lowen."

"Do you know what it's about?"

"I'm afraid so," said Emily. "I had lunch with Malone."

"Mrs. Trainer," said Rue.

Emily nodded, trying to look grave.

Barbara Wren, who was immense, took up most of the couch in Rue's office. Corinne and Inez perched on straight-back chairs. Inez Cort, who had an amazing cantilevered bosom, always seemed to Rue to have to fight gravity to remain upright. She and Corinne Lowen were unlikely allies of Barbara Wren, given that, along with Lyndie Sale and Malone Dahl, their daughters had done their best to make Nicolette Wren's life a hell the entire year. But Rue could tell from the body language that allies they were. This was not a dispute coming to her for mediation, this was an offensive line.

Barbara Wren began. "I'm an atheist," she said. "My father was a Communist."

"Religion is a matter of family values," added Inez. "It's fine to be a Christian or a Jew or an atheist, I don't care, but it's our choice what we teach our children about religion."

Corinne Lowen nodded vigorously.

"I'm with you so far," said Rue.

"There was a short, or something, in the heater in the fish tank in Mrs. Trainer's room," said Barbara Wren.

"Over the weekend. It might have been during the wind storm Sunday night."

"Or not, it doesn't matter," said Corinne.

"When the children came in this morning all the little fishes were cooked," said Barbara.

"They were floating on top, we don't know if they cooked or died of cold."

"Cooked," said Barbara Wren. "It wasn't that cold in the room.

If the heater had just gone off the guppies at least would have lived."

"But they all died," said Rue, seeking clarification.

"Nicolette said she offered to scoop them up with the net and flush them down the toilet, but Mrs. Trainer made a fuss, embarrassed her, and said they should think of their poor little souls."

"I'm sorry, fish do *not* have souls," said Inez Cort. "It's like . . . come *on.*"

Barbara laughed a big, gritty, contemptuous laugh. "She's some kind of animist? Their Little Souls?"

Rue was beginning to hope that this one idiotic remark was all there was to the incident.

"She made them all go outside and stand in a circle, while one of the boys dug a burial pit."

"Why a burial pit?" asked Inez scornfully. "Why not individual graves?"

"Why a boy to dig the pit?" asked Corinne Lowen. "Girls can dig just as well as boys."

"Then she produces, I swear to god, an Episcopal prayer book, and conducts a mass for the dead," said Barbara.

"Mass? Isn't that Catholic?" asked Inez.

"Episcopalians are Catholics who don't believe in the pope," said Barbara, the atheist. "Henry the Eighth and all that." The allusion seemed lost on the other two.

"How do we know it was an Episcopal prayer book?" said Rue, who was wishing she could roll under her desk and howl with laughter.

"Nicolette asked to borrow it," Barbara explained. Oh good, thought Rue. A little atheist Torquemada. "Then she came down to the lunchroom and told me." It was probably a 1928 prayer book, thought Rue wildly. I bet that's what they object to.

Unfortunately, they had a tighter grip on the situation than that. "The woman is a nutcase," said Barbara Wren.

Rue carried mugs of steaming tea into Mike's office at the end of the day and closed the door.

"Let's just stay in here and never come out," she said. "And don't answer the phone, I don't want any more bad news."

"I have something to tell you," Mike said.

"I know that tone. Stop, I can't take it. You're leaving."

"No," said Mike, "Bonnie's leaving."

"Bonnie! No!" There was a pause, in which they stared at each other, very unhappy. "Why? I thought she was happy here."

"She's very happy, but she doesn't have a green card. She's Canadian."

"But . . . she's been here for years. She took her degree here. . . . Don't we ask for proof of citizenship? Or work papers? I feel like Zoe Baird."

"Apparently Bill doesn't, for part-time employees."

"But he does get the TB test, the fingerprints, the child abuse statement?"

"Yes." Rue relaxed a little. But grew unhappier as she began to think about having Bonnie go. They sat in silence, drinking their tea.

"Did you know about this?" Rue asked.

"I've known for a while."

"There's something about her," Rue said. "She's a comforting presence. She gives people the sense that they're helping her, keeping her company, as they quietly dump out things they wouldn't tell anyone else on earth. I look out and see her perched on a wall or leaning against a tree, and there's something about her. Children trust her. Animals trust her. *I* trust her."

Mike nodded.

"Oh, hell," said Rue.

Rue had a talk with Catherine Trainer about the separation of church and state and the unwisdom of sharing her private beliefs, however deeply felt, on a multicultural campus.

"This is a secular school whether we like it or not," she said. "We teach ethics, and manners, but not religion."

"There's no line between them!" Catherine protested. "And a funeral is a cultural experience."

"It may not be easy to draw the line," said Rue, "but it is very easy to tell which side of it you were on."

"When we were studying ancient Egypt and the gerbil died, we prayed to Osiris and buried it like King Tut. You didn't see anything wrong with that."

"I'm not going to debate this, Catherine. It's not that complicated. I want you to review the Faculty Handbook cover to cover, and from now on adhere to it to the letter, or your contract will not be renewed."

Rue had said the fatal words. It sounded in the room like a thunderclap, and Catherine's face took on a terrible surprised expression, as if a dear friend had pulled a gun and shot her. She had finally heard the message and the pain in her face was something Rue felt it would take years to forget. She left the office in tears, and left Rue near tears herself.

From that moment on, whenever she left her office Rue kept coming upon members of the faculty in clumps on the campus, talking excitedly. They would break apart or turn away when they saw her. A few of the unflappable ones, like Evelyn Douglas, and Janet TerWilliams, whose husband was rich, maintained their good will toward her. But by and large a climate of fear for their jobs and resentment against Rue settled in with the January rains.

Mike Dianda still had the faculty's confidence, and he became the conduit for their grievances. They believed they were witnessing a witch-hunt by selfish parents with no concern for Catherine's length of service and no willingness to see past their spoiled children's complaints to the many fine and strong qualities that Catherine offered as a teacher.

They admitted that some of the newer ideas about whole language, for instance, or problem-centered teaching, were Urdu to Catherine. It was true she had been urged to take time off for faculty enrichment workshops, to let some new air into her pedagogical closet, and that she had not seen the need. But her husband had just died. Catherine's friends could not know that she rarely bothered to correct students' homework anymore or that she continued to use mimeos of tests she created ten years ago, the answers to which were widely circulated from older siblings to current fifth graders. They couldn't know the number or intensity of the complaints about her teaching or how often the complaints were entirely justified. There was no way Rue could let them know these things without wounding Catherine Trainer more than she was hurt already.

Rue's great hope for restoring morale was that she could get the Board to vote the faculty a six-percent pay raise. She was planning to ask for seven percent and fight for six percent. She couldn't believe it would go lower than that, given that Chandler had promised not to oppose it.

The budget meeting was always intense, but this year the country was in a hard recession. This year she had a family apply for financial aid whose gross income the year before had been $400,000. (They were getting a divorce. Last year there had been a one-time bonus. There were the rentals on two different houses. There was the $5,700 per month debt service on the couple's eighteen credit cards. The Scholarship Committee voted them a loan.)

On the evening of the Board meeting, a pipe backed up in the preschool bathroom. (Morning would bring the plumber and the discovery of a Ninja Turtle deep in the line.) The carpet was partly flooded and soaked in the adjoining music room, where the Board usually met. Rue had to stand outside in the chill evening air waiting for Board members to arrive one by one and suggest that they reconvene in the science lab down the hill. When she finally joined them, the trustees were crammed into child-sized chairs arranged in a circle, gossiping among themselves. On a high shelf circling the room, there were clear jars of formaldehyde holding specimens of rattlesnakes and fetal pigs. The room fell quiet as Rue emptied dregs from the coffee urn into a paper cup and carried it to an empty chair. When she was settled, Chandler called the meeting to order.

Rue fought for the faculty raise, and Chandler and Terry Malko fought back. When she turned to the usual faces for help—Sylvia French, Ann Rosen, Bud Ransom—she got nothing. Times were hard. There were families in the school for whom two tuitions represented a major proportion of their income. They couldn't afford the increase in tuition you'd need to cover these raises.

Rue countered that there were teachers in the school who were teaching evening classes in places like shopping malls, because they couldn't feed their kids and put gas in the car to get to work on what they were being paid.

Terry Malko raised the question of the discount on tuition for teachers' children who attended Country.

"If it's a question of need, how can you justify giving Janet TerWilliams the same discount you give Evelyn Douglas?"

"It's a question of principle," said Rue. "Pay them what they're worth. They're both great teachers. If we didn't give Janet a discount, she'd probably go back to business school and go to work where she could make as much as you do," she said, perhaps unwisely looking directly at Terry.

"Why does a teacher with four kids getting discounts, like Janet, effectively get eight thousand dollars more a year than Robert Noonan or Lloyd Merton? Aren't the ones with children taking the raises from the ones without?"

"We are running a school, not a factory. Teaching is the machinery with which we make our product. Why aren't you as interested in a capital investment in the faculty as you are in the goddamn water pipes?"

There was a pause.

"We can't *get* the pipes any cheaper," said Terry, and the whole room laughed, except Rue.

They voted the faculty a four-and-a-half-percent pay raise,

which after inflation meant a real raise of about one percent.

They moved on to curriculum review. Chandler presented the compromise Rue had accepted, that the faculty write annual curricula and quarterly reports. Rue, feeling sandbagged by the vote on salaries, made her point to the full Board about the extra burden on the teachers, hoping that this was an unsupported motion of Chandler's. The vote was illuminating. Terry Malko was voting with Chandler, and Ann Rosen, the leader of the loyal opposition, was silent. Sylvia French asked the odd question, but she didn't have Ann's brains or confidence, and the rest, many of them new to the Board, seemed confused by the issue or uninterested. The vote carried.

When Chandler brought up the five-year budget plan, Rue finally realized she was in a box. Chandler was constructing a series of obstacles she could neither get around nor over.

"Look at last year's budget, Chandler. You approved it. Yet we finished the year in the red because we didn't foresee that half the sixth-grade girls would withdraw to get away from Monica Nelson, and we didn't foresee having to destroy the parking lot and dig up the underground tank. How on earth are you going to guess what our needs will be five years from now?"

Nobody listened. At least not Chandler, or Terry. Terry who had suddenly decided that she had a vendetta against his son, Glenn. Rue was evidently responsible for everything that was wrong in Glenn's life, and Margee's, and Terry wanted her to feel his anger.

Well, she felt it.

$\mathcal{G}$lenn Malko destroyed the library copy machine by putting transparency film through it instead of paper. Mike Dianda wanted to kill him.

"I asked Mrs. Nafie, and she said she didn't know, go ahead . . ." Glenn protested when he was delivered to Rue's office.

"But you had already asked Mrs. Ketchum, and she said 'Absolutely not, it will melt and wreck the machine,'" she countered. She was as angry as she could remember being with a child. Glenn made a face and looked at a corner of the ceiling.

"Didn't you?" He shrugged. "Please answer me, Glenn!"

"I guess so," he muttered.

Children were amazing. They seemed to believe that adults could read their minds, especially when their parents failed to divine some need or desire of theirs and they felt hard done by, and at the same time to imagine that adults could be deceived by the most transparent excuse or lie.

Emily came to the door. "Mrs. Malko is in Los Angeles for the day, and Mr. Malko's office doesn't know where he is."

Rue silently and invisibly cursed.

"Glenn, what did we say was going to happen if you got into trouble again?"

There was a long silence. "You'd kick me out."

"This is not something I am doing to you. You are doing it to yourself. You had a choice. You had a thousand choices."

"I didn't know it would break the machine."

"You did."

"I didn't know Mrs. Ketchum was right."

"Would you have tried it on your father's machine?"

There was a long silence.

"Glenn?"

He finally shook his head. No.

Rue said, "I am too angry to talk to you any more right now. You are a valuable young man, and I believe in you, but I've had enough of you for the moment. Please go out and sit in the office until Mrs. Goldsborough finds your father."

Glenn got up and walked out.

Emily called Terry Malko's secretary every fifteen minutes, until two in the afternoon, when Terry turned up and called her back. By that time Glenn had been waiting four hours. Emily told Rue that he cried quietly for much of the first hour. After that, he had slept. Emily brought him lunch, but he didn't eat it.

Expelling Glenn Malko was not something Rue wanted to do. Glenn was a favorite, and a follower. His disruptive behavior was macho and silly, but nothing he wouldn't outgrow, unlike the escalating malice of Kenny Lowen. Rue felt Glenn would learn more about handling conflict if she could engineer a compromise punishment. She hoped to suspend him for a week, perhaps, and arrange for him to work on weekends until he had paid to repair or replace the copy machine. Unfortunately, the four hours she had to wait before she could discuss the matter with Terry gave her time to find that Glenn himself had boxed her in. He had bragged so widely that there would be no more suspensions for him and only expulsion was bad enough for him if he got in trouble again, that she had to follow through.

She couldn't discuss it with Henry. She knew too well what his reaction would be. "You expel a thirteen-year-old for using the wrong material in a copy machine, but you congratulate our daughter for dropping out of a full scholarship at Juilliard to become a Stool Sample?" Henry seemed to have convinced himself that Rue and Georgia shared a closeness that left him out, and that Rue had an influence with Georgia that Rue doubted she had.

The unrest among the parents over Glenn's expulsion, coupled with the depression and anger the faculty felt over their nonraise, gave the Merry Nineties dinner and auction party that Saturday night a decidedly unmerry cast for Rue.

Chandler Kip, looking very GQ in his beautifully tailored dinner clothes, stopped Henry and Rue as they walked toward the dining room. The party was being held in the Madison Room of the

Red Tower Inn, the fanciest motel in Seven Springs. Rue was dressed like a Gibson Girl and felt like an ass. When they stopped to sign in, she could see four school fathers inside the Madison Room, dressed in straw boaters and wearing suspenders, singing barbershop.

"Henry, excuse me a minute," said Chandler. "Could I just have a minute with your wife?"

Nice touch, she thought. Asking her husband's permission, not hers. She watched Henry stroll rather too willingly off without her as Chandler led her around a corner, out of the stream of arriving Country School couples and guests. They found themselves outside the Jefferson Room, from within which they could hear the strains of "Hava Nagila."

"I have good news," said Chandler. "I have persuaded Terry Malko to stay on the Board."

"I'm glad," said Rue, although she wasn't. "How did you do that?"

"I told him that Glenn would be welcome to return to school on Monday. And that from now on, any disciplinary decision involving his children would be made by me."

Rue felt herself go white. She couldn't have been more affronted if he'd ripped off the front of her dress.

"You shouldn't have done that," she said.

"You're out of control, Rue," said Chandler. "Somebody's got to do something." And he turned on his handmade heel and walked away.

Henry saw Chandler Kip come into the Madison Room, joining his wife, Bambi, and Sondra and Oliver Sale, whom he had brought to the auction, no doubt to rub Rue's nose in it. Bambi was wearing a corset that cinched her waist in to about the size of Henry's bicep, and huge mutton sleeves, and was displaying a lot of cleavage. Sondra Sale wore the dress of a frontier dance hall girl, very tight and low in the bodice, with black fishnet stockings. It wasn't quite the right period, but it showed off her figure in a way that, Henry thought, seemed like a direct challenge to her husband. Come on, big boy, let's show everyone the merchandise. Oliver, in a rented tuxedo, stared into space.

Henry looked around for someone to sit with. There was Carson McCann, a good-looking redhead who ran a bookstore downtown. Her husband was an aging preppie with rheumy eyes and a perpetual glass in his hand. . . . Henry wasn't in the mood. There was Terry Malko with his pretty wife, Margee. Terry was looking like the cock of the walk, laughing loudly and elaborately patting the bare shoulders of his wife. They were sitting with some people Henry didn't know, who looked too young to have school-aged children. He saw Corinne and Bradley Lowen trying to find their table. Henry liked the Lowens a great deal, especially Bradley.

Henry saw Rue come into the room, looking white. He watched her locate Mike Dianda at a table with the Percys and some other teachers and whisper something to him. Henry saw Mike leap to his feet, like a spring uncoiling. Mike took Rue's arm, and with a pang of something almost like jealousy, Henry watched them leave the room together. So. There was a crisis; fine, there had been dozens over the years. Team Rue would swing into action. Surgeons were cowboys, solitary gunslingers, and they didn't play on teams. He realized with plangent clarity, standing in the middle of the ballroom at the Red Tower Inn, that he was sick of it.

Mike marched Rue into the lobby and found some chairs near a plastic date palm, where it was just possible to talk over the din of a crowd watching a Sharks game in an open bar irrationally named The Loggia.

"You can't resign," Mike said.

"I have to. I can't go in there and give flowery speeches . . . this school is coming apart. The president of the Board has just violated every principle of sound management. . . . I have no authority. I can't expel. If I can't expel I can't discipline at all, I can't protect the teachers, it's impossible. Impossible, full stop. Let *him* run the school."

"Rue—he's an asshole."

"Thank you, Sherlock."

"Hold on. Please. You can't let an asshole like that have his way just because he wants it. We're a culture here, we're a civilization. We've taken years to evolve our laws, our standards. We have order, we have peace, we have arts and music, gardens and orchards, we're raising children to be decent useful citizens and carry this order out into the world. But we can't do our work without you, and *you* can't say, 'Oh, fine, I quit, Open the gates,' just because some moron in a loincloth shows up outside the walls and starts picking his nose and grabbing his balls and making faces at you."

Furious as she was, Rue smiled.

"It's not just you. The school belongs to all of us, but a body can't act without a head. But if we *can* act, we can solve it."

"I don't see how."

"He may think he can run the school without you, but does he think he can run it without teachers?"

Rue took a deep breath and looked at Mike. She saw his point. The teachers wouldn't stand for this either; how could they? If Glenn Malko set foot back on campus, it would take about half a day before their jobs were impossible. These kids would know in a hot minute that something at the heart of the machine had broken down.

"Welcome to *Lord of the Flies*," she said.

"Exactly."

"I can't go in there and go politicking from table to table, Mike."

"Of course not. If we're going to have a shit fight, we need you out in front in spotless raiment, not carrying the shit bucket. These teachers are not stupid and they're not weak, and neither am I. But if you quit, I'll quit, and half of them will quit or want to, and very few of them can afford it. If you hold on, we can get on our ramparts and pour boiling oil on the bastard."

Rue tried to remember how you did Lamaze breathing. She thought it would help her get control of her rage.

"You didn't go to military school, did you?" she asked. "You're pretty slick with a metaphor."

Mike smiled. He held a hand to Rue, and she took it.

"You don't actually know you can pull this off, do you," she said, and it was not a question.

"No," said Mike.

They sat holding hands, Rue feeling unspeakably grateful for Mike's friendship. She couldn't possibly have asked the teachers to stand with her now when they felt she had sold out Catherine

Trainer, but Mike could. And of course he would really be asking them to stand up for themselves, not her.

"Okay," she said.

"Thanks."

"Don't mention it." She tried once more to take a deep breath and then said crossly, "Do you have any idea how *fucking* uncomfortable these stupid corsets are?"

Mike said, "My land, I have never heard you use that word in public."

"I'm getting into the mood," she said. "Let's go. I have to hype these big spenders to unbutton their wallets for the best little school in the world."

As minutes passed and Mike and Rue did not reappear, Henry decided he was ready for a drink. At the bar he found Emily Goldsborough standing by herself. She was wearing black leggings and a long sweater and a Clinton/Gore button.

"I decided to go for the nineteen nineties instead of the eighteen nineties," she said, a little embarrassed.

"You're the only woman here who doesn't look like a fool. Can I buy you a drink?"

She smiled. "Please. White wine."

He was aware that she stood studying him as he ordered wine for her and a scotch for himself.

"You look nice in black tie," she said, taking her drink. He looked as nice in black tie now as he had twenty-five years ago, when he had danced one dance with her at a formal party in Philadelphia, somebody's coming-out party she thought, or was it a wedding? She remembered his hand on her naked back as he spun her around. He had kept his chin raised as he danced, as if he were scanning the crowd instead of thinking of the steps or the girl in his arms. What had she been wearing that her back was bare?

"I remember about a hundred years ago, when I offered to get you a drink and you asked for a gimlet," he said, smiling.

"A gimlet . . . my god, how do you remember that?"

He was looking down at her, warm and teasing. "I didn't know what one was."

"I didn't either. It was what my stepfather drank."

"What did it turn out to be?"

They were walking to the edge of the room together, seeing the past instead of what was before them.

"It was delicious. It had Rose's Lime Juice in it."

"Rose's Lime Juice . . . remember when we were young and people would drink that sort of stuff all night and be up for their nine o'clock classes?"

"I drank gimlets for about a year, as I remember, because they reminded me of you."

Henry stopped and looked at her, quizzical.

"Did you really?"

"Yes."

They found an empty table under a wall display of antique bicycles with huge front wheels.

"Do you really think I'm all right dressed like this?" Emily asked.

"Of course."

"I went to the costume place to rent something, but do you know what they cost?"

Henry shook his head. "Rue conceals that sort of thing from me. How are you getting along, that way?"

"Money?"

He nodded.

"Okay. Ann Rosen's got Tom pretty well hog-tied."

"Good."

"But this job has been an interesting experience," she added, gesturing at the Country parents, chatting and laughing and drinking. "Being seen as a social inferior."

Henry took a pull on his drink. "When I was growing up, my parents thought of doctors as tradesmen. Not the sort that one would know socially."

"Mine too." They looked at each other and laughed.

"How's our fence doing?" Henry asked suddenly.

"Our fence is great, you should come and visit it."

"I should," said Henry. "I loved that fence."

Emily smiled. They sat silent again for a longer stretch.

"Have we ever danced together?" Henry asked.

"Yes."

"How was it?"

"Nice."

"Would you dance with me now?"

After a beat Emily answered, "There's no music. People would talk."

Henry said smoothly, "Another time, then." And they looked at each other.

When Margee Malko pulled up in front of Home to drop off her children on Monday morning, half the boys in the eighth grade were waiting to greet Glenn with shouts and high fives. Wearing chinos hanging halfway down his boxer shorts, a plaid shirt buttoned only at the top so it flapped open over his undershirt, with Chuck Taylor low-top sneakers down at heel, and a blue Crips rag tied around his head so low over his eyes that it was practically a blindfold, his walk was a cross between a slouch and a swagger. His grin was huge as his phalanx surrounded him and accompanied him toward the upper school, like an honor guard. "My home boy, my homey," his friends kept saying as they slapped his back. Glenn was bopping, on top of the world.

"My home boy," said Mike, watching them go. "What a bunch of weenies."

He and Rue were sitting in her office, watching the rake's progress across the campus, waiting to see what would happen next.

What happened was, across the parking lot the door of the preschool opened and the three teachers, Helen Yeats, Mary Louise Boatner, and Kelly Lau, walked across the playground. They held up the line of cars in the parking lot waiting to drop off their wriggling cargo as they made their way to Home, walking in a line like something from *Make Way for Ducklings*. They reached the shaded benches where children waited in the afternoons for their carpools, and sat down in a silent row to the obvious surprise of the parents in line in their cars.

"Who's with the children?" Rue asked Mike.

"The TAs. Don't worry. The cook and the bus drivers are helping too."

Next Siobhan McKee emerged from her kindergarten classroom. Across the lawn in Primary, Janet TerWilliams, Charla Percy, and Cora Alba-Fish marched their students outside, and teachers and children sat down on the grass in silence.

Parents began to leave their cars and go to the teachers to ask what was happening. Parents looked surprised, then annoyed, and began to gather in knots among the stalled cars, talking, questioning, exclaiming. One or two people slammed car doors. Down the lane, beyond the reach of the grapevine, horns began to honk.

The middle-school teachers, Lloyd Merton, Catherine Trainer, Evelyn Douglas, and Joan McCone, brought their classes outside and sat down on benches in the sun in front of the library. The children formed up to play volleyball or jump rope or jacks. The upper-school teachers, Cynda Goldring, Lynn Ketchum, Consuelo Cole, Robert Noonan, and Toby Chen, emerged from their classrooms and sat down outside their doors.

"They've left the kids inside, oh god," said Rue. Mike, who was nearsighted, couldn't see as far as the upper school, which was across the creek, but Rue could. "Someone will fall off a desk or swallow a ruler, and we'll all be sued."

"Let Chandler worry about it," said Mike. Rosemary Fitch had come out of the science lab, Pat Moredock and Mrs. Nafie were sitting on the bench outside Home, and Blair Kunzelman and Kendra Flower had come from the gym to join the upper-school teachers. Rue related this to Mike as it happened.

In the parking lot Sylvia French, who had just heard what her leader and president had done, was saying angrily, "What I *love* about this school is that the children learn that actions have consequences. Rules are rules and they can't be bent for one person. I *want* my children to know that, and they don't learn it from television. And god knows, they don't listen to *me*. I'd like to know who Chandler Kip thinks he is!" Her listeners agreed. Down the lane, people abandoned their cars and walked up the driveway to join the ruckus.

Karen Bramlett, a local judge and member of the Parents' Council, appeared at the door of Rue's office, followed by seven or eight other parents from the parking lot. One, Toy Lablanche, seemed to be wearing her pajamas. All were thoroughly hot, emo-

tionally and otherwise, from standing on the asphalt on a cloudless
winter morning.

"May we come in?" Karen asked.

"Please," said Rue.

"Janet TerWilliams says that none of the teachers will go into
their classrooms until Glenn Malko leaves the campus."

"So I understand," said Rue.

"Well please call Margee Malko and tell her to come get him!
This is ridiculous!"

"I agree with you completely, but the president of the Board
gave Glenn permission to return after I expelled him. I work for the
Board; there's nothing I can do."

Karen stared. "Does he have the authority to do that?"

"I don't think so, but he's the boss." She shrugged.

"He certainly is not," said Karen.

"What do the bylaws say?" Corinne Lowen demanded. Rue
handed a copy of the Handbook to her, and she handed it to Karen,
who was after all, the lawyer. After reading for a minute or two,
Karen said, "Get Chandler Kip on the phone, will you?"

"Happy to," said Rue. She got up and threaded her way to her
desk, among the irate moms who stood or perched all over the
office, and dialed.

There was a feeling of elation on campus that lasted for days. The Malkos withdrew both children from school, and Rue was sorry about that. Chelsea had done nothing wrong and she was having a great year in Charla Percy's class. But the family had been so thoroughly humiliated by what had happened that they believed, or claimed to believe, that Chelsea would be persecuted by this faculty. And of course they blamed not Chandler but Rue for what had happened. Chandler was so embarrassed and angry at Rue that he wouldn't deal with her directly anymore. If he needed to communicate with her he did it through Sylvia French or Bud Ransom.

The faculty, however, felt "empowered."

"Ghastly word," said Rue to Mike. But she admitted that it fit the situation. They felt as if they had pulled together and roared like one mighty beast, and it felt great. And the best was that they'd done it without violating their dignity or their principles. It had even been good teaching. All over the campus, on one level or another, the children were discussing Gandhi and Martin Luther King or the American Labor Movement or the French Resistance. They talked about rules and how they must apply to all. They talked of the importance of resisting when leaders think they're Above the Law. Cynda Goldring taught a class on Watergate and the language of the Constitution, and Catherine Trainer, who was doing her Egypt unit, found a way to relate the faculty's action to the Jewish slaves under the wicked Pharaohs, preserving their culture and their beliefs until Moses appeared to lead them to the Promised Land. In Primary, there were interesting homilies learned about how to deal with playground bullies. The first grade spent a period talking of Safety in Numbers, which previously they had thought referred to the importance of arithmetic.

Rue felt confident enough that calm had been restored to honor a long-standing commitment. Wednesday she left to go to San Anselmo, where she was heading a team to evaluate The Prospect School.

The rest of her team consisted of Sister Catherine, head of a Sacred Heart school in Novato, and a math teacher from Marin, both of whom she knew at least slightly and liked. She hoped that it might be some fun to get away and pass judgment on somebody else's little cauldron of trouble. But instead it was a disturbing experience. Prospect was a starving little school and the present head, called out of retirement on short notice, was running the school and also teaching history, because he couldn't find anyone to take the job at the salary he could offer. Her team heard him call Asian people Chinamen and saw him throw erasers at students who gave wrong answers, and that was the least of the long list of shortfalls. Prospect made The Country School look like earthly paradise.

Late in the evenings, after the team had met and caucused and written their day's reports, Rue sat in her dingy motel room and tried to call Henry. He didn't answer the phone. She wondered where he was and thought they were two of the loneliest nights of her life.

When she got home Friday evening, Henry was not waiting to have supper with her, as she had hoped. He had left her mail piled on the kitchen table, but no note as to when he would be back. On top was a padded envelope from Georgia, addressed to Rue alone. It was a cassette tape, with a long letter.

Dear Mom,
I'm sorry I've been bad about writing. I've had a friend at the studio help me make this after hours.

We played a concert in Union Square Park on Martin Luther King day. We were actually paid by the Parks Department. An old black guy stayed for the whole set, down behind the bandstand, just staring at us. When we were breaking down afterward, Jonah asked him if he was a player. He said, "No, I've been in prison for thirty-eight years. This is my first day out."

You asked me what I listen to. Sometime I would really like to listen to this tape with you. I'd like you to like it.

1000 Homo DJs: "Supernaut"
This is a cover of a Black Sabbath tune, so the song is older than I am, but it sure is neat, especially when recorded in 1990 with an industrial groove. Try marching purposefully to this music, stomping your feet and looking evil. Fun!

Metallica: "Trapped Under Ice"

This song is pretty old too, first recorded in the early eighties. I love Metallica; they're the original epic speed metal band. This is perhaps the best straight-ahead metal the world has ever seen, vis à vis pure aggression.

The Toasters: "East Side Beat"

Though it doesn't show until the middle of the song, the Toasters are the quintessential ska band. They've got the guitars on the off-beats, the trombone fixation, the reggae groove, a full horn section, the upbeat dance thang, etc. Jonah loves ska. I love ska.

Primus: "Is It Luck?"

Primus are media darlings like you wouldn't believe. I think it's their bizarre jerking beat and strange time signature choices. Critics all over the place are thrilled to hear something truly new going on in rock.

The Red Hot Chili Peppers: "Subway to Venus" from "Mother's Milk"

This is also funk/punk, but in a very different groove from Primus. This is the band that began to legitimize idol worship of bass players. Everybody loves the Chili Peppers.

John Zorn/Naked City: "Latin Quarter," "Snagglepuss"

Zorn has a jazz background in saxophone, and is the conceptual father of the record. John Zorn is famous for changing grooves (and in fact the whole genre of the song) in between beats.

Neil Young: "The Days That Used to Be"

This is the same old Neil Young, except that now he's got a distortion pedal. The same old thudding, whiny rock and roll. I really like it.

Mr. Bungle: "My Ass Is on Fire"

This is currently my favorite song in the world. It's also the angriest song I know. Listen to it four times in a row. This is probably not one to play for the preschool, and don't listen to it while you're holding a baseball bat.

Bad Brains: "Revolution (dub)," "House of Suffering"

These two songs show the two sides of Bad Brains, and it may be difficult to believe that they are the same band: the first is straight reggae, the second is D. C. Hardcore.

Not many bands can get a head-banging audience to pump their fists while shrieking about peace and universal brotherhood.

The Jesus and Mary Chain: "Darklands"
J&MC is best known for distortion that makes their music sound like "chainsaws in a hurricane," but on this album they have (in the words of the reviewer) "fixed their guitars, and that's not such a bad thing." It's interesting to hear the ultra-grunge feedback juxtaposed with their soporific playing style.

The Fatima Mansions: "You're a Rose"
This is a good example of English pop/rock. They are politically conscious, make heavy use of keyboards, and use drum tracks that sound automated—the whole "ooh, I'm so deep" lyrical style.

Helios Creed: "Ub the Wall"
Jonah says this is the angriest song *he* knows. It draws on the industrial genre, with continuous background (or even foreground) distortion, and an undercurrent of table saw, or perhaps a whole machine shop.

Grotus: "Morning Glory"
Grotus is a magnificently weird band from San Francisco. On a 7" somebody gave me, they are listed as playing bass, bass, bass, and super x-tra bass. Mood music.

Let me know what you think. Hope you like it. You decide whether to play it for Dad.

Much love

It was signed with a drawing of a bloblike creature that Georgia had been peopling a line-drawn world with for years, on grocery lists and the margins of books and notebooks. The basic creature was (she claimed) a clam, with stick arms and legs and a bow in its hair.

Rue was beginning to wonder where Henry was. She thought she might feel less lonely if she listened to the tape. She was, thus, in the living room considering 1000 Homo DJs when Henry came home.

Over the weekend before Valentine's Day, Mike Dianda married Bonnie Fleming. The wedding took place on campus, outdoors under the live oaks. The wild parrots, frightened by the music, retreated to the highest branches. It was a potluck reception; all the teachers had brought covered dishes and arranged them on picnic tables, and Pat Moredock had made the wedding cake, covered with hearts. The music teacher brought the school's Kurzweil outside trailing a very long industrial extension chord. As the guests drove up, parked, and hurried across the soccer field, laughing and talking, she played favorite inspirational music ranging from "Come to the Church in the Wildwood" to "The Rainbow Connection" (first immortalized by Kermit the Frog).

Finally, Mike appeared wearing a new blue suit. His dark hair was combed and slicked carefully, and his blue eyes were solemn. He was accompanied by a friend, an extraordinarily handsome Episcopal minister. Mike and the minister stood side by side looking nervous as Lisa Stevens began playing the Mendelsohn "Wedding March." The bride's attendants were Mike's three daughters. They wore calico dresses and carried little nosegays of lily of the valley; they walked solemnly in single file ranked in order of height, first Terry, who was nineteen, then Mary, fourteen, and last Trinity, who was eleven. All three looked as if they were trying not to grin. Behind them, Bonnie walked alone, slim, shy, and dignified. Her hair was piled on top of her head, with lilies of the valley woven into it. She wore a long slender dress made of white buckskin, and she carried an ornamental cabbage.

The service was matter of fact and quite brief. Mike and Bonnie faced each other and recited their vows from memory. Rue found it very emotional. What a lot of hope there was in the world, and kindness. She was surprised to see how much heartfelt love they both seemed to feel for each other at this moment, and hoped that for them, it would last forever.

After the minister pronounced them man and wife, Mike and Bonnie kissed each other very sweetly, and it seemed the whole audience held its breath. Then Mike's daughters broke ranks, beaming, and made a circle around the pair, hugging and kissing each one in turn.

Henry and Rue were sitting with Emily. Rue was grateful for the buffer. She and Henry continued to cohabit, rather than connect, and were relieved for all distractions that broke the silence between them. Nothing like this had ever happened to them in twenty-four years of marriage, and Rue couldn't picture what would happen next to change it. She knew something would. Georgia would come home. Or Henry would start to miss Rue. Or something would make them laugh. Something would happen. She felt so fragile at the moment that it seemed best to do nothing to push it. She found when she thought about it, she couldn't really quite get her mind around what *had* happened between them. They had fought about Georgia. More than once. But it wasn't as if Rue had taken a position she could undo, as if she could give in to Henry and make things come out the way he wanted. So she got lost, trying to think her way back, trying to find the moment, the reason, that the distance between them had become an institution. Of all the painful and complex dilemmas she faced, this was the most painful and the most puzzling.

The wedding lunch was very festive; the whole school family needed a celebration, and this one provided a happy hiatus in the midst of the very stormy weather that had lately prevailed. There was a wide range of dishes, from vegetarian lasagna to barbecued pork, Blair Kunzelman's specialty at the grill. Catherine Trainer was happily recalling her wedding to Norman, and looking very pretty; she sat with Evelyn Douglas and Lisa Stevens, and there were roars of laughter from their table that made Rue look over with envy.

Both Henry and Emily were very quiet, Rue thought. She talked mostly to Cynda Goldring, who was concerned at the news that Rue was still getting phone calls from the silent breather.

"Henry never gets them. He gets hang-ups once in a while, but whoever it is is after me. When I answer, he stays on the line, breathing."

Cynda shivered. "Frightening."

Rue nodded. She *did* find it frightening, though she preferred not to admit it.

"Have you called the police? Can they trace the calls?"

"Henry did. This is not a high-tech crime-fighting force. They said they could call in Santa Barbara if the calls got threatening."

"Great."

"I stand there listening to this breathing, trying to figure it out . . . does he want to say something he can't say? Does he want me to say something? Does he think I can read his mind?"

"Have you tried asking who it is?"

"The police say, Never say anything. If you say *anything* it makes it fun for him, and he'll keep it up."

"Do you think it's Kenny?"

"Not really. After all, I *didn't* kick him out. I'd think of Glenn Malko, or even Terry, except the calls started before Glenn was expelled."

"What about Jerry Lozzato?"

"That a-hole, pardon my French. It could be. I just hope he doesn't pop out from behind a bush one day and shoot me. On the whole I prefer to think it's one of the Miss Plums."

"God, that's it," said Cynda. "It's Carla Plum, running the school from beyond the grave."

"I think it is. I feel that they're like my parents, hating rock music, sloppy grammar, and unable to program their VCR—I think they're counting on me to hold back the tide."

They were warming to this theory and would have enjoyed going on with it, except that lunch was nearly over and had been accompanied by a good deal of wine and beer. Just at that moment, Pat Moredock was hurrying to join the group to whom Bonnie would toss the bridal cabbage, when she tripped over an exposed root and fell heavily, breaking her arm.

Henry examined Pat and announced he would drive her to the hospital. Emily asked if she should go too—would Pat want a woman with her?

"Henry's a very comforting person, even if he is a man," said

Rue. "She'll be all right. Anyway, you should go try to catch the bouquet."

"Am I allowed? I'm still married."

"Of course you're allowed."

Emily went to join Lisa Stevens, Rosemary Fitch, Catherine Trainer, Bethany Loeb, Kendra Flower, Mike's calicoed daughters, and Malone. Bonnie, giggling helplessly, stood with her back to the group and then heaved the cabbage over her shoulder. Kendra made a heroic leap for it, but missed, and it was Emily, blushing, who caught it. Everyone applauded. "You're next," everyone said to her. Emily looked confused and pretty, with her cheeks flaming. Henry's car was disappearing down the lane.

Next the groom hoisted the buckskin dress, to the accompaniment of much hooting and whistling, and slid an electric blue garter over Bonnie's slim knee and down her leg, where it got tangled up in her white sandal. Mike was blushing furiously. At last he freed it and winged it over the knot of male guests jostling each other in the sun. Blair Kunzelman knocked Lloyd Merton aside and caught it, which caused a roar of laughter and cries of "foul," and a lot of teasing of his wife, Alma. "Meet my first wife," he kept shouting, with the garter around his arm, and the arm around the long-suffering Alma. Then the bride and groom climbed into a gleaming Model T Ford decked with flowers, lent to the pair by the TerWilliamses. As Carl TerWilliams turned the crank in front of the car and the engine roared to life, Blair tied a string of tin cans to the back bumper. Then they were off with a roar and a clatter amid much laughter.

Lynn Ketchum took over the Kurzweil and began to play a mean "Black Top Boogie." The guests, left behind, danced on the grass. Mike's daughters danced with each other in a ring, Lloyd Merton danced with Emily, the handsome minister danced very beautifully with Catherine Trainer, and Blair Kunzelman danced with four or five women at once. Finally, sun and the effects of unaccustomed wine wore them out, and Lisa took over the keyboard to play some of her favorite Barry Manilow tunes. Everyone else began to pack away the remains of the cake and the bottles and dishes. Henry drove up, without Pat.

"I took her home," he said. "She seemed in need of a nap."

"I don't wonder," said Rue. "How bad is it?"

"A hairline fracture. It will heal fine if she doesn't reinjure it. She's in one of those Velcro casts."

"Does she have much pain?" asked Emily.

"Not at the moment, if you take my meaning," said Henry. "But they gave her some Percodan for later."

"What if she takes that stuff and drinks too?"

Malone and David Dahl had seen the preparations for going and arrived to try to hurry their mother along.

"She could make herself pretty sick."

"But could she wake up dead?"

"Who, Mom?" asked Malone.

"A friend of ours," said Emily.

"Mrs. Moredock?"

Rue looked at Henry.

Later, when they were alone at home, she said, "I'm going to have to organize an intervention. If the kids have all figured it out."

Henry said he guessed so. Then he said, "I'm going to take my car to Liu's and have the oil changed."

"Do you want to do that now? You can drop it off on the way to church in the morning."

"He said this afternoon would be better."

"Do you want me to follow you?"

"No, I'll just wait. I've got a good book."

"Oh. Well. Okay."

"I'll be back in an hour or so. Do you want anything at Tagliarini's?"

"Could you get some two-percent milk?"

"Sure."

Rue settled down to pay her bills, but she had trouble concentrating. She missed having Henry to think out loud with, and now she missed Mike as well. Normally, he would have been the first she would have talked with, but he and Bonnie were on their way to some secret romantic spot, there to do she couldn't imagine what. Deepen an already loving friendship, she guessed. Finally she gave up and went to call Emily. She wanted to know what more Malone had said and exactly how much the kids had figured out about Mrs. Moredock's drinking.

To her surprise, the phone was answered by Patty Kramer, a buxom blond eighth grader who was babysitting.

"I think she was going to the Price Club," said Patty. "She said she'd only be an hour or so."

"Oh," said Rue. "Well, it's nice of you to help out on short notice, Patty."

"It wasn't short notice. She told me she'd be calling, she just didn't know exactly what time."

"Oh. Then it's nice of you to be so flexible."

"No problem. I'm saving for a CD player."

"Have you heard of the Red Hot Chili Peppers?"

"Not rilly."

"What *do* you listen to?"

"The Association," said Patty.

Henry was home an hour later. He apologized for forgetting the milk.

It was on the Thursday morning a week after the wedding that Rue arrived to the news that she would have to teach fifth grade. Catherine Trainer's car had broken down halfway to school, and she was waiting for a tow truck. Mike couldn't take the class; he was already teaching junior kindergarten for Helen Yeats, who had had a dental emergency.

"Did Catherine say if she left a lesson plan?"

Mike gave her a look. "Dream on, honey," he said.

Things were at a dull roar when she reached Mrs. Trainer's classroom. Her entry was greeted with pleasure and curiosity. Where was Mrs. Trainer? Was Mrs. Shaw going to teach them all day? Was Mrs. Trainer sick? Could they have a Free? Rue searched the drawers for a lesson book. She didn't find one, but she did find a stack of stories written by the children, ungraded, and dated December 16.

She quieted the class, then wrote on the board, "A Conscience Is Worth a Thousand Witnesses." "This is a maxim," she said. "Who can tell me what a maxim is? Carly?"

"A wise saying."

"Good. Who can tell me what this one means?"

There was a silence. It lengthened.

"All right, who can tell me what a witness is?"

Hands shot up. "Someone who saw you do something? Like if there's a murder, but somebody saw who did it?"

"Good. Now who can tell me what a conscience is."

No hands were raised.

"What about Jiminy Cricket singing, 'Let your conscience be your guide'?" Silence. "Nobody's heard of Jiminy Cricket?" No one had. Good grief, thought Rue, I never thought I'd be wishing for the return of the Mickey Mouse Club.

"Your conscience," said Rue, "is the voice inside you that tells you when something is right or wrong." They all nodded their heads. Oh yeah, conscience. Oh yeah.

"Now, who can tell me what this maxim means?"

Again, there was silence. "Kim," said Rue to Kim Fat Snyder, "if you're alone in a room, and you're tempted to do something, how do you know if it's a right or wrong thing to do?"

"If you might get caught," said Kim Fat.

"Say you know you won't get caught. How do you know if it's right or wrong?"

This seemed a hard question. She looked around the room, and the faces looked back. She began to wonder if they were putting her on.

"Okay, I'm alone in this room. Got it? You're not here." The class nodded.

Rue looked around, making sure she was alone in the room. Then she sidled toward the back of the room, where a desk was empty, its owner absent. She silently opened the desk top. She studied the mess of notebooks, workbooks, pencils, erasers, barrettes, and hair elastics. She shifted some loose papers, and came up with a calculator.

She held it up. She examined it silently. She looked around furtively, to be sure she was unobserved. Then she slipped the calculator into her skirt pocket, closed the desk softly, and returned to the front of the room.

"Now," she said. "What's wrong with what I just did? Harry?"

"You took something that isn't worth anything."

Rue expected the class to laugh, but the children seemed to think this a serious answer. Rue was beginning to feel incredulous.

"I'm not sure I understand you."

"You risked getting caught and punished for something that wasn't worth it."

"I told you I'm not going to get caught. What's wrong with what I did?"

Some of the children looked at each other. Rue wasn't sure what to do next.

"Whose desk is this?" she asked, hoping to awaken in them sympathy for their absent friend.

"Bharatee's," they answered, and Rue saw part of her problem.

Bharatee was a rather fat, very bright Pakistani girl whose distress they would welcome.

"Okay, let's say this calculator once belonged to Michael Jackson. Let's say it's Bharatee's prized possession, and it's worth a million dollars."

"If Michael Jackson owned it, you still wouldn't be able to sell it because everyone would know where you got it."

"Cut," said Rue. "Time out. Stop. What I did was wrong because I took something that didn't belong to me. It was stealing, and stealing is wrong whether you get caught or not. I didn't have to get punished to know it was wrong. I have a conscience to tell me it was wrong. Now how does my conscience know?"

They all stared at her.

"Did I take a course that taught me right and wrong?"

They nodded. That must be it. It must be a class they hadn't had yet.

"Who thinks that's right?"

They all raised their hands. Rue thought, I wish I were running a church school. I think I'll quit and become a nun.

"I didn't take a course. I know a simple rule, and so do you. I know that what I did was wrong because I wouldn't like someone to do it to me. That's called the Golden Rule." On the blackboard she wrote "Golden Rule: Treat Others as You Would Have Them Treat You."

"Please take out your pencils and journals, and write at least a page on what you have just learned."

They took out their notebooks and their pencils. There was silence and not much writing. After a while, Nicolette asked, "Mrs. Shaw? What if you really needed a calculator, and you know Bharatee has another one?"

"That's a good question. Why don't you write about it?"

Kim Fat's hand went up. "Mrs. Shaw? What if you knew for a fact that Bharatee would just think she had lost it?"

At ten o'clock Rue walked back into the office and said to Emily, "I've just spent the most depressing hour of my life."

"What happened?"

"You won't believe it; I'll tell you at lunch."

*   *   *

Emily didn't react to the tale of the maxim as Rue expected. She seemed instead distracted and upset. Mike claimed he didn't feel an iota of surprise and suggested they have the school renamed Go For Yourself Academy.

As Rue was walking up the hill toward Home after lunch, she saw Kim Fat Snyder hanging around the water fountain.

"Hello, Kim," she called. "Are you boycotting recess?"

"Mrs. Shaw, could I talk to you for a minute?"

"Of course."

"You know that maxim?"

"Yes."

"Well, remember when someone stole Bharatee's locket?"

"Remind me."

"It was right before Christmas? She took it off for PE and left it on a shelf in her locker, and when she came back it was gone. She told Miss Flower, and we all looked for it."

Rue realized she had heard this much, but that nothing had been resolved.

"We played basketball that day, A's against B's. Lyndie Sale went back to the locker room in the middle—she was the only one who did."

"Go on."

"Bharatee was so upset . . . it was a present from her grandmother. So after everyone left, I went back and looked in Lyndie's locker. I thought if it was there, I'd say I found it on the ground, and give it back to Bharatee."

"Did you find it?"

"Not the locket, but the chain was on the shelf in Lyndie's locker. It was all in pieces. It was all broken."

"Boy. You'd have to be strong to do that."

Kim nodded. Clearly the whole episode had disturbed her deeply.

"What did you do?"

"I didn't do anything. Bharatee wouldn't want it back like that. And I didn't want to be a narc. But when you told us the maxim, I thought maybe you knew."

"No, I didn't know, Kim. But I'm glad you told me. . . ."

She was interrupted by the shriek of a siren. She turned to see an entire hook and ladder, with five firepersons dressed in rubber coats with long-handled axes dangling from their belts, steaming up the drive past Home, heading for the Primary building.

Rue said, "Excuse me" and ran. Meanwhile, the firefighters all leaped off the truck and rushed toward the Primary playground, where the second grade stood watching as if gods had swarmed down from Mt. Olympus.

"What happened?" Mike asked, arriving on the run at the same time as Rue.

"Courtney Leavitt got her finger stuck in a Barbie doll," said Charla Percy, staring at the fire truck. "She was very upset so we called nine-one-one."

Some of the boys, excited by the sight of the dangling axes, believed the firemen would cut off Courtney's hand.

Courtney, who seemed to fear the same thing, was trying to hide behind Charla's leg. With a professional air, a large fireman knelt to examine the hand Courtney held out, its index finger vanished into the hole where the doll's left arm used to be.

"Is this your doll?" he asked. She nodded.

"Did you pull its arms off?"

Courtney nodded. Shannon Korfus, agitated, explained, "Well, she . . . she . . . well, it's an old one so she pulled one and I pulled the other."

"What happens if we pull now?" asked the fireman. Courtney gave a cry and snatched her hand back. "Hurts, huh? You already tried that?" Courtney nodded. A second fireman produced from his tool belt a needle-nosed wire cutter. The first one looked at the tool and nodded.

"Can you hold real still?" he asked Courtney. She wasn't sure, but it had been a rhetorical question.

The fireman began to cut across the doll's chest from the other armhole. Clearly Courtney thought he would come to her finger and snip right through it. But instead he deftly cut the finger free.

Courtney hopped up and down, half laughing, half crying, and holding the freed hand with her other. The fireman insisted on examining it to see that it wasn't permanently injured. The class crowded around wanting to see the finger.

"Thank you so much . . ." said Mrs. Percy, greatly relieved.

"You're welcome," said the fireman. "But technically, it was a Ken doll."

The day concluded with Hughie Bache's mother in the office, completely hysterical, talking on Emily's phone to Poison Control.

The day Pat Moredock broke her arm the hospital told her to make an ice pack of one-third rubbing alcohol and two-thirds water and apply it for fifteen minutes every hour. This she had done. She had one ice pack at home and another she'd been keeping in a baggie in the school kitchen's freezer. Between classes and at lunch break she would come get it and apply it to her wrist for ten minutes, then put it back. Hughie Bache, quite illegally, had gone into the kitchen to steal a soft drink. Since none were cold, he had filled a cup with slush from Pat's ice pack. That was easier than breaking out an ice tray. He poured a Seven-Up over the slush, and downed the whole thing.

"I know, but won't it damage his kidneys? My husband's a doctor," shrilled Patty Bache. "Shouldn't he take paragoric?"

A brief pause before she erupted again.

"There must be an antidote . . . what about milk? What about brain damage?" Finally she accepted that all she could do was give him liquids and let it pass through.

"They said he'll have a horrible headache." The patient was sitting looking frightened on the bench before Emily's desk. A half cup of rubbing alcohol. He did *not* feel good.

When at last the office was quiet, Rue finished clearing her desk. Leaving, she was surprised to find Emily still in the outer office, though it was nearly five and the office closed at four-thirty.

"What a day," Rue said, stopping to say good night. "It must be the phase of the moon, or something. Where are your little ones?"

"They both had play dates. I thought I'd just finish some letters I had to print."

"Did Mike tell you what Kim Fat Snyder told me?"

Emily nodded.

"Has Malone seen Lyndie, or talked to her? I worry about her."

"Malone does too. She's tried to call her a couple of times, but Lyndie hasn't called back."

"Maybe I'll call the principal over at Midvale and see how she's doing. . . ." Rue was thinking aloud when the phone rang.

Emily grabbed it. She listened.

"No, I'm sorry," she said. "Not at the moment," and hung up. As she reached for her coffee mug, which she had forgotten was empty, it seemed to Rue her hand shook.

"Em," said Rue, "are you okay?"

"Fine," said Emily tightly. "It was just some salesman."

"I didn't mean that. I mean, you seem . . . strained lately, at least to me. Is there anything wrong? That I can help you with?"

Emily looked at her. Rue's face was full of concern.

"No," said Emily finally. "I think you're right, it's just a star-crossed day."

"Thank god it's over," said Rue. "Good night."

⌒ B̶ut it was not over.

The Coburn/Kleins were giving themselves a going-away party, and Rue and Henry were there. Bob had won a full-year sabbatical and a grant to write a paper on epidemiology. They were taking their hulking teenagers out of school and moving to Barcelona. Rachel would take an intensive course of Spanish. They would go to bullfights. They had been reading stacks of guidebooks, and they served Sol y Sombres at the cocktail hour.

There were many toasts around the dinner table. The circle of friends that would be broken by the departure felt exhilarated and envious about this adventure. Halfway through the meal Rachel had to leave the table to get her calendar, as datebooks emerged from pockets and purses, and the friends got serious about when they would be over to visit.

Henry looked at Rue. "Easter?" he asked.

"I'm only off for a week. How about right after graduation?" She took out her book. "June fourteen. Leave June fifteen?"

"Done."

"Now, you may be overlapping with my parents . . . hold on. . . ." Rachel flipped to June. "Yes, they'll be with us to the twentieth."

"The next week?"

"Done," said Rachel.

"Great!" said Bob.

"Bob, the only trouble I see with this plan is, when are you going to write your paper?" said Ted French.

"I have that figured out. If the end of the year comes and I still haven't done it, I'm going to write to King Juan Carlos and apply for the job of court jester. I will pledge to legally change my name to Flan De La Casa."

Everyone laughed.

Henry reached for the sangría. "*We've* been thinking about running off to the Peace Corps," he announced to the table.

"Have you!" "How Great!" "Since when?" "When would you go?" "Where would you go?" The table responded with excitement.

"I didn't know you were thinking of that," said Sylvia French to Rue.

"I didn't either," Rue said, smiling.

"I'd like to go to Africa or Thailand. Or to the Marshall Islands."

"How about the Virgin Islands? Or Fiji?"

"No, I want to go someplace really horrible. Where we'll have to eat poi, and the only books in English will be forty-year-old paperback Penguins. I was once stuck in a monsoon on the Costa Brava with nothing to read but the short stories of Bertrand Russell. I've never gotten over it."

"Are you going to teach? Or farm? Or what?"

To Rue's surprise, Henry said, "There's an area in the Marshall Islands where whole families come down with a disease that looks like Alzheimer's. When you open their brains, it looks like a melt-down in a power station. In certain parts of the brain, the wires are fused and rigid in a mass. Genetic disposition is in play, but it's also environmental. Family members who move away from the area don't get the disease in anything like the numbers of their relatives who stay behind."

"Wow," said Rachel Klein.

"I've read about that," said Bob. "It's something in the diet, isn't it?"

"They think so. There's a foul starchy root they eat, especially in hard times, that seems implicated. I can't remember what it is. I want to get there and see for myself before I fuse any more ganglia and forget that I wanted to go."

"Rue, what will you do?" asked Rachel.

Taken off guard, she answered, "Commute." The table roared.

Driving home, they were quiet. Finally, Rue said, "Henry, are you serious?"

"I don't know. I don't know how to make a decision like this without you."

A stunning thing to say, a stunning thing to hear. They reached home, and Henry turned off the engine. Neither moved.

"Are you making it without me?"

"I'm thinking about it without you."

More silence. They watched a doe, confused to find herself so deep in the suburbs, come to the sidewalk, stand poised with a fore-hoof curled up, a tentative pose, then dart across the street. She disappeared into underbrush, bounding toward Marvin Schenker's garden.

"I didn't know you were so unhappy."

"I'm not unhappy. But I'd rather change my life at fifty than at sixty. I want to go while I'm young enough to take it, and while I still have something to offer."

She nodded in the dark. Clearly, they could stay up all night discussing the implications of this, or they could let it hang there between them. Rue thought that in many ways, it would probably come out the same. She also knew she had the Primary report cards to proof before bed.

She opened her door, and he did the same. They left the car by the curb and walked inside.

Rue went to the answering machine and played back the tape.

"Anything?" Henry asked.

"Three hang-ups." She took off her coat and took it to the closet. Henry went to turn on the lights in the kitchen and then the living room.

"Rue, look at this," he said from the living room. She went in. On the stone hearth in front of the fireplace lay the captain's clock, face-down, that had stood for sixteen years on the mantelpiece. Henry turned it over. The crystal was smashed and the hands were stopped at three minutes before nine. Rue stood over him, as they both stared.

"Did we have an earthquake?" she asked.

"I didn't feel one. Is anything else out of place?" Nothing seemed to be. They stared, puzzled.

"Well, that is truly weird," said Rue.

The phone rang and she went to answer it. Henry came into the kitchen to get a broom and dustpan to clean up the clock. She was standing in silence. Then she hung up.

"The Breather?"

She nodded. She sat down heavily at the table. The sequence, the hang-ups and the clock and the Breather, had upset her. Or the estrangement between her and Henry that upset her all the time these days, like a chronic low-grade fever.

The phone rang again.

"Let me," said Henry, and he grabbed it. But it wasn't the Breather; Rue could hear that a voice was speaking on the other end. Henry listened briefly.

"Not at the moment," he said. A question on the other end. "Please call tomorrow during business hours." He hung up. Rue looked at him, questioning.

"Why don't *I* ever get the Breather? I want to tell him I'll stuff the phone down his neck."

"Who *did* you get?"

"Somebody wanting to sell bonds."

"It's awfully late isn't it?"

"Ten of ten."

Rue thought that was awfully late. The salesmen usually called at dinnertime.

"I'm surprised you told him he could call back."

Henry always said, Not interested, sorry, and hung up. She thought.

"He won me over by not asking, 'How are you this evening.'"

He got himself a beer out of the refrigerator. He went to the closet for the broom and dustpan.

"I'll clean up the glass," he said.

"Thank you, honey."

He was in the living room with the broken clock in his hand when the phone rang again. He put the clock on the mantle. Rue had answered the phone; it had rung only once. He was sweeping shards of crystal from the hearth and the hardwood floor beyond, when he heard Rue scream.

Georgia had died a few minutes before midnight. She had been hit from behind by a drunk driver, who had dragged the body almost a mile without knowing it. Jonah had gotten part of the license number.

Jonah and Georgia were hitchhiking home from a gig in New Paltz, New York.

"Why the hell were they wearing black?" Henry asked in anguish. (This was later.) "Why the hell were they hitchhiking?"

He asked that over and over again, as if getting a simple answer to that one question would stop his pain.

"Why the hell were they hitchhiking? If they were stranded, I would have sent them money. . . ."

It was hearing him say that that made Rue feel she would lose her mind from grief.

All she had to do was call, and say Daddy, we don't have any money, Daddy we can't get home. And he would have sent them money. He would have. She knew it was true. All Georgia had to do was call. All she had to do was say Daddy. He would have told them to go to a motel. He would have wired them money. He would have gone to get her himself.

All she had to do was call.

Everything was over. Everything they had hoped for her, separately and together. Every joy she had felt, every smile, from the day they brought her home from the hospital, was for nothing. Every grade she had earned, every bite she had eaten, it was all a tease and a shame and a waste. She was gone. It was gone.

They took it differently. Henry raged and drank and broke things. It was very bad that she had died estranged from him. Rue sat still and wept, with her arms hugged close to her body. The second day, when the kitchen table was covered with food that people had brought, and the people who came to distract and comfort them were eating it, Henry came downstairs and marched to Rue, as if there were no one else in the house, and said, "I want all her things out of here. Everything that was hers. Clothes. Books. Everything. Get it all out of here." Then he took a bottle of scotch and went upstairs.

Sylvia French and Emily brought boxes. They sat in Georgia's room. For hours they worked emptying closets, folding clothes, packing them. Rue watched them. Sometimes she would see something that would make her cry out. A blue-jean jacket Georgia wore in fourth grade, with buttons pinned to it. Rue thought it was long gone. She held it in her lap and cried. After a while Sylvia took it from her and packed it. Then she'd stop them and reach out for something else. There was a shirt frayed at the collar that had been Henry's. Georgia had worn it as a nightshirt. She held it for a while, then let them take it.

Cleaning out the desk was much worse. Georgia's handwriting. Georgia's handwriting at fourteen, at twelve, at five. There were pictures made in kindergarten. There was a stash of notes passed from Georgia to Rochelle to Sasha when they were in eighth grade. What secrets were there, what jokes? What didn't she know of her daughter's secret life?

What life? Who cared? What was the point of knowing your child's secrets, except to advise, to protect? Rue sobbed till the muscles in her sides ached.

When all the clothes and notebooks and papers and snapshots and cartoons and ribbons and pins were put away, Emily and Sylvia asked again.

Get rid of them, Rue said. Burn them, send them to the dump, give them to Goodwill. All right, they said. And the boxes disappeared.

And when a day later, she couldn't stop crying, because she needed to hold her child and there was nothing of her left, they brought the boxes back.

The police were sorry they hadn't called earlier. Georgia's wallet had been lost when she was dragged, and for an hour, Jonah couldn't remember where they lived. Had she suffered? They didn't know exactly what had killed her, or how fast. An autopsy would show. But had she suffered? Had she died in terror?

Yes, the police guessed, since Henry insisted. They would surmise she had.

No need for an autopsy. They certainly didn't want to see her. Her ashes would be sent home, in a box marked Hum Rem, for human remains. The funeral home suggested Federal Express.

Henry wanted the drunk driver. He wanted to bash the driver's head against a pavement till it shattered like an egg, to scoop the brains out and grind his shoes in them. He wanted to crush the driver the way you kill the snail you find on the green leaf-blade of a daffodil. Crunch of shell, slime smear of body. The police hadn't found him yet. They had a partial tag; they were trying.

Why had they been hitchhiking? Henry asked the police, during that first long night. The police didn't know. The boy, Jonah, had $200 in cash in his pocket. They'd been paid for the gig. If they found Georgia's wallet, they would send it. They'd send somebody out to look when it was light.

How did they know what time it was when she was struck? They didn't, exactly. The boy, Jonah, running after the car in the dark, screaming, had heard a church bell ring before he got to the body.

Yes, she was dead at that time. Definitively.

The boy wanted to know if he could keep Georgia's guitar.

Their priest, a small round-faced man named Tom Ware, came to bring them comfort and to plan the funeral. This was the last week in February. Rue and Henry thanked him for coming and gave him some sherry. He saw that they looked unearthly pale, as if neither had slept in weeks. He noticed too that they sat on opposite sides of the living room. That they addressed him, but not each other. That they avoided eye contact. Mourning sometimes had that effect. Of shutting people off from each other, each in his own private oubliette full of grief. It was one of its horrors.

"The Twenty-third Psalm," said Henry. "And 'Oh God Our Help in Ages Past,'" and he bit his lip. In tears again. "Sufficient Is Thine Arm Alone, and Our Defense Is Sure," they had sung side by side, he in his strong bass, Georgia with her shimmering, confident alto. Sufficient for what? Defense of whom?

Tom brought out his prayer book. "You'll be wanting the Funeral Rite? Or would you like to compose something? It may be that Georgia's friends would like to help plan a remembrance."

"No funeral," said Rue. "She said she wouldn't want it."

Both men turned to look at her.

"Don't you remember?" She turned to Henry. "She said it over and over. She didn't believe in organized religion."

"But she came to church with you," said Father Tom.

"That was because she loved us. And to sing. She was clear about this. We listened to her opinion. We understood it. We can't just ignore her."

"But Rue," said Tom Ware, looking uncomfortable in his collar. "Funerals are for the living. It will be a comfort to you, and to Henry. . . ." Henry was staring at her.

"I know," she said, starting to cry. "It would be a great comfort. But it wasn't my life, and it isn't my death, it's hers. She didn't want it. We can't break faith with her just because she's dead."

The minister looked at Henry. He was looking steadily at Rue, as if he couldn't believe what he was seeing.

Finally he said to her, "She's gone, Rue."

She looked back at him, or toward him. She looked as if she wasn't seeing anything. Finally, she shrugged, and whispered, "A conscience is worth a thousand witnesses."

Sylvia French and Rachel Klein took turns answering the phone, since Rue couldn't and Henry wouldn't. Georgia's friends, and Henry's, and Rue's, called incessantly to know when and where the service would be. Over and over, Sylvia or Rachel would explain.

In twos and threes, Georgia's classmates would arrive at the door, dressed as if for church or graduation. They had never paid a sympathy call before. They would be shown into the den where Henry and Rue sat, writing answers to stacks of notes and letters of condolence. Henry would stare at them, as if trying to forgive them for being alive. Sometimes they asked for information about the death; sometimes they said how sorry they were. Sometimes they said how much they would miss her and that they would never, ever forget her, which Henry and Rue knew was a lie.

She'll fade from your lives and you won't even notice it, Rue thought. Whereas I pray for nothing except a moment when I forget her, and I don't get one, not one moment of oblivion.

"Did you hear about the clock?" Henry would suddenly ask, and the young people would shake their heads, no. Obsessively he would repeat this queer mystery, as if retelling it would reveal its meaning. The young people, who had come wanting to comfort, or be comforted, found that neither of these things could be done and found themselves trapped in a room where they understood how terrible that was.

"Thank you for coming," Rue would say, rising, to tell them that this was how they got out of it. They would leap to their feet and be gone. While they were there Rue felt she wanted only for them to go, and when they were gone, things seemed worse than before.

Neither Henry nor Rue could think what to do with the ashes. They had always had one theory about burial; you should be somewhere where your grandchildren can come to remember you, because you're part of who they are. What did that mean for Georgia?

One night, Henry and Rue sat in the living room. The night was very still. They stared, each at something that was going on inside themselves. Rue was listening to a silence so profound that it seemed she could hear her own eardrums roar, as a seashell does when you hold it to your ear.

There was a knock at the door. Neither of them moved, for a moment. Then Henry heaved himself up and went to open it.

In the hall, Rue could hear a young voice speak softly to Henry. She heard part of a sentence that had her name in it. She got up and went to the door.

From the top of the rise where the road wound down toward their house, there was flowing a silent stream of Georgia's friends. They were carrying lighted candles, and the candles lit their faces. There were the musicians, some in rags and patches, some with pins in their clothes and spikes in their hair. There were many from Georgia's high school class and many Rue and Henry had never seen before. Most of the girls from Rue's current eighth grade were there. They flowed down the hill and up the walk to the door, where they pooled and eddied into a pond, surrounding the doorway where Rue and Henry stood.

Rue stood in the doorway, her hands clasped before her, looking from face to face. Then, in the middle of the throng, Georgia began to sing *Panis Angelicus.*

Henry sank against the door frame, hands in his pockets, and cried. Rue stood as she was, like an icon, frozen. She couldn't see who carried the tape player. Many of the young faces looking back were now weeping. Rue was absolutely back in the moment, holding Georgia's mangy fur coat, feeling tears of love and pride in her eyes, seeing before her the little figure in the huge gray sweater. The singing ended. The tape had recorded a long crash of applause, but an unseen hand in the middle of the group clicked it off. The silence was enormous, though broken by sniffing and quiet crying. Then at the back, the first ones turned to go. The river re-formed and moved off up the hill. Slowly they walked into the night, taking the light with them.

Henry stood looking at Rue. She looked back, but felt like flinching. If he had been yelling at her, she couldn't have felt his grief and need more deeply. He seemed to be saying, "I cannot bear this. *They* can't bear this. You and your promises, you and your principles."

He walked rapidly past her into the house, into the den where the brown plastic canister holding Georgia's ashes sat on a table. Rue followed him as he took the box and marched past her into the garden.

He opened the box and stood looking at what was inside. He kept staring at it, as if in surprise, as if trying to understand what it had to do with Georgia.

He stood under the night sky holding the box with both hands, breathing deeply. Then he said, firmly and clearly, as if to an unseen assembly,

> *"All praise to thee, my God this night*
> *For all the blessings of the light*
> *Keep me, oh keep me, King of kings*
> *Beneath thine own almighty wings."*

Then, without looking at Rue, he upturned the box, and poured out the ashes onto the soil beneath the roses.

Much later that night, Rue couldn't stop thinking of Georgia alone outside as it started to rain.

Rue and Henry flew to Phoenix in a normal plane and then to Flagstaff in a little prop plane. Small planes frightened Rue, but Henry seemed in a mood to welcome danger. Even in early March the heat in Phoenix was suffocating as they left the plane. But it was piercingly clear and crisp in Flag, and the blue of the sky that formed a dome above them as they emerged onto the runway was intense. The chill and the tall pines that rimmed the runway reminded Rue oddly of Maine, though the land here was flat and the pines a different kind from those at home. They went inside and Rue stood around like an invalid, looking at historical displays of Flagstaff's early days, while Henry rented a car for the drive to Canyon de Chelly.

As always when they traveled, Rue was in charge of the guidebook, but Henry had done enough research to know that the Navajo reservation was dry. Before heading north and east, he found a gas station cum convenience store that also stocked a surprising variety of wine and liquor.

"They even had equipment for brewing beer," he reported as he climbed into the driver's seat and gave a bottle of scotch to Rue. She put it into her bag of books. Rue couldn't leave home without a supply of reading matter to last a month, as if she were constantly worried that she would be marooned somewhere and run out of things to read before she starved to death.

When they traveled, Georgia was in charge of maps.

Now Henry glanced at the photocopied road map the car rental woman had given him and then laid it on the seat between them, where it remained, as if neither of them knew what to do with it.

The view from the windows mostly stunned them into silence as the road climbed toward the Four Corners, the junction of Arizona, New Mexico, Utah, and Colorado. From time to time Rue would read from the guidebook.

"Chelly, pronounced *shay*, is a corruption of the Navajo word *Tseyi* (she struggled with that), meaning something like 'among the rocks,' or 'canyon.' Tsegi Canyon is named from the same word. Chelly (she pronounced it phonetically) is the Anglo version, Tsegi the Spanish. If it's Anglo why the 'de'? It should be French."

Henry grunted. Outside the car the world was like a table, jackrabbit country of sage and tumbleweed. In the distance they could see startling buttes rising red from the earth.

"The Hopi reservation is within the Navajo, and there has long been a territorial struggle between the two tribes. Most people believe that the Hopi are the descendents of the Anasazi people who lived in the Canyons from the time of Christ to thirteen hundred. The Navajo arrived in the Canyons about seventeen fifty; 'Anasazi' is Navajo for 'Ancient Ones.' Navajo and Hopi disputed rights to the territory for many decades, until the matter was finally bloodlessly settled by a pushing contest."

Henry smiled and nodded at that. "Send these people to Washington," said Henry.

"To Bosnia," said Rue.

They arrived at The Lodge, where they planned to spend several days, just at sunset. Navajo women ran the hotel desk; they were given their room key and elaborately told where to find the ice machines. Although the guidebook said they were at the canyon, they had no sense of being near anything but endless flat desert.

They had a brief but intense discussion over breakfast the next morning over whether to take a jeep tour into the canyon, or go on horseback.

"Or hike," said Rue. "We have plenty of time."

"You'll love riding," Henry said. What he meant was, he would love riding. He had grown up with horses, albeit eastern fox-hunters, not quarter horses with western saddles. Rue had spent enough time riding to be able to mount without falling off the other side, but that was about the extent of her expertise. "We'll be able to go places we couldn't on foot, or in a jeep," Henry added.

"You haven't ridden for more than two hours in thirty years," Rue pointed out. She wasn't sure that she had ridden for more than two hours ever.

"It's like riding a bicycle," said Henry. He called the horse rental place, and arranged for a tour and a guide. Rue went to the cafeteria to order three box lunches.

A young Navajo named Earl provided a saddlebag for the lunches and for a bottle of water Rue had brought. Three horses, tacked, were loaded into a trailer, and Rue and Henry were invited to board the four-door pickup that pulled it. They were driven miles across flat scrub land, still with no sense that a canyon was near. Rue guessed they had gone twelve or fifteen miles. If they were riding all the way back to where they started, this was not going to be a cakewalk.

Once the horses were decanted from the trailer and the driver disappeared down the road, the three mounted and Earl led off at a walk across tableland of sage and pinyon. The pine nuts were gathered in the fall, he said. "Navajo people live on top during the winter, while the children are in school. In the summer, they live in the canyon, farming. It's much cooler on the bottom," he said. "Fifteen, twenty degrees." Conversation was as difficult as always on horseback, when riding single file. At first Rue tried to induce her horse to walk beside Henry's, but both animals had an aversion to that arrangement. So they ambled in silence one by one until the moment they found themselves at the lip of the canyon, and saw the earth split open to reveal a wide crevasse hundreds of feet deep, with walls of sheer red and buff sandstone, a sight of heart-stopping beauty.

From that moment, the day took on a trancelike quality. The air was intensely clear, and the sky a wild light blue. Hawks circled above them, riding the air currents. The canyon floor was beginning to show the light lime green of new grass, and the pine trees were towering, black green. The quality of light, the arrangement of colors, exotic but natural, provided such a rush of sensory marvels that Rue could feel it flooding her, as if the brain were fully employed in trying to record and store the experience, and any such taxing of the system as linear thought would overload it and cause a short or an electrical fire.

Earl's last words, as they started over the lip onto the switchback trail, which descended to the canyon floor at a cant of about eighty degrees, were, "You can walk and lead your horse if you get nervous."

What makes him think I *could* walk this without plunging to my death, Rue wondered, and thought further that this likelihood explained the presence of the hawks. She decided to trust the horse and try not to consider that he seemed to be about thirty years old, which if true meant her life depended on the vision and reflexes of a creature the equivalent of her father's age. When the loose stones rolled under her horse's hooves, she stared across at the canyon wall opposite, and thought about what it could be like to live here, and run free, and be lithe and strong enough to climb to the protecting shelves carved into the walls of the canyon. The horse pottered and slid steadily downward, following Earl and Henry, swaying like a camel.

Halfway down, she pointed to a ledge across the canyon in the far sandstone wall.

"It looks as if someone has built a brush barrier partway across that ledge," she said to Earl.

It was a question. He said, "Anasazi people and Navajo people used to bury their dead in open air. Now we have three cemeteries on top."

Open air. Georgia. She couldn't look at Henry.

"If a Navajo wanted to be buried like that now, in the canyon, would it be allowed?"

"Oh, yes," said Earl. He started his horse and they followed.

Rue was liking the demand on previously unused muscles she was feeling so far. She could feel things tense and stretch in her thighs and abdomen. I can take this, she thought.

"Do you think there are still relics from the Anasazi to be found?" Henry asked. Earl turned to answer, knowing otherwise his words would be lost to them, and Rue felt the same fear for him she would if he were driving a car and let it choose its own way as he turned to talk to passengers in the back seat.

"I know there are," said Earl. "My brother-cousins were climbing up to a cliff, and they found a big ceremonial bowl." Rue felt envious. She knew that no one not of the Navajo Nation could go anywhere in this canyon without a guide, and that once here they might not disturb anything. Not take a pebble, or cut a switch with which to keep the horse awake. She knew too that it was scorned

among The People to sell to outsiders any treasures that had meaning for the Nation. But what were the rules of ownership?

"What happens to such a thing?" she asked. "Do your brother-
cousins leave it where they found it?"

"Oh no," said Earl. "We have it at the house."

Rue's mind floated from fantasy to memory, and hour after
hour she felt that what she was doing most was storing the colors.
Once on the canyon floor, they rode along the wash and began to
encounter log hogans. These were small, always round, with tiny
windows and the door facing east. Round for ceremonial purposes,
dark for people who live almost all the time outdoors. Around the
hogans was often a good deal of garbage; the owners were not effete
tree-huggers.

"How do the people who farm here in the summer get their
belongings in and out?" Henry asked.

"They used to put it in a blanket and tie it on the horse; came in
the same way we did. Now everyone has four wheel." So far they
had not seen another human, and the whole morning it was possible to imagine a time when there were no other humans here.
Certainly they didn't see or hear a plane, or an electronic noise, and
aside from their saddles and the cultural detritus in their heads,
there was nothing to distinguish their experience of these hours
from that of the first Navajo to discover the canyon.

Earl told them the legends of the towering Spider Rock and
Speaking Rock, which were said to talk to each other alone at night.
He showed them, high in the cliff wall, the first of many Anasazi
ruins they were to see. It was barely believable that a whole village
had once lived there, daily climbing up and down what looked to
be the distance of three or four stories of a modern building, carrying food and water and babies on their backs. The wall looked completely sheer. How did they do it?

They dug hand and toe holes in the rock. They were still there.
Had Earl been to that particular ruin? Oh, yes, he said, as if to say
of course—wouldn't you? He showed them a small low opening
that led to an ancient storage cave. Anasazi people in this canyon
farmed the floor but lived up in the walls of the canyon, to be safe

from predators, and from winter flash floods. In other canyons, people farmed the mesas, the tabletop above the canyons, and finally even built great pueblos on top, but not here.

They passed a deserted hogan beside the wash, in the shadow of the cliff, and from behind it came a beautiful appaloosa. It trotted out, ears forward, tail high, and followed them closely for several minutes.

"Someone you know?" Henry asked.

"Yes, my aunt lives there. He knows me pretty well."

When they reached the next bend of the wash and crossed it again, the appaloosa turned and galloped back to where he had come from, achingly beautiful.

They stopped by a bend in the wash, under cottonwoods, and dismounted to eat lunch. Rue was beginning to hurt and stiffen, and was grateful that the winter sun high in the sky warmed the windless valley. It was good to sit on something that wasn't moving. As they ate, Earl said, "I always rode bareback when I was a little boy, but when I became a guide, the insurance people said I had to use a saddle. The first day I used one I came home all blisters." He laughed. Rue was beginning to know how he had felt.

"Your aunt's horse just stays there, near the hogan, without being tethered?" Henry asked.

"Oh yes, they don't go anywhere. It's a good thing our horses are geld, because that one's a stud," he added, and Rue saw at once what he meant. She had a vision of the extreme discomfort that would ensue if one found oneself astride a horse fight. Like a dog fight, at three times the size, and at breakneck speed, with hooves. She had a moment of gratitude for her own mount's near somnolence.

"Does your aunt ride him bareback?" Henry asked.

"Of course. And she wears a skirt," said Earl. He talked a little about what the summers were like, when grandparents, great-grandparents, horses, dogs, and babies all moved down into the canyon to grow alfalfa and corn and beans, ride bareback, climb the cliff walls, and explore the ruins, when the only language is Navajo, and at night, in the dark hogan, the old stories are told.

*   *   *

Rue felt as if time had blessedly stopped. This is A Day of My Life, she thought, A Day of Days. The stunning physical beauty, the silence, the sense of being momentarily part of something human but mysterious and completely other was like a great tide that came up under the hulk of grief and mourning she and Henry soundlessly carried, and floated it, so although it was still there, it became weightless and small in this immensity. Their senses were so full it was possible to be entirely here and in the moment and nowhere else. It was a blessed relief.

When they rode on, the unfamiliar aches reasserted themselves and intensified. Earl pointed out ancient pictographs high on the sandstone walls, pictures of goats, men, dancers, antelope. The pigments, he said, were made from grinding different kinds of minerals found in the canyon and mixing them with pine pitch. They passed their first jeep tour, coming along the wash. Earl showed them a ledge inches wide, sloping high above their heads, where a nineteenth-century Navajo shepherd boy had painted white figures of goats. He pointed out the great streaks of natural black varnish pouring down and stained into the wall of the canyon as if someone on top of the mesa had overturned an immense bucket.

There were more ruins, including one at the floor of the canyon with its back to the cliff wall. It was possible to imagine—impossible not to—the traffic between the ancient tiny villages in sight of each other, the one on the floor beside the grain fields, the other across the wash and high up in the cliffs. They passed a farm field with several hogans, and Earl said, "That is owned by my clan grandfather." Henry asked about clans, but Earl gave answers less direct than those found in the guidebooks, and then told them instead that his clan grandfather farmed by planting each corn seedling within a tin can, lidless at both ends, driven halfway into the ground. That way he could water the plant without wasting water on bare soil, each seedling in its own three-inch oasis. His clan grandfather also raised peaches. They could see the trees over against the canyon wall; Earl said they were beautiful when they bloomed.

Earl expressed no interest in who they were or where they came from. He followed up no leading remarks. Rue could not tell if that was because in his culture it was rude to ask direct questions (as she strongly suspected it was) or because it was so satisfying to live and belong in this place and inhabit a world in which his ancestors and the Anasazi were as real and present to him as she and Henry were that there was nothing left over for curiosity.

"When Navajo people first came here and found ruins of Anasazi people," said Earl, "they did not disturb them because they were afraid to anger their ghosts. That is why they are so well preserved, two hundred years since Navajo people live here."

"So the ghosts turned out to be useful," said Henry, apparently after a long silence feeling the need to say something.

Earl didn't answer, which Rue had come to recognize as Navajo good manners in the face of a remark too dumb to notice.

When they came to a part of the canyon across from the White House ruin, where there is one trail tourists may walk without a guide, Earl greeted a group of young people in such a way that they paused, looking as if they'd been challenged for doing something they shouldn't. But he passed pleasantly and greeted the next group the same way, and Rue recognized that his was the manner of a host. That he was greeting them exactly as she would a friend of Georgia's whom she came upon unexpectedly in her own upstairs hallway. The canyon was where Earl lived. The tourists were guests. The people in their shorts with their cameras might feel entitled because they had paid to be there, but Earl clearly felt exactly as the Rockefellers in Seal Harbor did, on the days that they allowed the tourists to come in and tour the gardens.

She began to hallucinate about leading Navajo tourists through the pine woods of her girlhood. "What's this?" one would ask, and she would say, "Well, those are old lobster pots that belonged to my clan grandfather. After he died, his son Gordon started an old car graveyard here in the backyard. He had rusting hulks of automobiles piled up as high as the house, but then a man from Portland proved that engine oil was getting into the water table so Gordon had to pay to have them hauled away. Gordon tried to promise to hang them up on a hook first and drain them good before he put them on the pile, but no one believed he would."

She pictured waiting for someone to ask what Gordon wanted with an auto graveyard, and somehow knew that Earl, anyway, if it

were he touring the scenes of her childhood and her father's childhood, and her father's father's childhood, would be too polite to ask.
She had the strong sense that Earl was having to conceal the fact
that she had committed some breach of Navajo etiquette every second time she opened her mouth. She was used to knowing the
rules. To being rather an authority on the rules.

If she had to choose one word to sum up the experience of this
day, could she do it? "Awe" occurred to her. And "gratitude." And
increasingly, "pain." She and Henry had each ridden with Earl for
part of the afternoon, and once, for a stretch, with each other, but it
had now been quite a while since they had exchanged a word. She
wondered if his silence meant what hers did. They had been on
horseback now for upwards of six hours and she had begun to feel
that around each bend in the wash they would come upon the horse
trailer waiting for them, or even (and she couldn't imagine what
this would look like) the end of the canyon, the corral among the
cottonwoods where they had begun. But around every corner was a
new stretch of canyon, teaching them about the endless variety of
changes that could be rung on this one stupendous image. The towering red wall and the dappled sliver of wash beneath it, now narrow as a creek, now wide as a river, went on forever.

Rue and Henry's horses, either feeling their age or ready for a
nap, dawdled slower and slower. To keep up with Earl they had to
force the beasts into a trot, which Rue for one found excruciating
now that she was so sore, and her bust and every muscle in her
body hurt as they bounced. They were long since out of drinking
water.

They had been on horseback eight hours by the time they rode
up a slight grade at the end of a long silent silver stretch of canyon.
The sun was low in the sky and it made a streak of mirror of the
water. Rue's horse occasionally wandered into sink holes if she lost
her attention and failed to follow Earl exactly. She pictured herself
and the horse staggering over sideways and drowning in four feet of
water, too tired to bother to save themselves. Perhaps Henry was
trying to kill her. Perhaps Earl was trying to kill them both. If this
were a sort of cultural retribution, she could recognize with her
brain it was fairly witty, but was too tired and thirsty and incipi-
ently nauseous to care.

*   *   *

When they finally arrived at their room at The Lodge, long after they had ceased to believe the ordeal would ever end, they hobbled in, still in single file. Henry sat down, took off his boots, and got into bed with all his clothes on. Rue felt his forehead.

"You're hot," she said.

He said, "I'm freezing." She got the quilted bedspread from the second bed and piled it on top of him. Then she went into the narrow bathroom, moving as if she were a hundred years old. She slowly and painfully took off her clothes and got into the tub, half afraid her arms and legs would buckle as she lowered herself, and she would drop and shatter. She turned on the water and let the tub fill around her, so that she could adjust to the heat as the water rose. She wanted to be immersed in water hot to the point of pain for about a month.

When she finally came out, the bedroom seemed frigid. Henry was asleep. She hurried under the covers still half-dried, too easily chilled to wait to put on clothes. She too slept, and when she woke up she could tell by the light outside that it was nearly night.

Henry was awake. He was lying on his back, waiting for her to wake up.

"Well," she said, "that was a lot of fun," and they both started to laugh. It felt very strange to be naked in bed and hugged by a man who was fully clothed. She could feel the scratchy wool of his sweater and the cold of his fly buttons.

"You're a forgiving soul," he said.

"No, it *was* wonderful. The first four hours were maybe the peak hours of my life."

"I began to wonder if he was trying to kill us."

"Did you? So did I."

"At one point I looked back and saw that you were gray and I was frightened."

"I was thirsty," said Rue. "I thought of asking you to get me a drink from the wash, but I didn't want to be a wimp."

"I wouldn't have let you drink that. That's how you get giardia."

"Oh."

They lay holding each other. Rue cried for a while, because she had thought of Georgia and was too tired to hold it back. Henry knew what she was thinking and held her, and stroked her hair.

After a while he said, "It's night. Are you hungry?"

"I don't think so," she said. "I don't think I can move."

"Want some scotch?"

To his surprise, she said, "Sure, a little." So he walked, very painfully, with their brown plastic ice bucket out to the nearest ice machine. When he got back to the room, Rue was lying with her eyes closed.

"I'm watching the day," she said, and he knew what she meant. "It's hallucinogenic. It's so intense, those colors, all those images. . . ."

Henry put ice in plastic tooth glasses, poured them each some scotch, and got back into bed. They sipped very slowly and held hands.

"This is nice," said Rue after a while.

"What?" Henry asked.

"The scotch."

"You hate scotch."

"I know."

After a while she said, "I'm floating."

"I know."

"I'm so grateful for it. I'm floating."

"Shhh," said Henry. She knew he was right. She knew he understood her to mean she was too hurt and exhausted to feel the other pain. He was afraid she would say it out loud, which would bring it all back. After a while Henry got up and took off his clothes, and it was very nice to be able to feel his hair and smell his skin. The skin of his face and neck smelled of sun, as if the cells were storing it. She felt close to him for the first time in months, at peace, as if the barrier between them was gone. After a while she fell asleep.

Henry got up and poured more scotch. Then he turned off the light and got back into bed, and sat for a long while in the dark, feeling his wife breathing.

They were sore to the point of paralysis in the morning, but they forced themselves to move. They managed to get dressed, though it took three times as long as usual. Bending over to put on shoes and socks was agony, as it stretched the abused muscles of their thighs.

"I can't do it," Rue said. "I'm going to breakfast in my slippers."

"I was thinking of going in my bare feet."

"We're old," said Rue. "Everything changes because everything should. Earl didn't know; he's twenty-five. He never spent a day behind a desk in his life. He didn't know we couldn't do that anymore, and neither did we. But now we do. That's my deep thought for the day." Henry smiled.

They felt marginally better as they walked. The cafeteria was filled with schoolchildren on a field trip, already sugar high after choosing sticky breakfasts of sweetrolls or pancakes and syrup.

"Fourth grade," said Rue after one glance around.

"Fifth," said Henry, looking at a table of large boys. Rue shook her head and took a tray. She took a dish of stewed prunes, a muffin, and a pot of tea. An old woman's breakfast, she thought, content. Henry ordered bacon and ham. As they were paying, they saw one of the chaperones of the group preparing to speak to a table of girls who were dawdling over their food.

"Excuse me," Henry said, "what grade is this?"

"Fourth," said the woman.

Rue gave him a triumphant look. They'd been making bets with each other like this since the first week they met in Cambridge, twenty-five years ago.

The feeling of unity and peace of the night before was still with them. It was fragile, and they were both feeling as if they had been smashed to pieces and put back together by someone who'd never seen a person in the flesh before. But the connection was there and they moved together as if on one spoon they were carrying the world's most precious egg. If they could carry it and keep it whole, neither jostling the other nor faltering in any way, maybe things could begin to be as they used to be. They both knew that today would be a test.

"What shall we do?" Rue asked as they walked slowly back to their room in the weak winter sun.

"We could drive the North Rim. There are things to see from the Overlooks."

"I think I can manage getting in and out of the car."

"Good."

Henry drove. Rue sat close to him and touched his knee or the back of his neck from time to time. When she did, he kept his eyes on the road, but smiled. They both luxuriated in this physical reassurance that they were together and still breathing. Language would have been far more dangerous, so they didn't talk much.

They stopped at Antelope House Overlook. The parking lot was deserted. Entirely alone, they made their way over the rocky path, almost invisible at times as outcroppings of sandstone interrupted it, in the same way granite ledges broke through the soil in the fields and woods of Maine. But there was nothing familiar about this landscape. As they had the day before, they came suddenly to the lip of the canyon, and the drop, as before, made stomach and sphincter muscles clutch. You couldn't look at it without imagining falling or jumping. Antelope House was named for the pictographs on a nearby wall, and they found they could see the ruins and paintings clearly, closer to them here on the mesa than they had been to any of the ruins they saw the day before from the canyon floor.

"I'd give anything to be able to go into one," said Rue as they peered over the edge of the crevasse.

"I know."

"I just want to stand in one of those rooms, to feel the scale of it. They look so small from here."

"Anasazi people were smaller than us," said Henry, giving a perfect imitation of Earl. "Earl told me. He said they were about five feet tall."

"Ah."

"You could take a degree in anthropology. If you were good you might convince them to let you in for research."

"I think it would be worth it," said Rue.

Henry took her hand as they walked back to the car.

They drove on to Mummy Cave Overlook, where the ruined village filled a huge alcove in the rock. A very well preserved person had been found there, hence the name. The guidebook didn't say if it was a man or a woman, nor was it clear if it was the result of an open-air burial, or if someone had stayed on alone in the village when everyone else had gone and finally lain down and died.

At Massacre Overlook they weren't sure they were looking at

the right cave; it looked so small and so inaccessible. The sign said Navajo women and children had retreated to this ledge to hide from Spanish soldiers invading the canyon. They had been attacked then from above by a massive force on the cliff where Henry and Rue were standing, boldly blasting away at the cornered people. It was also called The Place Where Two Died because of a Navajo woman who had climbed from the ledge to the mesa, under fire, and killed a Spanish soldier by throwing herself from the cliff and taking him with her.

They stopped at the Visitor's Center at the head of the canyons, where artifacts from the ruins were displayed in glass cases. In the same room, a continuous video played, telling about Navajo life, past and present. The only people here besides themselves were some German tourists, a white-haired couple who were dressed as if for tennis. They moved around with the spritely energy of young athletes, and watching them made Rue and Henry feel crippled.

Henry and Rue moved from case to case, looking at the displays of Anasazi detritus: seed pods and pottery shards and beautiful baskets and cotton bolls and turkey bones and three different kinds of sandals. They read the information cards slowly, feeling so physically impaired that they mistrusted that their brains still worked. They didn't want to miss anything, and there was the distraction of the video soundtrack blaring away in English and Navajo.

"The men wore their hair long, but the women cropped theirs short," Rue announced. "Then they spun the hair along with other fibers and used the yarn to weave or braid with. Do you suppose that was a fashion statement? Or political?" Rue asked Henry. "One sex cutting the hair short? Like women's dresses, cut off at the knee. Don't you look at pictures of Hillary Clinton or Janet Reno, these national leaders with giant brains, with their bare legs sticking out of the bottom of their clothes, and wonder *what* they are thinking of?"

Henry laughed, so that the spritely Germans turned to look at him.

"Well I mean it. Can you imagine Richard Nixon greeting Khrushchev with his legs sticking out of his trousers? What *is* that?"

Henry smiled happily and touched her shoulder. She knew he was saying she delighted him. It had been quite a while since she felt she delighted him.

They ate lunch at a Burger King in Chinle.

"It might be a Samson and Delilah thing, the women cropping their hair," said Henry.

"I doubt it. With Navajo and Hopi, the women own the property and the men move from the house of the mother to the house of the wife."

"What makes us think their social structure was the same?"

"The kivas."

Henry helped himself to Rue's french fries. "Don't forget eighteenth-century Europe," said Henry. "Look at Louis XIV. All the men wore wigs and breeches that stopped at the knee. To show off their calves." He pulled up his pant leg a little and showed her his calf.

"That's true," said Rue, happily. "What does it mean?" And inwardly she thought, I need you, Henry. I miss my husband, and I need my friend. Please let this mood last.

But it didn't. After lunch, they started north to Monument Valley. But in the car they had the same problem with the map as they had at first, and Georgia was with them again. To avoid talk, they tried to listen to the radio. The rental car got poor reception and only very local stations; they looked for a National Public Radio station and found hard rock. Even turned low, the screech of heavy metal was like a gun going off in the car, reminding them both of the tape Georgia had sent, which was the last message they had from her, if you didn't count the broken clock. They turned the radio off.

Rue began to think about school. She couldn't go on much longer in a limbo between death and life. She had stopped floating. As scrub and sage and buttes rolled by outside, she began to think about Mike, and to worry about leaving him with things at such a flashpoint. In two days, she'd be back. She was hoping against hope that it would be a comfort to be at work. If she could be buoyed up by playing with three-year-olds, by seeing the new chicks born in the incubator in the kindergarten, by seeing a tiny eighth-grade girl in high heels doing Ethel Merman in *Call Me Madam* for the spring musical, she would be saved. And maybe if she were saved she could stay steady and in place long enough for Henry to come back to her.

She looked at Henry and saw he was a million miles away.

She'd seen that look so often in the last few weeks. But feeling her looking at him, he turned to her and met her eyes for a long few seconds. She felt he was studying her as if she were a rock he'd run over in the road. He'd stopped to get a better look because he'd never seen this object before.

He turned away again and said, "I have to tell you something." The tone was not casual; he did not mean he had to tell her he'd never liked Brussels sprouts. He wanted to tell her something that was going to make her sick. His eyes were fixed on the preposterous red buttes ahead of them. She looked at his profile and suddenly knew exactly what it was that was between them like a third passenger in the car, and it had nothing to do with Georgia.

"I need to tell you," he said.

"I need you not to," she answered.

It seemed to her he stepped on the gas, and she thought, Oh, this will be solved in a few seconds. We're going to flip and go up in flames together in a place with no name in northern Arizona. She hoped they would.

She looked at Henry briefly and she could see his face was hard, as if he'd offered her his heart and she'd stuffed it back into his pocket. Maybe that's what he thought he'd done.

"We've shared so much," he said.

"Please—don't say any more." She wondered what she would do if he ignored her. Climb into the back seat? Throw herself out of the car? He could tell her whatever he wanted to.

Finally, he said, with an acid edge to his voice, "Isn't the truth supposed to make us free?"

"Don't be silly," she said. "Nothing will make us free."

The car flew past the turnoff to Monument Valley. They were averaging eighty mph, sometimes faster. When they hit Route 98 north, Henry turned onto it; Rue had no idea where they were going and realized Henry had studied the map. When, exactly? When they got into the car this morning? After lunch? They sped through the cool alien landscape in silence. There were moments in which Rue felt a plea rising like a prayer, to whom she couldn't imagine. Stop, let's start over again, there was a way this day might have come out all right. But there wasn't. It had only felt like it, because for one day they had been in a world like an alternate universe.

When they hit the town of Page, it didn't take long to find the airport. It was small and clean, like Flagstaff's. Henry pulled up to the curb and got out, taking the keys with him to unlock the trunk. He got out his suitcase and set it on the sidewalk, along with the raincoat she'd brought for him for some idiotic reason, even though he pointed out that Canyon de Chelly was in a desert. He walked back to her window on the passenger side.

"I can't stand to be with you but apart from you," he said.

"I can't stand it either," she said, looking up at him. His thick blond hair had gone mostly gray, a dense ash color. His eyes, blue and pale behind his glasses, were red-rimmed. She wondered if he had slept the night before.

"Then we agree," he said, and dropped the car keys into her lap. She watched him walk into the airport without looking back at her.

She sat for a while at the curb, feeling how sore her body was. She wondered briefly if she should have let him confess, and then dismissed it. If she had ever believed that allowing someone to cause you that kind of pain would make you closer in the end, she didn't anymore. It would cost too much. The tears, the learning of dates and times and images she would then have to learn to forget. It might have helped him, it might not. It didn't matter. She couldn't afford it.

She got out and walked around to the driver's side, got in, and started the car.

The hardest thing about walking into the office on Monday morning was wondering how she could look at Emily. The anger and pain this thought caused her was so great she was almost grateful for it. The phrase "economy of pain" had occurred to her; why not take all the horror life had in store for you in one crushing dose, and if at the end you could still get up off the floor, maybe you'd be allowed some decades of happiness.

One day at a time, she said to herself. One day at a time. If you can keep waking up in the morning, if you can keep going through the motions, maybe one day the excruciating tide will recede and you will find you are alive again, walking on dry land in the sun. Some years from now. The thing to do now is prove to yourself that you cannot be crushed.

Emily was at her desk. She looked neat and pretty. Her blond hair was held by a velvet band and she was wearing a flowered shirtwaist dress. She had that friendly confidence that made her so good at this job, that had made her such a pleasure to have around. She did not seem to be working at anything; she seemed to be waiting for Rue. As Rue came through the door, their eyes met. Steady on both sides.

"How was it?" Emily asked, her voice quiet.

"Beautiful."

"Where did you go?"

"Canyon de Chelly. Monument Valley. Lake Powell."

"I've always wanted to see Lake Powell," Emily said.

"You must," said Rue. She wondered if Emily knew where Henry was now.

She walked to her office, pausing for a hug from Mike. On her desk she found messages literally stacked. She had been on leave for two weeks, which was a week longer, Chandler pointed out to the Executive Committee, than was industry standard for bereavement.

As she looked through the pink heap of messages, she blessed Mike for keeping the peace as long as he had. On the stroke of nine, she carried her mug of coffee into his office, and closed the door.

"Let's get into it," she said. "It looks as if expelling Glenn Malko hasn't solved our problems."

"Expelling him was all right. But unexpelling him was a disaster," said Mike. "That walk of triumph of his did more damage than Kenny Lowen caused in a year. The whole grade is running wild because we cut down their homeboy hero. And they learned there's safety in numbers too: we can't expel the whole grade."

Hughie Bache, Robey Hearne, and Jose French were vying to outdo each other in rudeness and intractability. Each had been suspended by Mr. Dianda with a warning of expulsion, and each had laughed it off. The way they saw it, if they got expelled they'd be heroes too, like Glenn. Robert Noonan would no longer allow Hughie in Latin class; he sent him to the library with extra homework during classtime, which made life difficult for Mrs. Nafie. Since Hughie had drunk the slush from Mrs. Moredock's ice pack, he and Jose had decided to specialize in terrorizing her during art class, which was by no means hard to do. They had frequently provoked her to unprofessional language and behavior. Some of the girls were even in on the uprising, and the upper-school faculty was now so hostile to the class that they were refusing to go along as chaperones on the annual three-day science field trip to Santa Catalina. Without chaperones the trip would be canceled. Every parent in the grade was up in arms about that, since the Santa Catalina trip was a god-given right of eighth-graders, and all had appointments with Rue to demand that she fix it. And the only person, bizarrely, who seemed to have no part in the mess was Kenny Lowen.

The faculty was exhausted because the minute Rue left campus Chandler made his presence felt in a dozen threatening ways. He now not only hated Rue, he saw the whole faculty as his enemy. The teachers felt left without protection or leadership, and on top of it they were frantically trying to write curriculum reports that would satisfy Chandler before their contracts came up for review.

Of course there was another Catherine crisis. One day Mrs. Bramlett, upset because her daughter had scored poorly on her

ERBs, demanded a meeting with Mike to denounce Catherine Trainer. Mike told her to go discuss the matter with Mrs. Trainer first. Karen Bramlett marched down to where the faculty was eating lunch, asked Mrs. Trainer for a minute of her time, and then railed at her through the lunch period and right through recess. By the time she was done, Catherine's food had been cleared away and she had a headache from hunger and a Civil War class to teach. The next day, Catherine had just emerged from the kitchen with a plate of hot lasagna when Karen Bramlett appeared again, demanding to talk to her.

"I am entitled to forty minutes off for lunch, Mrs. Bramlett," Catherine had said.

"This is the only time I can talk to you," Mrs. Bramlett answered angrily. "I have a meeting at the courthouse at one-fifteen."

"This is the only time I can eat my lunch," said Catherine, sitting down.

Karen whirled off, furious, to find Mr. Dianda, who was in the development office trying to help the temporary secretary work the mailing list program.

"Mr. Dianda, I have to talk to you right now."

Mike wheeled on her. "Mrs. Bramlett, you will have to make an appointment."

"This is urgent. Mrs. Trainer has been outrageously rude."

"Mrs. Bramlett, it will have to wait! I only have this temp for a day, we have to get out our Annual Report, and this goddamn program has printed a hundred and twenty dollars worth of mailing labels in ASCII!"

Mrs. Bramlett was momentarily halted.

"Where's the book, the whatchamacallit, the documentation?"

"There isn't any."

"What program is it?"

"It's a homemade thing that some Luddite software genius gave us ten years ago. The only person who can work it is Rue."

"That's ridiculous. Why don't you just go buy a program that you can understand?"

"Because we could buy a new program for thirty-nine-fifty, and then pay two thousand dollars in secretarial costs to reenter the data. The Board won't authorize it."

*　　*　　*

By the time Rue had spent a half-hour with Mike, which wasn't nearly enough, the line of people waiting to see her was out the door.

First was Carson McCann.

It turned out that Ashby had gotten a failing grade on a spelling test and claimed to his mother that Mrs. Percy had made him sit in the corner where he couldn't hear.

"What did Mrs. Percy say?" Rue asked.

"She said he's been in the corner before and can hear there fine. But it's his word against hers. Chandler said the fairest thing would be to give him the test again."

"What did Mr. Dianda say?"

"I didn't ask him. I told Mrs. Percy that I wanted him retested. . . . "

"Carson. For heaven's sake. Read your Trustee Handbook. Page thirty-one, Board members cannot dictate decisions to staff. You have no right to give a teacher an order. You're her employer, don't you understand? You carry a huge sword, and if you can't see it, she can. You can make your wishes known as a parent, you can discuss it with Mike or me, but I can't run a school if every member of the Board is running it with me! I can't run a school if every child who gets a poor grade can get the Board to order a retest!"

Mrs. McCann was slightly abashed. "Oh," she said. "Well, she refused to do it."

"Good. Do you have a copy of the Handbook?"

"Somewhere."

"Why don't you ask Emily to get you another one?"

Emily was at the door. Rue's meetings were scheduled every fifteen minutes. Some were going to have to be cut to ten, or she wouldn't have a chance to go to the bathroom.

"Mrs. Bramlett is here."

Karen Bramlett came in loaded for bear. "Here are Melanie's ERB scores from last year. Look at this . . . a twenty-percentile drop in math from last year. Rue, she's saying she hates math, that *girls* can't do math. Last year it was her favorite subject!" Rue studied the two sets of scores.

"I tried to explain to Mrs. Trainer how important it is to praise Melanie when she gets something right. She needs a grade, or a star, or *something*." Karen was near tears. "She did *fine* last year with Mr. Merton. But when she hits a snag and nobody helps her, she feels like a moron, and when she's depressed she can't learn. Nobody can!"

"What did Mrs. Trainer say?"

"She said that Melanie hadn't been turning in her homework. Then Melanie told me that she *did* hand in the homework, but Mrs. Trainer never graded it. Or else she handed it back so late that Melanie never knew what she needed help with before they moved on. Now she's at the point she can't do *any* of it because she didn't understand what came before! And when I came back to explain that to Mrs. Trainer, she *refused* to talk to me."

Rue felt utterly overwhelmed. It was nine-fifty in the morning, there were three-alarm fires all over campus, and she wanted to tell everyone to take their miserable problems and their spoiled living kids who had futures, and shove them. She wanted to get into bed with a bottle of scotch and cry.

Her next appointment was with Catherine Trainer.

Catherine came in in a swivet. Nobody appreciated her, the parents were out of control, Cora Alba-Fish in Primary was putting out food for feral cats, and the cats lurked around the campus and murdered her birdies.

"Catherine," said Rue, "Did you tell Mrs. Bramlett that Melanie doesn't do her homework?"

"No! I said she doesn't apply herself."

"Does she do her homework?"

Catherine blustered. "There are many blanks in the grade book for Melanie. I believe that when I have the children grade their own homework, she fails to enter the grade because she's done poorly."

"You believe that."

"Yes."

"But you don't know for sure. It may be she hasn't done the homework at all, it may be you returned it ungraded."

Catherine flared. "I am sure I have never returned a paper ungraded."

"Do you remember I warned you that you were to grade all papers yourself and return them within the week at the very latest? That I preferred them graded overnight?"

"No."

"Do you remember that I told you absolutely that you were to observe *all* guidelines in the Faculty Handbook, and that includes grading tests yourself? No self-grading, except for a sound pedagogical reason?"

"I had a good reason."

"What was it?"

"I showed that I trusted them."

"Mrs. Trainer, did you refuse to have a meeting with Mrs. Bramlett when she asked for it?"

"I had met with her for over an hour the very day before! She . . ."

"So the answer is 'yes'? You refused?"

"Yes, but . . ."

"Catherine, I'm sorry. You've been a valuable part of the school for many years, and I think of you as a friend. But you have been warned repeatedly, you've been given clear guidelines for improvement, and if anything, things keep getting worse. I am sorry. But you are fired."

Catherine was stunned. As she stared at Rue, the color drained from her face, like a person going into physical shock.

The faculty reacted to Catherine's firing as if it were one maddened animal. They were already feeling taunted and jeered, but this was a frontal assault. Rue had broken a cardinal rule; she had listened to an unreasonable parent and acted without hearing the teacher's side. In one swipe Rue had sliced herself out of the net of support and comfort that had been her hope for safety.

If anyone, including Rue, thought any allowance would be made for her emotional state, they got over it fast. Things piled up too quickly in a school; people's children, their jobs, their dignity were at stake. Everyone had problems. It seemed that once they started piling faggots onto this fire, no one could stop. Rue was biased, out of touch, old-fashioned. Rue thought that conventional spelling was important. She thought children should memorize poetry and do math worksheets. ("Drill and kill, drill and kill" was the name of that pedagogical antique.) She had told the third-grade teacher that the singular of dice was not dice, and turned out to be right. She had pointed out that kudos was not plural and turned out to be right. She had told the Latin teacher that you did not spell it "beyond the pail." She corrected when teachers used "lay" for "lie" or "hung" for "hanged," and people were stung, and they remembered. There was resentment. There was a sense of a pot on the boil, pressing for an outlet.

After a few days of this, Rue went to seek out Bonnie. She found her sitting with Evelyn Douglas at one of the lunch tables under the live oaks. The were both holding empty coffee mugs; Evelyn was talking and Bonnie was listening. Rue hoped she could join them, but as soon as she approached, Evelyn stood up. "To be continued," she said to Bonnie, and walked away.

Rue looked after her for a moment, then sat down.

"Can I get you a cup of coffee?" Bonnie asked her.

"Please," said Rue.

When Bonnie had returned with two mugs of hot coffee, she settled down across from Rue, watching her with her smokey diamond eyes.

"How are you finding married life?" Rue asked.

Bonnie smiled. "Just as I hoped it would be," she said. And after a pause, "How are you finding married life?"

"Are you a witch?" Rue asked.

"I had a great-grandmother in Nova Scotia who was supposed to be. I'm sorry to say I never knew her. Who named you 'Rue'?"

"My mother. 'With rue my heart is laden.' One hardly knows how to interpret it. My father preferred the line from Hamlet: 'O! You must wear your rue with a difference.'"

"Names are important."

"Yes. We named Georgia after the Ray Charles song."

Bonnie smiled. Rue smiled too, bitterly, and studied the weathered wood of the tabletop. Her heel tapped, as if she was hearing the song in her head.

"'No peace I find.' To answer your question, I think my married life is over."

Bonnie reached across the table and touched her hand.

"I hope not," said Bonnie.

"I hope not too. But hoping won't help." Rue sat silent for a bit. "When you marry young, especially if you marry the first person you really love, you imagine that being together gives you some special protection. That just holding on to each other will keep out the dark."

She took a deep breath, and it was hard to do, since she felt that her body was bound around by constricting bands of pain and pressure. "But now I see that nothing keeps you safe. Not love, not rules, not principles. And yet, you have to behave as if they do. You have to lead a principled life because you have to, but it won't keep chaos at bay. In fact, it won't make any difference."

Bonnie watched her gravely, and mercifully said nothing.

After a pause, Rue said, "I don't suppose you can tell me what Evelyn Douglas was talking to you about?"

Bonnie shook her head no. But she said, "The faculty seems quite upset."

"I've noticed."

"Someone told me that Catherine Trainer is going to sue."

"Of course she's going to sue. Everybody's going to sue everybody. It's a brave new world, if actions have consequences you can have them legally removed."

Bonnie sat quiet until Rue, sounding suddenly exhausted, went on.

"She should sue, because I fired her completely wrong. I had laid all the groundwork to counsel her out, at the end of the year or next year at the latest. At the very least, I should have listened to her side of the story. There are always two sides. There are *always* two sides. I knew it. I just didn't care. She whined."

Bonnie said thoughtfully, "The faculty is behaving like an abused child. Fits of anger. Reckless of feelings of others. Terribly upset by unpredictable behavior."

"They should grow up," said Rue.

Bonnie swung her legs out from under the table and turned her body to face the afternoon sun. She tipped her face up and closed her eyes. After a moment she said, "I'm hearing a lot of anger and mistrust. From the faculty and the parents. From the *kids*. A lot of it."

"I know it," said Rue. "I know it." She sat watching Bonnie breathe. Being near her made her feel calmer. She knew she could be as heartless and childish as she wanted to be, and Bonnie would go on breathing.

"I loved this school," Rue said. "I thought we were one body and blood. I thought I gave it health and strength. I know it gave that to me."

"You did," said Bonnie. "You did all that."

"Now I'm making it sick. If the head's sick, the body gets sick."

"You're not sick."

"I'm not well."

They sat for a while, listening to the sounds of the school. Cars were beginning to arrive in the parking lot, lining up for dismissal. The parrots yammered high in the live oaks. A dog barked in a yard up the hill, where the nearest newly built "mansions" pressed the edge of the campus.

"Are you saying good-bye?" Bonnie asked.

"Is that what it is? I wasn't sure."

"I don't know, I was just asking," said Bonnie.

"It's like a bad place in a marriage," Rue said. "You don't know whether to tough it out or whether to let it go. You can't tell if courage lies in hanging on or giving up."

That afternoon before he left, Mike came to the door of Rue's office. She was sitting very still, looking at whatever was on the surface before her. There was a picture of Henry. She had put away the ones of Georgia. There was a ceramic ashtray glazed in royal blue, given her in her first year at Country by a little boy who was now a Rhodes scholar. There was a silver pencil cup, and a clock, and her Rolodex. The telephone was black, and had dust between the buttons. Merilee used to clean it, but of course Emily had never thought of it and Rue would not have thought of asking her to.

The room seemed hermetic. Motes of dust were thick in the sunlight that slanted into the room from the windows over the soccer field.

"Are you all right?" Mike said from the doorway.

Rue nodded. Mike hesitated.

"Good night, then . . ." he said.

"Good night, Mike."

The phones were ringing, and Mrs. Leavitt had been waiting for her appointment with Rue for twenty minutes. Emily went to Mike's office.

"Do you know where Rue went?"

"No, isn't she in her office?"

Emily explained about Mrs. Leavitt. Bill Glarrow came to the door and said, "Do you know where Rue is?"

"Maybe she stopped somewhere when she went out to take attendance. I'll find her," said Mike.

He went looking for Rue. Along the way he stopped at Primary, Middle, and at the library. Finally he found Bonnie in the preschool, and together they went back to Home, where Bonnie thought to look in the mailboxes to see if Rue had left anyone a message. In Mike's box there was a letter on Rue's personal paper. He opened it and read it. Bill Glarrow, Emily, and Mrs. Leavitt had all drawn near and were watching him.

"She's resigned," he said.

When Rue left Chandler's office the first person she saw was Oliver Sale. He was standing outside the door in his gray suit and white shirt and massive black shoes. They stared at each other for a long moment. She nodded to him, and went past. Outside the office she pressed the button for the elevator, then decided she couldn't wait. She went out the fire door, marked EXIT, and ran down two flights of cinderblock stairwell. She had a thought that she would be all right if she just got back into her car.

But once in the car, she couldn't move. Here was the opposite of school. Here in daylight all the life was inside soundproof buildings, and outside nothing moved on the hot concrete. She couldn't lift her hand to turn the key in the ignition. She had no job, no career, and no place to go. She sat in her car in the parking lot with her hands folded in her lap, swaddled by a profound silence.

She sat extraordinarily still, taking very shallow breaths, as if she were perched so marginally on the edge of existence that she might slip out of it spontaneously. She kept thinking of an elegy she had read once. She could no longer remember the poem, or the poet, but she kept hearing this line, as if someone somewhere were ringing it like a bell:

> But Death, a magician, closed you in his hand and opened it suddenly empty.

Jonathan Sale had begun to hear the ghost. He heard it the first time one night after his mother turned off the light, shut his door, and clicked off down the hall in her taptap shoes. His mother was very beautiful with big hair and shiny clothes like a lady on television. She smelled good. But she didn't smile as much as ladies on television.

Tonight she was mad at him because he patted her with his hand and he forgot he'd just been licking it. He thought his mother might like him to pat her because Lyndie had made her mad and had to be locked in her room. That meant she liked him best, but not the licking. His new teacher told him if he didn't stop it he'd have to go to the Opportunity Room. He couldn't stop it though because he didn't remember doing it. His new teacher wasn't very nice.

It was very dark at their end of the house. There had been yelling earlier. Now the house was quiet and then he heard the ghost. It was outside his door, crying and crying. He was afraid it would come in and do something to him. He wanted to tell Lyndie he could hear it now, he believed her now, but to do that he'd have to open the door.

He was very frightened, and it made him have to go to the bathroom. But the bathroom was down the hall; to go there, he'd have to open the door and he'd see what was out there. Sometimes he could hear it walking up and down, crying, and just there, then, there was a THUMP as if it had thrown itself against the door. He began to whimper and lick his hand. Being frightened made him have to go even more.

It took just over a week for Chandler to ask that a special flag-raising be held, so he could introduce the new acting headmaster. On the day, he arrived with a man in his thirties in tow, a highly polished object with pale hair and lashes, who was wearing a gray suit and black Gucci loafers. When the nearly three hundred children (minus the preschool) and their teachers stood in rows before him in the winter sunlight, Chandler himself raised the flag, and then led the Pledge of Allegiance. Then he and the pale-haired man stepped up to the microphone. He told them he was pleased that the Board had been able to bring the school's moment of disarray to an end so quickly.

"Chip Horde holds a bachelor of science degree from Harvey Mudd, and a master's in business administration. He has many years' experience in the human resources field, and the Board and I feel that he is the right man to lead us through this difficult time. I know you'll give him all the support you can as he gets his sea legs here. Please welcome Mr. Horde."

There was anxious applause. Hundreds of faces studied this new one, wondering what his presence in their lives was going to mean. Mr. Horde gave a brief and gracious speech saying that he was glad to be on board, and that he would need their help. He said he was weak on names and would be grateful if they would introduce themselves to him each time they spoke. He said he hoped this would be a time of learning and growing together for all of them.

After classes began, Chandler brought Chip Horde up to Home to introduce him around and show him his office. Chip greeted each person on the staff by name before he was introduced.

"You must be Emily. Chip Horde, good to know you. Mike, good to know *you*. Bill Glarrow . . . so this is the Business Office? What database are you using?"

"Nutshell."

"You're kidding. Well." And he went on with Chandler into Rue's office.

"What does he mean, 'Good to *know* you,'" said Mike. "He doesn't know me. He just got here." He and Emily and Bill Glarrow looked toward the door of Rue's office. The first thing Chip Horde had done was close it.

Chip Horde was on the phone with the police when Emily the secretary came to the door. It annoyed him to have her stand there listening to him. The English teacher, Cynda Goldring, had had her house burglarized; nothing was missing but the house had been trashed, and the burglar had painted swastikas all over the walls with Cynda's nail polish. It was a disturbing crime, both unprofessional and uncannily malicious, and weirdly Mrs. Goldring suspected a child in the school, a Jewish boy. Kenny Lowen. It sounded to him like a hell of a PR problem.

The minute he hung up, Emily said, "Excuse me, Chip." She came in with a software manual in her hand. "I've spent about an hour and a half on this; could you just show me once how you do it?"

Chip Horde, who was trying to understand the budget, looked surprised. "Do what, Emily?"

"I can't get the program to print landscape, so we can print a run of envelopes. I could do one address at a time through the printer, but the software keeps overriding the printer command, and if I can't do it through the software, I can't access the mailing list. . . ."

"Have you called Tech Support?"

"Yes, I have, but the people who make the printer say it should work and the people who make the software say I need another printer driver, but when I install the one they say, it won't print at all. . . ."

Chip Horde looked pointedly at his watch.

"I could do it faster by hand, honestly."

"Don't you think that looks a *little* unprofessional?" he asked sarcastically.

"Not as unprofessional as having the mailing two weeks late."

"I can't imagine this is normally the Head's problem."

"Normally, everything is the Head's problem," said Emily.

"I can't believe she spent her time doing the secretarial work," said Chip to Chandler. "You should see the files. They're quite unbelievable. No wonder she never had time for anyone."

"That's just what I thought," said Chandler. "I knew it."

By the end of the second week Chip had fired Emily Goldsborough. He was extremely surprised to receive a protest delegation of parents and Board members, including Sylvia French and Carson McCann.

"She just wasn't trained for the job," he explained. "She's a very nice lady, I agree."

"Chip, maybe you don't understand what the job is. This school is an organism. We need someone who knows the DNA. Who's out of town, who's friends with whom, whose parents are getting divorced, what doctor to call when you can't reach the parents."

"Doesn't Mike know all that?"

"No. Besides, she's a single mother, she needs the money."

"Everyone needs the money," said Chip. He brought in his secretary from his former company, a failed start-up, a girl of twenty-four named Kimberly who could type like the wind. She worked weekends completely redoing the school's filing system so that no one else could find anything. When she realized what had happened, the development director went quietly and reasonably to Mr. Horde to explain that Kimberly had just made her job undoable. Mr. Horde said that was too bad, but the school would be better off in the end if it ran in a more professional way. The development director quit.

Mike Dianda explained to Chip Horde that faculty evaluation was a major part of the Head's job. Chip began spending an hour of every day observing classes. Then he would shut himself in his room studying the evaluations Rue had written for each member of the staff over the years. It baffled him. He couldn't figure out what the hell was supposed to go on in a classroom, especially since it seemed to be different for every grade. The only thing he could tell for sure was that one of the art teachers, not the one in the Birkenstocks, was half lit three-quarters of the time. He called Pat Moredock in during her lunch hour, confronted her with vodka bottles found in her paint closet, and told her she was fired.

Missy Kip went home to her father in tears.

"Mrs. Moredock was crying, Daddy. It's not fair!"

"It doesn't sound very fair, Missy. I'll see what I can do."

*   *   *

"Oh, come on, Chandler," said Chip Horde. "She was tight as a tick at ten in the morning."

"She's an effective and popular teacher, Chip."

"I don't see how she could be."

"It seems a little inhumane, that's all. Why wouldn't it be better to have a talk with her, see if she'll agree to go for treatment?"

"Why? We can replace her in a minute, at half the price."

"Be careful," said Chandler sternly. "Now I'm serious, be careful with that kind of talk. We had a union organizer on campus last week. The last goddamn thing we want is the whole group signing up with the Classroom Teachers' Association."

The two sat in silence. Chip didn't want to admit that he hadn't known private school teachers *could* join the Classroom Teachers' Association. Jesus, what a con game this was. How the hell did you get people bright enough to teach at all, to work for half what they could get in public school, if they had the choice of getting a union to stick it to everyone for them?

Chandler was thinking of Missy, and how much he wanted to go home to her and tell her he'd rescued Mrs. Moredock.

"I wonder if we couldn't arrange an intervention for Pat," said Chandler. "If she'd go somewhere and dry out, we could hold her job for her. What does she have for family? Who are her friends?"

"Now look," said Chip, "back off. Read the Handbook. Hiring and firing is *my* job. I'm trying to build a team, Chandler. If you keep coming in here, giving everyone the message that I'm not really in charge, you're going to find out no one is in charge."

"Sorry. I just wanted to give you my thinking," said Chandler stiffly.

"I've already acted. I couldn't take it back even if I were inclined to. You want a wuss in this job? Is that what you thought I was?"

Chandler stood. "Of course not. I was trying to be helpful."

"I don't think I need the help," said Chip, rising too. "No offense."

"None taken," said Chandler. This was a lie on both sides. The two men shook hands and Chandler left the office.

Lyndie Sale's room was aggressively messy. Her school books were spread out around her, but she wasn't working. She sat still, cross-legged on the bed. She had a *Playboy* magazine hidden under her mattress, and a pint of Bailey's Irish Cream that she had stolen from Tagliarini's in a knapsack on the shelf of her closet. But she didn't dare get these out while They were up. They had fixed her door so it could only be locked from the outside, and they came in whenever they felt like it, without knocking. She could hear the hum of voices and canned laughter from the television downstairs. Lyndie got up and left her room on stockinged feet, moving toward the sound.

In the den, her father was watching television. His high forehead gleamed in the blue light. At a card table in the corner, her mother sat in lamplight, surrounded by yarn of different colors, and bowls of dead tennis balls. Lyndie knew what she was doing. Her mother would wind long hanks of yarn around a tennis ball, secure it, then divide the trailing wool into eight long clumps and begin to braid. The eight clumps would be braided legs. She was making toy octopuses. You could see from the rows of them propped on the bookshelf that she had already made a great many, whether for a school or church sale or some other reason, Lyndie didn't know. Her eternal glass of red wine stood on the card table beside the tennis balls.

Without turning around, Oliver Sale said, "Lyndie . . . what are you doing?" Apparently he could feel that she had been gazing at his TV program from the doorway.

"I'm going to call Shannon."

"Is your homework done?"

"No, I need the assignment. I don't know what pages."

"You can't watch TV until you finish."

"I know."

She went on, into the kitchen. The kitchen was filled with every fancy appliance you ever saw, a microwave, a convection oven, a gelato maker, a vegetable juicer, a Kitchen Aid, a breadmaker, and a Cuisinart. You'd think her mother liked to cook. Lyndie's kindergarten drawings were lovingly framed and hung on the wall. A valentine she'd made for her mother two years ago hung on the refrigerator door, held by a magnet in the shape of an ear of corn. Lyndie took a popsicle from the freezer and started to eat it. She went to the phone and dialed. After a ring or two, a male voice answered.

"Hello?"

Lyndie just held the phone, and sucked on her popsicle. It was grape.

"Hello? This is Chip Horde . . ." the voice said on the other end, a little too loud. Lyndie said nothing, but made sure she was making enough noise that he knew someone was there. He said crossly, "Who is calling, please . . ."

"Lyndie, what are you doing?"

Lyndie slammed the phone down and whirled around. Her mother was standing in the doorway, her empty wine glass in her hand.

"I was calling Shannon."

"You just hung up on her?"

"No, we were done."

"You're lying, Lyndie."

They stared at each other.

Mike Dianda had asked for just a minute of Chip's time. He sat in the chair by the head's desk, where he and Rue had so often sat.

"What's on your mind?" said Chip, as he stuck a pencil into his electric sharpener.

When the whirring stopped, Mike said, "I'm going to be leaving at the end of the year."

Chip looked at him. "But you signed a contract."

"I know . . . I'm sorry. I've been offered a job in San Francisco, head of the middle school at Town."

"But that's a step down for you."

"No, it isn't."

"What are they offering you?"

Mike was taken aback. "It's not the money. It's a job I campaigned for, and I'm looking forward to it."

"I'm truly sorry to hear it, Mike. There are people who could tell me they were leaving, and I'd say 'Godspeed,' but you're not one of them. Let me see if I can get the Board to do any better on your contract."

"You're *kidding*," said Cynda at lunch. "If he *could* pay you more, why didn't he frigging do it in the first place?"

"I said I thought he'd really be happier with someone of his own choice in my office."

"You're bad." They both laughed. It was no secret that no fewer than seven members of the faculty would be gone by next year, in addition to Catherine Trainer and Pat Moredock. Four, including Cynda, had found jobs elsewhere, and three, including Janet TerWilliams, didn't care. They just didn't want to work at Country anymore. Nine families had withdrawn a total of fifteen children, and preschool applications were way down from previous years. Chip was looking at a budget shortfall of $70,000.

Mike was the second member of the office staff to quit. The first had been Kimberly, who thanked Mr. Horde for the opportunity but said she could get more money working at Digital, and it wasn't so, like, Reaganesque there. By which she meant, there were people of her own age, some of them straight single men, and you didn't have to keep going off campus to smoke a cigarette.

Chandler found himself struggling to keep this hemorrhage from spreading to the Board. Terry Malko was long gone, and now embroiled in a divorce proceeding. Sylvia French was resigning in support of Rue, but had agreed to finish her term, which would run until June. Ann Rosen had resigned, giving no reason. In this power vacuum Carson McCann had apparently become power-mad, lobbying behind the scenes on issues that affected her, such as whether children in first and second grades should have final exams.

"But don't you see," Carson had argued with Chandler in Curriculum Committee, "there are kids who will see a C in first grade and decide that they're dumb, and that becomes a self-fulfilling prophecy. If a late-bloomer (like Ashby McCann) has caught up by fourth grade, and he's never had a C, you spare him a problem there's simply no need for."

Chandler thought this sounded tediously like Rue's mewling about the decent survival of all. "So you want us to be surprised when they get to fourth grade and get grades for the first time? What if we find we've got a whole class of illiterates?"

"It hasn't happened yet, has it?" she shot back.

When the matter came to discussion before the full Board, Chandler was stunned to find that a vote had been proposed and taken before he got into gear, and that Carson's position had such a heavy majority that he had to abstain from the vote himself to keep from looking like a fool. He realized that somehow she had rigged this, on the phone, in the hot-lunch kitchen, in the parking lot, so that now there was a B Board and an A Board. Carson was running the A Board, and he was not on it.

It struck him, when he looked back on this year, that he had expected to feel a more complete sense of triumph.

D_{ear} Georgia, (Rue wrote)

It's almost May, and you will never see another spring. You have been gone for two months, and I miss you every minute—I miss you in every cell. I have wanted to die very often in the last two months, but it hasn't happened. I'm past the point in life when received wisdom can help me. My only help comes from ordinary souls around me, and they are learning it for themselves as they teach.

Darling child. My heart. I write this mostly at night, because those are the hardest hours. I write to comfort myself, because much as I want to believe otherwise, what I feel when I try to reach you is that you already know everything, and that you are beyond caring.

I've tried various things for the pain. Morphine is out. Scotch is out. Meditation and prayer are out, at the moment, because they require that you hold your mind still, and when I do that I miss you, and cry and cry. My current painkiller is to think. It's like taking baby aspirin for a triple amputation, but you only have what you have. It's a clock ticking in the rubble. Something still turns a gear, that turns a gear that turns a gear. I'm still part of the universe.

(And you are too, dear soul, but where? What part? All parts? I have to love it all to love you still? All right. More tears.)

The Anasazi buried their dead in open air. (Buried, no, but what word?) As if the dead were not asleep, in need of quiet and dark, but more awake than they had ever been, in need of light and sky and wind all day and night.

I wish you had lived to see those canyons. Those ruins up in the walls, above the wolves and the flash floods, safe, but empty. I understood them at once. Everything changes because everything must. Things get old, things die, things change, and old things give way to the new. But all change leaves pain and wreckage.

There I was, keeper of the flame. Thinking that something

priceless is being lost and nothing of equal value put in its place, when people said Less when they meant Fewer, and Infer when they meant Imply, and Home when they mean House, the dumbing down of language, the subtleties lost. What has been gained when native English speakers say "I'm like . . ." for I said, I thought, I cried . . . ? I thought I knew what was being lost. I thought I was right. I thought I could get others to see that it mattered. What a jerk.

Where are the brown-haired wavy-haired Anasazi? Did they melt into the Zuni and Acoma and Laguna cultures and become ancestors of the Hopi people, with their jet-black pin-straight hair? Or did they climb up into their rock caves and build the walls up around themselves and die of sadness?

The architecture and burial objects show that Anasazi people had no ruling class or person, no privileged group. All lived the same, all were buried the same. They must have found a way to conduct their communal lives so democratically that no hierarchy was needed. And they lived their lives so close together, so entirely in sight of others, that there would be no need for conscience. Every act would have a dozen witnesses. Every person shares a common tribal memory with all the others. Their religious life is inseparable from their daily life, so that every action is a moral one. Everything you do can be seen to affect the community, for good or ill. But now we live in a world where even people of good will cannot arrive at a common definition of kindness. Or of "home."

They were basketmakers, the Anasazi. They could weave anything. To make winter clothes, they first wove nets, three to four feet wide and sometimes 200 feet long, of hair and yucca fibers. And then a group, maybe the whole village, drove rabbits into the nets by the dozens. But instead of sewing rabbit skins together, they cut the skins into strips, and wrapped the strips around long flexible cores of plant stuff, so that each made a fat warm tube like rabbit-skin yarn, and those they wove into capes and robes. Everything woven, as if it was their metaphor for life.

They're gone, of course. Extinct, or dragged into slavery by raiding Shoshone nomads, or taken in as refugees by other tribes who believed other things. Or had had better luck with the weather. Or sang to more powerful gods.

The Anasazi could sing. Navajo legend tells of a boy a thousand years ago, when the Navajo were still wanderers, who followed his goats into Canyon de Chelly, and in the night, heard singing. He followed the singing deeper into the Canyon for four nights until at last he also saw firelight and shadows high up the wall, and he climbed up to the People. They took him into their kiva and taught him ceremonies, all secret, and gave him a name to take back to his clan, the first clan of the Navajo. Which proves that even though it was centuries before they returned to the canyon, the Navajo were always the spiritual heirs of the Anasazi, trying to find the way back.

I feel for the Navajo, trying to get the boy to lead them to the canyon, with him saying, "So I was like whoa, goats . . ." And then for centuries they wandered, keeping alive for each other the vision of the sacred place, where there was singing and firelight and everyone had the same gods and knew the same stories, and you knew without being told that this was home.

Did something fail because it ended? That is my question now.

I know God does not react well to being tested. But I need a sign.

Rue was reading Blake when the phone rang. It rang so seldom in this apartment that it almost frightened her. She picked it up on the third ring. She had fantasies that when it rang, it would be Georgia.

"Hello?"

For a long moment, there was no reply. Just that live silence of someone on the other end, not speaking. Then Henry said, "Rue— it's me." She hadn't heard his voice in three months.

This time the silence was on her end, for just a beat. "Hello," she managed finally, and started to cry.

"I'm sorry to call so late," said Henry.

"I'm up," said Rue. That much was true. She sometimes felt she hadn't slept in years.

"Are you all right?" he asked.

"It depends on the time of day you ask me. Nights are hard. Hang on a second." She put the phone down and went to the kitchen to take a drink of water and blow her nose. Then she came back.

"Where's one-oh-nine Chatham Street?"

"It's off Brattle. North of Radcliffe Yard."

"You have an apartment?"

"A little dump, yes."

There was a silence.

"Did Dad tell you where I was?" she asked.

"No, Mike and Bonnie did. I went home and there was some asshole living in our house."

"Well, it is the school's house."

"Yes, I know."

Another pause.

"So you didn't know what happened?" Rue asked.

"No, no one knew how to reach me. I didn't want anyone to. I didn't want to wake up in the morning and wonder if . . . anyone had tried. If anyone would."

"I understand that," Rue said.

There was another silence.

"What are you doing?" Henry asked.

"You mean this minute? Or in life?"

"In life."

"Moving slowly. I came here because I needed a library. I read a lot. I write a lot."

"What are you writing?"

She paused. "It's hard to describe."

There was another pause.

"Rue—I'd like to see you."

"Are you in Cambridge?"

"Boston."

"Oh."

"Could I come over?"

"It's late. And it's pouring." She wasn't sure she could handle this meeting with no preparation. After a while, she said, "All right."

It took him about a half hour to find the address. The apartment was a typical Cambridge railroad flat, with tiny rooms in a row off a long corridor. There was a gas heater in the sitting room in front. Rain rattled the bay windows. Beyond the sitting room was a tiny bedroom, a bathroom, a pint-sized dining room in which the last tenant had repaired his motorcycle, and a pullman kitchen.

"It's bigger than the place we had in med school," Henry said, after she had hung his dripping coat from the shower curtain rod over the bathtub. He was very suntanned, and thinner. He looked as if whoever had cut his hair last had had a learning experience.

"I know. I took the top floor because I get the most light, up here. I'm getting used to the stairs."

"How are the neighbors?"

"Fine. The ones right below me are chamber musicians. I get to hear all their rehearsals through the floor."

"Do you have any scotch?"

"No . . . I'm sorry."

He got up and went into the kitchen, and began opening cup-boards. Rue followed him in. He found a bottle of vermouth.

"I'll drink this."

"I got that for cooking."

"I know, I know you. It's still potable. What's *that?*" he asked, genuinely startled. Rue's cat, Helen, a beautiful mahogany Burmese, had jumped almost silently onto the counter, where Henry was star-ing at it.

Rue picked the cat up and patted her, and then set her on the floor and told her to scoot.

Henry looked at Rue.

"You thought I wasn't coming back," he said softly.

Rue nodded. She handed Henry a glass and opened the little freezer to get out an ice tray.

When Henry had his drink and Rue had a mug of tea, they went to sit in the front room. The cat, knowing in the unerring way cats do that Henry was allergic to her, settled herself on his lap. He looked at it, slightly alarmed, and then stroked it and smiled. They sat in slightly uneasy silence.

"Remember when you still lived in the dorms, and we used to meet for breakfast beside the Charles?" Henry asked.

Rue smiled. "And you would read to me." Rue remembered standing outside Elsie's Lunch, holding their bicycles, while he bought them huge paper cups of coffee and crullers with icing, wrapped in waxed paper. Then they walked side by side to the river where they would picnic in the pearly light of the Cambridge morning. He liked to read to her from a book of Hindu folktales he had bought at an outdoor stall for a dime. Hindu folktales, or Damon Runyon. She would lie on the grass listening, and watching the clouds.

He nodded. "Has the town changed a lot?"

"Yes and no. I find that my emotions when we were young here were so intense that they come back, quite pure, day after day, when I walk down a certain street, or stand in front of a building in the Yard, or look at the sky over Mass. Ave. It's good because the feelings are all charged with a sense of beginning."

Henry nodded. They sat in silence for a time.

"Are you finding old friends here?" Henry asked.

"A few. I haven't felt fit for company much. I'm not ready to answer questions."

Henry nodded. "I know," he said. "I've spent the last three months with people who don't speak English."

"Good idea," she said. She knew she should ask where he had been, and what he had been doing, but she wasn't ready. She wasn't ready to do much except look at him, and get used to his being here. She'd forgotten how beautiful his speaking voice was.

After a while he said, "Mike told me what happened."

"Good. Then I don't have to." He nodded. She wondered if he was thinking of apologizing for not being there. She hoped he wouldn't. He didn't. Instead he just looked at her, a long, steady thoughtful look. She felt he was different. As if he had lived so long without shaping reality through words that now he didn't think of trying.

After a while, he asked, "Could I stay here tonight?"

"If we could just bundle," said Rue.

"Of course," said Henry.

In bed, in the dark, they heard a cellist below them start running scales.

Rue said, "I can't seem to get used to this wet spring. It's almost June, but I'm cold all the time."

Henry, three-quarters asleep, wrapped himself around her. "I'll keep you warm," he said. "I'll dream about fire."

"Holy shit," said Mike.

It was a Saturday morning in September, in San Francisco. He was reading the *Chronicle*.

"What?" said Bonnie, looking up from her book.

He looked down the hall to the bedroom Mary and Trinity shared. The girls weren't up yet.

Mike read, "Dateline Seven Springs, California. It's a wire story. Headline: 'Wife of prominent lawyer arraigned for manslaughter. Sondra Sale, thirty-seven, was arrested here today and arraigned on charges of second-degree manslaughter after ambulance attendants found her five-year-old son, Jonathan, dead in his bed. Police quote Mrs. Sale as saying, "He messed his bed again. I was just turning him over to spank him and something broke in his neck." Mrs. Sale's husband, Oliver, who is chief legal officer at Kip Graphics, a Seven Springs computer company, was out of town at the time of the incident. The couple's older child, Linda, age eleven, has been placed in foster care.'"

◼ Perennial

Books by Beth Gutcheon:

MORE THAN YOU KNOW
ISBN 0-06-095935-5

In a small town on the coast of Maine, Hannah Gray begins her story: "Somebody said 'true love is like ghosts, which everyone talks about, and few have seen.' I've seen both, and I don't know how to tell you which is worse."

"An exceptional novel—thrilling, taut, austere: this is extraordinary writing of a tense, crytalline beauty." —*Shirley Hazzard*

FIVE FORTUNES
ISBN 0-06-092995-2

A warm and witty story of five unforgettable women and the unexpected friendships forged over a transforming week at the "Fat Chance" spa.

"[Beth Gutcheon] has absolutely perfect pitch when it comes to capturing the lives of these remarkable women."—Anne Rivers Siddons

SAYING GRACE
ISBN 0-06-092727-5

This "deliciously readable" (*San Francisco Chronicle*) story focuses on Rue Shaw, a woman who has it all – a great child, a solid marriage, and a job she loves – and wants to keep it that way, despite the changing world around her. Funny, rich in detail and finally stunning, *Saying Grace* is "by turns heartwarming and heartrending" (*Boston Globe*).

DOMESTIC PLEASURES
ISBN 0-06-093476-X (Coming Fall 2001)

Charlie and Martha, two divorced parents of teenagers from two very different worlds, are thrown together by drastic circumstances and suddenly find themselves falling in love . . . life is about to become more complicated than ever.

"[A] witty and often moving tale of love among the moderns."—*Washington Post Book World*

STILL MISSING
ISBN 0-06-097703-5

When six-year-old Alex Selky doesn't come home from school, his mother begins a desperate vigil that lasts through months of false leads and the desertions of friends and allies. The basis for the feature film *Without a Trace*.

"Haunting, harrowing, and highly effective . . . a stunning shocker of an ending. . . . It strings out the suspense to the almost unendurable."—*Publishers Weekly*

THE NEW GIRLS
ISBN 0-06-097702-7

A resonant, engrossing novel about five girls in prep school during the '60s, into whose protected reality marches the Vietnam War, the woman's movement, and the sexual revolution – and changes their lives forever.

"Funny without sacrificing intelligence, intelligent without being pretentious. It's all-around good reading."—*Boston Globe*

Available wherever books are sold, or call 1-800-331-3761 to order.